BY KATHERINE ARDEN

The Bear and the Nightingale
The Girl in the Tower
The Winter of the Witch
The Warm Hands of Ghosts

FOR CHILDREN

Small Spaces
Dead Voices
Dark Waters
Empty Smiles

THE WARM HANDS OF GHOSTS

THE WARM HANDS OF GHOSTS

·····

A NOVEL

·····

Katherine Arden

NEW YORK

Published in the United States by Del Rey, an imprint of Random House, a division of Penguin Random House LLC, New York.

Del Rey and the Circle colophon are registered trademarks of Penguin Random House LLC.

Library of Congress Cataloging-in-Publication Data
Names: Arden, Katherine, author.
Title: The warm hands of ghosts : a novel / Katherine Arden.
Description: New York : Del Rey, 2024.
Identifiers: LCCN 2023039811 (print) | LCCN 2023039812 (ebook) |
ISBN 9780593128251 (hardcover) | ISBN 9780593871508 (B&N edition) |
ISBN 9780593128268 (e-book)
Subjects: LCGFT: Science fiction. | Novels.
Classification: LCC PS3601.R42 W37 2024 (print) |
LCC PS3601.R42 (ebook) | DDC 813/.6—dc23/eng/20230828
LC record available at https://lccn.loc.gov/2023039811
LC ebook record available at https://lccn.loc.gov/2023039812

Printed in the United States of America on acid-free paper

randomhousebooks.com

2 4 6 8 9 7 5 3 1

FIRST EDITION

Book design by Simon M. Sullivan

To Evan

Because this was a book of battlefields

And you stood with me on all of them

Et diabolus incarnatus est
Et homo factus est

And the devil was incarnated
And was made man

—ARTHUR MACHEN

THE WARM
HANDS OF
GHOSTS

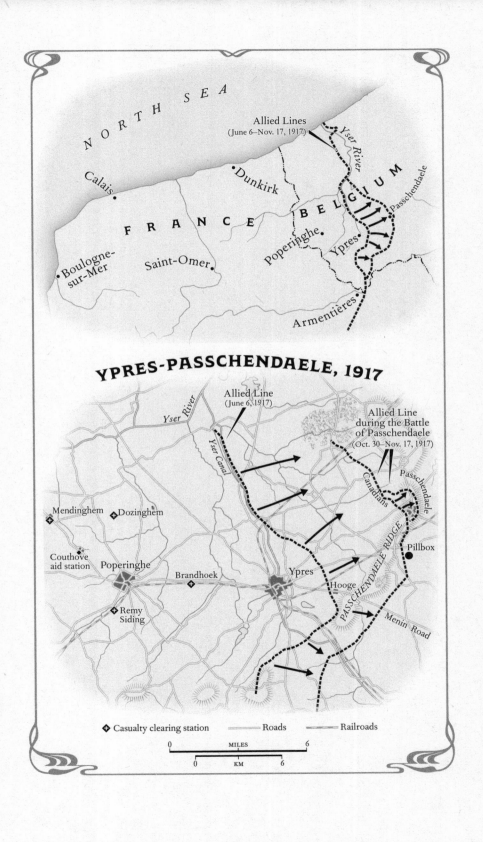

NORTH SEA

Allied Lines
(June 6–Nov. 17, 1917)

Yser River

Calais

Dunkirk

BELGIUM

Passchendaele

FRANCE

Poperinghe

Ypres

Boulogne-
sur-Mer

Saint-Omer

Armentières

YPRES-PASSCHENDAELE, 1917

Yser River

Allied Line
(June 6, 1917)

Yser Canal

Allied Line
during the Battle
of Passchendaele
(Oct. 30–Nov. 17, 1917)

Canadians

Passchendaele

Mendinghem

Dozinghem

Couthove
aid station

Poperinghe

Brandhoek

Ypres

Pillbox

PASSCHENDAELE RIDGE

Hooge

Menin Road

Remy
Siding

◈ Casualty clearing station ——— Roads ——— Railroads

0   MILES   6

0   KM   6

1

THE BEAST FROM THE SEA

·····

FREDDIE'S CLOTHES CAME TO VEITH STREET INSTEAD OF BLACK-thorn House, and the telegram that ought to have preceded them didn't reach Laura at all. She wasn't surprised. Nothing had worked properly, not since December.

December 6, to be exact. In the morning. When the *Mont Blanc* had steamed into Halifax Harbour, oil on deck and high explosive in her hold. She'd struck a freighter, they said, and the oil caught fire. Harbor crews were trying to put it out when the flames found the nitroglycerine.

At least that was how rumor had it. "No, I don't doubt it's true," Laura told her patients when they asked, as though she would know. As if, after three years as a combat nurse, she'd learned about high explosive from the things it wrote on people's skin. "Didn't you see the fireball?"

They all had. Her father had been in one of the boats trying to drown the blaze. Halifax afterward looked as if God had raised a giant burning boot and stamped. Fresh graves in Fairview sat snug beside five-year-old headstones from the *Titanic*, and the village of the Mi'kmaq had vanished.

And the post was a disaster. That was why she'd not heard from Freddie. He was her brother, he was a soldier; of course a backlog of his letters was lost in a sack somewhere. She had no time to think of it. She had too much to do. The first makeshift hospital had been scraped together in a YMCA the day after the explosion. The snow was bucketing down and Halifax was still on fire. Laura had walked past the uncollected dead. Shut their eyes when she could reach them, laid a hand once on a small bare foot. Three years of active service, and she was familiar with the dead.

Familiar too with the sight of an overrun triage station, although it was her first time to be met not with soldiers, but with parents clutching their burnt children. Laura had taken off her coat, washed her hands, reassured the nearest wild-eyed mother. Had a word with the overwhelmed civilian doctor and set about organizing the chaos.

That was a month ago—or was it six weeks? Time had stretched, as it did when wounded poured in during a battle, reduced not to minutes or hours, but to the pulse and the breath of whoever was under her hands. She slept standing up, and told herself that she was too busy to wonder why Freddie didn't write.

"That damned virago," muttered one doctor, half-annoyed, half-admiring. The Barrington hospital was full of willing hands. The Americans, blessedly, had piled a train full of all the gauze, disinfectants, and surgeons in Boston and sent it north. It was January by then, with snowdrifts head-high outside. The gymnasium had been turned into a hospital ward, sensibly laid out, ruthlessly organized, competently staffed. Laura was doing rounds, bent over a bed.

"That harpy," agreed his fellow. "But she's forgotten more about dressings than you'll ever know. She was in the nursing service, you know. Caught a shell over in France somewhere."

It was Belgium, actually.

"Caught a shell? A nurse, really? What did she do? Dress as a man and creep up the line?"

The first doctor didn't take the bait. "No—I heard they shelled the forward hospitals."

A startled pause. Then— "Barbaric," said the second doctor

weakly. Laura kept on taking temperatures. Both doctors stopped talking, perhaps contemplating trying to practice medicine under fire.

"Lord," the second doctor said finally. "Think all the girls who went to war will come back like that? Cut up, incorrigible?"

A laugh and a shudder. "Christ, I hope not."

Laura straightened up, smiling, and they both blanched. "Doctor," she said, and felt the subterranean amusement in her watching patients. She was one of them, after all, born by the harbor, before the world caught fire.

The doctors stammered something; she turned away again. *Virago indeed*. A fanged wind was tearing white foam off the bay, and her next patient was a blistered little boy. The child wept as she peeled off his dressings.

"Hush," said Laura. "It'll only hurt for a moment, and if you're crying how can I tell you about the purple horse?"

The little boy scowled at her through his tears. "Horses aren't purple."

"There was one." Laura snipped away stained gauze. "I saw it with my own eyes. In France. Naturally, the horse didn't start out purple. It was white. A beautiful white horse that belonged to a doctor. But the doctor was afraid that someone would see his white horse on a dark night and shoot him. Turn that way. He wanted a horse that would be hard to see at night. So he went to a witch—"

A lurch. "There aren't witches in France!"

"Of course there are. Be *still*. Don't you remember your fairy tales?" Freddie loved them.

"Well, the witches haven't *stayed* in France," the child informed her, in a voice that quivered. "With a war on."

"Maybe witches like the war. They can do what they like with everyone busy fighting. Now, do you want to hear about the purple horse or not? Turn back."

"Yes," said the little boy. He was looking up at her now, wide-eyed.

"All right. Well, the witch gave the doctor a magic spell to make the horse dark. But when the doctor tried it—*poof!* Purple as a hyacinth."

The child was finally distracted. "Was it a magic horse?" he demanded. "After it turned purple?"

Laura was tying off the bandages. The child's tears had dried. "Yes, of course. It could gallop from Paris to Peking in an hour. The doctor went straight to Berlin and pulled the kaiser's nose."

The child smiled at last. "I'd like a magic horse. I'd gallop away and find Elsie."

Elsie was his sister. They'd been walking to school together when the ship blew up. Laura didn't reply, but smoothed the matted, tow-colored hair and got up. Her brother's real name was Wilfred, but hardly anyone remembered. He'd been Freddie from infancy. He was serving overseas.

He still hadn't written back.

"Purple horse?" inquired the doctor-in-charge, passing. Unlike his civilian colleagues, he'd been behind the lines of the Somme in '16. He and Laura understood each other. They walked off together down the aisle between beds.

"Yes," said Laura, smiling. "It was early days. Some fool with the RAMC, straight from England. He was assigned the horse, white as you please, got windup about snipers. Tried aniline dye, the poor beast wound up violet."

The doctor laughed. Laura shook her head and consulted her endless mental checklist. But before she could set off, the three-month-old gash in her leg betrayed her. A cramp buckled her knee, and the doctor caught her by the elbow. Her leg was the reason she was in Halifax, discharged from the medical corps. A bit of shell casing, deep in the muscle. They'd got it out, but almost taken the limb with it. She'd been evacuated on a hospital train.

"Damn," she said.

"All right, Iven?" said the doctor.

"Just a cramp," said Laura, trying to shake it loose.

The doctor eyed her. "Iven, you're a wretched color. When did you come on shift?"

"Flattery, Doctor?" she said. "I'm cultivating a modish pallor." She didn't quite remember.

He looked her over, shook his head. "Go home. Or you'll be in bed with pneumonia. We can manage for twelve hours. Unless you *want* to go sprawling while holding syringes?"

"I haven't gone sprawling yet," she said. "And I still have dressings to—"

She could browbeat most of the staff, but not this one. "I'll do it. You are not the only person in Halifax who can dress burns, Sister."

She met his adamant eye, then gave in, threw him a mock salute, and went to take off her apron.

"And eat something!" the doctor called to her retreating back.

. . .

The wind struck her in the teeth when she went outside, dried her chapped lips. She pulled her cap closer round her ears. Clouds massed, lividly purple, over the water. She longed to go straight home and drink something hot. But she'd got off early. There was time to go to Veith Street. She hadn't been there since the explosion.

The wind rippled her skirt, made her nose ache. The task would not improve with keeping. She set off, limping. To her right, the Atlantic heaved under a field gray sky. To her left, the city sloped gently upward, blackened and torn by fire.

Laura Iven was sharp-faced and amber-eyed, her jaw angled, her mouth sweet, her glance satirical, a little sad. She wore a pale blue Red Cross uniform under a shabby wool coat. A knit cap, defiantly scarlet, hid tawny hair chopped short. She walked with the ghost of a brisk, supple stride, marred by the new limp.

The wind cried in broken steeples and sent eddies of blackened snow swirling round her boots. Boats in the icy harbor snubbed their mooring lines; no ship could dock at the burnt piers. The cold crept in off the water, reached dank fingers under her cap and down the collar of her coat. A lorry backfired from the opposite curb.

For a moment, she was back in Flanders. She jolted instinctively into the cover of a charred wall. One foot slid on the snow; her bad leg couldn't steady her. Only the wall saved her from going facedown. She got her balance, swearing colorfully, if silently, in the cant of soldiers from five nations.

The lorry rumbled past, puffing petrol. No explosion could keep Halifax down for long. The city lay at the world's crossroads. She'd never seen it silenced, except that one day. Perhaps her mother, who believed in prophecies, would have found a quotation for that howling quiet that came after the flash, and the rippling flat-topped cloud. She'd have whispered the Dies Irae maybe—*Day of Wrath*—even though Laura's parents were not so much Catholic as strange.

But she couldn't ask her parents. Her father had been on the water when the *Mont Blanc* exploded. Her mother had been at home, watching the ship burn from a front window. When it detonated, all the glass flew inward.

Laura kept walking. A flaw in the wind brought her a voice from the bay as though it spoke into her ear: *Come on, you fucking bastard*. She glanced out into the fairway, saw a tug fending off a freighter, everyone shouting. She kept on. Imagined sitting down to supper. A chicken, maybe, or buttered potatoes. Tried to conjure it clearly, but it slipped away. The war had fractured her concentration.

. . .

Their old neighborhood was called Richmond, and it teemed with industry, with kindness and goodwill. The whole region had answered Halifax's distress, had sent carpenters and seasoned wood, new furniture and canned goods. Undertakers.

Laura passed neighbors rebuilding. They called to her: questions about wounded relatives, snatches of news. She called back, answering, commiserating. Stopped once to look at a boil on the crown of a balding head. Promised to lance it when she had a moment. She had a surprising amount of experience with civilians. Plenty of Belgians, lacking alternatives near the fighting, came to army nurses for medical care. Laura didn't think there had ever been a war where the army delivered so many babies.

She kept walking, avoiding snowdrifts and shattered glass. Thought about Belgian babies. One or two small girls called Laure numbered among the children she'd eased into the world. Those were pleasant memories. She was concentrating so hard on them that she walked past the house before she recognized the place. But her feet stopped before her mind knew.

Memory supplied a small house, a little shabby. White clapboards, roughened with salt, a pitched roof. Her own upper window, looking out over the dockyard to the Narrows beyond. The path out the front door, lined with seashells, her mother's vegetable garden straggling up with the clover, fighting its way through the sandy soil.

But then she blinked and it was gone.

The stove was still there, half-melted, where the kitchen had been. Here were the remains of the parlor, a fireplace poker thrusting up from the ash. She pulled the poker free, jabbed it here and there. She didn't know what she ought to be looking for. Her mother's brooch? Silver spoons? The ash was layered with snow, new and old. Memory, which she'd spent the last six weeks outrunning, circled close; for a moment, her head was full of acrid smoke and falling sparks, herself stumbling through it, blood on her skirt, her hands, pooling on the floor of her parents' bedroom, her voice rigidly controlled, calling *Stay with me, come on,* glass in her fingers, under her knees, in her mother's eyes . . .

Laura shook the image away.

"Laura?" called a voice from the street behind.

She nearly lost her footing in the ashy snow. Her first wild thought was that it was her father at last, staggering bluish out of the harbor. But, she reminded herself, she didn't believe in ghosts.

"Miss Iven," corrected the voice. Then, more tentative, "Laura? You there?"

She turned. A man she knew stood in the fire-scarred street. "They said you'd come past," he said.

"As you see, Wendell," she called, hearing her own voice thin but perfectly steady. "How are you, sir? Delivering to Veith Street again?"

Wendell looked relieved to see her. "A bit, but I've been keeping a lookout for you in particular. A box came for your par—" He hesitated. "For you."

"That's very kind. How is Billy?" She crossed the snowy ground, brushing frozen ash and snow from her skirt. Billy was his son. Laura had pulled him through three nights of fever. He'd been walking to school too.

"He's all right. Fat as a dormouse now. Schoolchildren in Kansas collected pennies, sent up boxes of candy."

The ash on her fingers had left streaks on her blue dress. She thought, with distant irritation, that she must launder it. "What is it, Wendell?"

A lorry was parked in the street with a wooden crate in the back of it. He indicated the box. "This. Kept it for you. Wanted to do you a good turn." He hesitated. "It's from Flanders."

A chill skated across Laura's skin. She told herself it was the bitter wind off the water. "Thanks awfully. A bit bulky, isn't it? Any chance of a lift? I'm staying with the Parkeys, you know. In Fairview."

The Parkeys had hired Laura as a nurse-companion only a few days before the explosion. She'd been in their house, safely beyond the harbor, when the ship blew up. They'd waited up for her, when she'd come back late that night with glass embedded in her hands, blood drying on her clothes, and nowhere else to go. They'd fussed and bandaged and laundered. Offered her a room to live in.

Wendell said, "Of course I'll drive you, Miss Iven. You look like you could use a bite and a sleep, if you don't mind my saying so. The old ladies treating you all right?"

"Famously. They bake me pies, and I amuse them with ditties and bad words I picked up in Europe."

Wendell grinned. "Those Frenchmen swear a blue streak, I hear."

"Everyone does when you're patching them up. Stings, you know."

Wendell offered her a hand up into the lorry. Laura took it. She didn't look back at the ash heap. Perhaps thieves would come in the night and sieve the ruins. *Let them.* But though she stared straight ahead as they drove away, gooseflesh still rose, as though her mother were staring back, blindly accusing, out of the vanished upper window.

2

THIS FAIR DEFECT OF NATURE

·····

BLACKTHORN HOUSE STOOD SQUARE ON ITS PLOT, WITH PEEL-ing paint and a sagging roof. In summer, its shabbiness was windswept and romantic, but now the flower beds gaped bare and the birch by the door quivered naked in the air off the harbor.

"Servants' entrance, if you please," said Laura. She had a latch-key. She let herself into the kitchen, and Wendell followed. He laid the box by the hearth, and hesitated. He wasn't much older than she was. They'd been in school together, years ago. He'd a daughter, as well as his boy. "Iven—" he said. "Laura."

"Lord," she said. "Such a long face. I'll be along in a day or two, to see to Billy. Don't let him eat too many candies. Think of his teeth. And thank you. For the lift and for the box."

"I—" He caught her eye, swallowed, and went. The door closed behind him, and in the silence, Laura, standing still, was suddenly aware of every sound: the way the house groaned and settled in the chill, the whisper of the slow-burning fire. The box was indeed postmarked from Flanders. Addressed to Mr. and Mrs. Charles Iven.

Freddie was twenty-one. He wrote wretched poems and drew quite good pictures. He played football. He spent all his spare dimes on ice cream. She hadn't heard from him since she'd left Flanders on a hospital train. No letters had followed her to Étaples, or onto the ship, or across the ocean, but at first she'd been too ill to wonder much. And then she'd crawled off her sickbed in Halifax and the ship blew up.

They sent soldiers' effects if they died in hospital. But Laura hadn't had a death notice. This box could be anything. Freddie was somewhere on rest, drinking or playing cards or chasing the lice through the seams of his shirts.

Laura stared at the box and didn't move.

Then a woman cried out, somewhere in the house. Laura, half-relieved at the interruption, wrenched her gaze round and hurried out into the hall. Found herself in darkness, with amber light and a babble of sound pouring from beneath the parlor door. The heavy Aubusson dragged at her feet. A stentorian voice rose above the clamor. "Mr. Shaw!" it said. "James Shaw, if you are on the other side, if you are there, speak to us!"

Laura stopped. Another séance. The Parkeys amused themselves by giving séances. Séances were a growth industry, in 1918. The war was in its fourth year. People liked to point out that if mankind had learned to fly, and see bullets inside living skin, and sail underwater, then it stood to reason that they could talk to the dead. Séance money paid Laura's wages. The Parkeys had kept on paying her wages even though most of her time, after the explosion, had been spent in the YMCA hospital. Laura was grateful to the Parkeys.

Now the cries died away. The hall fell silent. Mr. Shaw, Laura thought, did not seem to be present. The commanding voice went up again. It sounded like Agatha, the eldest Miss Parkey. "Spirits! If any one of you knows a Mr. Shaw, knows the *fate* of Mr. Shaw, Mr. *James* Shaw, speak now."

Silence.

Laura took a step backward. The Parkeys could manage their séances without her.

"Wait," said a new voice, shrill and breathless. "I hear him, I hear footsteps. *Jimmy.*" A creak, and a crash, and a small, slender person shot into the hall and straight into Laura. With two good legs, Laura might have dodged. As it was, she hadn't a prayer. She went down in a heap, heard a soft "Oh" of dismay. Then small, ineffectual hands descended, trying to pull her to her feet. "I'm so sorry, I'm . . ."

"It's all right, ma'am," Laura said, trying to escape the helpful hands. Starbursts of pain exploded up her calf.

The stranger, surprisingly, stepped back. "I'm making it worse, aren't I? I do that."

The tone of wry regret was disarming. Laura said, "You are, rather." She flexed her ankle, rolled to her knees, and put up a hand. "All right. Pull in one direction?" Laura was hauled to her feet. She found herself standing before a finely dressed, old-fashioned person, half a head shorter than her, perhaps ten years older, and enchantingly beautiful. Outlandish hair, the color of fool's gold, framed neat cheekbones and a mouth like a rosebud. She was wearing black.

Laura got her balance and collected her wits. "Thank you, ma'am. Such a soft carpet. I'm glad I had the occasion to learn it firsthand."

"Oh, don't *thank* me," said the woman. "Are you sure you're all right? I mean, when I heard footsteps, I just— I was in there, and Miss Parkey was— Oh, I felt such a thrill, as though she was really *speaking* to the beyond, and then you were walking, so I had to run out and see. I *am* clumsy. I'm so sorry. I just— I thought it might be Jimmy."

"Jimmy?"

"My son. James. He's missing—I mean I haven't had news of him. Or— Well, he was in a battle. Near a place called— Oh, I can't pronounce it. Something with a *P*. Pass—"

"Passchendaele," supplied Laura, voice going a little flat. She'd gone home wounded in the midst of that ill-starred push. She refused to think of Freddie.

The stranger was still talking. "Oh, yes, of course—I never— Oh, those foreign words, you know— I hoped—that is—that the Parkeys could tell me where he is now. Because he's missing. I'm Penelope Shaw."

"Laura Iven," said Laura.

Mrs. Shaw smiled: an impish expression that crinkled her nose but didn't reach her worried eyes. "My aunt did always call me a heedless elephant of a girl. I'm really— Well, I usually do look where I'm going, but I— Oh, am I talking too much? I do that when I'm nervous, and—"

Three heads had popped out of the parlor: the Parkeys, neat as birds. Stout Lucretia, motherly Clotilde, vengeful Agatha. Agatha was blind. Her eyes, milky with cataracts, swiveled round the hallway in a parody of seeing.

"Not a ghost, Miss Parkey," Laura said to Agatha. "Only your elusive lodger. Good evening to you all."

"That's Laura," announced Agatha. "Could never mistake Laura."

Clotilde looked solemn. "The spirits have sent you, dear."

"Have they, Miss Parkey?"

"You are the link," intoned Lucretia. "Come in, dear, come in, we will hold hands and commune with the spirits once more."

That was what she got for escaping the kitchen. Tackled flat, then hauled into a séance. And yet . . . Mrs. Shaw had brightened with renewed hope, and the only thing waiting for Laura was that box.

She followed Mrs. Shaw and the Parkeys into the parlor. They had turned down the oil lamps—the Parkeys abhorred electric light—but the last of the daylight filtered in. A meager coal fire shone red in the grate. The Parkeys' wooden Ouija board was laid out on the green tablecloth. Mrs. Shaw's golden hair caught the lamplight.

"Come," said Agatha. "Quickly, quickly, while the spirits are with us. The hour is fortuitous, the hour is propitious."

She hissed her sibilants. Mrs. Shaw shuddered. Laura, used to comforting people, gave her a reassuring look. Agatha put the planchette on *H*. Laura put her fingers on the planchette. She wished she were sitting down to supper.

"Come, dear," said Agatha Parkey. "Let us begin."

Mrs. Shaw gasped when she saw Laura's hands. Her finger-joints were knotted, stiff with scar tissue, palms latticed red and white. "Oh, dear. What happened?"

Flanders happened. "I shook hands with a fine gentleman in a top hat," Laura said. "A mistake; they told me later he was Lord Beelzebub. You really meet all kinds of people at parties abroad."

But Mrs. Shaw didn't seem to register Laura's reply; she was obviously putting together Laura's limp and her hands, her uniform and the lines that stress had carved round her mouth. In a moment she was going to start asking questions. As though Laura, who had nursed in a war zone, was the closest thing in the room to Jimmy Shaw's ghost.

The last of the day was gone and the shadows lay thick in that room.

Laura, exasperated, shook her head across the table. Blessedly, Mrs. Shaw bit her pink lip and was silent.

"Don't be afraid," said Agatha, to the room at large. "The Departed love us. They want to be near us."

Mrs. Shaw looked down at the planchette.

"Now," said Agatha. "We fix our minds on the spirit we wish to summon, and we close our eyes." The little wavering gas flame gilded their hands. Agatha's blind eyes were fixed on the board. "We are in search of one who was in life called James Shaw, son of Penelope Shaw."

Silence in answer, and stillness.

Agatha lifted her head, eyes closed now, and addressed the darkness. "James?" she said. "James Shaw? Will you speak to us?"

The floor creaked. A hush lay like a hand over Blackthorn House, and in the silence, almost imperceptibly, the planchette crept toward *yes*. Laura hadn't felt them manipulate it, but that was unsurprising. The Parkeys were professionals. Mrs. Shaw had gone white.

"Who is here?" demanded Agatha.

J-I-M

"Jimmy!" cried Mrs. Shaw. "Jimmy! Where are you? Are you— Have you passed on, dear?" She had begun to shake. Laura felt it through the table.

The planchette drifted to *yes*. Then it kept going. L-I-S-T, said the planchette. Mrs. Shaw's gaze was locked on the moving arrow.

"Listen," gasped Lucretia. "But listen to what?" The world outside was utterly still.

B-E-W-R, said the planchette.

"Beware?" echoed Clotilde, sharp.

Mrs. Shaw said, "No, but— Jimmy? Darling? Are you all right?"

BWR MSIC MROR, said the planchette. HIM.

This was strange even for the Parkeys. MROR? Mirror? The detritus of Laura's brain offered her a vague association with the Lady of Shalott, Freddie declaiming the verses from Tennyson while she pored over an anatomy textbook: *The mirror crack'd from side to side,* *"The curse is come upon me,"* *cried* . . .

"No, but—" Now Mrs. Shaw was searching the empty air with frantic eyes. "Jimmy? Is it really you?"

DED, said the Ouija board. BUT HES ALIV.

Mrs. Shaw didn't speak.

"Who's alive?" demanded Clotilde.

FRED, said the planchette. FREDI FRED FR FIN FIND FIND. And if there was any more, Laura didn't see it because she'd wrenched back her chair, awkward on the carpet, turned away, and left the room.

3

DAY OF WRATH

·····

AT ANOTHER TIME, LAURA WOULD HAVE BORNE IT, IN SILENCE if not in good humor, out of respect to her employers. And gone to comfort Mrs. Shaw after it was done. But the presence of the box had shredded her nerves. She hadn't realized how shaken she was until she found herself shuddering in the hall.

If anyone from the parlor called out to her, Laura didn't hear, and didn't trust herself to turn. Combat nursing had given her tongue the edge of a sawtooth bayonet when she was moved, and she didn't want to turn it on kind, bereaved Mrs. Shaw, or on the scheming, silly old ladies who'd emptied their linen cupboards for her and given her a place to live.

But Laura was shaken enough, going to the kitchen, that at first she didn't notice the smell.

It was faint. A little earthy, a little sulfurous, very rotten. It was the miasma that lingered in men's clothes when they came out of the trenches. Laura had thought she'd never smell it again.

The smell was stronger in the kitchen. The box lying by the hearth drew Laura's gaze like a waiting scorpion, with the smell clinging round it. The heat from the fire must have . . . Was she breathing? She hardly felt it as she searched jerkily for a pry bar and wedged it under the lid.

Inside was a stiff, stained jacket.

She'd last seen Freddie—was it in July? August. He'd had leave and come to see her. They'd gone to a café in Poperinghe. Eaten a vast number of eggs, heaps of greasy chips. Drunk far too much of that terrible white wine, from the one-franc bottles. He'd been all right. Thin, but they all were thin, and a faraway look in his eyes. They all had that too. He'd smiled at her, just a little gap-toothed, still freckled as an egg. Her brave baby brother. It had been a bloody summer, but a successful one. The Allies had pushed the Germans back at Messines. But then the offensive stalled.

"They'll leave it there, for the winter," Laura had told him, deep into the second bottle of wine. "The attack. They'll wait until spring. Can't you smell the rain? Can't come soon enough." She waved her glass at the sky. "Get on with it, rain." She poured out her glass, a half-drunk offering. Freddie looked on disapprovingly. "Hush," she said, smiling. "I'll buy us another bottle."

The Belgians said the rain would come early that year. And when it did, the ground would turn to soup. Armies didn't attack in soup. They survived the summer, Laura had thought, hazy with wine. They'd survive the war. They *would*.

Freddie didn't reply. He was sketching. A little grease from lunch shone on his chin. When he turned his paper round, she could see her own face, done in knifing black lines, the tilt of her eyes, the angle of her jaw. The marks of exhaustion, the flush from the wine, the empty gaiety, her hidden, relentless fear. His damned gift, to capture what he saw. It was worse than a mirror. She didn't say anything.

Her other piece of news was on the tip of her tongue: that she'd been ordered up to Brandhoek, west of Ypres, to one of the casualty clearing stations in range of bombardment. But she bit it back. The sun was warm, her stomach was full, someone out of sight was playing an accordion, skillfully. They had the whole afternoon ahead of them. No one who'd been long at war gave too much thought to tomorrow. She wanted to enjoy the present. She could tell him by letter. "They'd better stop," she finished, and poured them both more wine. "When it rains."

"They'll stop," he echoed, shutting his notebook, to her relief. He grinned at her. "Now, what do you say we have a smoke and then eat the same lunch over again?"

· · ·

But there wasn't a telegram, Laura thought. They sent a telegram. If a soldier died.

How would a telegram have found her? Her known address was now an ash heap. Besides, the army had diverted everyone they could to digging bodies out of collapsed houses, not shuffling round with telegrams. And who could blame them? Halifax was just a city. Just people. They hadn't expected the war to come, slyfoot across the ocean, borne like contagion in a ship full of high explosive.

Laura steeled herself, reached forward, and drew the jacket out. Mud flaked off. The cloth was stained dark. The army might send soldiers' effects, but there wasn't time to launder their clothes. There was no smell of a gut wound, not enough blood to have killed him quickly. She tried not to let her mind catalogue all the ways a man could die slowly. Her fingertips were stained dark, when she laid the uniform aside. Mechanically, she turned to the other odds and ends. There were not many of them. Spare buttons. A tin of pastilles. A whistle. A pocket Bible. A set of homemade playing cards in a box made from a shell casing.

His identity tags.

Pvt. Wilfred Charles Iven
23rd Halifax Rifles

The world swam, her vision tunneling as her hand closed tight round the disc—discs? She opened her hand. Noted dimly that she'd bit her lip bloody. Both tags were there, the red one and the green. Both. But they took the red tag to send home. The other stayed with the body. Why— Well, there was no telling. The fog of war. She put the tags in one of her dress pockets.

Scarcely knowing what she did, Laura picked up the Bible next. It fell open. Revelation. Her eyes landed on a quotation: *For the devil has come down to you, having great wrath, because he knows he has a short time . . .* The smell of the mud seemed to collect in her mouth and coat her tongue.

She knelt there for a few moments, mastering an overwhelming nausea. She laid a hand again on the stiff wool jacket, felt something sewn into the lining, where the men kept field dressings. When her hands were steady enough, she slipped her scissors out of her skirt pocket and snipped the seam.

To her surprise, she found a postcard. A picture of a castle in the mountains, faded and much handled. Smeared with brown stains, obviously wetted through at least once. She turned it over. *Bayern* was printed on the back. A *German* postcard? Why would Freddie have it? A trophy, from a dead man or a captured trench? But Freddie had never gone for souvenirs, not like some men did. She looked closer. There was something written on the back, penciled lightly, in English, in a handwriting she did not know. *I will bring him back if I can. If I don't, and the war is over, you must ask . . .*

The rest of it was blotted by a stain, and no matter how much Laura peered, she couldn't make it out. Finally she slipped the postcard into the pocket with the tags. What else? His sketchbook—where was his sketchbook? She scrabbled again through the box's contents. It wasn't there. All those drawings, the truest measure of his soul, the mirror he held to the world. Gone.

He was gone.

They're all gone . . .

And then her hands were empty, and she didn't know what to do. She didn't cry. She felt nothing but blankness, and a faint confusion.

That was how Penelope Shaw found her, sometime later. Kneeling rigid over a bloody shirt and a Bible, a small heap of dirty oddments. Mrs. Shaw halted in the kitchen doorway. "Oh," she said. "Oh, I'm so sorry. I didn't realize. Are you—are you all right? Of course not, but I mean—Miss Iven?"

"I'm all right," said Laura.

There was a silence. Then Mrs. Shaw put a hand, bird-light, on Laura's shoulder. "I am sorry," she whispered again.

Laura laid her scarred fingers briefly over Mrs. Shaw's. Neither of them said anything else.

Outside, it had begun to snow.

THE BOTTOMLESS PIT

·····

H E COULDN'T SEE ANYTHING.

Couldn't hear anything either, since the shell came down. His ears were still ringing. He thought, *This is death*, and tried to let go.

And perhaps he did, for a time. His mind drifted. His body seemed far away. He'd been at the door of the pillbox, flinging a— No. He wasn't sure what had happened. He remembered the rattle of a machine gun, rain and bullets smacking together into the mud.

He remembered running like an animal, dead bodies, gray uniforms, the roar of the explosion. Dickinson, a bloody froth at his lips. No—was that earlier? And now: himself in darkness. Buried. Dead and buried, wasn't that the phrase? The shell must have collapsed the pillbox somehow. Or flipped it. Or killed him outright.

He was trapped.

He composed himself. He didn't mind dying. Or being dead.

Was he dead? His ribs ached. And his skull. His body was all around him, hurting, inescapable. And then his other senses came back too. He smelled stagnant water, blood, cordite. The muck of his own sweat. Heard breathing. Each breath pained him. He tried to breathe less. But the sound went on.

No, it wasn't him. It was someone else. He lurched upright. The movement arrowed pain down his stiff spine. He tried to see. Failed. It was utterly dark.

"Who's there?" he demanded, voice wavering. "Who's there?"

No answer. It was only the breathing, animal-loud, that told him he wasn't alone.

Perhaps, he thought, this was hell and that nameless *other* was waiting to devour him. But when the breaths faltered, he didn't know which would be worse, to be devoured by a beast or left alone in the dark.

"Hello?" he said. His head had cleared a little. He wondered if it was one of their boys or a German. Maybe, if it was a German, they could kill each other. Underground like rats. Better than waiting to die. Or— Had there been a grenade attached to his person? Somewhere? He groped. Not anymore. He had nothing but his sopping clothes, the contents of his pockets. He'd shed his pack when he charged the pillbox: his last clear memory. Had been carrying his rifle, he supposed, but it was gone now. Lost in the chaos.

"Are you wounded?" It came to him that a German wouldn't speak English, so why bother?

Then a deep, unfamiliar voice said out of the blackness, in English, "No." Pause. "I am dead." An accent, but slight. Just a hardening of consonants. German, after all?

Was that a joke? He decided it was. Soldiers joked about worse things than being dead. "Damned uncomfortable for being dead."

No answer, just a slight alteration in breathing, out instead of in. A laugh? Then the other voice said, "The air will go—soon, I think. And do you imagine"—a pause, coughing on the stink—"that anyone will—dig us out?"

"No," he said. Outside their tomb, the Canadian Expeditionary Force was scrabbling up Passchendaele Ridge, under a sky pouring water and high explosive. A search would be as good as a suicide, and there were easier ways to kill yourself. No, he and old Fritz were dead. It didn't matter that they were still breathing.

Shouldn't he be more afraid? He thought, *Laura, I'm sorry*. He was, but distantly.

"Maybe this is hell," he said, only half-joking. He supposed that in hell it didn't matter if you were Canadian or German. That put the war in perspective if you liked. The devil worked in mysterious ways.

"Are you hurt?" he asked again.

Pause. "Does it matter?"

"I suppose not."

Silence.

"I'm Wilfred Iven."

More silence. He thought Fritz wouldn't answer. Then—"Hans Winter." Just the name, no service rank. Well, Freddie hadn't offered one. A German, after all. Should he be more horrified? Then again, dead men didn't have enemies.

Freddie touched his own face, felt his hair plastered flat with wet earth, his tin hat gone. His fingernails hurt; he'd probably torn them away when he'd scrabbled for room in the first, convulsive moments.

Increasingly afraid, he tried to speak again. "Are you—" but he couldn't think of anything to say. He couldn't say *I'll cut your throat for you, if you'll do it for me*. But he couldn't just lie there either, not with fear rising in him. Goading him. The German said nothing. Where was he? "Winter?"

Silence. All Freddie could do was reach forward, blindly. The ground hurt his palms. His hand found a shoulder: a layer of mud, overlaying the sodden wool of an overcoat. "Wint—" he tried again, but, as cold as a snake, the other man's hand closed hard about his wrist, twisting his arm, wrenching him round and over, until his face was in the soup, and he was gagging for air.

"What are you doing?" demanded the German.

Freddie tried to pull away. But the other man was immensely strong. "Answer me."

"I'm not—I wanted—" Freddie choked.

Abruptly the hands were gone, the presence at his back was gone. He heard the rustle as the German moved away. He sat up, spitting out slimy water. If they were going to fight to the death after all, it wouldn't be much of a fight. He tried to think what to say. "I just— It was strange, talking to—to nothing. In the dark."

"Yes," said the German. He'd stopped moving.

They were both silent.

Freddie wondered what Winter looked like. It was odd to think he was going to die beside someone whose face he'd never seen.

Better than dying alone. He turned so that his back was against the same unseen rubble as the German's, close enough to hear the other man breathe. Perhaps the German felt the same fear of the silence, for he did not move away again. Freddie closed his eyes and let his mind drift.

Winter didn't speak again.

5

THE VOICE OF
THE SEVENTH ANGEL

.....

HALIFAX, NOVA SCOTIA, CANADIAN MARITIMES
JANUARY–FEBRUARY 1918

WHEN LAURA WAS SMALL, HER MOTHER USED TO TELL HER stories of Armageddon. It was coming, she'd say. This year. Or next. She'd describe the pageantry of it: the Four Horsemen, the Beast from the Sea, the devil riven and falling. Fire from heaven, trumpets and thrones, the infallible judgment of God. Rewards for the good, and punishments for the wicked. Laura used to dream of it, as a child—terrible angels, a great dragon—and she always ate her peas and helped with the washing-up, so God would see her virtuous.

And you were right, Maman, Laura thought. *It caught us up after all. War, plague, famine, death, the sky on fire, the sun black. Aren't you glad you were right? You couldn't change anything, you couldn't stop anything. But at least you knew it was coming. The end of the world. Was that comforting, in the end?*

Other times Laura would think, furiously, at her mother, *Pageantry? Justice? What a joke.* Armageddon was a fire in the harbor, a box delivered on a cold day. It wasn't one great tragedy, but ten million tiny ones, and everyone faced theirs alone.

The day after Laura opened the box, she worked a fourteen-hour shift at the hospital, but even work was not enough to keep her from thinking.

"Iven?" said the doctor-in-charge once, but she shook her head, and got on with it.

That night, she wrote the Red Cross, and her brother's CO, for news, sitting at her little writing desk, with a second glass of gin beside her. She didn't need to think what to say in her letter. She'd read a hundred just like it: *How did he die, where did he die?* She sealed the flap, and finished her gin staring out the window.

The answer from the Red Cross was strange. *Private Wilfred Iven is missing presumed killed following the taking of Passchendaele Ridge. Further information will be sent on.*

Laura crumpled the letter in her hand. Then she smoothed it out, frowning. *Missing* could mean *taken prisoner,* but it usually meant *blown to kingdom come.* Her father, who'd been alongside the *Mont Blanc* when all that high explosive ignited, was missing. Jimmy Shaw, who'd disappeared on Passchendaele Ridge, was also, technically, missing.

But if Freddie was missing in the *kingdom come* sense—she couldn't have his clothes, could she? Or his tags. His Bible. Unwillingly, she remembered the Parkeys' séance. BUT HES ALIV . . .

The Parkeys were a delightful trio of swindlers.

Then another letter came, in reply to one of Laura's. From the head sister of Laura's old mobile ambulance. Kate White had been with Laura at Brandhoek, working while the gas alarm blared, keeping an ear out for incoming shells, trying to stop wounded boys from tearing their stitches when they crawled for cover under their cots.

Laura had to put Kate's letter under every light she could muster in order to puzzle out the faint lines of pencil, daubed with mud and rain. The phrasing of the sentences was careful, and a little strange:

I am so glad you are alive, Laura. We feared the worst, when we heard the news from Halifax. I hope you will not give up hope.

Why, a patient of mine said he saw his captain, beloved and dead
three years, staring at him through a window. Anything, after all,
is possible. Do not give up hope, my dear.

Laura read through this missive twice and then sat back. Nurses
wrote kindly fictions to bereaved relatives all the time, but Kate
wouldn't do that to her. Of course, Kate's letters had to pass under
the eye of the military censor, so perhaps she was trying to convey
something obliquely. But Laura couldn't imagine what. Kate had
nursed in South Africa years before war broke out in Europe; she
was the least fanciful person Laura knew. Laura found herself thinking of the odd postcard, sewn so carefully into Freddie's jacket. *I*
will bring him back . . .

At that point, Laura wrote to everyone she knew, anywhere on
the Front. *Was he there? Did he die in this hospital? Or that one?*
Where? How? Do you know where he is buried?

She got replies, of course. Condolences, nonanswers. But she
could get no reply that satisfied her.

. . .

Another week went by, and a note came from the beautiful woman
from the séance: Mrs. Penelope Shaw. Mrs. Shaw was much more
concise on paper than she was in person, her writing a flawless cop-
perplate:

I am afraid of sounding heartless as well as frivolous, when you
are in mourning, and as the Parkeys tell me, much engaged at the
hospital. But if you have any inclination, would you like to have
tea with me? I can promise sugar, I think, and oatcakes and
sandwiches—plenty of both. And I have a chum staying with me
whom I should like you to meet. We were girls together, and she
has been overseas like you.

Laura hesitated. But anything, she thought, was better than what she was doing now, her days a blur of work, her evenings a blur of stealthy drinking. And Mrs. Shaw had been kind, the night Laura opened the box by the kitchen fire.

Laura went to the desk and dashed off a reply: *Thank you, very happy to join etc.*

6

MY KINGDOM FULL
OF DARKNESS

.....

PASSCHENDAELE RIDGE, FLANDERS, BELGIUM
NOVEMBER 1917

FREDDIE DIDN'T KNOW HOW MUCH TIME HAD PASSED.
Sometimes he could hear the German—Winter—breathing
with him, leaning unseen up against the same slimy wall. Neither of them spoke. Freddie couldn't think of anything to say. He
kept waiting for the air to run out, but it didn't.

How long did it take to die? The bruised shock that had cush-
ioned him through the first moments had left him, and in its place,
proper thoughts, panicky thoughts, circled in the depths of his mind.
He was freezing. He felt through his pockets, to give his trembling
hands something to do. Found a tin. *Bully beef,* he thought. And
with it a packet of biscuits. It was something. No water-bottle.

"Are you hungry?" he asked Winter. Freddie wasn't. His stomach churned. But he had to do something. Anything but lie there
waiting.

A startled hitch in the German's breathing. Then— "No," Winter said. And added, carefully polite, "No, thank you."

"I—I'm not either," said Freddie, although when he thought
about it, maybe he was. Must not be dead yet. It was damp where

they were sitting. The rain was getting in somehow, bubbling up out of the saturated earth. Was it drinkable? No. *Water water everywhere and not a drop to—*

Maybe they would drown. Drown while already buried, in a pillbox in Flanders.

"I'm from Halifax," he said, struggling to fend off the silence. Why couldn't they have just been killed at once? He thought he heard Winter turn toward him as he rambled: "Nova Scotia. Bluenose to the core, you know, although my mother's from Montreal. My father worked on a tug in the Narrows. There. My sister's out here too—in Flanders—a nurse—a proper nurse is Laura, not one of those who learned out here, practicing on us poor devils. An officer, even." A flicker of pride. "CAMC gave all the nurses commissions. She's a captain now, you know. Or the equivalent. Read you the riot act as soon as look at you. Cleverest and prettiest sister you could ask for."

Winter said nothing.

Cursing himself for his rising panic—*Why can't you just die quietly like a man, Iven?*—he said, "Where are you from, sir? Mr. Winter. Er, Herr Winter."

No answer. There was a thick smell rising from the sludge of water at their feet. Freddie dropped the tin of beef, swore, and began groping around for it. His hand met sodden cloth. It was a moment before he realized what he was touching. He jerked back. He'd touched dead hands before, of course. He'd once been given a stack of sandbags and tasked with the cleanup after a direct hit on an artillery installation. There was one trench, near Vimy, where some poor fellow had been buried in the breastworks with his arm sticking out. Men would shake the hand for luck when they went up the line; or did until the bone started showing.

But it was different now. Aboveground, even in trenches, you were certain that there was an essential difference between you and the blue-gray fingers sticking out of the revetments. *He* might be buried in the breastworks, in a sandbag, in pieces, but *you* would, one day, when the war ended, go home to Canada and make a fortune painting stormy landscapes, or at least enough money to publish your mediocre poems.

But here . . .

Freddie's world narrowed suddenly to the knowledge that in a day or in an hour, it would be him sliding into the sludge, and he'd be there floating with the other ones. Missing, presumed killed, until in five years or ten Laura gave up hoping. And all the while he'd be down here in the dark . . .

Something began to shatter, deep in his own mind, and he didn't know what animal sound of terror he was making, until the German, with surprising accuracy, reached around, seized Freddie's shoulder, and cracked him across the face.

Freddie's head rocked back and he tasted blood. The grip on his shoulder was hard, pinching. Then Winter's hand fell away, and Freddie heard it fall back, *thump,* to his side.

"I—thank you," said Freddie, after a strange pause.

Winter was silent. Then— "Did you drop the tin?"

"I—yes," said Freddie. "I can't find it now." It hardly seemed important.

He felt Winter stiffen. "Children in Munich are eating bread of turnips. And you will waste meat?"

Freddie had a moment of blank incomprehension. "Eating this—or not—won't help the children in Munich. Wait—is that where you're from?"

Pause. "From the mountains. And it is wrong to waste food." It was physically impossible to *feel* someone frowning, and yet.

Groping around the muck was beyond him. "You look, if you want it."

"I don't," Winter admitted. He didn't move. He hadn't moved much at all, except to subdue Freddie. His breathing hadn't settled. It was still fast and harsh and—

"You— Are you wounded?" said Freddie.

A silence. "Yes," said Winter, in his precise voice. "But not badly enough."

To die, he meant. Or at least to die quickly. But— "It hurt you. It hurt you to hit me."

"I do not want to be alive in here with a madman."

"What if I'd killed you? What if I'd got too frightened and killed you?"

He was startled to hear a huff, Winter's half-voiced laughter. "Kill me by all means, if you like. Do you want to—be here alone with my corpse?"

"Where are you hurt?" Freddie demanded. He thought, *Oh, Christ, what if he's dying? What if he could die any second?* It didn't matter how quickly they'd try to kill each other if they were anywhere else. Freddie knew that if Winter died, he'd go mad. He wouldn't have enough sanity left even to kill himself. And if some miraculous hand of God came down and freed him, it wouldn't matter because his mind would never get out of the pillbox.

"Don't die," he whispered.

He heard the scrape, as Winter shifted. Perhaps he understood.

Freddie said, "I'll— I can bandage your wound. If you'll tell me where."

A hesitation. "Left upper arm."

At least Freddie was good at bandaging. Laura had ruined several of his precious hours of leave, drilling him until he could stanch a wound efficiently, disinfect it, and tie it up. He crawled around awkwardly to Winter's other side, found the arm by touch. Felt his jacket soaked—although that could be water as easily as blood. Under the wool, Winter was bone under skin, his body held rigid. He didn't move when Freddie slit the sleeve enough to get at the gash, fumbling in his own jacket for bandages. All soldiers carried them, already soaked with iodine. He wrapped the wound by feel. It had to hurt. Winter didn't make a sound. At least now it would stop bleeding. "You should have said something before," Freddie said, hearing, with pain, his sister in his voice. He tied off the gauze. *Christ, why are we still alive?* "You've probably been bleeding this whole time." How long had it been?

"Perhaps." Winter's voice was still dry, although not so steady as before. "I was not wanting to draw things out."

Freddie sat back. "Why did you tell me, then?"

"You are a boy. It would be cruel, to make you hear me die." They were near enough to speak into each other's ears, and Freddie found himself reluctant to move away. Winter's body was the last warmth in his whole world.

Freddie's exhale was almost a laugh. "Not a boy."

"No? How old are you?"

"Twenty-one. *You* can't be much older."

"I am thirty-five," said Winter. He'd a deep, measured voice. Freddie wondered if he was—had been—an officer. Didn't dare ask. Noncommissioned, maybe. He wanted to draw the conversation out. Anything was better than the silence, leavened with the war booming on, endless, outside.

"And from Munich?"

"I had a farm. In the mountains. Meadows. Cattle." The deep voice dropped until Freddie could hardly hear. "Honey. Black pines, with the sun slanting in."

Freddie said, "Well—Halifax doesn't look like that. But we have the sea. I love the sea. Once, when I was in school, I tried to choose a different word every day for it, for the color on it. I'd pick a word and then mix up colors—how I scrounged for paints. It was easy, at first. Silver, I said, and mauve and sable. Smalt. Lapis. Rose. Pigeon's feather. Iron. I let myself have any time of day, you see. Dawn or dark or noon. That helped. But by the end I was making up words, and none of my colors looked anything like. Bloody pretentious little thing I was, really—I've my list somewhere, in the box under my bed at home . . . Wait. Where'd you learn English?"

"I was a waiter."

"I thought you had a farm."

"The farm was my father's. I went to England. I was a waiter in Brighton. I learnt English there. Many of us were in England, before the war. We went home to enlist. The Tommies used to cry *Hey waiter,* where the line was close together, and their snipers would shoot the men who moved."

Freddie found himself laughing—giggling almost. "Really? Hey waiter, and—and some poor dupe's head pops up—Yes, mister?—and *blam.* Really? This war's like a two-penny vaudeville, honestly." He was hiccuping, almost in tears. He slumped against the wall beside Winter and tried to get hold of himself.

Winter said, austerely, "My father was ill when I went back to Bayern. He is dead now. I gave the farm to my cousin before I enlisted. He promised to give it back. If I lived."

They were both silent.

Then Winter added, low: "Iven, there must be a little air coming in, for we are not dead."

The thought of being there until they died of thirst or drank the slime at their feet was beyond contemplation. "I suppose so," said Freddie. His mouth felt as if it had been stuffed with cotton. "I—I think I can kill you, if you want. Could we—could we do it at the same time?"

"Kill each other? What if one person died and the other didn't?"

Freddie said nothing. He was so thirsty.

"I have told you what I—who I was," said Winter. Perhaps he was as afraid as Freddie to let the silence return. "Now you. What did you do in—Halifax?" He pronounced the word with care.

"I was a harbor clerk," said Freddie. "I painted pictures. Some of them were decent. And I write—I wrote—poems."

Winter said, wry, "We all did. Barracks were a—hellish choir of verses—once. Tell me one of your poems."

"I—" said Freddie. "I can't." There was a gulf—a chasm—between the man in the pillbox and the boy in Halifax who'd sketched and scribbled things in his notebook. Even the soldier he'd been three weeks ago, on rest, standing in a barn doorway, looking out at the October rain. He'd crossed some invisible barrier. Wilfred Iven was dead. "But—I—I could recite one."

"Recite, then," said Winter.

Freddie groped for words. The darkness seemed to press on his eyeballs. *Poetry?* In this pit, at the edge of death? Poetry was nothing. *They* were nothing.

Then he thought that even useless words, written for another world, were better than the silence. He licked dry lips and said, "Remember *Paradise Lost?* After the Fall? Satan woke up in the dark. My mother used to say that the devil limps because he fell from heaven."

"Yes," said Winter.

Softly Freddie said, " 'Is this the region, this the soil, the clime, said then the lost Archangel—' "

He hesitated. No poet, in his bleakest dreams, could ever have imagined this darkness. But Winter said, "Go on."

" '—this the seat that we must change for heaven, this mournful gloom for that celestial light?' "

A crash interrupted him, a shattering roar. A heavy must have hit the remains of the pillbox. The bombardment had come close again. Freddie lost his grip on the words. The world convulsed. He tasted copper, realized he was bleeding. He jerked in the dark, some instinct to get away. But there was nowhere to go. He struck his head on—something. Winter was beside him; his last memory was of trying confusedly to catch hold of his hand, feeling an instant of gratitude—that they were dying and not lingering, buried alive. Then he was unconscious.

7

IT HAD TWO HORNS LIKE A LAMB BUT SPOKE LIKE A DRAGON

.....

HALIFAX, NOVA SCOTIA, CANADIAN MARITIMES

FEBRUARY 1918

PENELOPE SHAW'S FOYER WAS A VICTORIAN RIOT OF WALLPAPER finches. Her hat stand was carved to look like a candelabrum and had to weigh fifty pounds. Laura draped her knitted scarlet tam on the latter, where it hung limply and looked inadequate. "I should have brought a larger hat," said Laura. "If I had such a thing."

"I am so glad to see you," said Mrs. Shaw. She had got a little thinner since that night in the Parkeys' parlor, and she was dressed in full Victorian mourning, black from head to toe. But her back was straight, her clothes brushed, her manners impeccable. She said, "How are you, my dear? Have you been sleeping?"

"I'll do," said Laura. "The hospital has started to empty out. I think I shall take up a hobby. I read about a fine British lady who breeds hellebores."

"I volunteered at the hospital in the early days." Mrs. Shaw led Laura down a thick-carpeted hallway. "Spooning soup into people.

But I wasn't good at it, really. I'd see all those poor children—" Her voice faltered. "And I didn't do them any good, fumbling and getting teary-eyed. I was better at knitting—I've been making ever so many baby blankets. And little socks. This way."

Laura found herself walking gingerly. The carpet was the tender yellow of buttercups. She wasn't used to softness. The Parkeys lived in a rambling old pile, and the old ladies were as indifferent to comforts as a trio of hunting dogs. Laura was worse, after years in field hospitals. She could sleep on bare dirt if she had to. But Penelope Shaw's house was frivolous, and colorful, and soft. It made Laura uneasy.

"Oh—I'm so glad you're here," Mrs. Shaw said, half-turning as she walked. "It's the least I can do, the very least, after tackling you in that silly way. And then you found out—and I . . ." Her voice faltered again. "What do you like with tea? Sugar is so dear, but I managed a little—and oatcakes, and I—" She threw open a parlor door. "Oh, Mary, my dear, here's the lady I was telling you about. Miss Laura Iven, Mrs. Mary Borden."

She sailed into the room. Laura, startled, paused in the doorway. She knew the name Mary Borden. Mrs. Shaw had led them into a charming, old-fashioned parlor. Laura had a muddled impression of pastels: peonies on china, a pink and green rug. A fine coal fire going in the grate, the last word in luxury, with coal so dear. Penelope Shaw and her house together were like a picture postcard from the last century. From the world that had ended when the war began.

The woman waiting for them stood out starkly against all the old-fashioned loveliness. About Mrs. Shaw's age, and her hair was short as Laura's. No corset. A ruffian's smile. The look in her eyes, Laura recognized from her own mirror. "Mary Borden, Laura Iven," said Mrs. Shaw.

Mary said, "A pleasure. I've heard of you, of course, Iven. A Croix de Guerre, wasn't it?"

"Pleased to meet you, Mrs. Borden," said Laura. She'd been decorated in '15, after the first gas attack of the war. It was nothing she wanted a memento of, let alone to discuss with a stranger. "Is that curried chicken in that sandwich? How international of you, Mrs. Shaw. How many can I eat before you show me the door?"

"Call me Pim," said Mrs. Shaw. "My friends do. As many as you care to. You want fattening up." She turned the plate. "These have jam, and these have roast beef."

"You angel. Call me Laura," said Laura, sitting down on a raspberry-striped loveseat. She wondered if Pim would let her smoke a cigarette in her parlor. Probably not. She took four sandwiches. Pim's eyes got big.

"I heard rumors you'd died, Iven," Mary said. "Thirdhand, of course, but still. You look well, for a corpse. But not unscathed either."

"No? I'm blithe as a bird," said Laura, taking a bite of a sandwich. "What brings you to Halifax, Mrs. Borden? Done with the war at last?"

Mary Borden, not really a nurse herself, was still moderately famous. She had founded a private aid station behind the lines—in the Belgian sector, Laura thought, or was it the French—in the early days of the war. Managed to convince a lot of skeptical people to let her run it.

"No. I'm going back a week from Thursday," said Mary.

"How do you like your tea, Laura?" Pim put in.

"Hot," said Laura. "Extremely. With four sugars, and as much milk as you can cram in."

"Same for me, Pim," Mary said.

"My," said Pim, pouring and stirring.

"It's because of the water," said Mary. "In the forbidden zone. They chlorinate it, or we'd all have dysentery. Enough sugar you don't taste the chlorine. The sweet's a bit of a habit now. It keeps you on your feet when there's a push on."

"The where?" said Pim, looking fascinated.

Mary looked briefly self-conscious. "I mean the back area, behind the lines. It's just what I call it. There are signs everywhere in French: *zone interdite*, they say. So I call it the forbidden zone."

"How romantic," said Laura dryly. She sipped her tea, and took up her fourth sandwich. Strawberry jam. She ate it in four bites. Pim looked impressed and nudged the plate in her direction. Laura started on another round of curry.

"And your hands?" asked Mary.

"Ten fingers, all present and accounted for," said Laura, concentrating on her sandwich.

"Have a cake, Mary," said Pim, with a hint of reproof in her voice.

Mary was undaunted. "It's all right. Manners are going to be a casualty of this war, along with corsets and long hair. You're a relic, my beautiful Penelope. Never change. Iven's a modern creature. She's not offended. Can you still work?"

"Why should I?" said Laura. "I'm retiring to my estate in the country and growing hellebores. Pim will tell you."

"Mary," said Pim. "Manners may not survive the war, but I'll have them in my parlor, if you please."

Mary raised her cup in salute, picked up a sandwich. "I was sorry, Iven, when Pim told me they'd sent your brother's things."

Laura took an oatcake. She could not quite keep the edge from her voice. "They say you once carried a German cavalry spear into King's Cross station. A vicious rumor, no doubt?"

"The papers exaggerated," said Mary, accepting the change of subject. "But yes, I did. In the early days. Caused a sensation." She smiled to herself. "I drove ambulances at first. Then started my own aid station. Brought the Belgians hot chocolate in the trenches. Lord, the lines were close together. Once Fritz sent a message over—told me to wear a skirt so they wouldn't snipe me by mistake—I was right in the trenches nearly every day—puttees were better for getting around, you know." She shook her head. "Eventually I moved, moved again. A Belgian baron had abandoned his château—who could blame him?—so I took his house and grounds at Couthove. Now I've nearly got a full hospital. We call it an aid station, so we don't ruffle feathers, but we've got surgical bays, triage, and Madame Curie even donated an X-ray. They tolerate me well enough, at the various HQs, so long as I drum up funds myself. Not like they can turn down hospital beds these days. Especially not the French. I do some nursing, but mostly I run the place. I'm better at that sort of thing anyway."

Pim looked like she was struggling to decide whether to be horrified or impressed. It was a measure of their new world that a woman could talk with equanimity about running a hospital in a war zone.

Laura studied Mary over the rim of her teacup. "But you're far from your hospital now, Mrs. Borden."

Mary shrugged. "We run on private donations. With America entering the war, I thought it a good moment to come and pass the hat, as it were. Give some lectures. There's plenty of money, this side of the Atlantic. America's got most of Europe's by now, haven't they, what with selling them all those things to keep the war going? So I went round to Boston, New York. Chicago. Philadelphia. Set up in churches, talked. Meant to spend a week with Pim, and then take ship for Liverpool. We were friends as girls, you see, before my father moved us to Chicago." She shook her head. "What a bloody shambles, that explosion."

A small silence fell.

"These oatcakes are a delight, Pim," said Laura. "I'd ask for the recipe if I could afford the butter."

Pim said, "Have another, at least. I'll send some home with you. Aren't they nice with the currants? You should have seen me before the war; fat as a squirrel, honestly. I was always cooking. The oatcakes were Nate's favorite—and—and Jimmy's." She hurried on. "He was my husband. Nate. Nathaniel. Mary knew him. He—he died. January of '16. It was very sudden. His heart . . . But he did love my cooking."

"I don't doubt it," said Laura, biting into another oatcake.

Mary said, "What will you do now, Iven? Since you've been discharged."

"Hellebores, *hellebores*, I told you, Mrs. Borden."

Mary was not to be diverted. "Bit of a waste, isn't it? You held rank, didn't you?"

Laura said, "We cannot all tour America and pass the hat for money." The edge was back in her voice.

Mary said, still unruffled, "And you don't want to go back?"

Back? The word echoed through her brain. For a moment she was back in Flanders, at Brandhoek, right after the first shell came down, her eyes meeting Kate's before they ran off in different directions, the gas alarm ringing, Laura shouting at her staff to put on their masks, flinging herself on an armless man before he could throw himself off the cot in his panic.

"No," Laura said. "I don't want to go back. Pim, do you like gardens? I grew foxgloves in Veith Street, before I went to Flanders, and the Parkeys are mad for climbing roses. They planted all manner of shrubbery to keep the salt from the canes, so you can hardly see the three flowers the poor things manage every year."

Pim said, "Have they tried globe thistles? They stand the salt well, and I love the dear blue flowers, just the color of the harbor in July." Pim had clearly taken the measure of Laura's mood.

Later, Laura walked back to Blackthorn House, picking her way down a blue-iced street. Twilight lay over the city, and it was raw cold. She was glad to retreat to her bedroom and attempt the stretches that would ease the scar tissue on her hands and on her leg. Finally she gave up, and poured herself a drink. Half a bottle later, she managed to go to bed without going through Freddie's things one more time. Except for the tags, which she put under her pillow. But she couldn't help but glance at that damned postcard, which lay out on the dressing table, the lonely gray line of its mountain stark against a pale sky.

8

THE KEY OF THE BOTTOMLESS PIT

.....

FREDDIE WAS TRYING TO CRAWL OUT FROM UNDER A GREAT crushing weight, and he wondered if it was worth the effort. He was strangely warm. Then he heard a squeak. Something skittered over his face.

"Faugh!" he cried, lurching upright, alive, underground, and in a fighting rage. Nothing enraged soldiers more than the sound of rats. The bloody rats had come to eat him. Well, he wasn't dead yet. He struck out. His hand found the yielding flesh of a dead man, then recoiled off the resilient shoulder of a live one. Freddie heard a hiss of pain and remembered then that he was not entombed alone. Winter muttered a string of German curses as he struggled upright.

There was a chittering, and then a gnawing sound. Freddie's gorge rose. They were eating the dead. "The rats. Oh, Christ . . ." Then he realized he'd struck Winter, bad arm and all, when he was lashing out.

"Winter, I'm sorry, did I . . . ?"

"Yes," said Winter. "But I'm all right. Wait. *Ratten.*" A strange note in his voice.

"Rats? Yes? What do you mean . . . What are you doing?"

Winter had pushed Freddie away from him—they must have fallen unconscious in a heap. "We're not dead." Winter's voice had a new fierce note. "And now there are *rats*."

Freddie wondered, in horror, if *Winter* had gone mad. "There are always rats," he said, sharp. He could still hear the chewing. The skin was trying to crawl off his bones.

Winter said, "No—you see? We're not dead. There was—air coming in before. But now the way is bigger. The air is better. And there are rats now. The last bombardment could have done it."

"Made a way for rats," said Freddie, his mind starting to work again. "But for men?"

"We must feel for—for air moving. For—" Winter groped for the word. "Drafts." A pause. "There were five men in here with me. You might find . . ."

Bodies in the dark. Freddie had probably killed one or two himself. He was silent.

Winter said, "Talk to me as I go, and I will do the same for you."

But Freddie didn't move. He tried, but his limbs cramped and he stayed where he was. He was afraid. Afraid to crawl out into the void, away from Winter's living presence. As though somewhere in the dark, the German's unseen voice would be cut off, and he would discover that Winter was just the product of his fevered imagination. As though he'd find himself finally, and truly, alone. Except for those dead men. He imagined them, unseen, turning their slimy faces up toward him, little lights of hell burning in their dead eyes.

Then Winter's hand found his arm, gripping hard enough that he could feel it, even through the thick, soaked wool of his overcoat. "Iven?"

Don't be a child don't be a child, don't . . . "I'm afraid," he said, and was ashamed.

The hand tightened, the last real thing in his whole world. "So am I." Winter's voice sharpened. "Go."

Freddie had been long enough a soldier that his body responded before his flailing mind could think. He began to crawl. He put a hand down on something yielding, recoiled, slammed his shoulder against a wall. "Winter?" he called, ashamed of how his voice wavered.

He heard a few words in German that might have been an oath, or a prayer. "I'm all right, Iven. Go on. Go on, boy."

Freddie tried to be systematic, but it was so dark and he was so thirsty. He crawled, scraping his hands, bruising himself, bumping his head, groping ahead until he could hardly move his aching arms. He was lying there, his heartbeats shaking his whole body, when he realized that there was moving air on his face. "Winter."

A rustle of clothing, surprisingly near, and the faint grunt of pain as the German dragged himself across. How badly was he wounded? Then Winter's groping hand found Freddie's and he guided their twined fingers until Winter could feel what he had: air just stirring on his palm. And a sloppy layer of sticky mud. Mud that could be dug away. Perhaps. Freddie said, with regret, "I'd matches, but they all got wet. I can't see a thing. If we try digging, we'd be doing it blind."

Winter said, "We must try anyway." Something dauntless in his voice.

Their heads must be close together. He could feel the feverish warmth of the other man's body. "I'll start," Freddie added. "Since your arm is hurt. I'll tell you if I get tired."

9

THE DEAD, SMALL AND GREAT

.....

LAURA HAD NOT HAD A NIGHTMARE SINCE SHE WENT TO Flanders—she never dreamed at all anymore. She fell asleep to darkness and came awake again. Most of her colleagues said it was the same for them. Some protective quirk of the brain, to keep them from reliving their days.

But Laura had a nightmare on the night of Mrs. Shaw's tea party. She dreamed of the comet.

She was sixteen again, and it was 1910, the year the comet came, and her mother appeared at school, just as she had in life, to take Laura and Freddie home. They hurried back to Veith Street together. "Freddie," Laura said. "I'm so glad to see you. I had an absurd dream, that you had— Well, it's all right. You're here."

He smiled at her, but didn't say anything.

Their mother insisted on holding an umbrella over their heads. "Come on," she told them. "We have to hurry."

It was Laura who saw it, when the umbrella bobbled. She happened to be looking up. "Freddie," she whispered. "Look." There was fire in the sky. A blazon of white, stark against the thin blue of the winter noon. Seeing it, Laura was afraid. Her hand hurt where her mother held her wrist.

"Don't look at it, my darlings," her mother whispered. "Try not to breathe—the comet will drench the world in gas—comet gas, foul, green—stay under my umbrella, we're almost there."

Then suddenly they were in their own house, and her father was drawing the curtains. Laura had not been afraid when the real comet came, visible in the January daylight, even though her parents had trembled and called it a sign of the End. But in her dream she was terrified. The house got darker and darker. "No," she tried to insist. "It's just a comet. Dust in the sky. In school we—"

Her mother said, "Laura, Laura, they lie to you in school. To keep the public calm. World's ending, dear. Four Horsemen, remember? And *the first one's white*. What color is the comet?"

Laura tried to explain. *That's not the world, that's not how it works.* A single scarlet tear ran down her mother's cheek. *There's no horsemen. Nothing so grand as horsemen . . .*

"Maman? Are you all right?"

Her mother smiled at her even as another scarlet tear slipped down. "Of course I am. We're safe here. We're safe at home. We're all together."

But the scarlet tears poured faster and faster down her face, and Laura tried to go to her, to reach out to stanch the blood, but she couldn't move. She was knee-deep in mud now, the mud was in her house, and the comet, the comet was coming and there was nothing she could do . . . Her mother's eyes were pools of blood. "Laura, chérie, it's all right. We're all together, you see."

The comet outside exploded, a shattering noise, and all the glass blew in, and there was fire all around, and green gas, and in the middle of it all her mother was bleeding. No, it wasn't her, it was Freddie there, with a face full of blood. Laura was slipping and scrambling in mud, choking on gas, trying to get to him . . .

Then Laura lurched upright, wet with cold sweat. She was in her room and it was the blackest, coldest hour before dawn, with the fire burned down in the grate. The moon must have set, for even that cold trickle of light was gone from her window. She lay there panting. Saw the shadows of the armoire, the chest, the vanity.

And another shadow in the corner opposite.

The shadow moved. An intruder? A trick of the light? She tried to leap to her feet but realized that she could not.

It was a person, not a shadow. It had stepped from her nightmare. From her memory.

A familiar housedress. Blood in her eyes. Glass in her body. Accusation in every line of her ruined face: *You didn't save me, why didn't you save me?* The apparition came closer. Stiff fingers, full of glass, trailed over Laura's face. Laura couldn't move at all. And then the shadow was speaking with Agatha Parkey's voice, as she'd spoken in the séance, a loud, flat, blaring voice: "Ded but he's alive, ded but he's alive. *Ded but he's alive!*" The fingers were choking her, gripping her throat, and she could feel the glass in the hands pricking her neck, shaking her back and forth. "Fredi Fred Fr Fin Find FIND . . ."

Laura jolted awake just as her door flew open. Three white flannel wrappers and three nightcapped heads bobbed in the doorway, and Lucretia Parkey held aloft a lamp like an elderly Lucia di Lammermoor. "Laura?" said Agatha Parkey. "Laura. Are you all right?"

"I—" She tried for an easy answer, witty, polite, but her voice cracked.

"Oh, dear," said Lucretia, bustling into the room. The lamp chased away the shadows, and it was just Laura's ordinary, old-fashioned bedroom.

"I had a nightmare, Miss Parkey." She dragged her fingers through her hair, trying to clear her head.

"Well, you can't stay up here," said Agatha. Cataracts had left her eyes white as an egg, but she still seemed to be peering about the room. "The Departed are relentless when they want something. Often enough it's the only idea they've got in their heads. Come downstairs. We shall sit round the kitchen like girls, and have cocoa." Her sensitive nose twitched. "Without spirits."

Laura flushed. "I'm sorry I woke you."

"You didn't," said Lucretia comfortably. "The old don't sleep very much. Come now, dear." She stumped over to the bed, picked up Laura's dressing gown, nudged her slippers nearer.

Laura didn't want to have to lie back alone in the darkness. She put on her wrapper and slippers. Lucretia put a warm arm round her, and Laura felt the surprising strength in her, in the birdlike scapulae, the knotty fingers. They made a little procession down the hall.

"Waiting for something to happen?" Laura asked Lucretia as they walked.

"Well, yes," said Lucretia. "To you, you know. All your ghosts. You're trailing them like penitent-beads. Your family. Your patients. Not dear Freddie, of course. Because he's not dead."

Laura said nothing.

The kitchen was surprisingly warm, considering the hour, with a fire burning slow and hot in the oven stove. Hadn't she smothered the fire before going to bed? Laura helped Lucretia to a chair and then went to add more wood. Clotilde was bustling around with hot milk and powders. She put a cup into Laura's hands, when Laura came and sat down.

"I haven't had a nightmare in years," said Laura. How did Agatha contrive to make her blind eyes seem to be watching? Laura sipped her cocoa. Realized that she felt safe in that kitchen. As though the phantoms in her mind were no match for fire and chocolate, and those three ancient women, sitting round in their nightdresses and frilly wrappers and caps, looking serious. Lucretia and Clotilde were both watching Agatha.

Agatha said, "We don't often give advice." The room was still, except for the faint sound of the fire, whispering. Agatha smiled, a little. She'd only three teeth. "We answer questions, but we rarely offer advice."

"Sometimes, though," put in Lucretia. "To the worthy."

Laura was silent. There was something impressive about their quietness, the crags and valleys of their faces. Their hands on the scarred wooden tabletop.

"Laura," said Agatha. "I will tell you three things that are true. You may believe as you like. The first true thing is this: Your brother is alive."

There was no prevarication in her voice, none of the thickets of words with which the Parkeys hedged their bets in séances.

"Second: He will not come back to you. You must go to him. Third: To save him, you must let him go."

"I don't understand."

"You will," said Lucretia.

"And I will give you some advice," said Agatha. "Wars are stark things, are they not? Black and white. Allies and enemies. Not this time. You will not know who your enemies are, nor will they reveal themselves as you expect. You will not know whom to trust, but you must trust regardless. Do you understand?"

"No," said Laura.

"You will." Agatha's three-toothed smile was a little frightening in the firelight.

Laura said what she could never say aloud in daylight. "He's dead. They're all dead. There's nothing to save. I failed. The comet came. The fire. My mother was right. It's the end of everything."

"Perhaps. But there is something to save," said Agatha.

The kitchen was fracturing now into amber light and scarred wood. Three old ladies, straight-backed. Their caps had become hoods, their dressing gowns were sweeping robes, and all three of them looked at her with eyes that had seen sorrows like hers a hundred times: a quiet, remote empathy.

Agatha said, "I suppose that is another piece of advice for you, Laura. Do not despair. Endings—they are beginnings too."

Her voice echoed in Laura's head. The fire and the shadows were dissolving into nothing, and then Laura came quietly awake in her own rumpled bed. Clear morning light fell on her face.

She lay there a moment. Shook her head at herself. Dreams within dreams.

. . .

But this dream would not let her go. It lived behind her eyelids: green gas and fear, mud, the comet, her mother's voice. Agatha in her kitchen saying *Your brother is alive.* When that evening came at last, Laura stirred up her fire against the frigid dusk, closed her door, sat down at the desk, and set all Freddie's things in front of her. The jacket, laundered now. The Bible, with the place marked. The postcard from Bayern. *I will bring him back if I can* . . . She looked at the two tags, the cord twined round her stiff fingers. All her correspondence stacked neatly off to the side.

What did she know?

The Red Cross said he was missing. But he wasn't. She had his things.

Someone knew what had happened to him. Someone in Flanders. The person who'd packed that box. Who'd taken the jacket. *Knows but isn't telling me.* She understood. God knew she'd lied to enough families, to spare them.

Who is it? Who knows? She reached for her letters. One by one she paged through them all. *We don't know where he died. We don't know.*

She laid the creased papers aside and sat for a long time, thinking. *Someone knows.*

Before she could think too much about what she was doing, she got up from her desk and left her room. In the foyer, she put on her cap and coat and scarf, slipped out into the frigid evening, closed the Parkeys' front door soundlessly behind her. She was going to call on Penelope Shaw. Or, more specifically, Pim's friend Mary Borden.

SHAKEN OF A MIGHTY WIND

.....

T HE SKY WAS GETTING DARK, AND A CATARACT OF FRIGID AIR poured off the restless sea. As she walked, Laura found herself reaching in her memory for a warmer day, back and back, to the bright summer of '14, hot and dry and vivid, its long days freighted, somehow, with hope.

Laura had just received her nursing certificate, with a commendation. Enough success to silence even her skeptical father. She'd put herself through nursing school. Got up every day at four in the morning, scrubbing the hospital floors and emptying bedpans. She had been so proud of herself. Her mother had been proud too, quietly. She'd made one of her old Montreal dresses over for Laura for the graduation.

But 1914 was also the year her mother had fixed as the world's last, and she would not leave the subject alone. "I read it in *Zion's Watch Tower*," she told her children. "We must be wary, we must be prepared." She filled the house with tinned food, and read the papers with dogged intensity.

"Just don't argue," Freddie had advised Laura. He was always sensible, her brother. "Let the year pass. They'll come round." He and Laura were walking together in the public gardens, side by side in their scuffed shoes. It had been a Sunday in July, the sun hot on the back of Laura's neck. The roses had just opened, she remembered. The air hummed with bees. Laura ran a finger along the edge of a petal. She was twenty. He was eighteen. The world seemed to be opening before them. Like the roses.

"Try to understand them," Freddie had added. He was kinder than her too. "Look at the world now. It's terrifying, isn't it? We have flying machines. Phonographs. Moving pictures, even. Everything is changing so fast. Mother's frightened. In a way, it's easier to imagine the world's going to end. At least there's a certainty to it. End—*bam*—done. But change—where does change stop?"

Laura remembered her answer, her eyes still on the flowers. "When did you get so wise?"

Freddie snorted. "If only I could put it in meter."

Freddie had just got a job as a harbor clerk. Laura said, "I'm making money now." Although, admittedly, not much. "If you're working nights, we could do it. You could go to school to study— anything really. Art."

She could see he was tempted. Something changed in his face. But then he shook his head, gave her an affectionate look. "No, save your money. I have my art books, and I'll keep practicing, don't worry. You'll be a hospital matron before long and I'll have my pictures hanging in every fine house in North America. Just wait."

"I don't doubt it," said Laura. "Well, if not an education, let me at least buy you an ice cream."

"Lead the way," said Freddie. "Can you afford chocolate sauce?"

They left the park together, laughing. Eventually, Laura was sure, their parents would see that there was nothing to fear. "Did you hear?" said Freddie. "A poor archduke was shot last week in Sarajevo. His wife too."

"How dreadful," Laura answered. "Vanilla?"

. . .

Pim answered Laura's knock, a shawl flung over her shoulders, face colorless as the Della Robbia angels that Freddie sketched from art books. Her astonishing hair was plaited. "Mrs. Shaw—" Laura began, standing on the stoop. "Pim. Forgive the late hour—"

"Oh, it's quite all right," said Pim, smiling, poised, as though bedraggled acquaintances came to her door all the time. "Come in, come in, of course." Her eyes were red-rimmed.

"God bless you," said Laura, and meant it.

"Come into the kitchen," said Pim. "Have you had supper? I suppose it's something particular you came about? Are you all right, my dear? At least have some tea."

"I came to see Mary," said Laura. "It's important."

Was it her imagination, or did Pim's face fall? "Oh, of course you did. You have so much in common, it's only natural. I'll take you up straightaway, as soon as you've finished your tea. I even remember how you take it. And the milk just came."

. . .

Mary was in a sitting room, her back to the door, answering correspondence. "Mary," Pim said from the doorway. "Miss Iven's here to see you."

"A moment, if you please, Iven," Mary said without turning. Her pen raced over the paper.

"I'll just leave you alone for a bit," said Pim. The door shut behind her.

Laura was just sinking into one of the chairs by the fire when the echoing slam of another door made her lurch for the cover of the wall, narrowly missing the fireplace. Mary whipped around, in the same startled reaction.

Laura arranged her skirt, collected her dignity. "Pardon me."

Mary said, "If a car backfires in London, half the men on the street hurl themselves into the nearest doorway and crouch there quivering. Sit down, for heaven's sake, Iven. What did you come to see me about?"

Laura had debated ways to approach Mary all through her walk. Now she settled on the simplest. "You asked me if I meant to go back."

Mary stiffened. "I did."

Laura said, "What if I wanted to?"

She could see the thoughts running fast behind Mary's dark eyes. "Do you want to?"

"Yes."

"You were discharged."

"I recovered quicker and better than expected."

Mary's eye lingered on Laura's skirt-covered shins. "When did it happen?"

"November."

Mary's lips tightened; she was probably remembering November. "A bad time."

"Yes."

It had rained for two months without stopping by the time the much-delayed push began. The one Laura thought would never happen. By then, the ground was a viscous substance in which men swam and slipped and frequently drowned. Her patients came to her more mud than flesh, and already gangrenous.

"And you were in a casualty clearing station?" said Mary.

Laura said, "I was at Brandhoek. The army put an ammunition depot right near us. They said Fritz wouldn't bomb it, for fear of hitting the hospital."

Mary snorted. Laura was glad that Mary understood, that she didn't have to explain. She never spoke of Brandhoek.

"And you want to go back," said Mary. "At tea, you said you didn't. What changed?"

Laura said, "There is some confusion over how my brother died. I want to understand."

"You can write letters."

"I have tried. But I'll get answers in person that no one would ever give me in a letter."

"They might take you back into the army."

"Your time isn't your own in the army."

"So you expect me to get you into the forbidden zone, and then bid you farewell while you go haring about the countryside after news of your brother? No, thank you."

Laura said, "I can work, Mrs. Borden, and I will. I assume I'd have leave now and again? I will ask my questions then."

"Call me Mary, for God's sake. I couldn't pay you."

"All expenses covered, then," said Laura. "And we shall be liberal in our definition of expenses. I'm sure your openhanded American donors will fund my hire."

"I spent all their money on supplies," said Mary. But she still hadn't said no.

Laura waited.

"Pim said your parents burned in the explosion. Are you deranged with grief?"

"No," said Laura.

"How bad is your leg really?"

"Healed."

"Let me see it, then."

"It's not your business."

"It is, if you're going to be staffing my hospital. I will see for myself."

It was a small humiliation. Petty revenge for Laura's behavior at tea, or perhaps Mary was testing her resolve. Laura *knew* that, and still she almost stood up, walked out. Why stay? Because she'd dreamed of Agatha Parkey saying *Your brother is alive*? Was the girl her parents had formed still alive inside her, believing that the end of the world must come with miracles?

Or must she just spend her life kneeling at the altar of her ghosts?

She unfastened her garter and rolled down the stocking. With her skirt hiked up to the knee on one side, the scar showed clear in the pitiless firelight. It was nothing compared to what many men lived with. But it was ugly, the tissue stiff and red and twisted, a clean scoop on one side as though a giant had gone at her with a spoon. A few inches higher or lower and Laura would never have walked again.

Mary looked frowning from the scar to Laura's face. Then she sat back and said, "Very well. The ship is the *Gothic*, departing on the first. I hope I don't regret this, Iven."

RESTRAINT SHE WILL
NOT BROOK

·····

Two days after Mary agreed to take Laura with her to Europe, Pim wrote a note asking Laura to come by. Laura went after her shift and found, to her surprise, that Pim had got out a trunk, and that her bed was strewn with the most extraordinary collection of items—a mackintosh, winter stockings, an evening gown in mauve silk. A good flowered hat, a knit cap. Blouses.

"Pim, what on earth?" said Laura. "Are you going on holiday?"

"No." Pim looked pleased. "I'm coming with you and Mary."

Laura's heart clenched. "No, you're not."

"I already have my ticket."

"God, *why*?"

"I want to go," Pim said. Earnest as a child, Laura thought with despair. "To see where Jimmy was. And—Laura, I want to be of *use*. The way you are, and Mary. I know I'm not trained like you, but I can help. I couldn't help him but I can help someone else, don't you see? I can write letters and things for wounded men. Wash syringes. Anything, really." Her tone was fervent; the last four years had made them all cynical, but not Pim. "Do you think your brother is alive?"

Laura didn't. He wasn't. Despite anything Agatha Parkey had to say. "They sent me his tags."

Pim said, "The Parkeys said he was alive. And I don't think they lie just to make people happy. Or they'd have done it for me. But they said your brother is alive. Why would they lie?"

Damn the Parkeys. "How could they know? I don't think he is."

"But you think there's a chance," Pim pressed. "Or you wouldn't be going."

"Stop being romantic. I want to know what happened to him. Only that."

"Well, then," said Pim, "I can help you look."

Half a dozen arguments ran through Laura's mind, and all of them sounded hypocritical. Finally she bit the inside of her cheek and held up one of her hands. Pim, who had certainly been beautiful from birth, paled.

Laura didn't want to talk about this. She never talked about this. She said, voice flattening suddenly to tonelessness, "You asked once what happened to my hands."

Pim said, her voice small, "I did."

"It happened over time," said Laura. "The scarring." The words would barely come. Speaking of the war conjured it as crisply as life: the smells, the sound of the rain. Cold nights, long days. Flies. The screaming. She forged ahead. "You'll see the worst wounds in the world, over there. Wounds that shock you, that a man could be so hurt and not dead. You'll have your bare hands all over those wounds as they go bad—and they will go bad. It's all farmland, the battlefields; they've been spreading manure since the Middle Ages. If you've so much as a paper cut, or a blister on your own hand, well, that goes bad too. Over and over. It hurts very much. It scars. Do you want your hands to look like this?"

Pim looked younger than Laura. "It's all right. I'm not afraid."

"You should be," said Laura. "There's nothing noble about suffering. It's an ugly, petty, crawling business. You'll see men die with less dignity than dogs, cursing you sometimes, that you can't save them. Pim, stay here and knit blankets. Don't— You'll never forget the things you see over there." She couldn't say any more. She was on the edge of being sick. She turned away sharply, to the coolness from the window.

"I can be brave, Laura, I *can*."

Laura said, "You don't owe this to Jimmy, Pim."

She'd struck a nerve. "Don't I? I could have kept him home, you know. He wanted to enlist. He was so angry after Nate died. I thought the army would steady him. I let him go."

Laura said nothing. She met Pim's eyes in silence. Recognized the look in them. *God, Iven, who are you to judge what someone else thinks she owes the dead?* Finally she said, "I'll teach you to tie a tourniquet. On the ship."

Pim smiled a little, and relaxed. "Only if you let me cut your hair. It looks like you went at it with pruning shears."

THIS IS THE FIRST
RESURRECTION

.....

PASSCHENDAELE RIDGE, FLANDERS, BELGIUM
NOVEMBER 1917

FREDDIE HAD FOUND A TIN HAT; HE SCRABBLED WITH IT AT the wet earth until he could hardly move his hands, and then he and Winter took turns, inhaling mud and water, scraping at the mud and broken concrete, only occasionally encouraged by the fresh air coming in. *Useless,* Freddie thought. Still he dug. Liquid earth slid down and tried to choke him. He'd never been so tired in his life. He and Winter didn't talk anymore, except for grunts as they squirmed to change places. More than anything, Freddie wanted to stop. To rest. Perhaps he was tired enough to die, if he fell asleep. But Winter kept on, utterly silent now. Freddie didn't want to go out whining like a child.

Then, suddenly, he thrust a hand forward, and there was— nothing. Was that light? Was he dreaming? It was Winter's voice, panting but still matter-of-fact, that steadied him. "Can you put your head and shoulders through? You are not so big."

Freddie crawled forward. Wriggled. Realized that there was more air. Sucked it in. The gap was narrowing— "Push me!" he called back over his shoulder. "Winter, can you—?"

Winter was already shoving at Freddie's feet. Even exhausted, with only one good arm, he was strong. Freddie pushed back at him, clawed at wet earth and stone with the final strength of desperation—oh, there was light—not daylight but light, sourly red, but better than their muddy tomb, and so he reached for it.

And stuck.

He writhed, panicking. A freezing hand closed round his calf, and Winter snapped, in a voice like a Lewis gun, "You will *be calm*, boy, or I'll kill you after all. *Calm.*" Freddie forced himself to go still. Winter's voice seemed to speak to him from some underworld. "Go slowly, Iven. Slowly."

Freddie moved. His head. His shoulders. His hips. Squirmed. Squirmed again. Felt his clothes tear. And then his shoulders were past the narrowest point, and he was scrabbling through the foulest oozing mud and out into baleful night. He turned at once and reached back down.

The opening was not wide enough for Winter, but he shoved the tin hat through to Freddie, who widened the hole until finally a groping hand emerged. Freddie seized it, heedless of Winter's wound, and pulled with everything he had.

Winter slid out.

They collapsed, half-sunk in near-liquid mud, as though the earth were trying to finish what the pillbox had started. Freddie realized that he was whispering to himself without being aware of it, thought for a moment he was praying. Realized that he was just whispering *Fucking hell*, over and over. He wasn't sure how long they lay there, just two dirty smudges, invisible. But the whistle of a falling shell rattled Freddie back to alertness. He raised his head. Grew properly aware, for the first time, of their surroundings.

It was night. Night and cold. It had been warmer in the pillbox. Now they lay out under torrents of almost frozen rain, and enough wind to riffle Freddie's hair. A million craters stretched from one horizon to the other, full of water that reflected a sky glittering with shellfire. No landmarks but the ruined pillbox. Just holes and water, right to the flame-limned horizon. He couldn't see any people, although he could hear grenades and small arms and trench mortars, the sound muffled by the wet air. There must be people. But they were hidden by the night and the rain and the lips of innumerable shell holes.

It was too wet, too dark, to tell their direction. They could as easily have been looking toward Germany as Canada. Could they wait until dawn? *No,* Freddie thought. They'd die. The rain was close cousin to snow, and already he was trying to catch it on his parched tongue. He'd be starting on the water in the shell holes soon, never mind the spent explosives and dead bodies. And Winter was wounded.

"Winter," he whispered.

The German didn't answer.

"Winter," said Freddie again, seized with sudden terror. That Winter had died and left him alone. It was as though they were still in the pillbox, each the only thing in the other's shrunken world. "Hans," he said, loud and clumsy, catching the other man by his sodden shoulders, half-dragging him upright.

Winter raised his head just as a star shell went up and filled the darkness with cold light. Freddie realized with a shock that this was his first sight of the other man's face. He saw close-cropped hair, matted and filthy. Helmet gone. Broad features, deep-set eyes, sunken with exhaustion. Generous mouth, stubbled jaw, hollow cheeks. All color bleached to bone by the white light overhead. Except for his eyes, dark as blood. It had been easier, somehow, to think of the German as only half-real: a bony shoulder, a voice in the dark.

Freddie wondered what Winter saw. Russet hair, he supposed, turned to black by filth and by night, face sprayed with freckles, his beard coming in bristly, nose a babyish snub that Freddie had despised, back when that kind of thing mattered.

The light went out, and Winter was just a dark shape again, a living presence beside him. "We can't stay here," said Freddie.

"I know." Winter didn't need to say anything else. They were both bareheaded, wet. Weakened by thirst and confinement. They'd crawled out of their tomb. But they weren't back in the land of the living. Not by a long chalk.

"Do you know which way is which?" It didn't occur to Freddie that they might separate. The only thing worse than this place would be to face it alone. He'd fall into a shell hole and drown, and no one would ever know what had happened to him. The rain fell stinging into his eyes. His hands were still on Winter's shoulders.

"No," said Winter.

"We'll have to chance a direction. We'll die if we stay here."

Their eyes met, just as another star shell faded, and in the dark Winter asked, "Am I your prisoner? Or are you mine, Iven?"

And wasn't that just the bloody question? Freddie let him go. "Christ, each the other's, I suppose. But I'll follow, if you choose the direction."

He couldn't see Winter's expression anymore, just the general shape of his features, the loom of him against the insane sky. But he could almost feel Winter's surprise. Maybe Freddie didn't need to see him, after all that time in the dark. Awkwardly, he added, "You saved my life."

"Very well." But still Winter hesitated. Freddie understood: It was a guess. Whichever way they went, there was danger. Stray bullets. Stray shells. Drowning, in that mud and oily water. Simply being shot on sight, by whichever side they ran into first.

"This way, then," said Winter at length. "But do not speak, Iven, until we know where we are. I won't either. If the wrong side hears German—or English—they'll . . ."

"They'll shoot first," Freddie finished, and wiped half-frozen rain from his eyes. "Ask questions later."

"Stay close," said Winter, and started to walk.

13

AWAY INTO THE WILDERNESS

·····

THE GOTHIC, OUT OF HALIFAX

MARCH 1918

THE PONDEROUS GOTHIC, BELCHING SMOKE, WAS DRAWN UP at the quay with the gangplank down. Her convoy waited beyond the mouth of the harbor, gray smudges against the steely sea. They were to be convoyed to Liverpool first. Mary had business in London, before they went to Belgium. One heard that the system of convoys kept passenger liners safe from the U-boats, but Laura still had a horror of shipwrecks. Her palms sweated despite the cold as she went up the gangplank.

Two years after the comet, when the *Titanic* sank, all the fishermen of Halifax had gone out to the wreckage. They'd come back pale and hastily got drunk, as an endless stream of coffins came off their boats, to be buried with neither family nor ceremony. There had been so many dead that the undertaker had to invent a system of tying tags to toes to keep track of them all.

Charles Iven had been one of the men who'd gone out to the wreck. His drinking had got worse after that. Once, on a night he was very drunk, he'd even described it to his children.

"Just floating," he'd said. "Hundreds of them, in the water. Staring up, staring down. Like dynamited fish. We hauled them up, and some of them had their eyes pecked out by seabirds. Little children sometimes. There were so many. Thousands. Progress. Pah. What's progress? Give people God's power—to build ships like islands, or fly like birds, or set fire to the bowels of earth like the devil in his damned pit—it just writes their stupidity larger and larger until they drown the whole world. Our hands get bigger and our spirits shrink. Is it any wonder, really, that God's done with us? That was the white horseman, Marie. That ship. Not your comet. Who cares about a comet? Pray, all of you."

Laura mounted the gangplank, thinking she could face shellfire with equanimity if they could just get across the Atlantic.

· · ·

Mary and Pim arrived half an hour after she did. Laura was smoking on deck to calm her nerves. Pim's hair fell in wisps under her hat, and her face had a fresh color. Admiring looks filtered in from the other passengers. Mary seemed harried. She had, Laura understood, a mass of donations—bandages and sachets and pajamas and things—that she must chivvy across the ocean.

They joined Laura at the rail after they got their baggage settled. Mary accepted when Laura offered her a cigarette. Pim wrinkled her nose. Clouds were coming in. The turbines roared. They watched the other passengers board. There were more women than men among the new arrivals, and they were nearly all wearing black.

"So many," said Pim.

Laura drew on her cigarette. Some of their fellow passengers wore the extravagance of Victorian formal mourning, others merely shawls or armbands. They clung together, a flapping mass, like crows about to take flight. "They're going over for news," said Mary. "They besiege the Red Cross. They dog the generals with letters. *It's the modern world,* they say. *How can a man just vanish?*"

"'Go on your way to the shadowy abyss,'" Pim quoted softly. Her eyes hadn't left the mass of black-clad people. "'If with your singing you can placate the Furies, the monsters, and pitiless Death, you can take back your beloved.'" At Mary's glance of surprise, she said, "Gluck. Well, Orpheus. Going after Eurydice. That's what they're all hoping for, isn't it? Even you, Laura—" She stopped. Laura wasn't listening. Just for a moment, she'd seen a spot of stillness in the moving mass of people. Seen a woman wearing a bloody housecoat, her eyes empty pools of scarlet.

Pim said, "Laura? Laura?"

Just a phantasm brought on by the stress of departure. "Sorry, woolgathering," Laura said. "Can we go inside before we freeze, do you think?"

. . .

Laura had never traveled on a passenger liner before. She'd got to Europe on a transport, in February of '15, and returned on a hospital ship. She and Freddie had dreamed of traveling, of course. They'd been watching the ships come and go, peering out Laura's upper window, since they were children. "She's going to Russia," Laura would say with authority, while the smokestack billowed on one ship or another, her imagination skipping away in blatant disregard for the actual routes of ocean liners. "She's going to Saint Petersburg."

"And," Freddie would put in eagerly, "there's a woman aboard who's got a great diamond, the Northern Star, and she stole it from its rightful owner, a tsaritsa of the royal family—she is a disgraced servant girl, and now she is in a new situation, rich as Croesus because of that one jewel, but she cannot sell it or cut it so she is rich *and* poor and now she is going back to the land of her birth, always afraid the tsaritsa will get wind of her passage . . ."

Well, I'm getting on one of those ships now, Freddie, Laura thought to her brother's absence. *It's not Petersburg. Just Liverpool, but that's something, isn't it? I wish . . .*

She cut off that thought.

Their tickets were second-class. They had decent meals and a promenade deck, a library and a smoking room. Laura had nothing to do, and no one to care for, aside from the memorable night at dinner when she got a fish bone out of a choking old gentleman's throat.

She slept a good deal. Read novels that did not tax her fractured concentration. Smoked innumerable cigarettes, and drank more than she ought to.

Pim chased Laura down in their berth one afternoon, brandishing scissors. Laura, trying to nap, was unamused. "Nurse found dead in a second-class stateroom with scissors through the heart?" They'd been reading murder mysteries to each other in the library.

"If anything, it would be 'innocent widow from Halifax found dead'—you're much more murderous than I am, for all you like to joke. Laura, stop glaring. I'm cutting your hair."

"Oh," said Laura. She dived under the blankets. "Absolutely not." Her voice came out muffled. "Caps and veils will do extremely well for me, Mrs. Shaw, and you may brandish your scissors at someone else."

"Oh, no, you don't. *I* see your head, and it pains me. You shouldn't be asleep anyway," added Pim, virtuously. "It's teatime." Mercifully, she'd stopped waving the scissors.

"I'm not asleep now," said Laura with some resentment.

"You're worse than a five-year-old boy. Your hair won't take but a moment. Why don't you want to?"

"Because I want my tea." Laura sat up, feeling rumpled. Pim was neat from pinned-up hair to booted feet.

"You can— Laura, if I am being a prat, you may murder me after all, but—even battle-scarred war heroes like yourself are allowed to look pretty."

"Oh, Christ, don't be charitable," said Laura, rubbing her face. "I was having such a nice nap."

Pim said, "And you are. Pretty, I mean. A good man won't care about your hands, or your leg."

"So very earnest. But he will care about my hair?"

Pim met Laura's eyes, flushed suddenly, and put down the scissors. "No, not at all. Let's go to tea, then."

If Pim had insisted, Laura thought wryly, she'd probably have kept balking. "No, you're right." She stood up and plunked herself down at the chair in front of the tiny vanity.

"My," said Pim. "Now you look like a cat about to have a bath." But she picked up the scissors. "You'll see. You'll never be Empress Sisi, but how about roguish curls?" She gave Laura a critical look. "I think I can manage that."

"I should like to see you try."

"Just wait," said Pim, with the confidence of the very beautiful. Laura sighed, and let Pim have her way. It had been a long time since Laura cared about her hair. Although, now she was thinking of it, she *had* wept, when she first cut it. God, that was long ago. While she was in training, Laura had imagined, in her most secret impractical dreams, that she'd meet someone in France. A young aristocrat maybe. An officer. A flier. That they'd fall passionately in love, that they'd wed, bound eternally by shared adventures.

But truth was different. She wrote Freddie once, about love in a field hospital: *It doesn't seem right letting a man fall in love with you— falling in love with him—when you're the only girl he's seen for months, and he's hurting worse than he's ever hurt in his life. It's just hothouse emotion—like an orchid in a greenhouse—it can't survive in the real world.*

Laura had long since put romance aside, and vanity too. But she looked with some surprise at herself, after Pim stepped back. Roguish was a stretch, but it was an improvement. Her cheeks and lips had acquired some color—she was eating a bit more now and not working monstrous shifts. Her hair had little touches of honey in the lamplight.

"I know you modern girls laugh at corsets," said Pim. "But really, they support the bust *and* improve posture—" She broke off with a shriek. Laura had aimed a pillow at her nose.

"Teatime, Mrs. Shaw," said Laura. "Or you'll have me in a farthingale and pattens by dinner. Or a toga."

"You know," said Pim, "once, for fancy dress, I went as an Elizabethan noblewoman. I was a great success. Made the farthingale myself." But she was smiling.

"Not surprised in the least," said Laura, with feeling.

. . .

After supper that night, Laura and Mary went into the library to smoke. Pim eyed their cigarettes with disfavor. "It turns your fingers yellow."

"A filthy habit," Laura agreed, blowing out smoke. She had another murder mystery, *Death in Amazonia,* and her mind was pleasantly far from both Europe and Canada.

Mary was going over some list of inventory, running a pencil down a page, a finger of ungenteel whiskey beside her. Even though she kept company with them, there was always a part of Mary that stood aloof. Preoccupied. Mary tended her hospital, Laura reflected, the way some women hovered over their husbands and children. It was her enterprise. Her place and her purpose. Her obsession.

Pim was trying automatic writing. It mostly made her mutter a lot to herself as she turned the paper in all directions, trying to drag meaning from the scribbles. But eventually she got to the end of her page, looked sadly at the resulting nonsense, and put it aside. She and Mary fell to talking.

Laura only half-listened. Pim was talking about angels, and Laura, who knew all about archangels, and thrones, and dominions— her mother had been thorough—was wishing she would change the subject.

"Why shouldn't there be angels?" Pim was saying earnestly. "On the battlefield, I mean? God is everywhere."

"Why *should* there be?" said Mary, who took unholy delight in baiting Pim. "They probably have better things to do."

"But what about the angels at Mons?" Pim pursued. "I read all about that. There were pamphlets at church. An archbishop preached about it."

Laura tried to concentrate on Amazonia, but it was no use. Like everyone else, she knew about the Angels of Mons. During the retreat, in '14, the British Expeditionary Force would have been routed, or so the story went. Except that a pack—flock?—of armed angels appeared and drove the Germans off. No doubt the Germans had their own version of the story. Laura sometimes wondered, idly, what happened when the celestial backers of one army encountered those of the other.

"It wasn't angels at all," put in Mary, a gleam to her eyes. "I heard it was ghostly archers from Agincourt. Front's riddled with ghosts, you know. It was certainly the lads from Agincourt."

"But angels—" protested Pim.

Laura found herself strangely annoyed. "It doesn't matter, does it?"

Mary and Pim looked at her in surprise. Laura bit her tongue before she could say anything else. Like *Don't you understand? The world ends with high explosive, not trumpets, and even if an angel existed, it would be shot from the sky like an aeroplane.*

Pim said, "Of course angels matter. They are proof of God's—" She paused, looking unsettled. Laura wondered what the final word should have been. Love? Wrath? Sheer damned indifference?

"I'm sorry, Pim," said Laura. "I shouldn't have said anything."

14

AND FOUNTAINS OF WATERS, AND THEY BECAME BLOOD

·····

NO MAN'S LAND, YPRES SALIENT,
FLANDERS, BELGIUM
NOVEMBER 1917

FREDDIE, SKIDDING AND STUMBLING BEHIND WINTER, FOUGHT to keep his head clear. When they paused in a shell hole, he closed his eyes and tried to evoke better days; himself reading verse to a long-suffering Laura while she pored busily over a textbook on the other side of the fire. But the image wouldn't come clear. No poet, living or dead, could have imagined this place, real, upon the earth, and their very language was insufficient to describe it.

He would have died a dozen times if not for Winter. Twice the German pulled him down when a shell fell close, held him still when they saw the muzzle flash of a machine gun. But more, it was Winter's stoic presence, the splash of his footsteps, walking near enough to touch, that kept him moving. He'd no idea whether they were behind his lines or Winter's, somewhere in No Man's Land, or in the ninth circle of hell, with Satan on the horizon chewing on traitors. He didn't have enough strength to care.

And then, just ahead of him, Winter halted.

Freddie lurched into Winter, then caught his balance, panicky. Fall into that mud and he wouldn't get out again. "What?"

"There." Freddie, following the jerk of Winter's chin, saw what his shuddering brain first took for eyes, staring gleefully out of the darkness, but realized must be cigarettes. They'd found other people. At last. He was too far gone to be afraid for himself. But he was afraid for Winter. What if it *wasn't* Germans? He'd rather it be Germans. They'd maybe kill him, certainly make him prisoner, but they wouldn't kill Winter.

A shell splashed and exploded, showering them with earth. They flung themselves flat and began crawling. A whizz-bang whined and splashed into a shell hole, nearer still, but this one didn't explode. Cover—they needed cover. A machine gun chortled, far too near. There must be a hole there, not yet flooded, a trench . . . something. Another shell splashed down, and another howled as it flew. They reached the lip of a crater and Freddie tumbled in, his cry lost in the almighty noise. Winter came falling after him. The shell hole was full of reeking, freezing water, and Freddie's next cry was smothered in wet. He thrashed his way to the surface just in time to see Winter go under, rolled over, and dragged him up, just as a third man, indistinct in the dark, fleeing the iron rain as they were, fell into Winter.

Winter, gasping, swore reflexively in German.

Freddie saw it all happen slowly, as though the world had gone sticky. Saw, in the sudden flare of a shell light, the man's Canadian uniform, his eyes wide with fear. Saw him snatch up his bayonet and thrust it down in a panic at Winter's heaving body.

Freddie tackled the man just as the bayonet went down. And then they were both falling in the water, and the man was thrashing. He'd dropped his rifle and pulled a knife, stabbing wildly. His mouth was open on a scream, although Freddie couldn't hear it. The knife gleamed wet with water dark as blood and Freddie's mind filled with mindless fury. He got himself uppermost and held the other man down.

The body went slack. A moment passed, his mind cleared, and he realized what he'd done and flung himself away, choking. The thunder of the guns seemed to rise and fall with the blood pounding in his ears. He turned away and vomited bile; there was nothing in his stomach. Winter's hand closed on his arm. "Are you—" Winter's voice was strangely hesitant. His hand and his face were dark with blood and water, his chest heaving. "Are you all right?"

Freddie didn't say anything for a few shocked minutes. It wasn't real. It couldn't be real. If he didn't say anything, then he'd wake up and realize it wasn't real.

Eventually, his mind started working again. He'd killed someone. A Canuck, one of his own countrymen. Killed him dead in traitorous defense of the enemy. How was that possible? He looked at Winter as though the answer would be written on his enemy's face, then jerked out of Winter's grip, shuddering. It had happened so fast. Winter took Freddie by the shoulders, dragged him round to face him. "Iven? Iven, look at me."

Freddie didn't answer. His teeth chattered. His mind rebelled with every particle of itself.

"Stop thinking, Iven," said Winter. His fingers dug into Freddie's upper arms. "It was instinct. Men do that. It's war, Iven."

"I didn't mean to—and he— I'm . . ." He trailed off, tried again, but there were no words for it. He was hardly human. Finally he just bit down on his own hand, to stave off the scream.

Winter forced his hand down, still searching his eyes. "Iven?" For the first time there was fear in his voice.

Freddie's mind spun in circles. He *couldn't* be sane. A sane man wouldn't be in this hole, under this sky. He wished he could crawl into the foul earth and never come out. But he'd promised to keep Winter alive. That thought alone gave Freddie the impetus to drag the scraps of himself together, enabled him to choke out, "I'm all right."

Winter was silent. But he let Freddie go, turned away, reached for the dead man, pulled off his half-submerged pack with jerky movements, using his good arm. Freddie sat still, dazed, as Winter dug through the soaking pack and came out with a canteen, sloshing, half-full. Iron rations, the emergency ones. Chocolate wrapped in wax. A gas mask.

Winter was handing him the chocolate when Freddie crumpled suddenly onto the slimy, sloping earth of the shell hole, gagging. Winter caught him, braced him up with a bony arm, put the dead man's canteen to his lips. Freddie, head swimming, tasted water mixed with rum. Thought, *I killed a man to save my enemy.* Found himself drinking, tried not to vomit it back up.

A shell lit the night again. For a split second, Winter's face had color instead of just ridges and shadows. His eyes were a clear and startling blue. Freddie stared at that face as though there were answers there, a reason for all this. His mind was utterly unmoored.

Winter said, watching him carefully, "We're behind your lines. I am your prisoner, Iven."

"Yes?" Freddie tried to think. His mouth tasted of rum and earth and blood. Despite the danger, all he wanted was sleep. Oblivion. But Winter. "They'd—we'd— I don't know if we'd take a prisoner out here. It's too close to your lines. They might shoot you. We'll have to go back. Back toward the—" It would have been a support trench, if there were such things as trenches in that part of the line. But there weren't. Just wet strings of shell holes.

Winter said nothing.

"Unless—unless you want to go back to your side?" Freddie straightened his back, as much as he could, squatting half-submerged in a shell hole. "I wouldn't stop you." The thought of Winter leaving him alone terrified him.

Winter shook his matted head. "No. I am still your prisoner, Iven."

"I won't let you die," Freddie said. It was a vow he'd written in another man's blood, and now it was all he had left in the world.

15

THE PARADISE OF FOOLS

.....

L AURA, PIM, AND MARY DISEMBARKED IN LIVERPOOL, TURNED
their backs on the submarine-haunted Atlantic, and boarded a
train to London. As soon as they wheezed to a halt at Euston,
Mary charged off again, to see to her "bedsheets and potpourri," as
she called her donated supplies. Laura and Pim found themselves
standing on the platform, temporarily abandoned.

Pim looked about with muted pleasure, taking in the mix of uniforms, the glass and the ironwork overhead. Laura wished she could
see the station through Pim's eyes. London felt like limbo to her, the
glittering center of the modern world become merely the war's an-
techamber. She was hoping that Mary would be quick, and that the
hotel was not too far.

A train with blacked-out windows pulled up to the station, and
people in uniforms began gathering on the platform, obviously
waiting, exchanging the occasional low-voiced word. "Oh, it must
be wounded soldiers," said Pim. "The poor dears. Although I
thought—I thought a hospital train would be bigger. Shouldn't it be
bigger?"

"Not exactly wounded. It's the mad ones," said Laura, after a hesitation. She inhaled cigarette smoke. "We might go and wait in the ticket office."

Pim didn't move. "Mad—soldiers? Because of the war?"

"Yes. Pim, the men won't want to be seen like that. We should—"

It was too late—the door to the train gaped wide. Next moment, the men were being walked or carried out. The first one was wearing a straightjacket. He thrashed. The second was weeping, gray-faced. He stumbled off on his own feet, leaning on an orderly's shoulder. The third couldn't work his limbs at all; he shook like a fallen bird. The fourth was biting his fingers, his eyes like holes burned into his colorless skin. The fifth was talking, softly—quite rational in tone—except his face was covered in bandages and what he was saying was nonsense.

"The dead ones," muttered the soldier. "At night, you know, you see them. In the dark. They come back in the dark. One of them smiled. He told me I'd never go home." His voice rose suddenly, wheezing. "But I knew that, didn't I? I knew it I knew it I—"

He was hustled off by orderlies.

Pim watched him go, standing very still. "But—why do they go mad?"

"I don't know," said Laura. She did, but it wasn't something you said in words. It didn't have words.

Pim said, in an odd, fragile voice, "But they— The war drove them *mad*? What was he saying? About—about the dead ones?"

"Madness," said Laura, with finality. "It was madness. Come along."

. . .

They were supposed to spend three days in London. Three days too long, in Laura's opinion. "Patience, Iven," said Mary, busily opening letters at the breakfast table in their hotel the next morning. "I have people to call on; there's no telling when I'll be in London next. Private field hospitals don't run on donations alone. I need public and private goodwill. Why do you think they let me stay in business? I'm a newsmaking coup, a brave lady doing my bit. I'm off to the newspaper office this morning, soon as I've had my tea."

Laura applied herself to her soft-boiled egg and toast. "Well, as long as the newspapers are satisfied," she said.

"Exactly," said Mary.

Pim had brought a Baedeker to breakfast and was paging through it, making notes, ignoring her toast. Mary said, "Shaw, do you think you're here for summer holidays?"

Pim said, "Oh, Laura, do you want to see Trafalgar Square?"

"Why not?" said Laura. She'd never traveled for pleasure. "Is that the one with the lions?"

"Hopeless, both of you." Mary slit open another letter. Gave a crow of satisfaction.

"What is it?" asked Pim.

Mary said, "Rejoice, ladies. I have procured us invitations to dinner."

Pim shut the guidebook. "Yes? With whom?"

"At the house of a retired general, a good old creature called Munster, one of those who made his bones in India and South Africa. You may expect Turkey carpets, and statues on all sides, dubiously acquired." Mary shook her head. "*But* there will be a full complement of new-arrived American officers—that's why they've invited us, thinking the officers will appreciate ladies from their own side of the ocean. And—" Mary had clearly saved the best for last. "Gage himself will be there, of the Fifth Army, you know, much caressed at GHQ. He's made a quick run to London, going back the same day we are. We're fortunate to have caught him." Mary rubbed her hands together. "I can easily see— Why, what is it, Laura?"

Laura had dropped her carefully peeled egg. "Nothing," she said, collecting herself. "It's slippery. Go on, Mary."

. . .

Mary tried to drag them out for new clothes, but Laura was immovable. "I'll wear my uniform. We're in a war, and I am, God save us, a heroine, with a limp to prove it. Thus does one sidestep all dictates of fashion."

"All right," Mary said reluctantly. "But you'll wear a proper uniform. Not one of those field-modified things, hemmed to the knee."

"Am I a savage?" said Laura. "I'll look perfectly proper. I even have a medal." It was true that most of her uniforms had been made over long ago. The standard nursing uniform was charming to look at. It was floor-length, with seven pieces including a starched detachable collar. Pristine detachable cuffs. Every nurse near the front line had taken one look and started surreptitiously hemming, quick as she could. But Laura had kept one uniform back, for occasions like this one. She put it on the evening of dinner, and when she came out to the shared lounge between their rooms, Mary said, "Maybe you were right. You'll look better in uniform anyway. You have one of those faces. Authoritative. Evening clothes would just look frivolous. Shame you're not taller. Now tell me what's troubling you." Pim had gone off to bathe.

Laura gave Mary an inquiring look.

"Do not even try to look innocent," said Mary. "You looked like a thundercloud when I told you about this dinner. What is it?"

Laura said briefly, "The general—Gage—it was on his orders that we relocated to Brandhoek, in support." A criminal place for a mobile hospital. Tucked up snug between a railroad siding and an ammunition dump, inevitably a target.

"I see," Mary said, sounding unmoved.

Laura said, "I know. Put the hospital next to the munitions, and perhaps Fritz won't bombard the latter. Or, if he does, and smashes the hospital in the bargain, then someone in a fedora comes out and takes pictures of the wrecked wards and weeping nurses. Sends the best ones straight to the papers. Another coup of wartime newsmaking."

Mary said, "Yes, yes, all very nefarious. Can you keep your feelings to yourself at dinner? This is a great thing, Laura, this invitation. There will be donations from this."

"I'm not going to pitch a fit and refuse to eat my peas, Mary. I'd rather not go. But I think you knew that."

Mary said, coaxingly, "*They* won't be rationing sugar."

Laura laughed darkly. "Well, then, all is forgiven, I suppose."

. . .

The retired eminence, Mary's good old boy called Munster, lived in a soaring mansion in Mayfair. Laura, Mary, and Pim alighted from their taxi and were admitted into a lounge full of Benares brass, dark furniture, British and American uniforms. The room was monstrously hot.

Pim was pleased. "I've never met a general." She was wearing black and looked heartbreaking. Every head in the room turned to mark her progress.

"They're much like other folk," said Laura. "Perhaps more self-important." A bead of sweat rolled down her spine. The room was packed. Far too loud. It made her jittery. She made straight for the drinks cart, shot the nearest officer a smile. He mixed her a cocktail; she drank it off quick and got another, ignoring Mary's disapproving look.

The general, Munster, matched his house. He was old, fussy, busy, his skin yellowed. His mustache was impeccable. He didn't, Laura thought, look well. There was an odd flush on his cheeks, a glaze to his eyes, something strained in his bonhomie.

General Gage was far younger: not yet fifty, his accent faintly Irish and his manner quick and expansive. He circled the room with effortless charm. Laura could see why he was favored in General Headquarters, and in Whitehall; he was one of those people who listened with flattering attention, looked at you like nothing else mattered. He made the American officers—a rather stiff and dour bunch, very Methodist-looking—laugh uproariously, and then he circled round to Mary, Pim, and Laura.

His eyes fastened on Pim's flawless face. "No one told me a trio of angels were come to grace our rough company."

Laura tried not to look cynical. Pim appeared simultaneously flattered, delighted to make his acquaintance, and innocently unavailable. She'd probably practiced that expression in a mirror. Mary shook the general's hand, smiling. Laura took a deep swallow of her cocktail. The lieutenant behind Gage was looking at Pim, visibly awestruck.

"Are these ladies your volunteers, Mrs. Borden?" inquired the general.

"Yes, indeed," said Mary. She introduced Pim and Laura and then launched into a discourse about her hospital, its rich backers, its interested journalists, its good work.

Gage listened courteously, but when Mary wound down, he said, "What brings a fine lady like yourself across the sea, Mrs. Shaw? I honor your patriotism, but surely your family could not spare you."

Mary pressed her lips together. Pim said, "I am a widow, sir. I wanted to—to honor my son, James, who has passed."

Laura expected Gage to make sympathetic noises. Instead, he frowned. "James? A James Shaw, is that right? A Canadian?"

What was that in Gage's face? Not quite recognition. Unease? Pim said, "Yes, indeed, sir. Is there a chance—I mean, could you have known—"

The bell for dinner interrupted her.

"Yes—perhaps? I—we shall speak . . . after dinner," said Gage. "Lovely to meet you, ladies." He strode away.

"Maybe he knows something about Jimmy," said Pim, with bright hope in her face.

Laura doubted it. He was probably just hungry. "Anything is possible. Come on, I want my supper."

. . .

As they went in to dinner, Laura told herself, sternly, that there was no call to despise General Gage. It wasn't his fault that he was well dressed and well fed, well mannered and effortlessly charming. That he commanded his army from a comfortable château, that for him losses were numbers in ledgers, a question of mathematics.

That he would probably be created a peer after the war. It was just the way of things. She needed another drink.

As they were all sitting down at the dining table, a pleasant, rather silly voice at Laura's elbow said, "I *do* remember you. It's Iven, isn't it?"

It was the lieutenant, the aide who'd stood behind General Gage and stared at Pim with such ardent admiration. He had unfortunate jug-handle ears, a slim, overbred face, and an exquisite cut to his clothes. His eyes were already moist with wine. Hastily, Laura searched her unreliable memory. But the only association that came with that face, vague as smoke, was nonsensical: *asparagus*.

"Yes, sir. My name is Laura Iven," said Laura. "I was a nurse with the CAMC."

The lieutenant saw her blankness, and said, with a disarmingly toothy smile, "Name's Young. You don't remember, I imagine. We met in '15, you know. When Fritz—"

"Yes, I remember," said Laura, suddenly recalling. Asparagus indeed, the poor man. "How do you do, sir?"

"Can't complain," said Young, heartily. "I'm on my uncle's—I mean—the general's staff now." His eyes strayed sideways to Pim. "Is this your first time in London, Mrs. Shaw?"

Pim looked round and he immediately flushed up to his hairline. But Pim was unruffled. "Yes, it is. How nice to meet you. Laura and I were so pleased to be invited tonight."

Young was still pink. "Pleasure's mine."

The conversation proceeded predictably. Young was delighted that they'd be at Couthove, and that Pim was afraid of horses. "Don't worry," he said, finishing his wine. A little swagger had come into his voice. "I could teach you to ride. You'll be jumping gates in no time." Self-importantly, he added, "My uncle and I are going back day after tomorrow. Can't linger at home too long, not these days."

"Oh," said Pim, with flattering seriousness. "Is it very bad over there, sir?"

"Of course we'll always protect you, Mrs. Shaw. But, well, you know, those rascally Bolsheviks—"

Laura applied herself to the soup course.

"—they weaseled Russia out of the war . . ."

Young had a good deal to say about the Bolsheviks. Now that Russia was out, Germany was going to reinforce their western front with all the men from the east. There were at least a million of them. But Mrs. Shaw was not to worry. Because a single Allied soldier was worth ten Germans.

Laura wasn't so sanguine.

The soup was removed and roast chicken put down.

"Those Communists," Young was saying, expansively. "Infected the populace with dreadful ideas. All people the same. That just means chaos. They won't take orders, Communists. No discipline."

Laura had a patient once, an Austrian prisoner, who'd fought on the Eastern Front. *Lots of soldiers there,* he'd said. *Lots of Russians. But not enough of anything else. They send men out with one rifle among two, and tell the second man to pick it up after the first one's killed . . .*

Laura took more chicken.

"Why, even the French——" Young swallowed the rest. He'd spoken into one of those strange silences that occur even in the loudest of parties. Nearly the whole table had heard. Munster and Gage, and a handful of other officers, instantly fixed him with a hard eye.

Young flushed. "Our greatest allies," he added feebly, and then asked Pim, "Do you like the chicken?"

Pim murmured something polite. Laura cut up her second helping. Recalled the rumors that had spread from billets to estaminets during the long, bloody days of the summer before: *The French won't go up. They won't fight. They're singing "The Internationale" in their dugouts. Say they won't attack, say they're tired of dying. Calling for the working class to rise.*

Mutiny——that was the word, the rumor, that people had hardly dared to whisper. If Germany had known, that would have been it. They'd have broken the line.

Laura kept on doggedly chewing. A million Germans coming, the French wavering, and the Americans only beginning to trickle onto the battlefield. If they lost, all the stationary architecture of the back area would be crushed under advancing feet, and she'd never find out what happened to Freddie, would spend her whole life wondering . . .

A well-bred girl in evening clothes, who volunteered at London hospitals, was trying to revive the flagging conversation. She turned to Laura. "My patients tell me such funny things. Ghost stories and folktales, so interesting. Perhaps you've heard some good stories yourself, Miss Iven? One man said he'd seen his captain, who'd passed away years ago, tipping his hat to him through a window. Another said he met a man selling wine who'd grant you wishes. And another told me about the wild men. Have you heard of the wild men?"

"An invention of the newspapers, Annie," Munster put in repressively. A certain family resemblance there. Niece? Granddaughter? Munster mopped his face. Laura noted that his color was worse, thought perhaps she ought to tell his wife to call a doctor after supper.

"Oh?" said the girl innocently. "Because a patient of mine told me *he'd* certainly seen them. He was on a salvage party near Fresnes, and he said all the men were afraid to leave their camp at night, for fear of the screams and the rifle shots coming from No Man's Land. It was the wild men making the noise, he said. Frenchmen, Germans, Italians—all soldiers who had deserted—they lived together and they'd come out at night to scrounge food and fight for entertainment. Once, my patient said, he and his mates even put out a trap for the wild men—some food and whiskey in a basket. No one touched it, but the next morning they found a note inside that said, 'Nothing doing!'"

Annie laughed innocently. A few of the Americans joined her. Pim had tilted her head toward the exchange. Laura sighed internally. A much-cherished fantasy, that there was a brotherhood of free men waiting for those who deserted. But she could see Gage starting to fume, so she said, "Once I had a patient come in who'd gone over the top ten days before. He was only just getting his wound seen to, he said, because he'd spent a week in a shell hole, drinking rainwater and calling for help. He said it as though it was quite ordinary, too. There's your voices from No Man's Land. Soldiers who can't get back." Her mind presented her with an image of her brother, trapped in a shell hole. She shook it away.

The girl looked chagrined.

Munster broke in, raising his glass. "Shall we have a toast, then? To the end of the war. To the kaiser's ruin. To the army, gentlemen."

There were murmurs of affirmation, and everyone drank. A babble of fresh conversation broke out. But Laura set her glass down abruptly. The color had receded from Munster's face. Laura was on her feet and moving just as he slumped over sideways in his chair.

"He's taken ill," she said, to a volley of questions, the back of her hand on his forehead, the other finding the pulse in his thick neck. "Very ill." The skin of his cheek and throat was hot enough to scorch. He ought to have been upstairs in bed. *Not sitting at a table with you lot, drinking. And whatever he has, it's probably catching.*

Laura listened to the patient, didn't like what she heard. At least she had experience with fluid in lungs. Phosgene casualties generally came to her half-drowning. "Get him to a sofa. Prop him up. Here, help me," she said to the men hovering. "He cannot get his breath if he's bent over." Laura wrenched open the buttons on his collar. "Someone fetch a doctor."

Munster was taken off to a quiet sofa and propped up. Brandy and water revived him a little. Laura didn't like his high fever, though. It had come on so quickly.

"What is this?" said the doctor, when he came. "This man should be lying down."

"He's got fluid in his lungs," said Laura.

"Don't lecture me on my own profession, miss," said the doctor, bending toward the patient. "I'll see to him now."

Laura opened her mouth, saw Mary in the doorway, closed it again, and crossed the room to her. She was tired. "Where's Pim?" Laura wanted to go back to the hotel and get off her leg.

"Gage got hold of her in the confusion. Took her off to the library." Mary was nursing a glass of port.

"Do we need to mount a rescue?"

"No," said Mary. "I know Pim looks terribly unworldly—and is, in a lot of ways—but she's had men at her since she was a girl—it's that hair." Mary's tone was affectionate. "Anyway, she can handle Gage."

"Five minutes," said Laura, eyes on the door to the library, "and then we're mounting that rescue and leaving. And try not to breathe my air for a day or two. Munster was sick."

"Iven, did you really need to—" Laura didn't hear the rest of the question. Pim had reentered on Gage's arm, and for an instant, standing in the lamplight from the hall, Pim's face looked blank. Shocked.

Laura hurried across the room. Young was already there, quite drunk, paying Pim compliments, bowing over her hand. Gage did likewise, smiling with immense Irish charm, a particular tenderness. Pim smiled at them both, unruffled. Laura must have imagined the distress. Perhaps it was a trick of the uncertain light.

. . .

Laura couldn't sleep that night. She lay awake and imagined herself staying in London after all, perhaps as a nurse to a private family. A new life, one less troubled by memory. She recalled when Lucy Jeffries had been pulled out of one of the casualty clearing stations to tend to the king of England, after he'd sprained his back reviewing the troops. Lucy had spent six months in an English country house, eating her head off at royal expense, and got a medal at the end of it. Laura could do something like that. A country manor. Perhaps an older gentleman, an incurable hypochondriac. Yet the black current still had her, as much as it had in Halifax. Her face was turned eastward.

Pim was awake too; Laura could hear the whisper of her plaited hair as she turned her head on the pillow. "What do you think of the general?" Laura asked. "He hauled you off to the library so suddenly." Pim hadn't said a word about her interlude with Gage.

Pim's answer was mild. "Oh, he was very charming. He's been in

Halifax once, you know. Had an excellent dinner there, he said. Fried cod."

"He called you to the library to talk of Halifax? Pim—was he importunate?"

"Gage?" Pim sounded embarrassed. "Oh, no, of course not, Laura. A perfect gentleman. Where did you meet Lieutenant Young?"

Laura let Pim change the subject. "At a party, I suppose. We had a surprising number. In aerodromes and divisional headquarters and cafés. Quite desperate affairs, some of them. But he's famous for the asparagus."

"Asparagus?"

Laura laughed a little. "His unit was ordered up the line while he was on leave. In '15, it was. He was shopping at a greenmarket in Oise and missed their departure. Came back to billets and found his unit gone. The whole crew. Didn't faze him, though. He took his servant and his basket of cress and asparagus, ordered a taxi, and set off for the Front."

Pim said, "Goodness. And then?"

"Are you all right?" Laura asked.

"I— Yes, of course. Too much cream in the soup. Do go on."

Laura craned her neck to look across the room. But she couldn't make out Pim's face in the darkness. She wished she hadn't started the story. "Well, all this happened—bad luck—on the day Fritz first tried gas. At Ypres. Young was just driving up, tucked in his cab, properly civilized, when the gassed men started running back. Bit of a shock for him."

The story had been funny when someone had first told it in the mess. The absurd contrast: men staggering toward the rear, faces turning blue, clawing at their own throats, while the taxi driver stared, and the white-gloved officer in back clutched his fresh vegetables. They could laugh at anything, in their hospital mess. Told in London, to Penelope Shaw, it seemed less funny.

16

A RIDER, ON A RED HORSE

·····

BETWEEN PASSCHENDAELE RIDGE AND YPRES,
FLANDERS, BELGIUM
NOVEMBER 1917

THE NIGHT DRAGGED ON. THE BODY FLOATED BELOW THEM, half-submerged. Freddie wanted to go down, pull him out, lay him on the ground at least. But the ground was steep and slick, and when he tried anyway, Winter dragged him back. "It won't make a difference to him now." Freddie almost hated Winter for that, even as he subsided against the slope of their shell hole. They couldn't go anywhere. They couldn't leave until the rain lifted or the sun rose and gave them the direction. And then they must wait for nightfall once more, to cover their movements.

A day with the dead man. Freddie swallowed around his aching throat.

The rain still fell in sweeping curtains, but with full day came a slackening of the shellfire. In the relative silence, Freddie heard voices from other shell holes. Babbling, pleading, cursing. *It's the dead,* he thought first. Then he thought, *No, it's the wounded. Trapped by daylight.* Freddie found himself grinding his palms into his ears.

"Iven?" said Winter.

Freddie looked up, realized that he'd been whispering to himself. Lines of strain bracketed Winter's mouth, purple marks like bruising, framing worried eyes of that startling blue. Freddie could feel the heat of Winter's gathering fever where their shoulders pressed together. "It's all right," he said. "I'm all right. Are you?" Freddie found himself straining over the ambient noise to hear Winter breathe. Perhaps it was something that had been carved into his brain during that time in the pillbox, that Winter breathing meant that he, Freddie, was also alive.

"I'll do," said Winter, easing back.

Freddie tried to think what to do about Winter's wound. Laura had lectured him about this, too, making him learn what to do for a wound going septic. Christ, he missed her. He *didn't* know what to do. There were no more clean bandages. There was nothing to do at all but survive until they got back to the land of the living.

"Tell me a poem," Winter said. "Tell me one of yours."

"I can't remember," said Freddie. "I can't remember anything."

One of the unseen wounded was sobbing like a child.

Winter said, harsh, "Or tell me why the hell no one built proper defensive emplacements. Do you like sitting in holes? Something in the Anglo character?"

"Emplacements? Like that pillbox, our bloody headstone?" Freddie's voice was equally ragged. Someone shrieked from a neighboring shell hole.

"How many of your men fight ill because they walked up and down duckboards all night in the dark and then slept in a crater?"

"All of us," said Freddie. "They say it ruins the fighting spirit of the men to sleep in safety."

Winter laughed, something terrible in the sound. "The ones saying that aren't the ones in the craters, are they?"

. . .

Finally the daylight began leaking away again. "At full dark," Winter muttered. Freddie merely nodded. Neither of them would survive another night out. The corpse had begun to bloat. In the gathering shadows, they dragged themselves to the lip of the shell hole. Winter missed his grip and slid back. Freddie grabbed for him before he could go into the water; struggling mightily, he got them both onto the flat ground. "Winter?" Freddie whispered.

Winter shook his head and dragged himself to his feet.

Freddie turned back once, almost against his will. But the dead man was invisible in the renewed darkness. As they began stumbling toward the back area, Freddie realized why the wounded men had fallen silent. All those shell holes were full to the lip now with rain.

On another day, in another place, they'd not have got away with it. Their uniforms were indistinguishably filthy. They'd no rifles. Someone would have asked them what they were about, and what coherent answer could Freddie have given? But no one asked. It was nearly pitch-dark by then, rainswept, and every man still alive was hardly human. Just a bundle of impulses, living on nerves.

Freddie tried to distract himself, to remember Halifax. His books. They wouldn't come. He tried remembering Laura instead: those early days, when she was in training in Halifax, the raging letter she'd sent him from France, when he wrote her that he was joining up. He'd thought, at the time, that it was the most hateful thing she'd ever done, writing that letter. *A man died in my ward today,* she wrote. *He was called Culpepper. Do you know what happened, when they picked him up? The orderlies weren't careful, moving him, didn't know how big the wound was. His body fell in two pieces, Freddie, and they had to carry him away so, with the slime trailing . . .*

He'd been furious at the time that she'd say such things to him. He knew why she had, now. He hadn't listened.

He remembered her as she'd been in '16, posted in France, giving him first aid classes every time he got leave. "For God's sake!" he'd snapped. They'd had a free afternoon and gone to Deauville together. It was August, and the sun was warm. The send and suck of the sea reminded him of Halifax. He was trying to sketch it, sea bleeding into sky, gulls wheeling, and still Laura was beside him, lecturing about tying up arms. She'd got him a special kerchief, with different methods of bandaging printed right on the cloth. He still hadn't even seen proper combat. "Can't a man draw in peace?"

"If you tell me—" she began, and some gesture of hers called attention to her left hand, bandaged in two places, strangely stiff under the wrapping.

"What happened to your hand, Laura?"

"Nothing," she'd said. "Name me disinfectants, Freddie."

He'd recited, dutifully, "Alcohol, iodine, carbolic. Rum in a pinch." Then he kicked seawater onto her skirt and she splashed him back, and for ten minutes they were children again.

Perhaps it was the memory of light on water that drew his attention back, for of course there was light on water everywhere here. Scarlet and green, oily blue-white. Something gleamed particularly bright in the nearest shell hole. He turned his head to look.

The dead man stared back at him. The water stirred, rippled, and then, slowly, the dead man stood up. Water poured off him. His lips were black. The rats had been at him.

Freddie, staring helplessly, took a step toward the water. "I'm sorry," he whispered.

Freddie felt the impact of a thin shoulder, heard someone swear. A half-familiar voice was saying *"Iven."* Freddie took another step toward the shell hole. "Gott in Himmel," said the voice, right in his ear, savage, "will you listen to me?"—and then a fist came clipping across his jaw, hard enough to split his lip. Freddie came back to himself. The dead face was just a gleam of light. Winter had an arm round his chest; Freddie's heart was shaking like a fist under his soaked jacket. And the water that Winter had kept him out of wasn't water at all, but the indescribable substance that shelling had made of the ground, viscous and sucking, deadlier than quicksand. He'd been three steps from dying. They panted, leaning on each other.

"Don't look at the water. Watch your feet. Only that," said Winter, when he could speak. "Do you hear me?"

Freddie nodded.

"Come on," said Winter, shoving Freddie ahead of him. Freddie concentrated on his steps. Words from his past, flapping like laundry, useless sounds, ran through his mind: *Before me there were no created things, only eternity, and I, too, am eternal. Abandon all hope . . .*

"Walk, damn you," Winter said.

Freddie, without a will of his own, did.

Until a voice spoke out of one of the shell holes. Freddie's steps stuttered at the sound of it. "Kill me," said the voice. "Oh, Christ, oh, fucking hell, please will someone kill me?"

THE WOMB OF NATURE
AND PERHAPS HER
GRAVE

·····

Laura, Pim, and Mary landed in Calais, and spent the night in a hotel. They were tired with that unwholesome travel weariness that comes of sitting still for long periods while some conveyance heaves you into the unknown. Laura had a headache, steady and vicious, right between the eyes. Her face felt hot. Munster *had* been contagious. She drank whiskey and water, tried not to smoke, and prayed it would pass.

The streets of Calais were packed with soldiers on leave: faded blue uniforms for the French, khaki and drab for the rest. The French army was older than it had been. Most of the young men were dead; their fathers had been conscripted to take their places. Pim and Laura shared a hotel room, with Mary across the hall, in solitary state. Laura drank broth, refused supper, went to bed, and was lying still when Pim came up and felt her forehead.

"You look awful." Pim's fingers were cool and pleasant.

"It's my clever scheme." She did not take the cloth off her eyes.

"I am going to terrify the Germans into retreat. Give me another day of this headache, and I'll sweep them away with a glare."

"I brought you a headache powder."

"Thank God," said Laura in a more human voice, lifting the cloth from her eyes. "Mary doesn't have time for poor mortals' headaches."

"You must be all right if you can talk like that," Pim observed, helping Laura sit up. She was mixing the powder into a glass of water.

Laura recalled herself and said, "Go away. Other side of the room with you, madam. I was in earnest that it may be catching."

Pim tucked the blanket up round Laura's shoulders, put the glass by her bed, and retreated. "You've a wretched color. That's a nasty flu."

"A very nasty flu. Just ask poor old Munster. But he had pneumonia in the bargain, and I don't. I just feel vile; I'll be all right tomorrow." She gulped the headache powder and said, "Bless you."

Pim said, after a small silence and in a different voice, "How are you—how are you going to look for Freddie? How do you even start? Whom do you ask?"

Laura said, "I'm not looking for him. I just want to know what *happened* to him. There's a difference. Whatever—whatever mistake they made, in how they reported his death, he *is* dead." When Pim was silent, Laura said, "You must accept the same for Jimmy, Pim. If you don't, you'll see him in every face. He wouldn't want that for you."

"I already do," said Pim. Her face was in profile, her eyes on the darkling window.

Laura pulled the scratchy woolen covers up to her shoulders. "You mustn't blame yourself."

"I was proud of him." Laura couldn't see Pim's face anymore. "Nate was dead. Jimmy was all I had. He looked such a man, in his uniform, and I was so proud of him."

Laura said nothing. In Laura's mind, Penelope and Jimmy Shaw belonged to that old world, the fairy-tale Calais, with its color, and glossy mustaches and heroism bright as banners. Now Pim was lost, alone in the wrong world.

Laura said, after a pause, "You are still proud of him, I hope."

"Yes," said Pim. "Always. But does it matter?"

Laura didn't think it did. Pim's love and her pride were like the Angels of Mons. Like the wild men. Even if they existed, they hadn't changed anything. They belonged to the old world too.

. . .

A troop train would take them east to Dunkirk, and a lorry would pick them up there, for the last kilometers to Couthove. Their train car the next day was crammed with soldiers, sitting on the floor or straw or empty ammunition crates, playing cards. Laura kept to herself. Her headache was worse, and all her bones ached. Mary eyed her. "I ought to have left you behind."

"You couldn't," said Laura. "You wouldn't leave anything that might do your precious hospital some good. I'll be all right."

The soldiers stared avidly at Pim, and Laura found herself glaring them off, red-eyed, as though she were a chaperone at the most absurd of balls.

Finally someone unearthed a pocket tome of Tennyson, of all things. It found its way to Pim, who, after a small hesitation, began reading. The soldiers in the car around them fell adoringly silent to listen.

> Four gray walls, and four gray towers
> Overlook a space of flowers,
> And the silent isle imbowers
> The Lady of Shalott.

Laura listened in a haze of fever. She could almost convince herself that the poem was real and everything else illusion. Why should a tower, a tapestry, a fairy woman, and a magic mirror be made up when the thing crouching in the east, jaws wide, was real? A rumble was growing in the distance. At first, it could have been mistaken for thunder. But it went on and on.

Pim stopped reading and turned to Laura. "Is that——?"

"Guns," said Laura.

The light was beginning to draw in, gray mist over gray fields, where the crops hadn't sprouted. The war had left its detritus: here a tire, a flipped lorry, an empty petrol can, there a dead cow, hooves stabbing the sky. Small houses with barred windows. Pim kept reading, her eyes going from the page to the sopping gray countryside and back.

In the stormy east-wind straining,
The pale yellow woods were waning,
The broad stream in his banks complaining,
Heavily the low sky raining
Over tower'd Camelot;
Outside the isle a shallow boat
Beneath a willow lay afloat,
Below the carven stern she wrote,
The Lady of Shalott—

Pim shook her head once and passed the poems to someone else.

. . .

They got off the train, trailed by a chorus of yearning farewells. A lorry was waiting for them at the station. "Can't we just change trains?" said Laura, eyeing the lorry, thinking of how much slower it would be, and how a few hours of lurching on Belgian roads would hurt her aching head. The branch railway ran east as far as Poperinghe.

"You're not in the army now, Iven," Mary said, coming up briskly. "No room on the train going east for oddities like us. It's drive or march." Soldiers would march, Laura knew. But her leg would never take it.

Their lorry was driven by one of the orderlies from the hospital, called Fouquet. He was a Walloon, a French-speaking Belgian. Without a word, he helped them with their trunks. Mary's donated supplies would follow. A train whistled behind them, high and lonely, as they drove off into the dusk.

The road grew worse, and worse still as they went east, destroyed by tires and marching feet. It smelled of earth and petrol and that indescribable hovering stink of unwashed men congregated together. Laura tried to run her mind over what she knew of Freddie's last known billets, the name of his company commander, a list of hospitals that might have seen him, taken his clothes. But her mind slid away from it all, exhausted.

Pim tried to give Laura her coat, and was only restrained by the combined protest of Laura and Mary. The road swam in Laura's gaze like water, and for a second she imagined it *was* water, black water, sweeping them all along in its current. She blinked the illusion away. Then the lorry was slowing.

"Checkpoint," Mary said. "They've been trying for four years to keep the spies, the tourists, and the bereaved out of the forbidden zone. Pim, for God's sake, you're going to work in a field hospital. Try not to look like you're about to wash anyone's feet with your tears."

Laura was silent. They put up checkpoints to keep men from deserting too.

The checkpoint guards had a plum job, fairly safe and relatively dry. They emerged with a bit of swagger: big men with massive knitted comforters wound about their throats so that only the tips of their noses and their eyes poked out. One stuck the muzzle of his rifle into the back of the lorry. The other one shone a pocket torch. "What we got here?" said one and grinned, predictably. "Cannon fodder?"

"Just say that again when the next show starts," said Mary, leaning forward so that the light caught her face.

The man started. He looked like a grimy scarecrow, decayed by the rain. "Mrs. Borden," he said. "I thought you'd gone to America."

Mary said, "I came back."

A faint, disreputable grin was her answer, and a wet cough. The soldier had a violent cold. Was everyone ill, this side of the Atlantic?

"We're for Couthove," added Mary. "With new staff."

Their driver, Fouquet, had come round the back. He had spent all those miles hunched like a gargoyle over wheel and gearbox. He had been an under-gardener at Couthove before the war, or so Mary said. An expert in roses.

Fouquet said, "Problem?"

"I can't imagine," Mary said.

Laura could. The guards were bored.

"Canadian?" said the second soldier to Laura.

"Yes," said Mary.

Christ, now he was making agreeable small talk, barely hindered by his cough. "I should like to go to Canada one day. If Flanders gets any wetter, they'll have to call in the Canadian fishing fleet to bring up men, instead of lorries. Here, miss. You look like you could use this." He handed Laura a flask.

Well, that was more like it. Laura took it, drank. Unwatered rum. She coughed, eyes stinging, and the spirit burned as it went down, but it lit a small fire in her stomach, quieted the chills. "If you've a cigarette," said Laura, "I'll light candles to your memory after you catch a bullet, sir."

"Laura!" gasped Pim. But the man was already laughing; he pulled an army-issue cigarette out of his pocket and lit it for her. The smoke calmed her a little. She'd been wrestling involuntary panic as the noise of the Front crept closer.

Mary said, "Done with the pleasantries? Good. It's wretchedly cold. May we go on or not?"

The men looked disappointed, but Mary had fixed them with a steely look. "Be careful on the road," the first man said finally, stepping back. "There's old Fritz's aeroplanes, there's the ghosts, there's the madmen, and then there's the fiddler."

Pim said, "Fiddler?"

"Well," said the soldier, "they say he roams the back area, and if he catches you, *wham*. Alive or dead you'll always—"

"*I* am going to be a ghost if I stay here much longer," interrupted Laura, just as Mary said, "Can we get on or not?"

"I suppose," said the soldier reluctantly. "Watch out," he added to Fouquet, man-to-man. "They've been flying sorties toward the coast."

Fouquet just grunted and went back to the front of the lorry. The engine snarled to life and changed gears.

Behind them the soldiers were calling "Good luck, Mrs. Borden! Let the little lady watch for officers; they love nurses!"

Pim blushed, but Mary replied, unruffled, "Until you're peeling off their dressings."

Twinned barks of laughter chased the lorry out onto the road. Laura looked toward the receding checkpoint and was startled by a trick of the shadows, and perhaps of her rising fever. It looked, in the uncertain light, as though a great gate arced across the road, barring the way back.

AND MANY MEN DIED OF THE WATERS

.....

"KILL ME. OH, CHRIST, WILL SOMEONE KILL ME?"

Freddie turned to look, and Winter walked into him.

There was water everywhere. Some of the water was on fire. Freddie was about to put the voice down as a product of his disordered brain, when something moved amid the sickly red-black shimmer. *It's him,* he thought, cold. *It's him, it's him.* Winter swore and his voice pulled Freddie back to reality. It was a living man, not a dead one, floundering in the not-quite-liquid earth. Freddie's flailing mind offered words: *People, mud-bespent, in that lagoon. All of them naked . . .* Freddie told his mind to shove it. The man might as well have been dead. He was going to drown in the mud.

"Kill me, will you?" he gasped, reaching a sticky arm.

They couldn't, unless Winter was a dab hand at throwing pocket knives.

"Please," said the man, thrashing. He sank a little more. They *had* to get him out, Freddie thought. He couldn't leave someone else behind. Floating . . .

"Winter—" he said. He knew it was foolishness. They didn't have rope, they didn't have *anything*, and surely this man's comrades had already tried . . .

But Winter didn't say no. He was looking at, of all things, a dead mule. The flesh was gone around the muzzle and the eyes were pecked out. It still wore its harness. "We can try," Winter said, as though Freddie had asked a whole question, as though he knew why Freddie couldn't leave this man drowning. He knelt stiffly by the mule. Freddie, puzzled, dropped beside him. The shells still fell, screaming like the damned. But Winter ignored the shellfire. He began undoing the girth, flinching a little as he put pressure on his bad arm. "Get the harness."

"I—all right," Freddie whispered, fumbling at the buckles. Inaudibly he whispered, "Thank you."

"Can't just pull him out," Winter said, as he worked. "Wants an angle to—end the suction." He lifted his good hand briefly to illustrate.

"How?" Freddie said.

In answer, Winter called to the stricken man. Even Freddie could hardly distinguish Winter's accent, in the all-pervading roar. Winter said, "Listen to me. You must—be calm. You must move carefully."

"All—all right," said the man.

"Take your pack," said Winter. It was barely visible, half-sunk beside him. "Pull it in front of you. Slowly . . . slowly."

The panic came back to the man's face. "Throw me a rope!" he cried, and then gulped mud, coughing, sinking lower.

"Wait," said Winter, and again there was that authority.

The man stilled.

"Your pack," said Winter.

The man pulled his pack round, and Winter said, "Lean on it. Try to get your weight off your feet."

The man did, but the pack sank almost at once, and then the man was thrashing, until Winter snapped, "Stop."

Miraculously, the man did.

Winter cast about, seized a fallen entrenching tool, threw it to the smudge. "Push it straight down." Another shell screamed and fell. Close. Christ, so close. "Next to your feet," said Winter, his careful pronunciation eroding.

"It won't hold!" cried the man.

"It will let in air," said Winter. Finally the strain could be heard in his voice. A single stray shell could have killed them all right then. "Break—break the pull. The suck. Of the mud."

The man pushed the spade down, and then he leaned forward again to where his pack was sunk below the surface, spluttering all the while. As he did, his legs kicked up, the angle of his body changed, and that was when Winter threw him the length of leather straps. The man seized it, choking, his head and shoulders barely above that hungry surface. "Slowly," snapped Winter, and then the man was slithering over his submerged pack toward the side of the shell hole. Winter was pulling grimly with both arms, the good and the wounded. "Iven," he said. "When he's close enough, get down and take his hand. The harness is going to part."

So Freddie threw himself flat, and Winter bared his teeth with pain, as he held the makeshift rope alone. Freddie's groping hand met the drowning man's just as the harness buckle broke, and Freddie slung his other hand forward, and they two were clasped, wrist to wrist, just as Winter snatched Freddie's collar. They all writhed backward and ended up in a heap on the duckboards.

No one moved, for a moment. The stranger looked as though he were sunk in some insane dream. "It's all right," Freddie said, and felt hysterical laughter bubble up. He bit blood from his tongue to stifle it.

Winter's eyes were already on the eastern horizon, looking for dawn in the seething sky. "We must go."

The Tommy's head came round. Winter had forgotten his careful intonation. His accent had been unmistakable. But the Tommy didn't say anything.

Winter said again, more carefully, "We can't stay here."

"Where are we going?" asked the Tommy, like a child.

Freddie didn't know how to answer. He pointed them west, along the duckboards.

"Come on," Winter said, his eyes still on the horizon. Was that light in the east dawn, or was it just the German guns, firing from the heights?

The three of them started to walk.

AND THE STARS OF
HEAVEN FELL TO EARTH

·····

BETWEEN DUNKIRK AND COUTHOVE,

FRANCE TO BELGIUM

MARCH 1918

THE SUN HAD SET. NOT A PROPER SUNSET, THOUGH, MORE LIKE the sky was wounded and bleeding out its light. The lorry swayed along the rutted road. Laura wished she hadn't smoked a cigarette. Her throat ached. The gunfire was louder still, a distant drumroll beyond the horizon.

"Are we close?" Pim asked Mary.

"Less than an hour perhaps, if the road's all right. Lord, the guns. Iven, you don't think Fritz is planning another attack? How would they? I heard they were eating plaster and turnips in Berlin, after three years of blockade."

Her eyes half-closed, Laura said, "Their only chance is to attack before all those well-armed, well-victualed American boys come out in force. They have to know it." Surely she'd find out what happened to Freddie before then. And she'd go home. She'd saved enough lives.

Home, whispered a sly voice in her mind. *Where's that? The cellar-hole in Veith Street? The Parkeys' spare bedroom?*

And then she jolted upright. "Aeroplanes," she said. A higher pitch than a lorry, a propeller rattling, unmistakable.

"Probably ours—" Mary began just as an explosion ripped the night. Pim's head swiveled round, her eyes huge in the shadows. "Just a stray bomb," Mary said. "We're all right." The noise of the aeroplanes got louder. Laura found herself concentrating on the motion of her lungs. In. Out. She'd been here before, crouched beneath an iron rain. But she had no task now, no one to nurse, nothing to do but listen and live. It wasn't easier. Then she caught sight of Pim, face stark with bewildered terror. Always, Laura Iven had found her courage when others needed her. She said, "It's all right, Pim." Pim was shaking so hard her teeth might well crack under the strain. Never mind her fever, Laura put an arm round Pim's shoulders and pulled her into the shelter of her body.

The planes were coming closer still—they were strafing the road, or else going after the train station at Beveren. She knew in excruciating detail what shrapnel did to bodies. "Merde," said Fouquet. Laura braced herself, the muscles in her stomach cramping, as they barreled into the dark. The road before them wavered like water in the light of the headlamps.

But there was someone in the current. A shadow, a blur. For an instant, Laura could have sworn she saw a housecoat, and eyes black with blood. "Someone on the road!" she shouted, before she could think, and Fouquet swore and slammed on the brakes. The lorry slewed sideways and halted just as the bomb came down with an annihilating roar, in the road where they would have been. Dirt rained on the lorry, and the windscreen cracked. Everyone's ears were ringing.

Laura recovered first. "Enough of this. Get out, get underneath! Take cover."

Fouquet was already moving. They pitched out of the lorry. Laura's leg didn't hold her. Pim half-fell on top of her, and then they were crawling underneath just as another explosion obliterated the world in a wave of sound and spattering earth.

. . .

Was she hurt? Laura didn't know. You didn't feel it at first, if it was bad. There was rain in her eyes. Her head was ringing. The aeroplanes had moved off.

She remembered the figure in the road, just before the shell came down, looked in that direction. There was nothing but a crater now. She blinked her eyes free of grit, crawling clear of the lorry. "Pim?" she called. Fear and incipient pneumonia gripped her lungs.

After a small, horrible pause, Pim's voice answered. "I'm here." Her skirt was soaked and filthy, her face absolutely colorless.

"Are you all right?" Laura asked. "Mary? Fouquet?" She couldn't hear or see anyone but themselves, and wasn't that strange? She knew the night teemed with people, with men, with *armies*. But it felt as if she and Pim were standing alone at the edge of the world. Perhaps it was shock.

"I'm all right." Pim squinted, trying to make out Laura's face in the darkness. "Except my ears are ringing. You?"

Laura felt a knifing pain when she breathed. She wasn't all right, but she'd do for the moment. "Mary?"

"Still alive," said Mary, her voice jagged with adrenaline as she emerged out of the wet darkness. "But the lorry's never moving again."

Laura could just make out the engine smoking against a patch of lighter sky. "Where's Fouquet?" But then her eye fell on him, huddled in the shadow of the smashed lorry, only half underneath. Dead indeed, with a blown-off piece of the engine halfway through his body.

Pim made a little sound, her knuckles against her mouth. Laura, limping, went across, checked his pulse for form's sake, and covered his face with his hat. Mary was looking from the road to the wreck to the eastern sky. Pim was standing shocked, her face a mess of mud and tears.

"We must walk," Mary said. "It's too cold to stand. Not too far to Couthove now. We'll send men back for Fouquet's body. Let's get on, Iven. Shaw, pull yourself together."

Laura coughed, shallow with pain.

"Mary, Laura won't make it; she's sick."

"Where do you suggest, then—" began Mary, when Laura broke in.

"What's that?"

Pim and Mary turned. Far across the field, a gleam, quickly gone. Something like a light in a window. Laura squinted. Thought she saw, if she concentrated, a deeper darkness against the sky. The vague shape of a building. A farmhouse, maybe? It had begun to rain again, the soft remorseless spring rain of Flanders. Laura could already feel it soaking through the seams of her clothes. "We could ask for shelter until morning," said Laura, eyes on that distant light.

The road was still empty, and silent. *Where is everyone? This is a war zone. Pim should have six men at least vying to carry her, literally, to safety.* But there was no one. Just the three of them and the dead man lying alone.

Mary looked torn. She gazed eastward again, toward Couthove. Then she glanced at Laura, seemed to give herself a mental shake. "No point in us all getting pneumonia." They set out stumbling across the wet fields, toward that elusive light. It was cold, the mud was sticky. Laura's limp worsened.

"There," said Mary. Laura forced herself to look beyond Mary's straight back, blinking ice from her eyelashes. Her heart sank. She could make out the jagged line of a roof, nothing more. Had they come upon a ruin? Flanders was covered with ruins. A gleam from the changeable sky showed gold lettering on the front of the building—HÔTEL DU ROI, it said. *A ruined hotel,* Laura thought. Just like a hundred others. Abandoned in the early days of the war.

"Well," Mary said grimly, "hopefully we can find a corner that's out of the wet, at least. Or if not, we'll leave you, Iven, and go for help."

Laura made no reply. They struck a chipped cobbled drive, silvered by the rain and glancing moonlight, murder on Laura's leg.

And then, they came to a door. "Won't it be locked?" said Pim between chattering teeth.

Without a word, Mary turned her shoulder and pushed.

Laura was expecting damp chill and the smell of mold. Instead she felt a rush of warmth. Thought it was a by-product of her fever. Realized it wasn't. "Oh, lord," said Pim. They'd walked out of the rain into warmth. Into not a ruin, but a foyer.

The room—no, a bar, smelling of wine—was lit entirely with firelight. At first glance, all Laura saw was gilt: on cornices and chandeliers, glimmering in the low light. Then she saw the men. Soldiers in drab and khaki and blue. They were sitting around tables, their heads close together, faces softened with the firelight, drinking. Not a single head had turned at their entrance. Everyone was watching a man standing at the far end of the room.

This man wore a shabby civilian suit. He'd a sharp jaw, arching bones. Bow-curves of dissipation gouged lines round his mouth. He was playing a violin, flawlessly. Silky, grave, strangely familiar, the music poured like water from between his fingers and seemed to banish everything outside itself. Even the rustle of Laura's strained breathing was lost as the room filled like a cup with melody.

Laura, Pim, and Mary stood transfixed. When the last notes died away, there was nothing in the room for three heartbeats but stunned silence. Then a roar of acclamation. The player bowed. Sweat stood out on his face. "Please. I hope you enjoy yourselves tonight. Drinks, anyone?"

That got him another roar, as he put his violin in a cracked leather case. His amused gaze flickered over the crowd and paused at the three women, standing soaked and mystified by the door. For the briefest instant, he wore no expression at all. Then a smile lit his face. With a tilt of his head, he indicated an empty table and then went off in the direction of the bar. The room filled with murmuring talk, laughter, calls for more wine. Laura, Pim, and Mary drifted to the table, looking around in exhausted bemusement.

Illicit drinking was as old as armies; secret bars dotted the forbidden zone, although Laura had never heard of one so—grand. Surely she ought to have heard of this place? She'd never imagined anything like it. She wanted to be wary, but the air was too warm and too mellow with talk, the scent of good wine was too delightful. She felt like a storm-tossed boat that had slipped, unexpectedly, into harbor. "Christ, this is more like it," said Mary.

Laura agreed silently. The music still echoed, somewhere, in the bones of her feverish face.

No one had called to them when they entered, and no one turned to look when they sat down. That was strange. Women were rare as hens' teeth, and women who spoke English in constant demand. But the room was gripped with that easy, delightful kind of drunkenness that makes people idle and drowsy and contented. Perhaps that was what kept the men where they were, murmuring with their heads close together.

The musician crossed the room, paused to speak to another table, made a joke that set them all to laughing. Laura studied him. It was not an ugly face, although its bones were sharp under the skin, and he'd the mobile mouth of an actor. But his eyes were not the same color. One was dark, like a well dug deep. The other was green as peridot, and shone.

He caught her eye and came across. "Seldom do I have guests so lovely," he said. Laura could not quite place his accent. "I'm called Faland. What brings you here tonight?"

"Accident," said Mary. "A bomb fell on our road. Our lorry was disabled, and the driver killed. We should like something to eat, Monsieur. And a place for the night."

A line, faint as thread, showed between Faland's brows. "A fortunate coincidence." Was there an odd note in his voice? "That led you straight to my door." His strange gaze didn't seem to look directly at you, but caught you sidelong, piercing. "Supper. Of course. Straightaway." The eyes ghosted over Laura, returned. "Are you well, Mademoiselle?"

"Nothing a bite and a drink won't fix," said Laura. The musician was carrying glasses and a bottle. He smiled, laid out the glasses, and poured the wine. Laura had to sit on her hands so she wouldn't seize it and drink it off like a savage.

Unexpectedly Pim said, "Monsieur Faland, why are all those men looking in that mirror?" Pim was staring across the room, at a dark mirror behind the bar. Several of the men were clustered around the glass, peering. Laura hoped there wasn't a naked girl behind it; poor Pim would be shocked.

Faland's eyes lit with unholy laughter, as though he'd caught her thought. But he answered Pim courteously. "Just a superstition, Madame. One of the attractions of my establishment."

As Faland spoke, one of the men turned away from the tarnished mirror, the tracks of tears clear in the grime on his face. Laura frowned. Pim looked as she had before the Parkeys' séance. Eager. Curious. "What superstition, Monsieur?"

"Why," he replied, lightly, "that the mirror will show you your heart's desire." He bowed. "Enjoy your wine."

"And supper," called Mary, picking up her glass, as Faland slipped away.

"I would avoid that mirror, Pim," said Laura. "It's probably obscene."

Pim said nothing. Mary lifted her glass and toasted Laura and Pim. They all drank. The wine was glorious. Like getting hit in the face by an ocean wave; it was a shock, then a pleasure, then a numbness. Laura's headache receded.

One glass became two, and then Laura realized that she'd lost count. Dinner never appeared, but it didn't seem to matter. Faland's smile was delightful, his supple voice raised from every corner. Laura, head full of wine, thought vaguely, *He doesn't carry it the way the rest of us do. This place. These years. Why is that, I wonder?*

A madman, perhaps.

She wasn't sure how much time had passed before she found Faland sitting beside her. She was startled. She hadn't seen him cross the room. But he was there, rolling an empty glass between long fingers. "It's Laura, isn't it?"

"Yes," said Laura. When had she told him her name?

"Do you like the wine?"

"Yes," she said. She was so warm, the knife-edges of the world all blunted.

He refilled her glass deftly. "And you were wounded?"

He'd noticed, of course. How could he not? "I was."

"Brave heart," said Faland. "But surely you would stay home after that, in the arms of your family. Or are you so wild for adventure?"

"No," she said. A hairline crack ran now through Laura's enjoyment. There was something in his face, almost too subtle to notice. Malice? His sidelong stare seemed to see everything. The ghosts that Agatha Parkey swore she trailed: her mother, her father, her brother. The hope and long-denied despair that had dragged her back across the ocean. He seemed to see it all, to catalogue it, even to be laughing at it, in some secret place.

Didn't he have patrons to serve? Pim was nowhere to be seen. Mary had put her head down and gone to sleep. Trying to turn the force of his gaze, Laura said, "Have you ever considered leaving Flanders? A man with your talent—" She fell silent, staring past Faland's shoulder.

Standing in the middle of the room was the figure she'd seen in the road, the figure that had prompted her, half-instinctively, to cry out. It was the watcher from the gangplank in Halifax. The face from her dreams. Her mother with glass in her eyes, glass jutting from her body.

The glow of the wine vanished. Laura stumbled to her feet, backing away. She was wet, hungry, tired, ill.

Faland shook his head, as though he'd understood something that vexed him. Then Laura blinked and the figure was gone. She stood panting, swaying on her feet. Lightly, Faland said, "You could stay here awhile. It would do you good, I think. You could stop being afraid."

"I'm not afraid."

He didn't dignify that with a response. He'd seen her staring in horror at nothing. Laura set her jaw. Madness stalked the Western Front, but she would not, could never, succumb. She was the steady one when others lost their heads. She must concentrate on what she'd come for: to learn what had become of Freddie. "I can't stay. I have things to do."

"Do you?"

Did she? Why was she in Flanders, really? To torment herself with the—

Across the room, Pim screamed. She was staring into the mirror over the bar, her expression reflected in the glass raw with equal parts hunger and horror. Laura didn't think even a great obscenity would put that look on her face. "Pim—"

Faland had turned as well, almost impatiently, but then his shoulders stiffened. Laura could see in profile his lips pursed in a soundless whistle. But there was nothing to see but a woman, her golden hair coming down, looking into a mirror. "What does she see?" demanded Laura, already making her stumbling way across the room.

He didn't answer; she didn't know if he followed. Mary didn't stir, her head still pillowed on her folded arms. The mirror itself glimmered, black with tarnish in spots, spider-webbed with cracks in one corner. Laura squinted into the depths but could see nothing that would have prompted Pim to—

A face, reflected in the mirror, swam into focus as she walked closer. It wasn't hers.

Then she thought her heart would stop, because it was Freddie.

Freddie with eyes hollow and blank. Freddie with white threaded through the russet of his hair. Freddie with his expression strangely dim, puzzled. A reflection that wavered, as though her brother were caught in the tarnished glass.

She knew it was just a figment. Some sort of hypnotic suggestion. Faland had *said* she'd see her heart's desire, and he'd meant it literally. It was his voice working on her brain, along with the dimness, and the wine, and her fever. She *knew*. And still she turned to look behind her. No power on earth could have kept her from looking.

And of course he wasn't there. Just a sea of men, drowsy, with—

No. There. For an instant she could have sworn she saw russet hair, straight shoulders, haunted eyes. His name came tearing from her throat. "Freddie!"

But he was already gone, vanished between tables, between men, between shadows. He'd never been there at all.

She tried to follow anyway. Came up instantly against people dazed and stupid with wine, came up against her own drunkenness and doubt, her cramping leg. Found herself pushing like a woman in a nightmare, not even sure what she was looking for. There were so many doors. The room was ringed with doors. Which door? Take the right door, she thought confusedly, and she'd find herself in a different world, she'd find herself back in Halifax, before the end of everything. She clawed her way out of the sodden crowd.

Fetched up against a person who caught her by the shoulders. "Gently, Mademoiselle," said Faland. "You are hallucinating, feverish, you are not yourself."

"My brother— I saw my brother."

He didn't let go. "That damned mirror. I'm sorry I said anything about it. You are very ill, you know."

She pulled away, fighting for her balance. "No, I saw him. In the room. Not just in the mirror. *I saw him.*"

His face expressed nothing but puzzled concern. "Could your brother be here tonight? By coincidence? Forgive me, but why would you have to chase him? He'd come to you, surely."

Of course he'd come to her. If he could. He wasn't there. He was dead, and there was no such thing as ghosts. "No," she whispered. The fight went out of her. "He couldn't be here tonight."

Faland's face softened. "Then I am so sorry, Mademoiselle." He offered her an arm. "I shall take you back to your companions. You should sleep. You should stay. You are in no condition to endanger—"

Endanger? His words reminded her of Pim, and she looked up. Pim was still standing in front of the tarnished mirror, utterly still, an expression of horrified longing on her face. "What's wrong with my friend? What did she see?"

Faland's green eye glittered with firelight, but the dark eye had no reflection. "It is often illuminating, to see your heart's desire. But it is not always pleasant. You might have just discovered that yourself. Come, I will take you to her."

WHICH WAY I FLY IS HELL

.....

LIGHT CREPT RELUCTANTLY BACK INTO THE WORLD, AND WITH the light came a shrouding fog that left the landscape as formless as it had been by night. Winter and Freddie and their rescued soldier stumbled westward through a gray void. Slick duckboards alternated with mud that tried to claw off their boots and the road had long since been registered by German artillery. A shell came down ahead of them. They heard it fall, heard the screams where it landed, but saw nothing but fog and one another. It hardly seemed real.

The Tommy was even filthier than they and possibly more off his head. He was whispering, half to himself, "Where are we going? Is it quiet, where we're going?"

"Keep walking," said Winter.

Freddie didn't speak. It was all he could do to put one foot in front of the other. He didn't dare look behind him. He kept hearing footsteps in the mist. His reasoning mind pointed out that no one was following them. No one could *see* them. They could hardly see each other in the fog. And when he looked back, there was nothing.

But part of him whispered anyway, that the dead man followed. That the dead man would never let him go.

The mist finally thinned, like water draining off rock, and now Freddie saw the skeleton of Ypres, black against the sky. The civilians had abandoned Ypres long since. It was shell-torn and dangerous, smashed to rubble. But it was still a human place, swarming with men and dressing stations, cookfires and ration wagons. Military jurisdiction. Superior officers. Billets. A place ruled by men and not the howling dead. It was a place where they could begin to think beyond their own survival.

He was responsible for Winter. He must see Winter safely taken prisoner. Put in with the other prisoners, safely hors de combat. And then—

Freddie glanced sideways at Winter's drawn face. The answer came to him unbidden: And then they'd take Winter away. Maybe a doctor would tend his arm. But not for a long time. There were so many wounded, and who'd see to a prisoner first? There weren't enough doctors. No one would look at his arm. Not for days.

Winter would die.

The thought drew him up as though he'd walked into Ypres's crumbling wall. Winter would lie out in the rain until he died. Of slow sepsis and fever. And then, if he was fortunate, a hastily dug grave. Without a hospital, soon, he would die. And there was no hospital to be had, not for days and days. Not for him. Not on this side of No Man's Land.

And Winter *knew* it. He'd probably known it for days, what that gash in his arm meant. And he'd walked on, stayed with Freddie, said nothing. *I am your prisoner, Iven.* He'd done it for him, Freddie knew. So he'd live. And now—

Winter was still moving. They were almost into Ypres itself. No one looked at anyone else, senses strained east for the sound of incoming shellfire. The remains of the fog, hovering near the ground, wrapped them like grave-clothes.

No, Freddie thought. *No.*

Winter seemed to shrink as soon as they passed into the town; he stumbled, and Freddie had to catch him, support him on his good side until he got his balance. It was as though he'd not allowed himself weariness before. Freddie caught sight of an overrun aid station in a ruined church. "That way," he managed. He had a vague notion that maybe a medic could be brought to at least look at Winter's arm, and then . . .

But the church, half its roof fallen in, was packed with patients lying out exposed to the weather, and one glance told Freddie it was no good. The stretchers lay in endless rows. Some men were dead. Most were visibly nearer death than Winter. One was saying, in a very peculiar voice, "No, no, it's all right, Doctor. I'll wait my turn," and Freddie realized he could see daylight through the hole in the man's body.

Their rescued soldier's legs gave out; he thumped gracelessly to the ground. He tried to get up and fell back, clawed at Freddie's knees. "Don't leave me here."

A medic caught sight of them and swerved. "What's wrong with him?" His bloodshot eyes were on the twitching Tommy. Winter was still behind Freddie, half-invisible in the murky dawn.

Laura would have wanted Freddie to answer. So he stammered, "He was trapped in the mud. He was drowning."

"Shell-shock, then," said the medic. "Look, if you can walk, keep on to the next dressing station."

The soldier was sitting on the soaked flagstones of the church, rocking back and forth. "Can't," he whispered.

The medic struck him smartly across the face. "You! Yes, you there, sir. Pull yourself together. Drink this, come on . . ." He was carrying a canteen like a sidearm; he put it to the boy's lips.

The soldier didn't take it. His white-ringed eyes were fastened on Freddie. "But aren't—aren't you the wild men?"

"Christ," said the medic. "Pull yourself together. Go on," he added, over his shoulder, to Freddie. "I think you're making it worse."

But the soldier had gone rigid, looking between them all, his face a rictus of fear and betrayal. As if he'd believed, in the madness of the night, that Freddie and Winter actually knew a way out. "No—? You're a traitor, then! I heard him! That one! He's a—"

Freddie didn't hear the rest. The medic was starting to frown. He could say it, right then: *I took a prisoner, here he is, helping save your life.* But if he said that, then Winter would be gone, Winter would have to go be a prisoner, with the others. And then Winter would die, alone, in the rain.

A shell burst on the ramparts, and everyone ducked. That distraction was enough to make Freddie bolt out of the aid station, snatching Winter's good hand as he went and dragging him away. He knew it was mad even as he did it.

But he did not stop. He would not let go of Winter's hand.

· · ·

They took no direction but *away,* ducking into the shadows. Their flight was a spasm of insanity, no more. They ran as far as their strength would allow, then pulled up panting, both of them wild-eyed. Winter was absolutely scorching with fever. Where to go? What to do? It would be full day soon. They were fast crossing the line that divided *Canadian with German prisoner* from *two fugitives.*

Freddie stood panting, groping through the fragments of his mind for—anything. His very soul rebelled. He'd left all the rest of himself out there somewhere, in the blood and water and darkness; he refused to leave Winter to his fate. He imagined it: going off to fight again while Winter died by inches, alone. He couldn't do it. He'd go stark, screaming, staring mad.

A shell fell in the street, sent a half-ruined building down with a rush. They ducked into the cover of a crumbling wall, covered their heads against flying bits of masonry. But when the danger passed, Winter did not move. He was leaning on the slimy brick, his eyes closed.

"Winter?" whispered Freddie.

No answer.

"Winter?" He bent closer, touched Winter's hot cheek. "How's your arm?"

"Fine," said Winter. His eyes opened a little more, struggling to focus. "Are you well?"

"I'll do."

Winter visibly forced himself to straighten up from the wall. "Where now, Iven?"

"I don't know."

"You will put me with the other prisoners. Then go find an officer, say you are reporting for duty."

"No," said Freddie violently. "No—I won't let you die. *No.*"

"Iven," said Winter. His voice hardened. "There's nothing else to be done."

An idea came to Freddie: completely mad, desperate. "Yes, there is," he whispered. "Yes, there is. We'll go to Laura. We'll go to my sister."

"If I'm not a prisoner, then I'm a spy. I do not want to be hanged. Or put your sister in danger."

"She won't be. She's a hero. She's got a medal and everything. She can manage. Would you rather die of a wound gone bad? You're my prisoner, anyway. You'll go where I want. And I want you to go to Laura. I want you to live."

A muscle ticked in Winter's unshaven jaw. "Better I die than both of us."

"No, it isn't." It wasn't based in reason, his wanting Winter to live. There was only a certainty that if Winter died, he, Wilfred Iven, would one night wake up back in the pillbox. And this time he'd be all alone. "I promised I wouldn't let you die." He wished he didn't sound so young. "I *promised.*"

"You don't owe me your life, Iven."

"But I do," said Freddie. "It's all right. Laura will make it all right." He remembered back in '15, when she'd written the family about her decoration. She'd been strangely laconic: *The French are pleased with me, after some unpleasantness with poison gas; they have voted me a Croix de Guerre.* But she'd told him a little more when he asked, after he'd come over: three days without sleep, fighting tooth and nail for gassed men's lives. She'd spoken of it only once, and reluctantly, after a bottle of wine. But even with what she hadn't said, he knew it had been a feat. If she could manage that, then she could manage this. If Freddie believed in one thing in this strange world, he believed in Laura.

The plan leapt fully formed to his mind. He and Winter would find a place to hide for the day, slip out of Ypres in the darkness. It wasn't too far to the casualty clearing station at Brandhoek, where Laura was stationed with her mobile ambulance. Freddie would slip in, find Laura quietly, explain. Laura would find a way to help them. She'd put Winter in with the prisoners, she'd feed them both. She'd see that Winter got surgery, that he was properly nursed. She'd save his life.

Freddie turned to Winter, ready to persuade him. But before he got out a word, a singular voice met his ears. So singular, in that context, that Freddie's arguments died away unvoiced, and Winter went still beside him. To Freddie's left, a deep-set door hung askew from rusting hinges. Through the crack, Freddie saw a room with rotting floorboards, three men, and a shabby printing press. Two of the men were in British uniforms, but the third was a civilian in a worn checked suit. He was addressing the two soldiers with a faint accent that didn't sound like French. Flemish? "I would like," he said, "to place an advertisement in your paper."

Freddie knew what the soldiers were doing. They were printing the *Times*. The trench newspaper. Everyone read and laughed over the *Times*, when it could be got out between bombardments. But it wasn't a real paper. It was satire. A long black joke, printed in the wreckage.

The men printing it clearly didn't know what to make of the civilian. "A submission, you mean?" said one of them. "I—what?"

"An advertisement to attract clientele," said the stranger.

Silence.

"For evening revels," the man went on.

The two printers still looked nonplussed. "But— Our paper's a joke, sir. We take poetry submissions. There's limericks . . ." He trailed off.

The stranger shrugged and handed them a scrap of paper. "Print it. Some will understand."

Another shell rattled the masonry and there was the peculiar wailing scream that meant someone had copped it. The two soldiers in the room ducked instinctively. Winter's hand fell on Freddie's sleeve, the effort audible in his voice. "Iven, we have to go."

"No, there's no location," the stranger added. "People will find it."

"Revels, sir?" said one of the printers, in a new voice. "Are you— I've heard— Are you the one who . . ."

"Probably," said the stranger.

Then one, joking weakly, said, "Well, then, the going rate's three bob a word, sir."

"I can do you one better," said the stranger. "If you will only come and drink with me." Freddie could not see the stranger's expression; his back was to the door. But the men printing wore looks of terrified yearning.

"That sounds—all right. If you like, sir," whispered one of the men.

"Very well," said the stranger. "Good morning to you both." He turned for the door. One of the soldiers made a jerky gesture, as though he wanted to reach out. But his mate clapped a hand to his wrist.

The stranger emerged in the alley four feet from where Freddie and Winter stood silent in the shadows. He started off, but then his steps slowed. He turned. Winter went deathly still. "Good morning," said the stranger. "It isn't polite to stare."

A group of soldiers under a sergeant came up the street. Winter and Freddie pressed themselves deeper into the shadow of the wall. The oncoming men slowed. Freddie had one despairing second to think, *What do I do now,* before he realized that the men hadn't seen him and Winter at all. They were all gawking at the stranger. A civilian hadn't been seen in Ypres for two years. It was like seeing a unicorn. And the eccentric didn't disappoint them. "I was hoping for a tour of the ramparts," he said. "Will someone guide me?" There was a flicker of mischief in his voice.

"Now, sir," said the nonplussed sergeant, "this city's under military jurisdiction—" He broke off, shook his head, said, "Do you have a death wish?"

The stranger's eyes opened wide. "I am a committed tourist. Well, I shall find my own way."

Without warning, he slipped down a side street, leaving the sergeant calling "Sir—sir! Monseer! You can't just—" In answer the stranger, now quite swallowed by the early-morning shadows, began to whistle. They heard his footsteps retreating.

"Mocking us, he is," said the sergeant, with anger. "The madman. Well, arrest the bastard, damn you all." They took off after the sound.

"Iven," said Winter. "We must go."

Had that just happened, or had he dreamed it awake? Winter was pulling him on. They must find somewhere to hide. No chance of getting anywhere unremarked before dark. And perhaps a rest— somewhere dry—would do Winter some good . . .

Freddie wasn't sure how far they'd gone—not very—when the stranger reappeared beside them.

Winter halted. "No," he whispered.

"Oh, dear," said the stranger, in English. "You've a terrible fever, my good man." Winter's face was set like granite. Freddie looked in bewilderment between them.

"Delighted to meet you," added the stranger as though the patrol had never interrupted. "I am called Faland. I am, in my way, a native of these parts. May I inquire where you are going?"

Freddie could almost feel Winter trying to muster more words, and failing. Finally, to Freddie's shock, he raised a trembling hand and made the old peasants' sign against evil, the two fingers extended. A shell burst a few streets over as though for emphasis.

Both Faland's brows rose, unruffled. "Do you need a bolt-hole for the day?" he said. "I think there's a cellar about."

Winter shook his head. "No," he said again.

"Winter, why not?" whispered Freddie. "If he knows a place." Logic told Freddie there was nowhere safe in Ypres. But there was something about this civilian. A confidence. Either he was utterly mad—not unlikely—or he *did* know a place. "We could rest properly, and I could have a good look at your arm."

"But—" said Winter. "Can't you see?" He looked afraid. Not once, in those last hellish days, had Freddie seen Winter looking afraid.

Freddie said, "What else are we going to do? Winter, you're sick. You need to rest. You need to get dry."

"There are worse things than dying," said Winter.

"You are not going to die."

Winter didn't say anything more. Maybe he'd come, at last, to the end of his strength. He bowed his head. He was shivering.

"Excellent," said Faland. "This way."

THE WINE OF THE
WRATH OF GOD

·····

T HEY SLIPPED THROUGH YPRES, KEEPING TO THE SHRINKING
shadows. No one stopped them. The mist distorted their footsteps. Faland's step was just a little uneven in the rubble-strewn
street, as though he favored one leg. Freddie's skin crept as he
walked. A miasma of fear hung over Ypres. The skeleton-city might
be a place ruled by men, but Death lived there too, and sat at their
cookfires, and ruled his own subjects, side by side with the living.
The shells whistled and crashed, now near, now far.

"Where are we going?" Winter looked like a man in a nightmare
who couldn't wake up.

Freddie didn't know. He was wondering if he'd lost his mind.

And then Faland was standing in front of a nondescript doorway;
he produced a key from his pocket. The door swung open. Icy air
poured out. "As I thought," Faland said, with satisfaction. "This
way."

Freddie stood a moment, disbelieving. Winter balked.

"Come on," Freddie said, and took his arm. "There's nowhere
else to go."

Winter let himself be led. The two passed under the lintel and
started down some steps. Faland had lit a candle, of all things, as

though there were no such things as pocket torches. The door swung shut behind them, and they were back in the dark, except for their own strange shadows moving in the candlelight. Freddie tried to see the light playing on the walls, to think only of that, and not the blackness all around, the renewed weight of earth overhead. He reached for Winter and their hands twisted together, the way men overboard snatch at rope in a stormy sea. *I am still alive. He is still alive. We are still alive.*

Faland had gone down first, with the light, and his shadow crawled monstrous before them all. There was mortared stone over their heads, a pit of blackness below, with Faland's light swimming through it. Freddie didn't know how long the stairs went on. Suddenly they were at the bottom, stumbling on flat ground, and Freddie was startled to see that when Faland turned back, holding his candle, he illuminated a wine cellar.

And such a cellar. Its ceiling was lost to blackness, its walls were packed with racked bottles. How had this place escaped three years of shellfire? The prying eyes of a hundred thousand men? It felt— removed, somehow, from the world above. The noise of shelling could hardly penetrate. The sound of water dripping somewhere in the darkness was louder than the muffled roar of the heavies on Passchendaele Ridge.

Faland ran his fingertips over the racked bottles, candlelight still flickering in one fist. "It's still here." He sounded faintly surprised.

"You came to Ypres for wine?" said Freddie. His head felt thick, his thoughts slow and disjointed.

Faland didn't answer but pulled a bottle, drew the cork. Took a long swallow and held out the bottle. "Drink?"

Suddenly Winter sank to the ground, still leaning against the wall, and Freddie caught him. The sweat was standing on Winter's face, even though the cellar was cool. He made a harsh noise when Freddie pulled his wet jacket off and cut away the sleeve beneath. Even in the dim light, the wound was swollen, foul, red streaks running up and down. Winter's eyes had drifted shut. Faland, obligingly, had pushed his candle over, so Freddie could see the details of advancing gangrene.

"Sir?" said Freddie, in a voice that wavered. "Do you have any bandages, or clean cloth, so I can—"

Faland had been watching them with intent, curious eyes. He said, unexpectedly, "I can do better than that," and got up. He was gone, leaving them the light, before Freddie had time to react. Winter didn't speak.

Freddie fumbled with their nearly empty canteen. "Drink this, then, at least," he whispered, putting the metal rim to Winter's lips. Winter did drink, a little. "Why do you say not to trust him?" Freddie asked. "Do you think he's gone to tell them we're here?"

Winter's good hand came up and gripped Freddie's forearm. "Couldn't you see? All around him?"

"See what all around him?"

"Ghosts," said Winter. "What does he want with everyone's ghosts?"

Winter was raving. Comfort poured awkwardly from Freddie's lips. "No— Winter, no. He's an eccentric, he's—"

"Iven, he's—"

Faland's uneven step sounded on the stairs, another candle held before him. Freddie turned to Faland, almost with relief. He didn't want to be afraid of Faland, didn't want their one piece of good luck to be false. "It must be murder keeping matches dry," he said a little at random, with a nod at the candle.

Faland shrugged, slid a bag off his shoulder, and opened it. Freddie watched in helpless gratitude as its contents were laid out: a bottle of iodine, a wad of clean, dry bandages, a large canteen of water, biscuit, canned meat, and even, wondrously, a dry wool blanket. The candlelight flickered on Faland's face, picked out the deep orbits of the eyes, the lines round his mouth. Freddie touched the bounty reverently. "How did you get all this?"

"Nothing easier. I was a soldier once." Faland's eyeteeth were just a little sharp. "A bad soldier. Takes one to know one, I suppose." His knowing gaze rested on them both, then he turned away, uncorked a fresh bottle, and offered it to Freddie. After a hesitation, Freddie took a sip. It was a glorious wine; it left him warm and languid, even unafraid, for the first time he could remember. He offered it to Winter, but Winter shook his head. Faland pushed the second candle closer so Freddie could help Winter take off the rags of shirt and jacket, could rinse the wound and pour iodine over it and bandage it fresh and give Winter the blanket. He made Winter drink the water, eat some biscuit that he'd soaked to soften it. He'd heard the Germans were going hungry, but it was something else again to see the hollows between Winter's ribs, feel the ridges of his collarbones.

Winter's wandering glance went again and again to Faland, and there was still that look of fear. Freddie couldn't bear to see Winter afraid.

"Winter?" Freddie whispered, bending close, to distract him. "Winter—" He groped in his mind. "Winter—don't be afraid. I could try to remember a poem. One of mine. You wanted to hear one of mine . . ."

Winter's dazed eyes returned to Freddie's. He nodded a little.

The only poem that came to Freddie's mind wasn't one of his best—it wasn't jolly, to encourage a wounded man, nor did it even rhyme in a way that made it a pleasure to recite. But it came fountaining from his lips into Winter's ear. And he supposed into Faland's too, although the stranger never made a sound.

"Rain," Freddie whispered.

Midnight rain, nothing but the wild rain
On this bleak hut, and solitude, and me
Remembering again that I shall die
And neither hear the rain nor give it thanks
For washing me cleaner than I have been
Since I was born into this solitude.
Blessed are the dead that the rain rains upon:

But here I pray that none whom once I loved
Is dying tonight or lying still awake
Solitary, listening to the rain—

He'd forgotten the rest. Apologetically, he said, "I'm no good, really, just a hack, but I—I'm better at painting . . ."

He fell silent. Winter's cold bony fingers folded around his. "Danke," he whispered, and his head sank back.

Freddie heard the slosh as Faland drank more wine somewhere in the grand, dusty dark. He turned so he was leaning against the same wall as Winter, so Winter's head could fall heavily onto his shoulder, so he could hear the slow, strained rhythm of Winter's breathing. Faland sat cross-legged leaning on a barrel opposite, the wine open beside him. He'd just lit a cigarette. A red point of light shone in one of his eyes but not the other. "Who are you?" Freddie asked.

"Since I seem to have preserved you, I might ask that question first." Faland shoved his pack of cigarettes across, and a matchbox. After a small hesitation, Freddie took it, lit up. Winter slid further down, until he was lying on the floor, covered in the blanket, his head on Freddie's thigh. Freddie's free hand was on his ribs, tracking the shiver of his pulse. The line ran through his head over and over, and he couldn't make it stop: *I pray that none whom once I loved is dying . . .*

"I'm called Wilfred Iven," said Freddie. "My—friend—is called—" He stopped, feeling obscurely that Winter's name wasn't his to offer.

"Never mind that," said Faland. "I'd rather have a story than a name." He grinned around his cigarette. The ember made something savage of his smile. "Beeindrucke mich," he added, with a glance at the silent Winter.

Winter jerked, raised his head, blank as a man in delirium. Freddie, taking the words for a threat, groped for his knife.

But Faland just took another drag on his cigarette. "Stop mantling like a rooster. Tell me your story."

"It's all right," Freddie whispered to Winter, who slowly settled back down. His skin was scorching hot.

"We were ordered up the Ridge," said Freddie to Faland. "I was—we met there, my friend and I. We came down together." It was all he could bring himself to say. Poet or no, there were things that he would never put into words.

"Is that all?" said Faland.

Freddie was silent.

"I see," said Faland. "I will summarize: A man back at General Headquarters moved a few figurines on a map, snapped his fingers, and off you went. Bad luck. And now you're here. What are you going to do?"

"I don't know!" Under his weariness was an endless anger. At himself. At the entire unrecognizable world. Winter's hand moved, took Freddie's, closed round it, dirty palm to dirty palm. He calmed a little.

Faland took another drag. "And so?" he pursued. "Going to put your prisoner in a pen where he belongs?"

I'd kill myself first. The thought came clear and sudden to his mind.

"I thought not," said Faland. "Going to desert? Off to Holland, are you, to scratch around in ignominy until the war ends? But your friend won't make it. He needs a hospital. A little iodine won't do it."

"My sister," Freddie whispered. Something about Faland's steady, detached gaze dragged the truth from him. "She's a nurse. In the sector. Not far. At Brandhoek. With a mobile ambulance. I'm taking Winter to my sister."

"An interesting idea. Perhaps you'll succeed," said Faland reflectively. He blew out smoke. "And then? Go back to barracks? You'll have to run through more bullets, you know, when the old man in his château says 'Jump.' Such a pity."

"What do you care?" demanded Freddie, voice rising. "What would you do? What are you even doing here?"

"Oh, go to sleep, boy," said Faland. "I serve wine, I listen, and occasionally I play a violin. Your harebrained plan won't work until it's dark again, anyway. Go to sleep." A pause. "I liked your poem."

Sucking exhaustion rose in Freddie, like a tide. He whispered, "Winter said there's ghosts all round you."

Faland snorted. "When you swim in the ocean there's water all round you, but no one mentions it."

Freddie didn't know what he said in reply, was hardly aware of the moment he slid prone to the cellar floor and curled under the blanket with Winter, hardly aware of when, under the twin influences of wine and Winter's feverish heat, he finally stopped shivering. But even in sleep he felt his hand pressing, pulse to pulse. Once he even thought he heard Winter speak: "Ich weiß, wer du bist."

And Faland laughing, replying in the same language, "Wer bin ich?"

Then nothing.

AND THE HEAVEN DEPARTED

·····

TRY AS SHE MIGHT—AND LAURA DID TRY, AGAIN AND AGAIN— she could never fully remember the rest of that night in the hotel. Her last clear and certain memory—and even that began to fade after a few days, like an overhandled photograph—was of Pim staring stricken into a tarnished mirror. Everything else was snatches and flashes.

She remembered firelight on fair hair—although she never knew whether it was Faland's or Pim's or perhaps the two with their heads close together. And a voice coming out of darkness— But why darkness? Where had the firelight gone? "You know what I saw, don't you?" someone was saying. "It's not real. It's *not*. I could never—"

"No?"

She remembered being thirsty. Thinking, *Was* that Pim speaking? A woman, certainly. But she also remembered the woman saying viciously *But I hate him, that* bastard. *I wish he'd*— Pim would never say that.

And the other voice, answering, "I know."

"Pim?" she thought she'd tried to say. But no sound came, and when she tried to move, she could not.

And then memory dissolved into fever-dreams; for she remembered her mother stepping out of the shrouding darkness, embedded glass scraping when a hand trailed over Laura's face. "Look," she whispered. "Look look look *look*!"

But try as she might, Laura could not answer.

And then her mother was gone, and Laura was alone. It was so dark. A reasonable voice was speaking in her ear: "If you stay, she won't trouble you again."

Her mouth was so dry. But she whispered, with a kind of exhausted defiance, "There's no such thing as ghosts."

The reasonable voice replied, "She'll follow you until you go mad."

Laura, dreaming, thought that might be true. She was so afraid.

"Tell me where she came from," said the voice. "Why does she haunt you?"

That was a story she'd never told anyone, and never would. But something about the tender detachment in that voice pulled words from her anyway: "She's my mother. I saw her die. A ship exploded. She was standing by a window." She bit blood from her tongue rather than say anything more. "Where's Pim?"

The voice didn't answer. It said, "What are you fighting for? World's already ended."

Try as she might, Laura could never recall if she answered. She didn't think she had. Perhaps she muttered *Not yet.* But she remembered nothing more until she awoke to a crashing rumble to the east and jolted upright in fear. Regretted it. She was boiling with fever and it felt as if someone had thrown sand in her joints.

"Mary," said Laura. "Pim?"

She was sitting on the bare floor. She was very sick. She could barely breathe around the fluid in her lungs. She'd a pounding headache. Somewhere in her memory was violin music like a requiem, almost mocking in its sobbing grandeur, and a voice speaking over the instrument: *You'll regret it*. Dimmer still was a memory of Freddie's face, seen as though in a dream.

Mary scrambled to her feet. Pim was sitting upright, her expression blank. "What happened?" She sounded as though her throat were full of dust. Gray daylight filtered in through shuttered windows. There was no one there but the three of them. Laura crawled to her feet, every bone and sinew chorusing protest. Pim got up too, flinching. "I remember a mirror," said Pim. "And I saw——" She was staring blankly, as though she could see it again.

Laura turned to ask, just as Mary said, "What in God's name?"

A draft of dank air eddied round them, a smell of sour wine, dust, and something rotten-sweet, like flowers past their best. They were still in Faland's foyer. Laura had thought it magnificent. She had distinct memories of magnificence: fire on gold.

It wasn't magnificent, though.

It was a ruin.

"I don't understand," said Pim.

The floor was covered in broken glass and splintered lumber, softening with rot. Upholstery was torn, chairs lay frayed, with the signs and smell of mice, nesting.

"I don't understand," Pim said again, voice rising. "What—what happened? Monsieur Faland?" She turned in a circle. "Is he hurt? Is he dead? It's all ruined." Her eye fell on the mirror hanging over the bar, now black with tarnish. She took one aborted step as though she wanted to look into it again. But she stayed where she was.

Laura stood silent, disbelieving.

"Shouldn't we search?" asked Pim, urgently. "We need to search."

"We need to get on," said Mary, obviously capable of rationalizing away the impossible. "It's not safe here. The walls could collapse. The ceiling. Look at the *cracks*."

"But *what happened*?" said Pim.

Laura tried again to organize her memory, from the shelling on the Beveren road up to this dusty silence. But it wouldn't come clear.

"It's as though no one was ever here," said Pim. She gave a small, nervous laugh. "The way people wake up and they find they've slept for a hundred years."

"We haven't," said Mary. "Can't you hear the guns?"

There hadn't been noise outside before, Laura thought vaguely. Or had there been? Was that part of her fever-dreams, that they'd spent the night free of the rumble of the guns? The only sound she remembered was music. Softly, Pim said, "Like faerie revels that end at sunrise."

"Drugs in the wine, maybe," said Mary. "We need to go."

"But—" Pim said.

"Now," said Mary, turning toward the door. "If it was a hoax, damn him. If a hallucination, I don't want to think about it. If he wants his bill settled, he can find me at Couthove. Come on." She strode across the lobby floor, glass crunching under her feet.

There was nothing to do but follow. Laura had no strength to search, even if she'd wanted to. They passed through the airless stillness, across the lobby, and back into the daylit world. The hinges screamed as the door shut behind them. Pim's forehead was lined with bewilderment. They found themselves out in a brisk wind and clear sun, standing on cracked cobbles rimed with melting frost, anonymous crumbling buildings all around. Pim had turned back to the hotel with an uncomprehending face.

Half the hotel was collapsed. The other half was barely standing, as though the first high wind would scatter it like dandelion fluff, back into its component bricks and wood and tile.

"I don't understand," said Pim again.

Laura stood beside her, staring. She didn't understand either.

But Mary was already walking away. Just beyond the still, ruined village lay a road. They could hear the rumble of it, see the traffic. The distance between the ruined village and the teeming road was like the border between sleep and waking.

Mary had already crossed over. "Something must be happening further up the line," she called. "Come on. Look at all that traffic. They're going to want us at the hospital. Can you walk, Iven? No—I didn't think so. We'll beg a lift, then. Come on."

"Are you all right, Laura?" said Pim. She put the back of her hand to Laura's forehead. The maternal gesture made her ache. "You're burning up."

. . .

Hitchhiking was a perfectly usual way for nurses to get about, and it took hardly a moment's trying before a unit of sappers took them up. The three women were met with a wave of delighted chatter, eager conversation. But there was a constraint on the men too, a grimness, and they glanced often to the east. Laura leaned against Pim, her eyes half-closed.

"Sir, what is happening?" Mary asked the officer, as they jolted along.

"Fritz is trying to get through," came the reply. "Trying proper, this time. They say they've attacked the French at Amiens, pushed the Frogs back. Some say they've broken the French line already. We're reinforcing the Salient. Haig's said hold to the last man." The sergeant turned his head and spat.

Laura and Mary exchanged glances. The line had surged back and forth but had remained unbroken for four years. And it wouldn't break now, Laura told herself. It *couldn't*. Not before she went looking for Freddie. But she was so damned sick . . . The chatter of the men fell disembodied on her ears as the thin spring sun fell warm on her neck. She must get well, quick as she could. She shut her eyes. "—The Americans are hopeless, I hear. Big, well fed. But hopeless. Charge machine guns like maniacs, no notion of tactics."

"That's what the Frogs did back in '14. Don't need tactics, if there're enough of them."

"They'll get killed in droves."

"Better them than us. If only they come in time."

"They won't."

"Haig's at Chenonceau, I hear. Foch is there too. And the king of Belgium. The whole shooting match."

"Jawing and eating frog legs, are they?"

"Trying to agree on a high command. Put one bloke in charge, they say, that's the ticket. Better one bugger in one château, deciding things, than— Sorry, ma'am," he added, when his compatriots chided him for his language.

"Strange place to have picked you up," another of the men was saying to Mary.

"We were wrecked on the road," said Mary.

"There was a light across the field," chimed in Pim. "We came upon a hotel—"

Laura was only half-listening, trying to make plans despite her feverish haze. She had to find the men of Freddie's unit. Talk to his CO. Find one of the boys from Halifax who'd been in Freddie's platoon. Unwillingly, she recalled the hallucination of the night before, Freddie's face amid a seething crowd. She'd thought it was him because she wanted it to be.

Then she heard the strange silence that had fallen on the men in the lorry. One man said to his neighbor, "Do you think it was—"

There was a meaningful pause.

"A hotel, she said," came the reply. "And music—wasn't there music, ma'am?"

The officer was glaring. "You just met a Belgian, like as not, making money off smuggled wine. They do move around a good deal, to save themselves a raid."

None of the men looked convinced. One said, "Was it— What was the wine like? And the music?"

"Beautiful," said Pim at once. She seemed to want to add something else.

A man nudged his neighbor. "*Sounds* like him."

"Shut it; he doesn't exist."

"Who?" said Pim.

"No one," said the officer. "Just a story."

"Will you tell us?" said Pim.

"He's a charlatan," said one.

"A madman."

"A Frenchman."

"No," said a new voice. An old, authoritative voice. "He's the devil himself, and right at home."

Silence went round the lorry. Laura heard a driver cursing his horses outside. A dog barked, high and sharp. The sun went behind a cloud and the sweat chilled the back of her neck. Then another man snorted and said, "Devil don't live in old hotels, you can lay to that. No, if the devil's anywhere, he's in a château, in General Headquarters, maybe. Eating frog legs with the others."

Derisive laughter.

"The man in the hotel—he's called the fiddler," said one of the men, persistently. "That's what all the stories say, anyway. Can make you forget all this"—his gesture took in the world around them—"but what they all say, every story, is those who've drank with him, heard the music, seen what he shows you, and then come back out here—" He spat out to the leeward side of the lorry. "Well, they're always pining for it." Laura caught the Irish in the speaker's lilting voice. "But you only see it once. You can't get back. They say men have gone mad. Looking for the fiddler. Like they can't ever be happy again."

"And they say that sometimes a man finds him," said another voice, "and no one ever sees that man again."

"Twaddle. People go mad for all sorts of reasons. But going for want of a jig . . . no. It's just a story."

One man elbowed his neighbor. "I'd be here if I was the devil," he said. "Why, half the army'd sell its soul for a decent drink. Bet he's racking up the score."

Laughter erupted, over the officer's protests.

. . .

They got to Couthove at sunset, after a day spent inching down a packed road amid the horse-drawn ration wagons, the lorries and marching men, the dogs pulling machine gun carts, the motorcycles. To the east, the scattered lights of Poperinghe, British HQ in Flanders, reflected off the low, boiling clouds.

The lorry halted. Helpful hands lowered Laura to the ground. Pim was stumbling. Mary looked ten years older. Laura's cough had settled deep in her chest. The men called good wishes to them all, health to Laura. Then their motor roared and the road swallowed them.

Mary's hospital was built into the château itself, looming dark against the sky. Even in the dusk, Laura could see that Couthove had been grand once. There was a grace about it still: in its long, repeated windows, steep-sloped roof, two curving wings. But the windows were boarded up, the drive potholed. They walked up from the gate, the château looming larger.

The door was flung open hospitably before they'd got even halfway. A pair of figures, one stout and one tall, appeared. The stout one wore a white Red Cross uniform; she spoke first, coming quickly down the steps. "Mary, good lord. I had almost given up hope."

Mary had lit up like a hound at a fox hunt. "Wild horses couldn't have kept me away. Now tell me—"

The tall figure was wearing a doctor's coat; his voice was flatly American. "I thought you were bringing us fresh hands, Mary. Not more work. That one can barely keep her feet." The doctor had a thin-lipped face, dark hair, a prow of a nose, and eyes that saved the rest, large and liquid and dark. He eyed Laura and Pim, frowning.

"It's all right, Doctor," said Mary briskly. "Doctor Jones, Miss Iven, Mrs. Shaw. Miss Iven's got a Croix de Guerre, Jones, and three years' service with the CAMC. A jewel. She's just a bit poorly, is all. Influenza."

Jones's eyes narrowed as he looked Laura over. "You should have left the poor woman at home."

"Lovely to meet you all," the woman in the Red Cross uniform said kindly. "Lord, I'm glad to see you—come in, come in—and Mary, I must talk to you about ether—we've enough for the time being, but—" The two women went through the front door together.

"Well, come on," said the doctor to Laura and Pim. "Let me get a look at you. It isn't as though I had enough work."

Laura, the world going a little hazy, found herself in a foyer, floored in cracked black and white. Grimy walls, once seafoam green, were festooned with wires for the lights and the telephone.

"Pleased to meet you," said Laura. "I've just got a touch of—"

"Pneumonia, yes, I have ears, it sounds like you are trying to breathe underwater," said Jones. "Not particularly all right if you ask me." His eyes had fallen on her hands.

Jones turned to snap orders to someone out of sight. She heard a voice speaking, low, somewhere ahead: "The wounded are going to come down on us like three tons of bricks, Mary; you couldn't have come back at a better moment." Her voice dropped lower. "The men—at night—anxious—" Then Laura lost the thread of speech.

"Get some rest, Iven," called Mary. "I'll need you back on your feet."

"Well, you're not getting her tonight," muttered Jones.

AND HIS KINGDOM WAS
FULL OF DARKNESS

.....

FREDDIE AND WINTER SLEPT THROUGH THE DAY AND WOKE UP at dusk, alone in a greasy cellar whose low ceiling shook with shellfire. A welter of empty bottles rolled and clinked on the floor amid broken glass, and there was a smell of damp earth. Had Freddie actually thought it was grand? Gothic? Full of untouched wine? Christ, he'd been off his head.

Faland was gone. They might have imagined him too. Except that a single candle had been left burning, a guttering stub, the only thing that kept the darkness from swallowing them. Winter sat up stiffly, tipped his head back against slimy brick.

"He's gone," said Freddie.

"I'm glad." Winter didn't open his eyes.

"He helped us." Freddie heard the edge edge of bewildered protest in his voice. It was as though Faland had taken that otherworldly cellar with him. In the damp chill, both seemed equally unlikely: the civilian with his listening silences, and the safe place, set apart, where they'd spent the day.

"I don't—" Winter's eyes were glassy and his lips cracking with fever. "I don't think it was for kindness."

Freddie thought, *Why else? We've nothing he could want.* But he said nothing. He picked up their damp, filthy shirts. "We ought to go ourselves," he said. He could wonder about Faland later. When Winter was safe at last.

. . .

A gray river of wounded stumbled toward the back area, mingling with troops coming up, the world shrouded in renewed darkness, stabbed through with electric light. Winter and Freddie walked with their heads down, in the margin of the road. No one looked at them. No man had an eye for anything beyond his footing in the slime, or an ear for anything but incoming shells.

Freddie and Winter were past caring about shellfire. Either they'd cop it here or they wouldn't. Winter walked as though in a dream, and despite the ambient noise, Freddie fancied he kept hearing the dead man's splashing footsteps.

"Has he gone?" Winter asked once. The night held them close in an icy hand. "I don't think he's gone."

"Gone?" Freddie was imagining those footsteps. He *was*.

Winter answered himself, "No, he's not gone. The dark country's empty now. All the devils are here."

"A little further," said Freddie. "A little further."

It wasn't far from Ypres to Brandhoek. Not in miles. But their way stretched on and on, slowed by the limping press of wounded, and every puddle had to be tested to make sure it wasn't a shell hole ten feet deep. They had not gone half the distance before Winter was weaving drunkenly, his face set in determination. Freddie, supporting him, had the impression that if they stopped, Winter wouldn't be able to go on again.

But Winter did go on, on and on, his eyes staring blind and raindrops running down his jaw, brilliant as sequins in the intermittent light. Freddie stayed with him, and he kept his eyes only on Winter, so he'd not try to make out the dead man's face in every human wreck that came alongside.

They came, still alive, to Brandhoek when the night was at its darkest, when the road was at its most chaotic. The hospital was no shining beacon in the storm, it was merely a series of sheds and marquees, grimy white, lit by the lanterns of its quick-moving staff. Freddie saw the place in slices. The ammunition dump. Triage tent, toolshed, flagpole.

The men.

Acres of wounded men, lying out in the rain, while nurses in mackintoshes went from stretcher to stretcher. There was no room inside.

But Freddie was too tired to worry, too tired, almost, to understand what he was seeing. The only question in his head was how to find Laura in the frenzied darkness. His eyes darted from place to place; his only thought was *Where.*

So he didn't see it at first.

And even then, his shuddering brain didn't understand.

Winter understood before Freddie did. His hand closed on Freddie's upper arm, and *then* Freddie saw. Some of the marquees were smashed. There were raw shell holes in between. Guns still boomed away at no great distance. "Oh, Christ," he whispered. "Oh, fucking hell. They took fire . . . Laura. Let me go."

"Wait, Iven," said Winter. *"Wait."*

They bombed a hospital, his mind gibbered. *They bombed a hospital.* All the absurd rumors he'd ever heard about Germans over the years came back magnified a thousandfold: *They hang priests as clappers in their own bells, they chain the gunners to their machine guns . . .* He rounded on Winter with something very near hatred. *"Let me go."*

Winter let go and Freddie ran. Winter didn't follow. Freddie saw marquees freshly sandbagged, men on stretchers borne into makeshift surgical bays, orderlies loading men onto train cars.

Laura ought to be easy to find. She wasn't the tallest, or the broadest, but he would see the staff orienting themselves around her steady presence. He would hear her snapping orders, joking, see her face determined, her hand on some poor sod's forehead . . .

But he couldn't see her. Maybe in one of the marquees? They weren't all wrecked. There were plenty of nurses around. They were all right, weren't they?

Where would she be? His searching eyes fell on the head sister. Her uniform was unmistakable, her veil. He even knew her name. Laura had written about her often enough: Kate White. In the cold white light of her lantern, she looked shattered. He threw caution aside and plunged into the maelstrom of people, and came up alongside her. "Sister, where is Laura? Laura Iven, where is she?"

Kate White just looked at him. He could only imagine what he looked like: an insane stranger, filthy, pallid as a corpse. "Gone," she said after a pause.

Freddie took the word like a fist between the eyes. "Gone?"

"I— Yes. A shell . . ."

He tried to muster another question, but his mouth had gone dry. The word *gone* echoed in his brain. Sinking horror collected somewhere in his stomach. He was still trying to frame his next question, but Kate White beat him to it.

"Who are you?" she demanded. "Are you wounded?"

Even as she spoke, a chorus of shouting erupted from one of the wards.

She swore and turned toward the commotion. "Stay there, then."

Freddie stood as though rooted to the spot. *Gone gone gone. Ask her if she's dead. Ask her that, you coward. She said "gone."*

He stood there like a pillar of salt. Despair and madness whispered, *Gone means dead. The Rapture, remember the Rapture? Mother always talked about the Rapture. The good are taken up, and only the sinners are left. And who was better than her? She's gone.*

Before Kate White could come back, before Freddie could think what on earth he meant to do, a hand closed about Freddie's arm.

It was Faland.

Freddie, too much in shock to speak or even be much surprised, looked from the thin fingers to the angles of his face, the hair dark with rain. As improbable at Brandhoek as he'd been in Ypres— more so. His calm was almost eerie; who could be calm when the whole world had— Faland said, "Stand there long enough, little poet, and you'll be back with your platoon by nightfall and your German left to die with the rest."

Freddie was too shaken to say *What are you doing*. He stammered, "I— No. I don't know now. My sister's gone."

Faland said, "Unfortunate. And you're going to stand there, lamenting?"

What were words? What was the world? Freddie said, "I promised Winter . . ." Then he remembered. He'd left Winter alone. All that way, and he'd left Winter alone. Chest heaving, he wrenched away and plunged at once between the wards, through curtains of lamplight and rain, back into the night. He didn't see if Faland followed. He hardly believed that he'd seen him at all.

. . .

Winter had sunk to the ground. But he raised his head when Freddie stooped beside him. His eyes darted beyond him, into the darkness. "No," he whispered. "Iven, no. Not him."

Freddie half-turned, but there was no one near. Freddie didn't have an answer. He didn't have anything. Laura was gone.

What to do?

In that extreme of stress, an idea came to him.

He stripped off his own jacket, with all the scraps of belongings that he still possessed in its pockets. He wrapped the jacket round Winter's shoulders. He was too cold to feel colder, although the rain plastered his shirt to his skin. He pressed his tags into Winter's flinching hand. Kate White wouldn't do anything for a nameless German. But she had real authority. She might do something for Laura. And if the nameless German appeared to know the fate of Laura's only brother . . .

Winter whispered, "Iven, what are you doing?"

"I'm going to save your life. Pretend not to understand English, all right?"

"Please," Winter whispered. "Don't—"

Freddie plunged back into the vortex of the hospital. He found Kate White again, her hair sticking to her cheeks with rain, a smear of blood on her forehead. "Sister, there's a German prisoner out there with the wounded." She was already shaking her head to dismiss him, but he forged on. "He's got the jacket and the tags of a bloke called Wilfred Iven. He don't speak much English. But he showed them to me. Said he was to give them to a nurse called Laura Iven. I didn't know what to do with him."

"Iven—" Kate White whispered, and then her exhausted gaze sharpened. "Out there? Take me to this man. Quickly."

Kate followed Freddie out, through the wreckage of men on stretchers, to the place where Winter knelt, head bowed. She summoned orderlies in her wake, and dropped down at once beside Winter. Took his pulse, touched his forehead, looked at his wound. Shook her head. "Get him up," she said to the orderlies. "*Now.* Where did you get these things, sir?" The question was directed at Winter. She had Freddie's jacket in her hands.

Winter said nothing. Freddie didn't know if he was conscious. Kate turned her head, but she sought for Freddie in vain. He'd slipped out of reach of the lantern, behind the shield of the rain and the darkest part of the night. *Don't ask who I am. I'm nothing, I died on the Ridge. Think only of him. He's the only one who can tell you what you want to know. If you save him. You have to save him.*

Only then did he realize that Faland hadn't been a figment of his shattered mind. For Faland was *there* again, with him in the sheltering darkness, near enough for Freddie to see that one of his eyes reflected the glittering point of the lantern, and the other did not. He was watching the little lamplit tableau: the nurse and the wounded man. "Well, you are a clever boy, aren't you?" he murmured. "Think she'll save him for her dead friend's sake?"

"My *sister*," whispered Freddie in a voice he hardly recognized.

"Laura." The orderlies were rolling Winter onto a stretcher. Kate was bending to take the tags clutched in Winter's hand. Freddie's tags. All that was left of Private Wilfred Charles Iven. She slipped the tags from Winter's failing grasp, although he made a faint sound of protest. She said, "Come on, you're not going to die on me, sir. Get him up. Gentle with that arm."

And then they carried Winter away through the rain. Just like that he was gone. Just like Laura. Everyone was gone.

Freddie was alone. The purpose that had driven him off the Ridge left him suddenly; he swayed like a puppet with cut strings.

But he didn't fall. A hand caught his elbow. "What now?" said Faland, still beside him. "Off you go, back to barracks? Or to Bedlam more like, considering the look on your face."

Freddie didn't answer. He had nothing. What future waited for him but to lie down in the mud and let the drowned man take what was his? "I'm already dead," he whispered.

"Straight to perdition, then?" Faland said lightly. "Well, it can hardly be worse, can it?" And when Freddie turned his head to look, Faland smiled.

NOW IS COME SALVATION

.....

THEY TOOK LAURA UPSTAIRS TO A BARE ROOM WITH A SLOPING ceiling, and there she was sick for four days. Early on, Pim hovered with tea and broth and mustard-plasters, but by the third day Laura grew delirious as her fever climbed, and Jones ordered Pim out. Laura was racked with nightmares of her mother, of reaching hands and ruined eyes. She dreamed she was in an endless corridor full of doors and someone was crying, in a half-familiar voice, *"Why can't I remember?"*

She said, "Who can't remember?"

"The blessed," Faland's voice said. "The blessed forget and the damned remember."

"Where are you?" she demanded. But his voice had already faded into a sharper one saying "Iven, come back," and Laura opened her eyes. Doctor Jones sat by her bed, his thumb pressed to the pulse point on her wrist, a towel and a basin on an overturned crate beside him. Laura realized that her hair was wet; little runnels of cold water ran across her throat and jaw.

"I didn't know surgeons went in for nursing," she said. Her mouth was paper-dry.

He looked into her face, and she thought his expression lightened. "There you are. Not usually, no. But we're understaffed and you're in the crisis; I came up to browbeat you through it. Your fever's come down in the last hour. You're past the worst of it now, I hope." He wet the cloth again, laid it on her hot forehead. "But in case I am wrong, you are still *not* to die, I need someone to assist in surgery. Have some water, you look like you just crossed the Sahara in August."

He got her to sit up, put a cup to her lips. She gulped until her head swam, flinched at the pain in her lungs. His hands smelled faintly of disinfectant. "All right, enough, lie down again," he said. His tone was acerbic, but his hands were steady, professional. He'd taken the same oaths she had. He was trying to save her life.

"Thank you," she whispered, lying back, letting her eyes drift shut.

"Why the devil did you come back here?" It sounded as though he were talking half to himself. "Wounded, honorably discharged— why come back?"

She didn't have an answer, but he didn't seem to expect one. "Just keep breathing," he advised, as more cool water ran with the sweat down her face.

. . .

Laura came through the crisis, and that evening she woke up alone, found herself staring at a spiderweb on a roof beam, trying to piece together all the hours since she'd arrived in Europe. She hoped they'd been able to give Fouquet a proper burial. The room was small, the ceiling sloped, and it contained nothing but two narrow brass beds, one on each side, with a nightstand each and hooks like crooked fingers on the wall. It must have been a maid's room, when the château was a home instead of a way station. Laura's trunk sat by her bed, retrieved from the wrecked lorry, and Pim's lay at the foot of the other.

They'd come to Dunkirk, gotten on a lorry. She remembered Fouquet. Bombs. A dark shape in the road. Music. But try as she might, the rest would not come clear. Finally, in frustration, she rolled to her feet, stood stiff-kneed against a bout of light-headedness. Began groping in her trunk for a flannel and a clean uniform. She couldn't do Freddie any good in bed. When she was dressed, she sat down for a few minutes to clear her swimming head. Then she hauled herself upright again, and turned determinedly for the door.

A narrow staircase took her out of the servants' quarters, down and down, and finally spat her out in the main foyer, the evident nerve center of Mary's small hospital, full of the sound of quick feet, a mingling of men's and women's voices, the smell of decay, chocolate, and carbolic.

A door swung open, revealed a sterilization room, made over from what might once have been a music room. Splintered parquet, chipped putti near the ceiling. Syringes in boiling water, an old table, probably dragged up from the kitchen. A hodgepodge of fine furniture, raveling upholstery. A coal fire in the fireplace. Laura felt a little puff of warmth on her face, even from the doorway. Jones's unmistakable American voice was berating an orderly in heavily accented French:

"My knee," he said. "I left it here, just there, on the table, in a saucepan. Where is it?"

Laura felt her brows climb. She still wanted to sit down.

"Your—knee, Monsieur?" stammered the orderly.

"Yes, yes," said Jones. "Just there. I meant to seethe off the flesh—some very interesting . . ."

The orderly murmured something.

"A leg of mutton. *A leg of mutton?*" said Jones. "You mistook my knee for a leg of mutton? It was the perfect specimen! Such an interesting presentation of the anterior ligaments."

Mary spoke right behind Laura, who jumped. "You didn't eat it, I hope, Colas," she called sternly to the orderly.

"Bloody hell," muttered Laura.

Jones stepped out of the sterilization room. She hadn't misremembered the flat American voice, the bony face, the fine eyes. "I am sorry about your specimen," Laura said.

"So am I," said Jones. "And you may stop thinking *ghoul* at me, Iven; *I* didn't eat it. How's your chest? Take your dress off."

"In the sterilization room," said Mary, herding them.

Laura obediently undid her dress, shrugged it off her shoulders. Jones put his icy stethoscope to Laura's back in several points. Her chest still hurt. "Do I have you to thank for my recovery, Doctor?" asked Laura, trying to be cordial.

Cordiality was wasted on him. "Yes, of course. Me and a reasonable constitution." He stepped back. "You'll do, if you eat properly and don't get chilled. Get dressed and let me see your hands."

Her shoulders went rigid. Letting him examine her hands was much harder than taking her dress off. "My hands are all right."

"You have considerable scarring," said Jones clinically. "And you will almost certainly be arthritic in the next five years. Let me see."

"*I'm* not an amputated knee," said Laura.

"You'd argue less if you were," said Jones. He put out one of his own hands. Long fingers, perfectly kept nails. Jaw set, Laura put her hand in his. He manipulated the scar tissue, tested the range of motion.

"Well, the damage is done," Jones said, letting them go. "A shame. You'll want to massage them every night, so the scars don't stiffen further. With lanolin, or beeswax. *Can* you assist in surgery?"

"Yes," returned Laura, hating the way his black eyes covered the wreck of her fingers.

"All right," he said. "Join me on rounds, will you? If you're up to it?" He let go her hands, and was out the door.

Laura said a very bad word.

"It's just his way," said Mary. "Weak in the bedside manner."

"I am not in bed anymore. And I have a credential or two. How does he think I got the scars on my hands? Not lounging around a civilian hospital."

Mary said, "Iven, you may rant to me all you like, but I beg you will attempt to tolerate Jones. In the interest of harmony. Highly qualified American surgeons do not simply fall from the sky, you know."

"Never mind him anyway," said Laura, mastering herself. "Shouldn't we discuss inadvertent cannibalism amongst your staff instead?"

Mary snorted. "I don't want to know. Do you?"

"Not particularly." Laura flexed her hands, trying to erase the sensation of Jones's grip. "How is Pim?"

"Thriving," said Mary. "The men think she's their earthly angel. Come this way. I'll show you about. I need you taking a shift as soon as ever you can. They are saying the Germans are going to try to break the line at Ypres and sweep us toward the sea."

Laura said nothing. Four years and how many million lives, and they could lose it all now. And then she thought, *Time, I just need time . . .*

"Won't happen, Iven," added Mary, seeing her face. "This way."

Mary opened the front door onto a glorious dusk: a scarlet, saffron, and violet sky that hardly seemed to belong to the gray earth. "The ambulances come up the drive. And we have triage in the carriage house," she said, pointing. "You'll be out there quite a bit."

They turned back into the house. The main ward of Couthove had been set up in the once elegant ballroom, full now of close-packed beds and sickroom smell: alcohol and iodine, bodily fluids, and sweat. The glorious parquet was stained. There had been a buzz of conversation as they entered, and Laura caught just the edge of it:

—paradise, if you find it.

So? Every whorehouse is paradise to some.

Another voice, low and grave: *My mate found it. Coming back drunk from leave. Was crying when he told me. He forgot the war, he said. Just like the stories. Saw his girl, even. In that magic mirror. A perfect night. But he never found it again.*

You don't ever find it again.

He don't charge money. No, not money . . .

He split with the girl, you know, not long after. It was like he'd forgotten all about her. He's dead now.

The conversation subsided into a general murmur, and then Pim was hurrying over. "Laura!" she cried. "I was so worried. You'd such a fever. But Dr. Jones said you'd do. Isn't he marvelous? How are you, dear?"

"Blooming," said Laura. Pim's face was thinner than it had been in Halifax, but she was smiling. Mary hadn't exaggerated. The men were all looking at her as though she were their own personal miracle.

"I've been writing the men's letters," said Pim. "They dictate, or if they—if they can't dictate, then I just write their mothers myself. And I draw little pictures—look."

She pulled out a sketchbook, unfolded a loose page to show a very credible sketch of a young man with a bandaged shoulder, smiling.

"I am sure they are grateful . . ." began Laura, and then Jones appeared, and cut her off.

"Rounds, Iven," he said. "Half an hour, then supper, then back to bed with you."

Laura sighed internally. Reminded herself that Jones was not the most dictatorial surgeon she'd ever met, even if he had a knack for getting under her skin. "Yes, Doctor," she said mildly, mouthed *Later* to Pim, and crossed the room.

They went from patient to patient, checking charts, taking temperatures, asking questions. Jones at work was dispassionate but careful, decisive. She began to relax into the routine of it. But then, six beds in, they came to a man called Trovato. His leg was very clearly gangrenous, and Laura was nonplussed. Why hadn't Jones amputated? The smell was unmistakable: ripe, swampy, unlike anything else. "Doctor—" she began.

"Yes, yes," said Jones, not looking up. "Unorthodox, I'll give you that. But the gangrene hasn't spread; there's a chance it will slough and we will save the leg."

"I'd like to keep my leg," put in Trovato earnestly.

Laura just managed to keep her thoughts to herself. No doctor she'd ever known would have hesitated to amputate. "Dress the wound, Iven," said Jones, as though he could hear her disapproval. He was making notes on the chart. Laura began laying out bandages and disinfectant. Jones, after a glance at the patient's set face, called, "Mrs. Shaw, come here."

Laura bit her lip. But Pim had signed on for this, and so Laura said nothing when her friend hurried over and took Trovato's hand, smiling. He relaxed a fraction.

Laura set to irrigating the wound. Trovato made a small, animal sound. Pim held his hand tighter. Laura didn't stop. Army medicine was as much about ruthlessness as anything else. "You've been out here before, Sister, haven't you?" Trovato said to Laura, with the air of a man trying to distract himself. His eyes were closed, but he must have seen her hands.

"I came out in the spring of '15. With the bluebirds." The Canadian nursing service, she meant. "Was discharged this November." She shot him a brief, reassuring smile, but his eyes were still closed. "Suppose I couldn't stay away from you lot."

"Got a story for us, Sister?" he asked. "From those far-off days?"

Anything to distract him, Laura thought, beginning to dress the wound fresh. She shot Jones a sideways look. She wasn't in the regular army anymore—she didn't have to behave. "Have you heard the story of the ammonal at Hooge?" She let her voice carry to the room at large. Saw men stir under their blankets.

Jones raised both brows.

"It was early days," Laura said, winding the bandage. "Just when they'd first got the bright notion to dislodge Fritz from Hooge by undermining his positions and blowing him up. Steady. That's the worst over." Trovato had gone an extraordinary gray-green. Pim bent to murmur something in his ear. He gave her a wavering smile, an incisor missing.

"In '15," Laura went on, "the lines passed right through the grounds of Hooge Château, and Hooge, as you maybe know, was the worst place on the worst salient on the worst sector of the Front."

Some of the men were lifting themselves up to hear better.

"Fritz held the château itself, and Tommy held the stable, and they'd dug trenches in between. Each one was making plans to blow the others out. Well, the British hit on the idea of mines: Dig holes, pack them with gun cotton, fire it, there you have it.

"Higher-up had a big stunt planned for just a week later, and the bright lad in charge of the mining realizes there is no way on earth that they can dig a hole big enough in a week to hold all the gun cotton they need to blow Fritz out.

"So he suggests using ammonal, like they'd use in the coal mines. Harder to handle, but more powerful, you can put less in, see? All very well, but the supply master has no notion what manner of thing ammonal is. They've never encountered it before. He asks a chemist friend, and receives this reply . . ."

Laura paused, grinning. The room was listening, rapt. Jones gave her a look.

"A medicament, says he," Laura resumed. "For the lessening of sexual desire."

The room broke up into laughter.

"Now," said Laura, "I do not know what the reaction of the supply master was, or if he asked what they were doing in Hooge to require so much of the stuff—"

More laughter.

"—but," said Laura, "they did blow Fritz out, in the end, so someone must have straightened it up. Eventually."

There was a chorus of laughter and indelicate suggestions. Pim looked scandalized. Jones surprised Laura by barking a laugh, shaking his head. Laura had finished Trovato's dressing. His head fell back against the pillow. His sprouting beard was stark in the clammy hollows of his throat, but he was smiling too.

The next patient was an attempted suicide, and he was going to die.

Laura didn't need Jones to tell her. She could see it in the angle of his wound, and the color of his face. Hear the stertor. From the look of things, he'd put the rifle under his chin, tried to fire with his bare toes. "What's his name?" she said.

"We don't know," said Jones. "He came in such a mess. No tags.

He kept shouting a name though. A girl's name. It was all he'd say. *Mila,* he shouted. *Mila.* Maybe he shot himself for her, who knows? But we've been calling him Mila, for want of anything better."

Trovato had turned his head to watch. "Poor bugger. Saw the fiddler. Couldn't stick it. Some say he takes their souls. But maybe the war's already done that." Laura had given him morphine; he was rambling.

Pim had been sponging his face; her cloth stilled and she said, "But who is the fiddler, sir?"

Laura found herself listening intently, although she didn't look up. She had to shake off an involuntary sense-memory, like something dreamed in fever, of the rising cry of a violin, the heavy smell of wine.

Trovato muttered, "There's all sorts of stories, but none of them's right for a girlie like you. Fiddler's for the likes of us. If a man wants to risk it—well, that's for him to decide. But you—stay away."

"Sir—" Pim began, but Jones said, "Let him rest, Shaw."

Laura had questions of her own. But Mila's wound distracted her. It was as though the doctor hadn't . . . She finished the dressing and glanced with some surprise at Jones.

He looked strangely uneasy. Finally he said, "A word, Iven."

Laura followed him across the hall and into the sterilization room. Jones shut the door. He was watching her. Finally he said, "What do you think?"

"His prognosis? Poor," said Laura. Cautiously, she added, "It would have been better if he'd gone into surgery straight off. Or at all."

Jones said nothing.

She added, more carefully still, "I noticed that he hasn't."

"No."

"Strange," said Laura. "Since I suppose they told you to do your best to save him."

"They did." They would have. Suicide was a capital offense. The army didn't want men just *getting away* with it. No, they had to be saved so they could stand up and face a firing squad. Maybe Jones was sounding her out because he thought she'd be—shocked, that he was going against protocol, letting a man die in bed? Lord. Poor Jones. A few months ago he had probably been doing surgery in a clean Boston hospital, far from the stew of competing ethics and ad hoc morality that was a military hospital.

"I want us to understand each other," said Jones stiffly.

"I think we do," said Laura. "Poor man. No hope. Couldn't be saved, despite your best efforts."

They looked at each other. Suddenly Jones's face relaxed; his lips twitched. "You've seen men like him before."

"I've seen a lot of things," said Laura.

"More than I have," said Jones, with candor, surprising her again. "I'll remember it in future. I don't *mean* to be insufferable, Iven, however I come across. What's Mrs. Shaw's interest in this fiddler person? It's some bugbear of the patients'. Whenever anyone mentions it, there she goes, scampering over, listening for all she's worth."

A coldness spread across Laura's skin. "I don't know."

Jones said, "Keep an eye on her; people take on strange manias out here. In the meantime, we have rounds to finish, and then you are to eat some supper, Iven. I could count your ribs, earlier."

To Laura's surprise, she felt her face flush. Without another word, Jones stepped through the door and was gone.

. . .

Supper was army rations, somewhat improved with fresh bread and an egg each. Laura, still coughing, had little appetite. But she got her soup anyway, her mug of tea, sat down at the long, scarred table where the staff not on duty were cramming in nourishment. "Pim," she said, "Jones told me you are hounding the men with questions about the fiddler."

Pim tasted her tea, made a face, and added more sugar. Quite prosaically, she said, "I've been thinking he's really that man Faland."

Laura put her spoon down. "What do the men say about him?"

In answer, Pim pulled out a notebook filled with her handwriting, licked a finger, and started reading off tidbits, going from page to page. "You can only find him at night," she said. "No one's ever heard of anyone seeing him by day."

"Is he a vampire?" asked Laura dryly. She spooned up more soup.

"Hush. He plays the violin— Well, we know that, don't we? Not much agreement on what he looks like." She turned another page, and there was Faland's face, the hair done in swift strokes, the dark eye and the light. Pim really did draw well. "His hotel—sometimes they say it's a bar—is the best place anywhere, although some say it's also the worst." She flipped another page. "You have the best night of your life there. They say he'll show you the thing you want most." Her voice wavered on *most*. "But you can only find his hotel once. And people who've drunk there, they pine for it, once they've gone. Then they go mad, some of them." Pim frowned at her closely written pages. "That's quite a lot of rumors, isn't it? About the same person. I'm curious."

"Only curious?"

Pim flushed. "Faland's hotel *was* like a miracle, I thought. So— so warm. His music. And then it vanished at dawn."

Laura didn't trust the look on her friend's face. *They pine,* the men had said. "He's just a swindler, Pim. A mesmerist selling uncustomed wine. Probably spikes it too. Wormwood. Sugar of lead. How are your bowels?"

Pim pressed her lips together.

"Pim, I don't think Faland's a good person," said Laura more seriously.

"Maybe not. But it all felt like magic, didn't it? The music, the night, the—the mirror. The morning. All of it." There was a thread of unwilling longing in her voice. "When was the last time anything in your life felt like magic?"

Laura was silent. Her conviction, born of long days and longer nights, was that if the world contained any magic at all, then it could not also contain their war. She asked, "Pim, what did you see in that mirror?"

"Oh—" said Pim, her gaze far away. "Jimmy, of course. I saw my son."

"Pim, it was hypnosis."

"Oh, I know," said Pim, although she didn't sound wholly convinced. "Anyway, never mind that. There is one piece of the legend that's easy enough to check."

Laura was pulled from her own thoughts. "What's that?"

"I want to go back to the hotel, of course. Because the men say you can't find it twice. I'm going to see if I can. By day, even."

Pim turned away to her dinner before Laura could voice her vehement opinion of that notion.

· · ·

It was dark when they finally took themselves upstairs to bed.

Pim was disgruntled, because Mary, to Laura's relief, had put paid to any notions of leave to go anywhere. "Shaw, the wounded are going to keep coming down on us like three tons of bricks. If Fritz breaks the line up here, we may have to evacuate the hospital. I need every hand ready, and no one is going off pleasure-bound for *any reason*."

Laura had never much appreciated Mary's caustic authority, but in this case she agreed entirely. In their shared room, Laura stripped off her dress, peeled out of waist and stockings and chemise, stood there naked as Eve with a wet flannel, and attacked the sticky remains of fever-sweat. Pim sat primly on her bed and looked at anything in the room but Laura. "You'll be doing it next," said Laura, amused. "Unless you want to go to bed mucky."

Footsteps sounded in the corridor and Mary pushed the door open. Pim yelped in surprise.

Laura glanced up, went back to sponging.

"It's all right, Pim," said Mary. "Iven will defend your virtue."

"I'm not defending anyone without three hours of sleep, a cup of coffee, and a cigarette," said Laura, drying herself off. "Mary, what are you doing up here? I hope no one is hemorrhaging. Go rouse Jones. If I try to work a shift right now, I will poison someone by accident."

"I am aware," said Mary. "No, I was going through my correspondence and there was a letter for you." She held it out. "Go to bed. Tomorrow will come quick, and you have shift schedules to think of, Iven. And Jones tells me you must put on ten pounds at least, and that your cough is still unpleasant."

"Officious man," said Laura. She tossed the letter onto her cot.

Mary was studying Laura's limbs, the way a horse-coper looks at a horse. "He's quite right. Lord, I thought you were bony before."

"Good night, Mary."

Mary departed, and Laura put on a ratty jumper over her chemise, laid her uniform dress, apron, and boots ready to hand. "Get some sleep while you can," she told Pim. "If Mary's right, we won't be getting much in the near future." She picked up her letter, slit it with her pocket lancet.

She knew the handwriting. *Kate.*

My Dear Laura,

How are you? Imagine my surprise when you wrote and told me you were coming back, that you'd taken a place at Couthove. So near. I should very much like to see you, if you can get away. I've got one or two things of yours here, and of course news. I met a friend of yours a few weeks ago, and I know how much you love a good gossip, my dear. Come and I shall tell you all.

Laura blinked. She had left nothing at Brandhoek. And what friend?

They've moved me back from Brandhoek, thank goodness. I'm at Mendinghem now, a much pleasanter place, on the whole, and a scant few miles from your château. At least we don't have to do rounds with our gas masks at the ready. I am so eager to see you, Laura.

Laura wanted few things more than to see Kate White again. But the tone was unlike her, there was an eager undercurrent, just like her last letter. *What are you trying to tell me?*

Thinking hard, she put the letter aside and climbed into her cot. If she was to go anywhere, it must be soon. The tension gathering in the air was palpable. The next great battle was a matter of *when,* not *if,* and it would, quite possibly, be decisive. And when it was joined, she wouldn't be able to go anywhere at all.

AND IN THOSE DAYS SHALL
MEN SEEK DEATH

·····

BRANDHOEK AND PARTS UNKNOWN,
FLANDERS, BELGIUM
NOVEMBER 1917

FREDDIE STOOD LIKE A PILLAR OF SALT, A MAN STRIPPED AT once of purpose, past, and future. He wished the dead man would come, and take his vengeance. He was a murderer. A traitor. He should have drowned too.

Beside him, Faland resettled his shoulders in his shabby suit. "Well, then," he said. "I shall leave you to it." He stepped into the dark. But a stray gleam caught his rain-silvered hair, and Freddie came out of his stupor and snatched Faland's sleeve.

Faland's expression turned inquiring.

"Where are you going?" said Freddie. He was thinking of that deep, quiet cellar, the way it had looked in the light of the candle held in Faland's fist. Otherworldly. Even safe. Freddie would give anything to have that feeling again. He wanted to leave the world and never come back. But he was too much of a coward, he thought bitterly, to put a pistol in his mouth and pull the trigger.

"Here and there," said Faland.

"Will you— May I come with you?"

Faland raised both brows. "That is the behavior of a very bad soldier indeed. You've comforted your enemy, and now you'll desert your country?"

Enemy? Was Germany his enemy? In the last few days, Germany had become Winter, breathing with him in the dark. Freddie said, "Germany didn't put my sister's hospital next to a munitions dump."

Faland's smile was beautiful in itself, but brutal in its contrast with the night. "Perhaps you may. I do have my fees, however."

"How much?" whispered Freddie. "I've nothing."

"No? Every night you stay with me, I want you to tell me a story. Something about yourself. Good or bad, I don't care. But it must be true."

Freddie didn't know if it was the cold rain or his own rattling heartbeat that made him shake. Nothing felt real. "Why?"

"Call it inspiration," said Faland.

"For whom?"

"Yes or no?"

"I—yes. Yes." *Not him, Iven,* Winter had said. But Winter was gone. "Anything," Freddie added aloud, and even he could hear the desperate truth in his voice.

Without another word, Faland turned and crossed a muddy ditch, light on his feet. Freddie scrambled after him. They passed out of earshot of Brandhoek, found themselves in a gray field, swaddled in bitter mist. The world already seemed set at a remove, even the shellfire flattened to distant thunder. Freddie was so relieved he wept. He didn't know where they were going, and he didn't care. All his heart told him was *away,* and that was enough.

He would dream of that walk, after. Dream imaginary horrors: an orchard of dead men hanging like fruit, a river of silky black water. But memory told him only that he walked until the end of his faltering strength, that the world narrowed to nothing but the uneven sway of Faland's stride ahead of him. That at last they stood together in front of a heavy door set into a timeworn wall.

That Faland pushed the door open and went inside.

Freddie hesitated. Raindrops pelted his face, but within lay a flickering darkness. He almost turned around. But his life was out in that rain, his losses, his ghosts. He crossed the threshold. The door swung shut.

"Welcome," said Faland.

Freddie's first impression was of a vast space, his second was of magnificence. Mellow gilt, soft firelight, marquetry and parquet, diapering and gilding, velvet and glass, almost painful in contrast with immediate memory. It could not be real. And yet Freddie could *feel* the nap of the velvet on the wall, on a chair, when he ran his fingers across. The heat of the fire made his numb face tingle.

His third impression was of decay. The velvets frayed, the gilding peeled, tarnish showing through cracks in the glass. A faint dust, raised by Faland's feet as he crossed the room.

Freddie followed him in a daze, registering dimly that the room had a startling number of doors. Faland laid his hand on one of them, but before it opened, Freddie caught sight of a mirror. He did not see his reflection in it. He saw Laura.

She was with Winter. They were sitting together at a table. They were well. Whole. God, even friends. They looked up at him, in unison. Laura and Winter, alive. His sister: quick, wry, competent. Winter, his face clean, his hair straw-colored. In the mirror Laura smiled at Freddie and said something to Winter, and he laughed.

Something inside him cracked, horribly, wide open. They were *right there.*

Faland caught his wrist. Freddie realized that he'd been reaching toward the glass. "Not now," said Faland. "Later, if you like."

"*What is it?*" said Freddie.

"It depends on the person looking."

"That's impossible."

"More so than anything else?" The tilt of Faland's head seemed to encompass everything outside; the whole world gone mad.

To that Freddie had no answer. Perhaps he was dreaming. He hoped he never woke up.

. . .

The bedroom at the top of the staircase was as grand as the foyer below, and as shabby. More velvet—on the heavy curtains, on the counterpane. Fine wood furniture, elaborately carved. But all of it chipped, splintered, faded.

Faland said, "Rest," and left him in the doorway.

Freddie stopped thinking. He clawed off the rags of his uniform, found tepid water, a basin, scrubbed his skin raw, and then collapsed naked on the bed.

But he found himself too exhausted to sleep, ill at ease on a mattress, under sheets, in solitude, after so many nights sleeping rough with a dozen others, in barracks, in dugouts, in strange catch-as-catch-can billets. So instead of sleeping he thrashed and sweated and finally dozed, only to awaken in darkness, thinking he was back in the pillbox, thinking he was being smothered underground. Knowing he was all alone. Winter wasn't breathing. Winter wasn't there.

A sound, not far from a scream, nearly tore blood from his throat, and he folded in on himself, caught in an airless void. For a moment he yawed right on the edge of madness. He was already dead. Everything was broken, blackened by rain. He thought he saw a star through the fallen-in roof.

Then a light flared from the corridor, and his door flew open.

Freddie threw a hand over his eyes. Faland was in the doorway, a candle in his hand. The light showed an intact roof, a room of shabby magnificence.

"Hush," Faland said. "Take the candle."

Bed, he thought. *Walls. Floor. Air.* His feeling of choking eased. He tried to get up. But he couldn't move. *Shell-shock. Laura had patients who couldn't move after they were shell-shocked.*

Faland crossed the room, put the candle on the nightstand. His hair had dried from the rain, lightened to silver-gilt. Freddie found that his rigid limbs would heed him again. His chest was sheened with sweat. He must have made a racket in his sleep. He shivered at the draft from the door and drew the blankets up. "I—I'm sorry."

With the candle on the nightstand, Faland's face was in shadow.

With a strange note in his voice, he said, "I woke in darkness once. I dream of it still. Now go back to sleep."

. . .

With the light beside him, Freddie slept, and the next time he woke, it was to music, and he was alone. Someone in the hotel was playing a violin. Precisely, achingly, flawlessly, the music trickled through the room: a melody he almost recognized. He saw fresh clothes folded at the foot of the bed. At first he thought they were a uniform, then he realized that they were just pieces of one. Canadian trousers, a British jacket. Castoffs. Like himself. He put them on. Ventured to the door, stiff in every limb. Peered out. The hallway was soft with carpet. The music rose. Freddie followed it down a flight of stairs. Found a door and opened it.

The music struck him in the face, like walking into rain.

He was back in the foyer, but it wasn't empty. Men in proper uniforms packed the room, sitting at tables, drinking, talking, laughing. Sometimes crying. Their lips were stained, the floor was sticky. Their noise made the chandeliers quiver. Was it advertisements, Freddie wondered, that brought them all? He didn't know if it was night or day. The room revealed nothing of the outside world.

Freddie clung to the shadows. The sheer, tenacious life filling the room frightened him, as though if he got too near he'd be swept back into its bloody gyre. But no one beckoned, no one was looking at him. They were all watching Faland. He was the one playing a violin.

Freddie was surprised somehow, that the musician was him. Faland seemed so remote. Detached. But there was nothing detached about his music. It reached a clawed hand right inside Freddie's forgotten heart, alive with things he was too wounded to feel anymore. Regret, tenderness. It was beautiful, and it hurt so much.

He stood there frozen, and that was when he caught sight of the mirror over the bar.

Winter and Laura were eating supper. The war had never happened. Freddie and Winter had met in the ordinary way. There was no white in Laura's hair, there were no lines on Winter's face.

He didn't hear the music ending. He didn't hear anything at all until Faland's voice in his ear shattered the illusion, left him reeling once more. "Well, you are among the living after all," said Faland. He was carrying his violin in a case.

"Who are you?" Freddie said. He realized his face was wet. "I don't understand."

"I am a notable hotelier," said Faland. "And fortunately you don't have to understand. Would you like some wine?"

"God, yes," said Freddie.

. . .

He drank until he was no longer afraid. He drank until longing became only a pleasant ache. Faland drank too, color on his cheekbones, the paler eye brilliant. It was a compelling face. You wanted to look at it, and know its secrets. You wanted to look through it to where the music lived. The room around them was sunk in murmured talk, heady with warmth and wine.

"Will you tell me a story now, Iven?" said Faland. He'd taken a seat beside Freddie, lounging in the half-light.

Freddie hesitated. A story meant remembering. He wanted to stay adrift in the unmoored present. But Faland's silence was expectant. *I have fees,* he'd said. Well, it was little enough, for the hours of glorious oblivion. Freddie found himself groping through his wine-hazed memory, thought of things he could tell—good and terrible—and finally he blurted, "Laura stole an ice cream for me once."

"Misdeeds run in the family, I fear," said Faland. He propped his chin on his fist and waited.

Freddie hadn't thought of it in years. But he found himself slipping into the memory as though it were playing out in front of him. Faland leaned forward.

"Laura— God, she spoiled me. I'm nearly three years younger, you know, and I was a fat little brat of a red-haired thing. Awful freckles. And she had me by the hand once and we were walking past the shop, and I told her I wanted an ice cream. She didn't have any money, of course, and neither did I. But you know it never occurred to me, even then, that she couldn't get me one. So she looks at me. Looks at the shop. And then she marches in like a queen, holding me by the hand. She was—twelve? Twelve, I think. And she orders ice creams for both of us. With chocolate sauce. And then she gets to the till. Of course she's not got a penny. And she reaches into her pocket. Nothing's there. Her eyes fill up with tears. I started to cry myself, seeing her get started. She turns to the shopkeeper and says, 'Sir, my dollar fell out of my pocket.' She's weeping like a Madonna the whole time, and she turns to me and says, 'Freddie, go home, for I must make amends. Please, sir, spare my brother at least—' She was heartbreaking, I can tell you. And the long and short is we got those ice creams and got off scot-free. I used to think she was terribly clever; now I think the shopkeeper was just impressed with her barefaced cheek and crocodile tears."

Freddie raised his eyes and saw Laura's adult face in the mirror, without a single mark of strain on it. As though the woman there had grown from the girl in his memory, with no Armageddon come between. He didn't know how long he stared and when he looked away, Faland had disappeared.

Freddie didn't remember how or when he got to bed. But he must have managed somehow, for he woke up back in that luxurious bedroom, dry-mouthed, with a headache. He had no notion of the hour, or even the day. He dimly remembered telling Faland a story. But he had absolutely no memory of what the story had been about.

AND HIS DEADLY WOUND
WAS HEALED

·····

LAURA WOKE IN THE DARKEST PART OF THE NIGHT AND KNEW that something was wrong, even though she was high in an attic, out of earshot of the ward. Before she was properly awake, she was out of bed and hurrying into her clothes, laid ready on the trunk. In less than a minute, she was slipping softly down the stairs, straining for the sound of aeroplanes, of explosions. Nothing. But she heard the commotion clearly as she got closer to the ballroom, saw the play of electric lanterns as the night staff belatedly heard and came across. She was with them as they entered the ballroom, their lights sweeping the stained parquet. The staff looked disoriented, even sheepish. They'd been taking their ease in the warm sterilization room while things went to hell in the main ward. Laura had to bite back orders and reprimands both.

The room was in chaos. Mila—Christ, why had no one been with him?—was screaming.

"Where are you?" howled the dying man, with a volume and clarity he absolutely shouldn't have had, not with his ruined face. "Please, please, please, you *promised* . . ."

He was the loudest. But the whole room howled. Patients' voices fell on her ears as she made for the screaming man.

"God, did you *hear?*"

"It's a sign, it is, we've lost."

"He'll come for us all."

"God save us."

Someone was sobbing.

Laura went to Mila, who'd actually got himself out of bed, bellowing like a calf, and pulled the bandage loose from his face. The blood was already starting to run. She caught his clawing hands, said, "Sir, you must go back to bed." Laura could not stop him physically; her head hardly came to his shoulder.

"He knows me," said Mila. "I don't care what he wants, at least he knows me. That was him, calling . . ."

Laura said, "You must go back to bed."

"I don't care. He can have me. He doesn't lie. Everyone else is a liar," said Mila, voice choked with blood. "They lied when I joined up—they said we were all heroes." Then he staggered, eyes rolling back, and she caught him, shouting. He'd have taken her down with him, but there was a familiar voice, a familiar smell of disinfectant, and then Jones was there, taking Mila's weight, calling for orderlies.

More and more staff were coming in; Mary was there herself, with a wrapper thrown over her nightgown, and under their collected efforts, the ward quieted a little. The patients were tucked back under the blankets, given water, bedpans, morphine. Laura glanced out the window. She could hardly see out, with the lights in the ballroom. She thought she saw, briefly, movement in the dark just as a frail voice behind her said, "Is he gone?"

Who? she thought, before the rest of her brain caught up. That was Trovato's voice. Something wrong in the timbre of it. She spun, saw the flow of black blood from his leg, the hemorrhage unnoticed in the confusion.

"Doctor!" Laura called, not looking up. Her hands flew.

"*He's* not a liar," whispered Trovato. He tried to catch at Laura's wrist. "That's the worst of it, that he's not a liar. He doesn't pretend virtue, you know. Take the little one home. Take her . . ."

He fell mercifully unconscious. The flow of blood eased; she'd got a tourniquet round. Now Laura cut away the soaked bandage round his calf. Saw that the gangrene had sloughed, as Jones predicted; the whole rotten piece sliding free to lie seeping on the bedclothes. But the slough was deep enough to have taken the artery with it. Trovato's lips and nails were already bluish. Suddenly Jones was behind her, a strong light in his hand. He cast a professional eye over the situation. "It came off," he said, looking with satisfaction at the hollow where the gangrene had been.

Trovato was unconscious and Laura was furious, which is why she permitted herself to retort, low and savage, "Yes, well, I'm sure that will be a great comfort to him, to be buried with two legs and no gangrene." Even if he didn't bleed to death in front of her, how was he going to *heal* with the artery severed?

Jones merely put his stethoscope to Trovato's chest. "He needs blood," he said. An orderly vanished. Laura's stomach knotted. She'd seen attempts at transfusion before. It meant shredded veins, tubing everywhere, and the patient nearly always died.

"Objections, Iven?" said Jones.

"Doctor, he's not a science experiment. Let me give him saline and—"

The orderly reappeared, carrying, of all things, a glass jar full of blood. Laura had never seen blood in a jar. Transfusions were between people, lying parallel. How could there be blood in a jar? It ought to be clotted black. It ought . . .

Jones began to set up tubing with quick, practiced movements. His voice was surprisingly mild. "We ghouls with our experiments sometimes have the last word."

Laura said, "I've seen transfusions. They go into shock. They die."

"A question of blood type," said Jones. "Been begging the continentals for *years* to take account of blood type."

Laura said, "You don't know his type."

"Don't need to. We only store blood from the O's—they can give to anyone." He took up the bottle of blood. Laura stood silent now, holding the light for him. Jones's transfusion setup was an ugly scrawl of tubing, a mess of blood and iodine. But if it worked—

Laura said, "How do you keep the blood from clotting?"

Absorbed in what he was doing, Jones had lost much of his supercilious manner. His eyes were bright as a boy's when he said, "Paraffin on the inside of the bottles, citrate and dextrose in the blood. If it's kept cold, it will last for days. Weeks, even." He slipped a needle into the vein in Trovato's arm.

The implication silenced her. If they could store blood . . .

"Christ," she said.

"Yes." Jones glanced up. Now the light in his eyes reminded her of Faland, in his ruined hotel, when he played his impossible music. Maybe it was just the act of wrenching something beautiful or useful out of the grime. "Imagine," said Jones. "Shelves of blood. And then when an attack comes . . ."

He trailed off. Laura could see it. All the men who expired from shock and blood loss—they'd have a chance. She had never met anyone who had held the wreckage of the war between his hands, and could still imagine making the world better. But now she watched the color come—like magic—back into Trovato's face, and she said, swallowing her pride, "Doctor, will you show me how to use the tubing?"

"Naturally," said Jones. "I have to dazzle you somehow, Iven; *I'll* never win a Croix de Guerre."

She didn't have an answer to that, but he didn't seem to want one. "Look here," he added, businesslike, and bent to show her the arrangement of tubes, the vial, the syringe. The blue had left the patient's lips. Laura stood there in fragile wonder, until Jones said, "I know you're lost in admiration, Iven, but enough for tonight. You ought to go back to bed."

Laura shook her head. "After all this excitement? Not a chance. I'm going to have cocoa and have a word with the night sister. Such carelessness, leaving a roomful of wounded men all alone."

. . .

Sterilization rooms had been gathering places in every field hospital Laura had ever worked in, and the one at Couthove was no different. Sterilization rooms always had hot water. An endless supply going, to clean instruments. One could draw the water off for cocoa, for tea. One could stand near the steaming burner and feel a little warmer. But this time, when Laura ventured in search of cocoa, the sterilization room was empty. Or almost empty. To Laura's surprise, Pim was there, standing flushed and fully dressed for the outdoors with a coat over her uniform. There was mud on her boots.

"Out for a stroll?" Laura asked. She busied herself with cocoa powder and hot water, extra sugar, tinned milk.

A line deepened between Pim's brows. But she replied in a rush, "I went out to look."

Laura stopped stirring. "Look?"

"I heard the men—they kept saying *he* was there. I thought it might be the fiddler—their legend, you know?" Lower, she added, "I thought it might be Faland. So I went to look."

Several replies came to Laura's lips but she bit them back. Finally she settled on the most sensible: "Did you see anything?"

Pim shook her head. She stood in the middle of the room, looking fragile.

Laura said gently, "Pim, *why* would he be here? Of all places—at this hospital, in the dead of night?"

Pim said, "I just thought he might be. A feeling."

Laura, at a loss, said, "Do you want tea or cocoa? You need something; you look half-frozen."

"Hm?" said Pim. "Oh. Tea, please. No sugar."

In silence, Laura drew off more hot water, set some tea to steeping, added tinned milk. Handed it to Pim, who took a sip. Made a face. Not even tea steeped beyond recognition could mask the taste of chlorine.

Laura gave her a speaking look, handed her the box of sugar cubes, and said, "Pim, that disturbance tonight—the patients have had morphine, they're in pain, they've seen terrible things, they have nightmares. It's not uncommon, in hospitals, for one man to set the others off. Someone had a fit and the others took it badly. Pim, please. It wasn't Faland. Let him go."

What could Pim possibly want from him? Something like she'd got at the Parkeys' séances? Another sight of her son in his mirror? *They pine.* With a shudder, Laura recalled her own glimpse of Freddie.

Pim said, with a sudden wry expression, as though she'd read Laura's thought, "I'll be all right, Laura. I'm not going to pine away. Stop looking so worried. It was foolish of me, I know." Her hand hovered, hesitating, over the box of sugar.

"What is foolish?" said Mary, sailing in with Jones at her back.

"Cavities," said Pim, without missing a beat. She ran her tongue over her teeth.

Jones was looking from Pim to Laura, as though he'd caught the tension between them.

Laura said, "Mrs. Shaw, there is a fine French word that the English adopted, and that word is *triage.*" Pedantically, she added, "From *trier,* to sort. In this case, to prioritize."

"I don't understand."

Mary interjected, "Iven is telling you that teeth are less important than—" She gave Laura an inquiring look.

"Getting through the night," said Laura. It was barely sunrise, and the remains of pneumonia whispered like wings when she breathed. She drained off the sweet dregs of her cocoa and lit a cigarette. Army issue; the tobacco was harsh in her mouth. Pim looked from Laura to her tea, then visibly steeled herself, dropped in three lumps, stirred, and took a sip. Made another face.

"You both look as though you'd been dragged backward through a hedge," observed Mary.

"It comes of lurching off one's sickbed straight into a hospital ward at four in the morning," said Laura. She sounded testy even to her own ears. "I'll be sleek as a bride after breakfast. Which I am going to eat now." She left the sterilization room, disquieted still at the look on Pim's face.

. . .

That afternoon, Laura cornered Mary in her little booth, what must formerly have been the housekeeper's office, where she was going over inventory. Mary didn't look up when Laura came in, but said straight off: "I suppose you're here wanting to know when I'll give you leave to wander the countryside after your lost sibling."

That was, in fact, what Laura wanted to know. "If you please."

Mary put down her pencil. "I did promise I'd let you. But you know how things are, Iven. I'm going to need you. Strong. Well."

Laura just nodded.

Mary asked, "Have you ever ridden a motorcycle?"

Laura blinked. "No."

Mary said, "It's better than hitchhiking round the forbidden zone."

Laura said, "Mendinghem isn't so far. Neither is Pop, for that matter."

Mary said, "Maybe not for a troop of Girl Guides on a fine day. But I don't think either your legs or your lungs would agree. Look, here's what I'll do. Once you're well, I'll start you off riding my motorcycle. Then you'll need a week practicing before I can trust you not to kill yourself. After that I'll give you two days for your searching, but if Fritz attacks while you're out, you come straight back. And if the battle's joined before you go in the first place, well, you stay until things settle back down. Fair?"

Laura thought about it. The motorcycle tempted her. The freedom it implied. The power. To go where the evidence took her, explanations owed to no one. And Mary was right. Once she might have walked, but her leg would hardly take it now. "We'll start tomorrow," Laura said. "I'm in a hurry."

Mary sighed. "All right. If you eat quite a lot and sleep tonight, Iven."

THE MIND IS ITS OWN PLACE

.....

FREDDIE NEVER LEARNED TO DISTINGUISH NIGHT FROM DAY IN Faland's hotel, although he had a vague sense of sleeping in daylight and rousing at dusk, when the music wound its way up the stairs and summoned him. But he was never certain. Day and night had no meaning in a place where all the light came from fires and the outside world was so effectively shut out.

Freddie didn't miss the sun. He kept to the shadows and drank and watched Faland's mirror, lost in longing. It was an endless, daydreamer's longing, satisfying in itself, with no need for fulfillment. The people in the mirror could not disappoint in any way, and he would never fail them, or lose them, or mourn them. It was easier so. He had only to watch and yearn. And tell Faland a story.

Freddie had no idea why Faland wanted to hear them. "Inspiration," he would say, and nothing more. Perhaps it didn't matter what Faland wanted. Stories were a small price to pay for the surcease of night terrors, for the wine, for the silence in Freddie's head that might almost have been taken for peace, so Freddie told him of the time he and Laura were picking beetles off the cabbages in their mother's garden, and decided to play avenging angels, with the beetles as their victims, until Freddie burst into tears and said he hardly thought the beetles deserved eternal damnation for eating cabbage.

He told Faland of the time Silas French got taken with Laura and kept following her home from school trying to carry her books, until she finally got tired of it, opened one of her books, and started reading, in a syrupy voice, about bowel resections, until Silas turned green and went away.

He spoke of the ships they watched from Laura's upper window, how they'd imagine whole stories for them: manifests, and destinations, and secrets, and murders.

It wasn't easy. Often, he hated it. Each memory felt like pins and needles, a deadened limb stirring sluggishly to life. Thoughts he did not want would run through his head: *What would my family think of me?* And, worse, his sweet fairy-tale longing for the dream in Faland's mirror would become a sick sorrow, when he remembered afresh that he had nothing *but* mirror and memory, that his sister was lying in a pine box, under the same earth that he, sometimes, wished he'd never escaped. That Winter had gone to an unknown fate. He'd tell Faland a story—even a lighthearted one—and then press the heels of his hands to his eyes to stop himself feeling, reaching desperately again for forgetfulness.

Faland would pour Freddie a cup in silence, the glittering eye and the lightless one both fixed on his face.

One night, Faland tuned his fiddle as he listened, the instrument laid tenderly across his knee, the murmur of it a background to Freddie's voice when he spoke of the battle royale that took place in their house when Laura got into nursing school, how their father had flatly refused to pay, and how Laura had told him that he didn't have to, that she was going to do scut work in the hospital and pay her own way. And she had. By God, she had.

When he fell silent, the wandering sound of the fiddle seemed, briefly, to take the story up, chords of determination and stubborn pride, more like Laura than the smiling girl in the mirror was.

Freddie turned away from the sound, shaking with regret and

love and sorrow, poured himself a cup, tossed it back quickly, and while he waited for it to work, he blurted, "Why are you here?"

Faland scraped his bow over all the strings at once, and the tune vanished. Freddie was glad it was gone, and wished he'd play it again. "Here?" inquired Faland.

Freddie hardly knew what he was asking. But the thoughts still were trying to crowd his mind, so he opened his mouth instead. "Here. In the war zone. You could keep a hotel anywhere. London. New York. You could play your violin at Carnegie Hall."

Faland's bow drew another shimmering run of notes from the fiddle, something nostalgic that evoked a bright city, far away. "Perhaps. But in New York, they'd pay me in money. Or perhaps in love, or secrets, as men sometimes do. But here—" The violin changed key, seemed to whisper slyly to itself. The firelight sharpened the edges of Faland's face. "Well, here, people will give me anything at all."

"But you don't ask for anything. Just stories."

The violin murmured again, something vaguely familiar this time. Where had he heard that tune? "Yes," Faland said, meditatively. "Just stories."

. . .

The next night, when Freddie was half-asleep in the shadows near the bar, his eye settled dreamily on the people in Faland's mirror, a question occurred to him. He tried to dismiss it. But he could not, so when Faland came to him and waited, Freddie blurted, "What did I tell you last night?"

Faland just looked at him.

"My story," said Freddie. "Last night. I don't remember what I told you."

Faland had poured himself a glass of wine. He sipped it. The subtle lines of laughter deepened round his eyes. "No?"

Freddie cursed his sodden brain. He tried to think back—one night—then the next. And he said, slowly, "And—and the story before that—do you remember what I told you?"

"Yes," said Faland. "I remember everything."

"I don't," Freddie whispered. "I don't remember any of them." His mouth had gone dry.

"Well," said Faland, "you paid with them, didn't you?"

"I— You can't possibly—" But Freddie's eye caught Faland's and he knew abruptly that he *could*. He searched his memory. *How* would he even know what he'd lost? "How many nights?" he whispered. "How many stories have I told you?"

"Do you really want to know?"

"Who are you?"

Faland was leaning on the bar now. "I? A relic in a brave new world. Does it matter? You told me willingly."

Freddie said nothing. He found himself wishing he hadn't realized. He wanted to sink back into torpid peace. His gorge rose.

Faland's hungry gaze seemed to swallow every detail of Freddie's horrified face, before he straightened and said, "Off you go, then." He pointed. "There's the door, go."

But Freddie stood still. *Go?* he wanted to scream. *Go where?* But if he stayed, he'd— Oh, God.

Faland's voice dropped effortlessly, took on an intimacy that made Freddie's whole body quake. "You asked me once why I'm here. Well, I shall ask you. Why are *you* here? Don't you know?"

Freddie's eyes never left Faland's face.

"Because out there you can give up every piece of yourself for nothing, let the mud swallow you, nameless and naked, or you can sell yourself to me, story by story, for all the delights of peace. There are two evils"—his voice turned wry—"and I am the lesser. Besides, where would you go?" The words seemed to drip down Freddie's body, and pierce his heart. "Imagine for a moment that your sister were not dead. Do you think, for even an instant, that she'd be glad to see you?"

Freddie was silent.

"Shall I say it for you?" said Faland. "Deserter. Traitor. Coward. You've already decided. If you go out and they catch you, you won't be honorably dead anymore. You'll be another poor fool who ran.

They'll put you up against the wall in the courtyard of the mairie in Poperinghe, and they'll shoot you."

Freddie didn't say a word.

"And your German," Faland said. "Winter? He tried to warn you, didn't he? Told you to be brave. But you weren't. This world wants nothing of you save your death, Wilfred Iven. Yet I want more. I think you know that too."

Freddie groped for a reply. He'd always had words. He'd been a poet. But now the only thing that came was fragments: "No—I'm not a coward." He couldn't think. He couldn't even move when Faland put out a crooked finger and tilted his head back.

"No?"

Freddie was like a puppet under the other man's fingers. He stood perfectly still. "How can you do these things?" he whispered.

"That is not the question, is it?"

Die, Freddie thought. *Of course it is better to die than to sell my soul, piece by piece.* Then he thought, *Is it?* He realized, to his horror, that his loneliness was trying to answer for him. He had tipped his face into the other's hand, yearning after the mortal warmth in the violinist's palm, and even more, the terrible understanding in his eyes. Faland might ruin him, Freddie thought. But he'd know him first. Out there, Freddie was just a body dressed in drab.

Faland pushed back Freddie's hair, bent lower, and murmured, "Stay then." In his eyes was an endless hunger. "Tell me a story."

Freddie tore free and ran for the door.

· · ·

He didn't know which door, of course. He groped for the nearest, opened it, and ran through. The door opened onto a long corridor, carpeted, with sconces burning low on the walls. The whole way was lined with doors. Freddie ran past them all. He ran until his first blind panic had faded and was replaced by disjointed thoughts. *I have to get out of here. But there's nowhere to go. Better to stay. What does it matter?*

Winter had tried to warn him. Laura wouldn't have wanted this for him. He came to another long hallway, full of doors. He must get out. Was it this door? He tried it. Locked. All the doors were locked. Creeping dread filled him. Take that staircase? Where was he even going?

He looked back, like a child checking that the bogeyman hadn't followed him home.

The drowned man was there. Standing, dripping, in the hallway, his face fish-belly white, blue-lipped. Grinning, endlessly patient. The drowned man would always be there . . .

Freddie bolted again. He ran until his legs seized. Until he caught his foot on nothing and fell and couldn't bring himself to rise. He curled his body into a ball, and waited for the corpse's clammy hand. It was no more than he deserved.

He almost screamed when the touch came down between his shoulder blades. But the hand was warm. Freddie did not move. Tears had dried on his eyelashes.

Faland pulled him to his feet as though he weighed nothing at all. Freddie had the sensation of being borne along by a cold, black river, by a will stronger than his. He still hadn't opened his eyes.

"Tell me a story, Iven," said Faland.

And Freddie, his face buried against Faland's throat, did.

AND LO A BLACK HORSE

·····

CHÂTEAU COUTHOVE, FLANDERS, BELGIUM
MARCH–APRIL 1918

WHEN MARY TOOK LAURA OUT TO THE FIELD BEHIND Couthove to teach her to ride a motorcycle, Laura was determined to learn faster than any woman in history. The news from the south had only worsened—there was talk of the enemy advancing, of lost positions and hurried retreats. Couthove was unsettled, its people straining after news. Laura was eager to be away. Every hour, her window of time felt narrower. She faced Mary over the bony metal conveyance and waited.

Mary leaned on the handlebars, looking raffish. "First off: Have you made a will?"

"Droll, Mrs. Borden."

"All right, all right, get on the seat—yes, like that. Do you know which is the left and right?"

The motorcycle was an awkward thing to bestride, especially in skirts. "Mary, your comic stylings are delightful, but for God's sake . . ."

"I see my sense of humor is wasted on you, Iven. All right. That's the speed lever—make sure it's in neutral, yes, there—unless you want to take off at top speed. Here's the clutch—no, down there, near the front wheel. Shove it in. Good. All right, look now, you spark it, give it some gas. Then put your foot on the crank and push."

On Laura's fifth try, a sound like an explosion rattled from the engine, and the motorcycle sprang forward, bucking. Laura fell off.

"Not the moment for dismounting," said Mary.

"Mary, you—"

"Now try again. Look, once it's going, you push the gear out, throw the speed from neutral to low, *slowly*."

Mary kept Laura at it until she was soaked in nervous sweat. Finally, Mary shook her head, got on herself, pressed the clutch, gave it gas, and ripped off like she was spurring a horse in a hunt. "You'll get it in time," Mary shouted back over her shoulder.

"The sooner the better," said Laura, watching Mary fling up arcs of cold mud. "How do you stop it?"

"Well," called Mary, coming back in a wide circle. "A time-proven method is to pick out a stout tree dead ahead." She laughed at Laura's expression. "A better one is to turn off the spark, throw out the gear, and apply the brakes. Like this. Come on, get up behind me, Iven; you'll see how it feels."

Laura got up, felt the rumble, the nervous tremor of the machine between her knees.

Mary let out the clutch, gave it gas. "Don't let go." They shot off.

Laura shouted. She could feel Mary laughing where Laura gripped her round the waist. "Maniac!" bellowed Laura, but her heart was racing with delight. However much the war had cost, it had paid with this freedom: to run a hospital without interference, to ride a motorcycle without judgment. Strictures belonged to the old world too. Mary whipped round, heading toward the front of the château, and Laura was laughing as well by then, leaning forward.

Then she saw that a horse had come in through the gate and was cantering down the drive. Its rider was tall, white-gloved, straight-backed, like a knight-errant who'd taken a wrong turn. Or yet another refugee from a vanished world. His horse halted neatly at the door, arching its neck.

"What now?" muttered Mary, killing the motor. They left the motorcycle standing and approached their visitor. With surprise, Laura recognized Lieutenant Young, from the party in London. His ears still stuck out, but he was graceful in the saddle as he'd not been on the ground.

"Lieutenant," Mary said, masking any surprise. "What brings you to our door, sir?"

He'd looked a knight on horseback, but he was still awkward once he dismounted. "Mrs. Borden," he said eagerly. "I've news. That concerns this hospital. And, er—" He swallowed. Said, self-consciously, "I've come to visit Mrs. Shaw. She wrote me. Said it was urgent. May I speak to her?"

Mary and Laura looked at each other.

"Did she, sir?" said Mary, recovering her wits first. "I believe she is on duty, but I will have her come to you. What do you have to tell me?"

"Well," said Young, dropping his voice. "There are fears of an attack in the sector."

"Yes," said Mary, with a trace of impatience. As though anyone was unaware.

"And there is a German spy loose," said Young.

That was news.

"He was wounded," Young added. "Got himself taken into hospital. Quite clever actually, the blackguard. When he got better, he slipped away. Certainly bent on mischief. A man with one arm. Speaks English, it seems. There is some fear that he will reach his countrymen with intelligence regarding our strength and positions, before they launch their assault. We are all to keep a close watch for this man."

"What is his name?" said Mary. "What does he look like?"

"Well," said Young, "a fair-haired man, apparently, but so many of them are. They are saying he's called Winter."

• • •

Mary didn't think much of Young's news regarding the German spy, and Laura tended to agree. What could a single spy do, running ragged around the forbidden zone, certain to be captured? A useful spy would be quietly filing paper in Washington, in Whitehall. The whole story smelled like Young's excuse to come and see Pim.

"Well," said Mary judiciously, once she had seen Pim off on a walk round the orchard on the arm of the worshipful Young, "if Pim wants to cultivate that young man and help me keep in good odor with HQ by doing so—Young is Gage's nephew, you know—then she's welcome."

Laura was on fire to know why Pim had written to Young at all. But she had to wait until she could get Pim alone. In the meantime, the hospital, like every place Laura had ever worked, loved a good romance, and rumors were running riot. One of the nurses had crept down quite openly to the orchard to eavesdrop: "I heard him promise to teach her to ride and even shoot a pistol. He told her she'd be the fairest cuirassier in Europe!"

"Who'd want him? Have you ever seen such ears?"

"But rich, they say."

Laura forgot temporarily that she was a new volunteer, and rounded on the gossips. One look at her hard eye, and they fled. But the whole hospital kept talking.

"*Did* you write to Young, Pim?" asked Laura at last. It was evening, and she was sitting on her cot, unlacing her boots. She'd come upstairs and found Pim brushing her hair with exaggerated care. Laura didn't blame her. Soldiers came to the hospital crawling with lice.

"Well, I like him. He's very nice, actually."

"Pim."

"He's going to help me," said Pim. She flushed. "He's— Well, he invited me to dinner. Mary won't stop me going; she wants to be in well with the staff officers. And—I think Young would take me to Faland's hotel. In a car. After dinner. If I asked him."

Pim didn't look at Laura but kept on brushing determinedly.

The thing was, Pim was absolutely right. Anywhere she wanted to go, all she needed was the help of an aristocratic staff officer, nephew of the man in charge of the sector, wholly besotted. But Laura didn't know which was a worse idea: Pim hunting determinedly for Faland, or Pim putting herself in debt to Young.

Laura said, "Are you going to end up married to the poor boy for his pains?"

Pim looked indignant—probably at the insinuation that she could not manage a hapless creature like Young, although she was far too kind to say it aloud.

Laura said, "Pim, it's not a good idea."

"It will be all right," said Pim, going back to brush her hair. "Young's harmless. Means well."

"And Faland?" said Laura. She'd been rolling up her stockings; she stopped and watched her friend narrowly.

Pim said nothing. She laid aside her brush, began plaiting her long hair for the night.

Laura said, "Pim—doing this won't . . ." She hesitated.

Pim turned to face her. "Won't—?"

"Won't bring Jimmy back. Faland isn't going to conjure your son's ghost for you."

Pim stiffened, determined dignity in every line of her face. "If the Parkeys could contact Jimmy, then why not Faland?"

"The Parkeys are a trio of old frauds! They are good, they are kind, but there isn't a veil, there aren't . . . Pim, don't throw yourself on Young's mercy, all to chase a ghost. Don't let Faland do this to you, whoever he is."

Pim didn't fire back. Pim was Victorian to her bootheels, Laura thought, and had no notion of how to get into or out of a proper row. "I—I know your advice is well meant, Laura, but I—" Pim's voice frayed. "I need to see the mirror. I need to ask Faland something."

"Don't, Pim," Laura said. "Let him go." She didn't know if she was talking about Faland or Jimmy.

Pim had finished pinning her hair. She didn't look round when she said, "You're going out on Mary's motorcycle. You're going to look for news of your brother. I'm just looking for—for news in my own way. I'm just like you, Laura. Hoping."

It's not the same. I'm not expecting a miracle, Laura wanted to say. But she didn't. She was a little afraid that she was. And she'd never set herself up as a hypocrite.

. . .

Pim refused to argue again, but Laura could see her mind made up under the softness, stubborn as a stone. So Laura worked and watched and worried and practiced on the motorcycle, until the day came when Mary pronounced her fit to take the machine out into the world.

It was just Laura's luck that the same day, Pim was leaving the château for her dinner with Young.

Laura hated the thought of letting Pim go out alone, with her hope and her scheming, her courage and relentless innocence, and she hated that she might not be there to see to her when she returned. So, short of other ideas, Laura went looking for Jones.

He wasn't on duty. He also wasn't in the wards, or in the sterilization room. Finally Laura slipped out the château's front door and to her surprise found him sitting outside on the cracked marble step. She rarely saw Jones sitting at all. He was a dynamo in surgery, in the main ward. But now he sat, elbows on knees, his face turned up. The weather had warmed steadily, from dripping March to greening April, and the slanting sun heated the stone on the west-facing façade of the château. The grass-grown drive swept elegantly out toward the teeming road; the old orchard, unpruned, showed green on its boughs, backlit by the sun. The western sky was a startling deep rose.

Jones had his sleeves rolled and a cigarette between two fingers, a little raw from endless scrubbing. His forearms were thin, the wristbones sharp. He looked surprised to see her there. "Iven. To what do I owe the privilege? Aren't you going out tomorrow? Shouldn't you be scrounging petrol for Mary's infernal machine, or—" His eye fell on her face and he stopped. "What?" he said, sharper. "Is it one of the patients?" He was on his feet, the languor gone, the cigarette burning unheeded.

"No," said Laura, already wondering why she'd gone to him at all. "Not a patient."

He frowned. "All right." He fished in his pocket and held out a cigarette case. Rather a nice one. Silver, monogrammed. Laura took a cigarette, accepted his light.

Jones sat back down. After a moment, she sat beside him. "Well?" said Jones, taking a drag on the cigarette. He turned his head, considering her. "Tell me what's troubling you."

Laura didn't know why exactly she'd sought him out. Perhaps because Mary was too ruthless to confide in. Perhaps it was the memory of his face, intent over Trovato's transfusion, his quick sideways smile. Or an even deeper memory, of waking up to the smell of disinfectant, his irascible voice crisp even through the fog of her fever.

She exhaled smoke. "I'm worried about Pim."

"If you're being prudish because she's going out tomorrow with that boy—"

"I'm not," said Laura, sharp, and Jones fell silent.

After a moment, he said, "This father confessor business is damned hard work. All right, why are you worried for your friend?" The strong sun reddened his brown hair.

Laura pressed two fingers between her eyes, not sure how to answer. The smell of spring earth mingled with the disinfectant smell of the hospital.

"Iven," Jones said, "just today, one of the patients was swearing Mrs. Shaw had the face of someone who'd seen the fiddler. Is that it?"

Laura's hand jerked. Ash dropped from the end of her cigarette. "What does that mean?"

Jones looked taken aback. "How the devil should I know? Puny, I suppose. Like she's about to shuffle off this mortal coil. Soldiers are a lot of superstitious bastards. I should like to meet this fiddler person; he's got them all on the jump."

Laura took another drag on her cigarette, to steady herself. "I thought you were a man of science, Doctor. Don't tell me you believe there's a man out there with a magic violin." Gooseflesh rose on her arms.

"Don't *science* me, Iven. Magic's just science we don't understand. What if a man a thousand years ago saw one of the flying contraptions that we have winking about everywhere? He'd think it was magic. And you diverted me—well done. Why are you worried about Mrs. Shaw?"

Laura relented and told him. From the night the lorry was wrecked, to her conversation with Pim upstairs. The only thing she left out was her sight of Freddie in Faland's hotel.

Jones kept silent while she talked, and smoked another cigarette. When she was done, he gave a low whistle. "Sly, Iven, not saying a word. You really did meet the fiddler."

"A mesmerist with drugged wine. But Pim wants to be swindled. She wants to believe. She wants to find him again."

"And so she's going about with Young so he'll help her look," Jones finished for her. "That boy is probably delighted at the chance. If she's not the prettiest woman in Flanders, she's damned close."

Laura jerked a nod.

"However," Jones added, "I don't know what you can do. Her choices are her own, so long as she does her duty by the hospital. Lot of letters she's writing, does the men a world of good."

"Will you keep an eye on her?" said Laura. "I'll be gone tomorrow and I won't be here to—"

"See her off? Welcome her back? So it's not just a father confessor you wanted? Yes, all right, I'll look after her if she needs it, but I still don't know what I or you or anyone can do. Perhaps Young will think she owes him for this, and try to collect, but she knows that. She's not blind, for all that blinding innocence. You're a mother hen, Iven."

Laura was silent, acknowledging.

Jones fixed her with a look. "Not to mention that you're going off on your own quest, aren't you, never mind your pneumonia, and all my careful nursing. Shouldn't *you* be more worried about what you're getting into? Setting off on a motorcycle with battle on the horizon?"

"I can take care of myself."

A muscle ticked once in his jaw. "Mary said that your people died when that ship exploded. That you're an orphan."

She tapped ash from the end of her cigarette. "The world is full of orphans, Doctor."

"No doubt," said Jones. "Iven, what do you mean to do?"

Could he not leave anything alone? Could he not stop looking at her in that steady way, taking in the marks of stress etched on her face, the stiffened scars on her hands? She said, "I am going to take Mary's motorcycle and go on leave."

"No—I mean once you solve your mystery. Are you going to stay at Couthove until your leg gives out? Or go back to Halifax?"

Jones could talk, Laura thought. He'd go home after the war, patent his technique for transfusion, marry a rich girl with perfect hands, and be invited to give lectures. While she . . .

"You've no notion, have you?" said Jones. "Not a one. And yet you're down on Mrs. Shaw for being reckless."

Why was she angry? He wasn't wrong. "Yes."

To her surprise, he did not make suggestions, or bluster, or tell her she was being defeatist, or hypocritical, or anything else. He just nodded, pulled a flask, drank, handed it to her. Brandy. She took a healthy swallow.

"I'm buying cheaper liquor if you're going to drink it like that," he said.

She huffed a laugh and took a more delicate sip, rolling it round her mouth, relishing the burn. "Better?"

"Much." His eyes still lingered on her face. Then he snatched the flask from her fingers, took the weight. "Christ, Iven, you're a lush." He drank again himself.

Laura didn't say anything. The brandy had been good. She felt, not unpleasantly, as though she were floating.

"Why not go to Borden?" Jones asked abruptly. "If you needed someone to keep an eye on Mrs. Shaw?"

"Because Mary won't care if Pim is hurt, not really. Her hospital is the only thing she sees." Laura hesitated. "I thought you might be different."

His smile was crooked. "Trust me, Iven?" he said.

She found her mouth quirking in answer. "I think I do, God help me. Now pass that brandy."

A SLOW AND SILENT STREAM

·····

FREDDIE AWOKE IN BED, AND BEFORE HE EVEN OPENED HIS eyes, he was clawing, frantic, through his memory. He didn't even know what he'd lost, but he could feel the absence. A dry-socket ache. He felt—smaller—somehow.

The violin was playing, tormenting his ear with strange familiarity, calling to him as it always did. He found himself putting on his crumpled pieces of uniform, walking to his door.

No, he thought, with a flare of rebellion. That night he was going to explore the hotel. Behave like a man, not a ghost. Decide, logically, what he ought to do.

When he stepped into the corridor, he went the opposite direction, as though fleeing the sound.

The corridor was just as it had always been: dim, soft, dusty. The doors were set a little too close together, so that you imagined strange rooms on the other side. Prison cells maybe. But when Freddie put his hand on the nearest handle and tried to turn it, the door was still locked.

He tried another. Door after door. All locked.

He began to walk faster. Kept trying doors. The corridor never *changed.* It was the same length, the same carpet, the same deceptive light. Even the same violin, taunting him with things he could not remember, a sound he could not escape. Even when he put his hands over his ears the melody sounded, endlessly, in his head. Finally he stumbled, gasping, through an archway and found himself back in the foyer. Felt the place as a trap instead of a refuge: a luxurious version of the pillbox. He found himself longing to hear Winter breathe.

It took Freddie a moment to pick out Faland. He was across the room, his back turned. Freddie's first emotion at the sight of him was relief. As though familiarity were stronger than any reflexive horror. He tried to claw his anger back. He needed the courage. *He's going to turn round, and I'm going to ask him again which one is the door outside. And he's going to tell me, and I'm going to go. I'm no puppet.*

But Faland didn't turn.

Freddie's skin prickled. Faland was facing the grand mirror over the bar. He had put down his violin. He wasn't laughing or talking or pouring wine. Freddie found himself stealing toward him. The room was packed, but Faland was all alone in his corner of it. Freddie came up behind him. He didn't see Winter and Laura in the mirror. He didn't see anything he understood at all.

The mirror flickered with images. A throne. A dead forest, a red-laced sky. A city shining gold like the peeling gilt of the hotel and a light that made Freddie want to sob . . .

Faland turned. Freddie tore his gaze from the mirror. Faland snatched up a bottle of wine and drank, throat working as he swallowed. "Come to pay up, Iven?"

"What do you see?" whispered Freddie. "In the mirror—what is it? What do you want?"

Faland put the bottle down. "Oh, no. No, I never promised *you* stories. I don't have any you'd care to hear, anyway. They'd freeze your blood. No, tell me a tale, Iven, I'm waiting." His hand had fallen on the violin case; his fingers flexed. His face was flushed with wine, his eyes glassy with it.

"Why?" said Freddie. He'd had noble visions of standing before

Faland in defiance, demanding his freedom. But what he said was, "I'd work for my keep or—or anything. You can't just—just take my—you have no right!"

Faland said, bitter as aloes, "It's the pattern of the times. Were you expecting honest justice? There's none. It's a new world now. It eats you up, sinners and saints, all alike."

"Tell me who you are."

"You know," said Faland. "Or you think you do. But you don't. No one's the same now. Not even I."

"You lied when you said it's my choice to leave. I couldn't. All the doors were locked."

Faland drank again. "You didn't really want to go. You still don't. You think you can best me, and you know there's no victory to be had outside."

The mirror was dark now. Faland had nearly finished the bottle. He wiped his mouth with the back of his hand. In his face, in that light, was the shadow of a terrible beauty, timeworn like his hotel. The light silvered his hair. Freddie, with clairvoyance borne of despair, recognized Faland's expression. With slow surprise he said, "You hate this place, don't you? You hate everything. You hate the war as much as I do."

Faland drew the cork on a new bottle and raised it in toast. "Yes, I hate it, clever boy. It's a hell with no master, that men made themselves." He drank. "Of course I hate it."

Freddie whispered, "But can't *you* leave?"

Faland set the bottle aside, *thump*, on the bar. His voice dropped confidingly. "Oh, yes. But do you know the worst of it, Iven? I love it too. Have you been thinking me a poor victim, just like you? No. Do you know what men do here? They turn to me. They choose me. They say *Better you than that*. Over and over they choose me." Avarice now as well as despair in Faland's eyes. "They hand their souls to me. As you did. That's why I'm here. Because I cannot bring myself to go."

Freddie's throat had tightened with shrinking horror, and the worst of it was he still hovered halfway between recoiling and yielding. The glitter of Faland's lighter eye was frightening in his flushed face. His voice dropped. "But, you know, you've only ever told me things you want to remember. You could tell me things you want to forget."

Freddie's throat closed. Faland waited.

There weren't words for some memories. The very language he'd learned in his boyhood did not feel equal to describing some memories. They were better off left wordless. Formless, hidden. Forgotten.

Forgotten . . . He looked at Faland with sudden hunger. *You could tell me things you want to forget.*

Of course, to do that, first he had to remember.

"It's not all bad, is it, Iven?" said Faland softly.

Freddie stood caught between conflicting impulses. He thought Faland knew it, and savored his distress. His gut knotted in fear. He was yielding, he was glad to yield, and he was so afraid. "Please," he whispered, but he didn't know what he was asking for.

Faland just watched him. No mercy at all in that face, but who needed mercy when someone looked at you like that, like he understood every thought that passed through your mind? Like he would know every nuance of your soul before he devoured it?

Freddie bowed his head. He thought a moment. "It was raining in billets, when the order to advance came and we . . ."

. . .

He told Faland everything he could remember of that advance on the Ridge, and every word hurt. The formless days that had lain like bitter fog in the back of his mind must be given phrases, given color and shape and hours and minutes. Conjured there, in the flickering dimness of the hotel: *This happened, and that and that.* No euphemism would satisfy Faland, no barrier, however small, between experience, mind, and voice.

The words dragged him back, made him live it all again, caught helplessly in his own mind until he was sweating and sick and gasping, as though mud and gas and rain could be embodied from memory. The tale took him all the way to the pillbox. "And then it was dark," Freddie said, gasping for air.

"And then?" said Faland, gently.

Tell him everything, Freddie thought. *And forget it ever happened.* He'd never again wake up choking, afraid of the dark. He'd never remember why he *ought* to be afraid.

But Winter had been there in the dark. There was no way to separate the horror from the memory of Winter's voice, his courage. He could not bring himself to let that memory go. It seemed wrong, disrespectful to the thing they'd shared, to let it go.

"I told you a story," said Freddie.

. . .

The next time Freddie woke, his hours on the Ridge were gone. He remembered getting their orders, then nothing before the pillbox. He felt lighter, but also unsteady. As though he'd chopped off a diseased section of limb, and now there was no limb at all, some essential balance lost.

I should tell the rest. About the pillbox, and escaping, and the shell hole, he thought. *Why keep it? It's not as though I'll ever see Winter again.*

However, that night, he told Faland of the dead man in the breastworks near Arras, whose hand they shook for luck as they went up.

One night followed another, and each night, Freddie flung his worst memories at Faland: bad days in trenches, mates in hospital, the day he told his mother he was enlisting and she sobbed on his shoulder. But he didn't tell Faland of the pillbox. He didn't say a word about Winter.

Faland listened, as always, in silence.

Then, in one of the unmarked hours, when the hotel was hushed and somber, Freddie's candle went out and he woke again in the dark, screaming Winter's name.

Only silence answered. Silence, and then a voice. But not the one he longed for.

"Why keep it so close?" said Faland in his ear, silky. He hadn't come with a light this time. He sat on the edge of Freddie's bed, smelling of wine and rosin and old flowers, reached out as though he could see in the dark, slid a hand over Freddie's hair, took hold of the back of his neck. Freddie bowed his head, hating the way he turned helplessly to the warmth.

"Tell me what you remember," said Faland. "Tell me of the dark, and yourself, and that German. That's what I want to know. That's what I've always wanted to know."

Freddie didn't speak. He'd never see Winter again. What good was memory? But he didn't speak. He held his silence and held it until finally Faland got up and left, taking the candle with him.

AND TO THE WOMAN WERE GIVEN TWO WINGS

·····

MENDINGHEM CASUALTY CLEARING STATION,
FLANDERS, BELGIUM
APRIL 1918

IN HER YEARS IN FIELD HOSPITALS HEAD SISTER KATE WHITE had been Laura's mentor and her friend. Kate knew everyone, every medic, every nurse, every orderly in the back area. If anyone, at any hospital, had seen Wilfred Iven, treated Wilfred Iven, buried Wilfred Iven, Kate could find out.

Chaos found Laura quickly, on the road running northwest from Couthove. It was thick with mules and munitions and marching men. Bicycles, motorbikes, high-booted officers on horseback. She felt the percussion of the guns in the bones of her face as she threw herself into traffic, weaving doggedly. By the time she got to Mendinghem, her headache was a spike, right between the eyes, from the fierce concentration it took to ride the motorcycle. She threw the gear out and killed the motor, left it by the gate, and walked in.

Like all casualty clearing stations, it was a collection of sheds and long tents, sharply familiar even though she'd never served in this one. Stretchers everywhere, men being moved, nurses with syringes. And then a familiar figure appeared between two tents, her eyes lit in welcome.

Laura's first sight of the forbidden zone had come in '15, when she was sent up the line to her first CCS. Head Sister White had met her at the train station in Poperinghe. Beatrice Hoppel, who'd got off the train with her, had whispered, awed, "There she is. She was in South Africa, I heard. A *legend*."

Laura had watched Kate White cross the main square. She'd expected austerity, a proud bearing. Iron-gray hair, perhaps, and the disposition of a mother superior. Nursing had a nunnish history, after all.

Laura had *not* expected a stout, cheerful, pink-cheeked woman, with broken blood vessels about her nose, and eyes that missed nothing. "Welcome to Pop," she'd said, "where the ratio of men to women is something in the nature of a hundred thousand to one. I warn you now that all hundred thousand of them, give or take, would like to bring you to bed."

Beatrice gave an indignant huff. There was a sly warmth to Kate's clever gaze, as it swung between them.

"How unfortunate for them," said Laura, and Kate laughed.

Bea didn't stick it; she married a flier six months later and he widowed her, pregnant, three months after that. But Laura and Kate found kinship. It was Kate's voice that had berated them all to keep going the first time they got gas casualties, with orderlies turning away in fear, nurses weeping as they worked, boys choking as they died, on and on until she collapsed. Then Laura had taken charge of the wards, organized the nursing, seventy-two hours without sleep. It was Kate who had stood shoulder to shoulder with Laura for their first mustard gas cases, when they'd discovered together that the gas lingered in men's clothes, on their skin and hair, burning the nurses' eyes and palms and lungs.

It was Kate's voice that had snarled at Laura to hold on, with her leg drenched in blood.

It was Kate now, crossing the space between them, older than on that square in Poperinghe back in '15, the lines carved more starkly around her eyes. But those eyes were the same.

Heads were turning and Laura recognized some of them. Word went round, *Iven, that's Laura Iven,* and then the staff were coming up to her, eager, while questions like whizz-bangs came at her from all sides: *you're alive, where'd you come from, how's the leg, we heard about Halifax, why'd you come back.* Laura was smiling with helpless pleasure.

"Christ," she said, when she could speak. "I'm glad to see you. But this war's on the brink, that's certain—half the British Isles are out there going up the line. And here you all are shirking."

That prompted a chorus of laughter, then Kate's incisive voice cut in. "Off you go, all of you. Iven's alive, and working with that strange lot at Couthove, and you may pester her when we are not about to be overrun. Off you go."

They scattered, with backward glances.

Laura said, "Overrun?"

"Lord, yes," said Kate, the smile fading. "They've been evacuating field hospitals down south, and leaving behind the men who can't be moved. It'll be us next. They're even saying we're going to withdraw from the Ridge, as it's indefensible." She shook her head.

"Withdraw from the Ridge?" demanded Laura. "That how many men died taking? What was it all for if they're just going to—" She swallowed the rest.

Kate looked startled at her vehemence. "Don't think that way, Iven, you'll run mad. Come. I'd take you to supper if I could, but I only have half an hour, I'm afraid. Although it's poor hospitality for your pains." She cast an assessing eye on Laura's gait. "Healed all right, did you?"

"Never mind my leg," said Laura.

Kate passed into the sterilization marquee. "No? A blighty wound, back home with honors, and now you're here again?"

Laura must have been silent an instant too long. Or perhaps something showed on her face. Kate knew her very well. "Oh—Christ—we saw about Halifax in the papers. But you didn't say anything in your letters. Did—" Kate read the answer on Laura's face. She looked older suddenly. "Laura, your people, did they—"

Laura said with a dryness she did not feel, "Pitiful, I know, but you will perhaps understand now why I am so very interested in the fate of my brother."

"Laura, I—" Kate read Laura's face again, and shut her mouth. "As you say. But—" She fell silent, frowning.

Laura went to get tea, and take a moment to collect herself. She found the tea-things without trouble, added sugar and tinned milk, brought the two cups back. Then she sat and without preamble said, "I got a telegram in Halifax, from the Red Cross. It said Freddie was missing, presumed dead. But if he's missing, then they can't have sent his things along, could they? And they did. I have his tags. Both of them." Laura pulled them out from where she wore them strung around her neck. "I couldn't make sense of it. So I came back."

Something moved through Kate's eyes, like a flicker of recognition.

"Kate," said Laura.

Kate said, "I didn't think you'd come back. I didn't dare say anything in a letter. And now that you're here, I *still* don't—" She stopped, began again. "It happened just after you were wounded, after they took you away. It was such chaos, that day."

Laura grew very aware of her pulse, beating at neck and wrists. "I remember."

Her friend's expression was reluctant. "I—don't want to put you in danger."

Laura's only answer was a disbelieving snort.

Kate looked angry. "Yes, I know you don't care, you daft girl. But you're running reckless as a man on a trench raid. Do you think I can't see it?"

"Surely that's my own business."

"It's mine too. And every other person's who loves you, prickly wretch. Do you think I want to tell you something that makes you go charging off, get yourself arrested, or killed?"

Laura stared. "All that? Kate, tell me."

Kate said, "You were gone." She sounded almost incensed, that Laura had got herself injured. Laura could understand. The worst night of all their lives, and Kate's indefatigable deputy, her ward sister, had been gone. Just like that. "It couldn't have been more than a day or two after we'd sent you off to base hospital. I could hardly tell which way was up by then, or what I said to whom. I didn't think you'd live. I grieved. I was so tired. And I can't remember things properly anymore." She shook her head. "But I remember that a young man came into the hospital. He was so dirty, like all the men off the Ridge. And he'd that look about him, shell-shocked."

Laura knew that look well. Glassy-eyed, the thousand-yard stare.

"But he wasn't wounded," said Kate slowly. "He was—he was strange. Honestly, I wasn't even sure, afterward, that he wasn't a ghost. He asked about you. I don't remember what I answered. 'She's gone,' I think I said. And I told him to wait. There were fifteen emergencies on my hands, and I went to deal with the worst of them. When I happened back, he was still there. He told me there was a man, a German prisoner, wounded, whom he'd found carrying the jacket and the tags of a Wilfred Iven."

Laura hardly dared to move, lest she interrupt.

"Of course, for your sake, I went to see. The German was delirious, nearly dead of exhaustion, had a wound in his shoulder gone bad. But he did have your brother's jacket. Was clutching it to himself, with the tags in his hand. I asked him what had happened to the owner of the jacket, but he was too far gone in fever to hear me. So, I had him brought in at once, and broke a hundred rules to get him a bed, and to get his arm off in time . . . I was thinking of you, how you'd loved your brother, and that if you lived, you'd want to know what happened to him. And that the German might be the only one that knew."

"What happened to the other soldier—the one who came and got you?" asked Laura. "What did he look like?"

"I could hardly tell, with the night and the rain and the dirt. I never got his name. He vanished. Duty done. Maybe the German saved him, and he was trying to do right by him."

"Did he live? The German?"

"Oh, yes. Had his arm off at the shoulder joint. I kept him with me; he was at death's door with fever for—weeks? More? But he lived."

"Did he say how he came to have Freddie's things?"

"He hardly talked at all, at first. His eyes were— He had that look they get after combat—looked straight through you. But I did my best for him, made a point of doing his dressings myself. He came through his fever eventually. Was it Christmas? After? We'd had the news from Halifax by then, so after. January perhaps. Up until then, he'd only spoken in his fever, and that only in German. One of the nurses had a little German, she said he must be some odd form of Protestant, he spoke so much of the devil."

"Never mind that. What did he know? Where is he now?" There was something strange in her friend's face. "What, Kate?"

Kate said, "He ran."

One arm. Young said their spy . . . Oh, surely not. "Did they catch him?"

"No, they haven't."

"What did the German know about Freddie?"

Her friend hesitated. "I asked him about Freddie. Again and again. For a long time he wouldn't answer. But finally one night, he told me that he and your brother had been trapped in an overturned pillbox, that they'd clawed their way out together. But your brother died in a shell hole, he said, and he took Freddie's things away with him. And after that, the German said, he had been taken prisoner."

Well, that explained it all. The arrival of the box, the mixed messages. Laura had built it up in her mind into some unknowable mystery and all along it was . . . She burst out, "Why in God's name did you send me cryptic letters, then? Why not just tell me? I'd not have come if . . ." She shouldn't have come. She had told herself she didn't hope that Freddie was alive, so why did it hurt so much?

Kate said, "No, of course— I'd never . . . Laura, the German said something else."

"What did he say?"

"It was late. I'm not sure he knew it was me. He'd had morphine. I was changing his dressing, he was still in a good deal of pain. He was speaking German, and the good lord knows I've picked up enough of it, nursing prisoners. The German said, *He's not dead.*

"And I said, *Who?*"

"*Iven*, he said. *I promised him.*

"*Promised him what?* I asked.

"*That I'd save him*, he said. *I promised.* He didn't say anything else. In the morning, I convinced myself it was all delirium. But— then—a few weeks later, once the German had more strength, he ran."

"That's all?" Laura saw the answer on her friend's face. "You believed him, didn't you? You believed that German. You think he lied the first time, when he said Freddie died in a shell hole."

"It's so hard to know what to believe sometimes," said Kate. "Even when you see something with your own eyes, or hear it with your own ears, you think, well, I was mortally tired, or I'd had a few at dinner. A man once told me, in great earnest, how he saw his brother, dead three years, in his dugout, leading him away just before the heavy came down. *Ghosts have warm hands*, he kept telling me, as though it were the greatest secret in the world. I remember nodding like a ninny. Still, now, whenever I touch a man's cold fingers, I catch myself thinking, *Well, he's not a ghost yet.*" Kate spread her hands. "So yes, Laura. Somehow, I believed him. The German lived. He healed. He ran. They're still searching for him. They haven't found him. And, rightly or wrongly, I think he left the hospital to go and look for Wilfred Iven, whom he believed was alive." She paused. "He might have been a madman. But I've seen enough madmen, out here. And I—I don't think he was. There was something in his face."

"What did he look like?"

"The German? A fine-looking man," said Kate. "Pale blue eyes. Crisp, you know. Intelligent. A little older—mid-thirties, I'd say. Polite."

"And one arm," said Laura. "Do you remember his name?"

Kate sighed. "Winter. He was called Winter."

. . .

Poperinghe had gone to seed: a town of prosperous burghers turned gimcrack, where the only industries had necessarily to do with war or the entertaining of soldiers. Cafés and bars abounded, and souvenir shops, and brothels.

But it had a life, did Poperinghe. The main square teemed with men, talking and milling, drinking and laughing. Pop was as good as Paris, the soldiers said. Shell-scarred, but alive. You could get a drink there. Take a room and sleep in a bed. Not like Ypres to the east, which was fit for no one but ghosts.

After she left Mendinghem, Laura took the motorcycle to Pop. She'd arranged to meet Freddie's officer, a man called Whiting, over an early supper. She arrived covered in spring mud and nervous sweat, but she'd managed to preserve herself and everyone around her despite the motorcycle's best efforts.

She didn't know what to make of Kate's story, and she didn't yet have time to think about it.

Whiting was the lean, lantern-jawed sort, with the slightly blank stare, fixed in the middle distance, that many men acquired after combat, and a touch of neurasthenia: a tremor in his hands. He also had a vile cold, but there was hardly a man serving who didn't. He ordered some of the one-franc wine for them both and drank his off fast.

"Your brother died quick, Miss Iven," said Whiting straight off. "No pain." He sneezed. He wore an expression of wary forbearance: a man doing his duty by a dead comrade. He probably was expecting tears and pleading.

Laura put down her glass. "I am not here to cry on your shoulder, sir. I simply wish to know, in as much detail as you can, what happened to my brother." She left her hand flat on the tabletop.

His eye wandered to it, back to her face. "Better not to know, Sister," he said.

In an even voice, Laura replied, "Nothing you have to tell me is worse than what I have imagined, sir."

Whiting visibly steeled himself. In a new voice, quite toneless, he said, "It was raining. We were ordered to take the Passchendaele Ridge. Bad ground—I've never seen worse. Mud hip-deep, and Fritz well dug in—pillboxes and machine gun nests."

Laura knew it was an ugly thing she was doing, making him re-live it. But she didn't ask him to stop.

"There was a pillbox, had us in its sights. Machine gun inside, clawing us bad. We had to take it. Your brother—I ven—he charged, with a grenade. Brave lad. I didn't see what happened, exactly. The light was bad, it was pouring so you couldn't tell earth from air, with the mud so thick. I don't know if his grenade went off, because right as he hit the doorway, a heavy hit the pillbox. It—it flipped. Happens sometimes, especially with the ones Fritz put up too quick."

"Flipped, sir?" said Laura.

Whiting looked reluctant. "Yes—unlucky—turned door-down, don't you know. No way out but the door and the concrete's thicker than three men standing. Anyone in there—they weren't coming out."

Kate said the German was trapped with my brother in a pillbox. But he said they got out. "And my brother was in there."

"Yes, ma'am," said Whiting. "But don't worry. I'm sure he was dead before it went over."

"And if he wasn't?"

Whiting looked down into his glass, with an expression of steady remote pity. "Well," he said. "He's dead now, ma'am." He dashed some cognac into his empty wine glass and took a hearty swig. "He was a brave boy. Lot of brave boys gone that day. A damned shame. A damned shame."

"Yes," said Laura, in a voice strange even to her own ears. "Thank you for telling me."

Whiting hesitated. "There was one more thing. I wouldn't have mentioned it, but you're a sensible woman, that's plain, and you won't read much into it, except to know that he's not forgotten among us."

Laura wasn't feeling remotely sensible just then.

Whiting said, "Bowles, my servant, he says he saw Iven's ghost."

Laura wanted several more drinks. "Did he? Where?"

"At dinner in GHQ. It was quite an occasion. Christmas. They even had a goose. I was pals with one of the boys on the staff, that's why they invited me. They'd hired a violinist—Christ, he was good, I remember, servants blubbering like babies in the corners—anyway, Bowles was helping with the serving, and he's just at the window, with the soup tureen, and he goes white as a sheet and drops it. And when I ask him what the devil's the matter, he says he's just seen Iven's ghost."

Laura had no notion what to say. "What was . . . the ghost . . . doing?" she asked, after a pause.

Whiting looked troubled. "Just staring. Staring in the window."

Not sure she was joking, Laura said, "Seems a long way for a ghost to come—down off the Ridge—just to haunt headquarters."

"Those bastards, carving their goose, congratulating each other on a good season of campaigning," said Whiting with abrupt, concentrated venom. "I hope he haunts them all." He poured himself more white wine, drank it fast again. Ducking his head he added, in his ordinary voice, "Apologies, Sister. That's all I can tell you."

"Thank you, then," Laura said. She left the café soon after. She could see from Whiting's face that he was eager to get down to some hard, steady drinking, and that he didn't want her around for it.

THE LOST ARCHANGEL

·····

FALAND'S HOTEL, PARTS UNKNOWN,

FLANDERS, BELGIUM

WINTER OF 1917–1918

WHEN FREDDIE CAME DOWNSTAIRS AGAIN, DULL FROM nightmares, there were no people in the hotel. The foyer was empty but for Faland, who sat on an overturned ammunition crate, violin laid across his knee. He was dragging bow across strings, frowning, and the half-formed melody that filled the room was jagged in a way that made Freddie flinch. "Will you tell me what you hate, Iven?" asked Faland, not looking up, although the melody had trailed away to nothing. He stared thoughtfully down at the instrument in his hands. His voice was gentle.

"Not yet," said Freddie. He was groping for a bottle. "I can't tell a story yet."

"Just answer the question."

"Why?"

Faland raised his eyes from the violin. "Call it curiosity."

Freddie cursed himself that he could not keep silent when Faland looked at him like that. "Everyone. Everyone who put me and Winter on the Ridge, who put Laura at Brandhoek. All the men with clean hands, hanging back in headquarters, making plans with our lives."

"What would you tell them, if you could?"

He felt like a mouse with an owl stooping. "I said not yet!"

"No? But aren't you curious why I want these stories of yours?"

Wild answers ran through Freddie's head, fit for the poet he'd been: *You eat them. You hoard them like jewels. You want them because you've no soul of your own . . .*

"Why?" he said.

"Would you like me to show you?"

When had he come near? Freddie could smell wine and rosin and flowers past their best. He didn't look up, half-afraid he was looking for any reason to trust Faland again, that he would be glad when Faland found another chink in his brittle armor. "All right."

Faland took up his violin case and went quite prosaically to a door. This door looked no different from the others, but when Faland pulled it open a gust of frigid air blew in and Freddie saw darkness and stars, and the world outside. It was night. He hadn't known that. He hadn't realized how musty the hotel was, how close, until he smelled the night air, and felt a stray snowflake on his cheek. He stood arrested, wanting to gulp the air down, and also to beg Faland to shut the door, and lock it against everything.

"Come," said Faland, and added, when he saw Freddie hesitate, "Afraid I'll abandon you to the wilderness? Not tonight. Come."

. . .

Freddie remembered nothing of the walk but the uneven beat of Faland's step, although he dreamed afterward, sometimes, that he walked past a lake of red embers. But when Faland stopped walking, Freddie found they were standing in the shadow of a building that hummed like Halifax Harbour in July. Electric lights dazzled him after so long with only firelight. Faland said, his lip curling, "Recognize it?"

Freddie had never been there. But it was unmistakable. "General Headquarters," he said. "But it's—that's *miles* to the south."

Faland didn't answer. Freddie fell silent, staring. GHQ wasn't just a château, it was a whole village of trim buildings, standing clean against the stars. There was no smell of death. Just petrol, and earth, and food cooking. Freddie had forgotten that buildings could be grand, or bright, or well kept. Even Faland's hotel, for all its magnificence, had an air of relentless decay. He thought he saw silver gleaming behind a bright window, a table laid.

Faland said, "Go stand under that window. You'll understand."

"I'll be seen."

"So? It's Christmas." Faland bared his teeth a little. "When poor ghosts walk the earth. What do you think you are?" A light snow was falling by then, muffling the world in white.

"I'm alive," said Freddie. Sometimes he wasn't sure. "What are you going to do?"

Faland didn't answer. But then, Freddie suspected that Faland liked drama the way he liked wine. Faland just strode across the ground, knocked on the front door, and was admitted.

Freddie thought about walking away. He knew where he was. He could find civilian clothes, maybe, and then—what? He imagined having to face himself, in a world that felt real, and could not. He took one step, another, found that he had turned, not through the gate, but toward the window, keeping to the shadows. He peered inside.

They were preparing to serve dinner. There was cutlery. White cloth. Jellies in crystal. When had he last been hungry? This elegant table could not be further from the last Christmas he'd had, with the rain thundering down and a stale cake, shared out, that someone had got from home.

Officers, already flushed with drink, began to stream in. He recognized a few. Others, in American uniforms, he did not. The regular serving officers, their clothes less than pristine, could be picked out by their faces, something rigid and remote in their expressions, the claw mark of the trenches. They spoke little and applied themselves at once to their food.

But the general staff, the men who did not go up the line, started up an instant tumult of conversation. Jokes, snatches of news, a toast to victory. Freddie realized he was biting his lip bloody. There was no malice in them but a fatal, all-encompassing ignorance. *They're fighting their war in the last world, but we're dying in this one.*

Faland appeared in the doorway.

Heads turned. In his anger, Freddie waited eagerly to see what Faland would do. No blithe ignorance, Freddie was sure, could survive under Faland's gaze, and Faland could be cruel. Didn't Freddie have cause to know it? Faland bowed to the room, said something, smiling. The officers looked at one another.

Hurt them, Freddie found himself thinking.

Faland put his violin to his shoulder, and began to play.

The music curled out, into the room, into the night. Talk died away as the sound built slowly. Almost sweetly. Freddie was disgusted. *No,* he thought. *Not here. Not tonight. How dare you play them something beautiful . . .*

And then, as though Faland had heard him, the music turned savage. Sweetness became fury, became shattering loss. Freddie had never heard the tune in his life, but somehow he knew every note.

Then Freddie understood. The music, its familiarity, the reason it hurt to hear. It was *himself.* His loves, his flaws, the way his world had ended. His deep, ruinous anger. His memories weren't gone. They were there, in Faland's moving hands, at his service. In that moment, Freddie understood Faland's power at last; he'd shared it once. It was the poet's alchemy, to seize the intangible or unspeakable and drag it, real, into the living world. But in Faland's hands the gift was monstrous. The very silver on the tablecloth rattled with the force of Freddie's anguish. It felt like a threat. It felt like magic, a cry of defiance, the voice of his soul, in a world that did not care if he had one. But the music diminished him too, flattened him to a scream in an endless wilderness. There was no place in Faland's rendering for Laura's laughter, or Winter's eyes. There was only wrath. As he listened, Freddie began to be afraid. Began to wonder if he really was nothing more than the furious cry of Faland's violin.

Yet alongside his fear, he was savagely joyful. Because the keening note of his agony was piercing the diners' soul-deep ignorance. Freddie saw restless movement, clenching fists, darting eyes. The war was *there*, all around them: the rain, the dark, the hunger, the thirst. The dying. Things that didn't have proper words, but the violin didn't need words. It howled. Freddie's soul wasn't gone, but it had shrunk to raw pain, distilled to power in another person's grasp. Freddie had forgotten he was anything but the scream of the violin. He felt himself teetering on the edge of madness, but he didn't mind. He thought the men at the table might be doing the same. *Stop*, he thought to Faland. Then, *Don't stop*.

A sudden crash rattled the window.

The spell of the music shattered, and Freddie leapt instinctively for the cover of the rhododendrons. But it was too late: A man was standing next to the window, eyes perfectly round. It was Bowles, his commanding officer's servant. He was staring at Freddie.

Freddie forced himself to stillness, did the only thing he could think of. *When poor ghosts walk the earth* . . . Like a man gone beyond guilt, Freddie raised a hand in lonely salute, and ducked into the shadows. He was shaking.

No one came after him. But the music did not begin again.

. . .

Sometime later, a familiar step scraped the icy gravel and Faland appeared beside him, under the shadows of winter-black trees. Freddie leaned against one of them, still shivering. It hadn't occurred to him to leave. "That's why you want me to tell you stories. For your music."

Faland was silent.

"But why do I have to *forget*?" said Freddie. Did he even want to remember?

He thought Faland wouldn't answer, or if he did it would be a joke or a lie. But finally Faland said, "I made music for myself once." He glanced up briefly, and Freddie saw a single star, there and gone in the grayness. "And put it into the world. But now I cannot create without destroying."

"Why not?"

"Prying is so impolite."

"That's what your mirror does, isn't it? You see who people are and play it back on the violin."

With a faint, familiar malice, Faland said, "They have to pay for their wine somehow."

Chilled, Freddie said, "Does everyone forget themselves?"

Faland shrugged. "People forget anyway. The war shatters them, remakes them. At least I make something of them. Otherwise they merely—fade to gray."

Freddie said, "Make what? In the dining room, in the music— that wasn't me. That was—that was just a scream."

"Oh, child," said Faland very softly. "It was you."

Reality tilted again for an instant, as though his soul made Faland's music but the music in turn remade him, round and round, ouroboros forever, until he was small enough to fit into the strings of the violin. He gritted his teeth, managed to say, "What's the point of it all?"

Faland turned to look at him.

"What you played, tonight, it was just *dinner music*. No matter how strange or—or pretty. No matter that you got it from—from me, from all those things I told you. They heard, but it didn't change anything. It didn't matter. You don't matter. But you could. I saw you in Ypres. You were like a king. Nothing touched you. You have that—and you just play games with people's lives. Making and destroying. For what?"

"Well," said Faland, a needling edge coming into his voice. "Perhaps I lack the right inspiration. You certainly have not given me the best of yourself, have you?" In his face was a flicker of hunger, almost lust. "Tell me what makes you wake screaming in the dark. The memory at the bottom of your soul. Give it to me." His voice crawled over Freddie's skin. "Tell me about the German."

Freddie, his mouth dry, whispered, "What will you do with it?"

"Rend men's hearts. Don't even tell me you don't want me to."

Freddie said nothing. He was trembling. He'd go mad if he gave that memory. He knew it suddenly and clearly. It was a cornerstone of the tottering edifice of his soul. All that he'd become was in that memory: fear and courage, darkness and kindness. Lose it and he'd collapse like a house of cards. He couldn't lose it. He couldn't bear it.

Faland had stopped walking. He watched Freddie in silence. Waiting. *He'd wait forever,* Freddie thought in a daze, not sure if he was awed or horrified. He didn't know what he was going to say before he opened his mouth, but he found himself whispering "You said that you were a bad soldier once. What did you do?" He thought Faland wouldn't answer.

Faland said, "Why do you ask questions that you already know the answer to?" He relented. "I rebelled."

He couldn't think, with how his heart was beating. "How did you hurt your leg?"

"I fell," said Faland. The dark eye ate up the light, darker than the haze of a tarnished mirror. "And then I woke up in darkness."

The boy Wilfred would have been sick, and terrified. But Freddie didn't know what to fear now. Perhaps the poet in him was exalted. Perhaps the poet understood. Perhaps Faland was a poet himself. He couldn't speak. Faland's voice was like frayed silk. He added, "And that is all the story you will get from me. I have shown you what I can do. I will show you more, if you will tell me why you wake up screaming, Wilfred Iven."

AND I SAW THE HOLY CITY

·····

DAY WAS DESCENDING TOWARD EVENING WHEN LAURA LEFT Whiting and went out to Mary's motorcycle. She ought to get on, kick the thing into gear, and return to Couthove for the night. But she hesitated. Mary would be cross if she was late. But she had a last errand in view. Not for herself, or for Freddie. For Pim.

Laura left the motorcycle and the main square and stopped about midway down Priesterstraat, at a house with a long queue of men leading up to it. A lamp burned scarlet beside the door. Heads turned among the men in the queue, but Laura didn't look at them.

Madame Maertens was the best-known businesswoman in the sector, and her business was prostitution, fueled by the twin influxes of Edwardian virgins in uniform and Belgian women without recourse. She had grown into affluence, over the course of the war. Madame wouldn't know anything about a dead soldier named Wilfred Iven. Battlefield deaths, in her world, weren't interesting. But she traded in rumors and scandals. Her girls collected them diligently in their little booths. Madame might know the stories of a man nicknamed the fiddler. She might have heard stories of a hotel, and a person called Faland. She might know enough to ease Pim's mind. Madame's grown son was at the door, keeping order. Laura said, "I'm here to see her, Gerald."

Gerald knew Laura. She'd dosed half the girls for syphilis, and delivered more than one infant for them. "Heard you'd gone home. Some were saying you'd died."

"Not yet," said Laura.

Gerald nodded and Laura slipped inside.

Madame's office had been a pantry before the war. She was muttering over her books when Laura knocked. Her eyes flew up. "Mademoiselle Iven!" she cried, with surprised pleasure. "We heard you'd lost your leg."

"A bit the worse for wear, is all," said Laura.

"Sit down then, shut the door." She fixed Laura with a very shrewd eye. "What brought you here? Something particular, I don't doubt."

Niceties didn't interest Madame. Laura said, "I am looking for a man called the fiddler."

Something hardened behind her eyes. "Ah," she said. "Everyone is asking, aren't they? Never mind that men come back like ghosts. They're all still looking."

"Why?" said Laura.

Madame shrugged expressively. "Who knows? They say he takes their souls and pays in wine." Laura couldn't tell if she was joking. "But," Madame added, "the ones who have been out long enough, they've lost their souls anyway. So who knows?"

Superstition was unlike Madame. Impatient, Laura said, "But who is he? My friend met him, and she's desperate to meet him again. She has uncovered—strange stories about this man. For her sake, I want to know. Where does he come from? What is he doing here?"

Madame crossed herself. "No one knows. If I were you, I'd—"

Then she hesitated, eyes on Laura's face. "You're in earnest, petite?"

"If I was trying to joke, I am certain I could come up with something better."

Madame watched her a moment more. Then she bent to her desk, rummaged. Emerged with, of all things, a copy of *The Wipers Times*. The joke paper printed by soldiers on their crumbling press. "This is all the answer I have," she said. Madame folded the issue back, pointed to a page.

The *Times* was the printed equivalent of whistling past a grave-yard, and every issue was a frantic mishmash of pitch-black humor. There were fake letters to the editor. There were fake answers to correspondents. But Madame had pointed at a page of false adver-tisements. *DANCING!!!!* one of them said.

Prof. Porky's weekly classes

The professor will give a pas seul exposition of the
TRENCH TANGO
———
ADMISSION: THE USUAL PRICES WILL BE CHARGED INCLUDING WAR TAX

It was absurd. Laura found herself smiling. But beside the first advertisement was another. *MUSIC!!!!!!!* it said.

M. FALAND
The CELEBRATED VIOLINIST, Purveyor of LIQUID
COURAGE, ILLUSIONIST
COME FOR THE INIMITABLE BACCHANALIAN REVEL
STAY FOR THE SELF-KNOWLEDGE, SOUL-RENDING TUNES
COULD BE ANYWHERE
SEEK AND YE SHALL FIND
———
MONEY NOT ACCEPTED

Laura looked from the text to Madame. It was just the kind of satire the *Times* trafficked in, just the kind of joke that would make the men laugh and make the staff officers puff up in indignation. Carefully, she said, "I don't understand."

Madame said, "You asked who he was. I think that's his answer, or all the answer you'll get."

"What can he possibly gain by—" Laura began.

Madame said sharply, "I am a woman of business, and so my answer is a businesswoman's: He is getting a good return for his trouble, jokes and all. If you want a better answer, perhaps you should
ask a priest."

Laura hardly knew what to reply. Madame's big-boned face was
utterly serious. Laura thought of herself as rational. But the mirror
over his bar was in her mind, Pim's face and peeling gilt, the dust of
that morning's awakening. *Seek and ye shall find.* Well, they had.

"I also think," added Madame carefully, "that this is a good place
and a good year for monsters. And that you should go back and tell
your friend that if she values her life, she will forget this man."

Laura found herself whispering, "And if she won't?"

"Then I am sorry for her."

. . .

It was dusk. Laura's inquiries had left her with more questions than
answers, a sense of bewilderment and a creeping dread. She tried to
think what to do next. Speak to Young about his escaped German
prisoner? Try to find Pim, warn her again off Faland? Find a way to
get her sent home? But what right did Laura have to interfere? Pim
wasn't a child.

Laura turned her feet to where she'd left the motorcycle. The
wind hurried, catching at her skirt and coat and the scarf over her
hair. The light was strange, and the boarded-up houses had an aura
of malevolence, empty windows glaring down. She stumbled over a
piece of fallen masonry. The war had left its mark here too.

When she looked up again, a figure barred her way. She lurched
backward, a choked-off sound surging in her throat. A familiar figure. Transposed from its place in her nightmares. Ten feet away,
clear as daylight. Bloody housecoat, bloody eyes. The hand raised,
a finger pointing in condemnation. "You're not real," Laura whispered. *"You're not real—stop. Stop!"*

She was backing away, she found herself at a corner, and hurried
down a different street, thinking of nothing now but of returning to
the lights of the main square. But where was it? She'd walked the

streets of Poperinghe a hundred times. But now she turned and turned again, found herself in a warren of turnings, of empty windows and shattered glass, with the main square nowhere in sight.

Then the figure was standing before her *again,* just the same, eyeless, pointing, and Laura spun again, a knifing pain in her lungs. She was almost running when the figure loomed a third time and Laura could bear it no more. She halted, cried out, "What do you want? I'm sorry. I'm so sorry. I didn't mean to let you die."

Did she think the dead figure would vanish, apology accepted? Did she think the dead figure was there at all? She pointed again, not at Laura but somewhere beyond. Laura turned her head, thought she saw furtive movement in the shadows just as she fell sprawling over another piece of lumber and struck her head a glancing blow.

When she got to her feet, head ringing, the figure was gone. There were voices in the street. The lights seemed brighter. A soldier turned the corner; there were ordinary passersby too. Belgians, staring. Then more soldiers turned into the street: military police. Their voices fell overloud on her ears: "He came this way. Who's that?"

A familiar voice said, "I know her."

Next moment, men were clustered round her and a pocket torch dazzled her eyes. A face half-seen, half-familiar hovered behind the light. "Why," said the voice, "Miss Iven, are you all right? What are you doing here? Did you see him?"

"See whom?" said Laura, trying to collect herself.

"Oh," said Young—for it was he, flushed and eager, his ears as big as ever—"the escaped German. They say he's gone to ground in . . . But no, you don't know. Sorry to distress you." Young was being chivalrous and soothing. It came to Laura that he was rather a nice boy, certainly a sincere one. He kept talking, and she was grateful for the inconsequential, well-bred flow; it gave her time to settle her breathing: "Such a coincidence to see you here! Mrs. Shaw is coming to us this evening, as I'm sure you know. Should you like to see her? Perhaps you'd like a bite of supper yourself?"

Laura wouldn't have turned him down even if she'd had the presence of mind to say anything at all; she wanted to see Pim. Young gave his men orders and offered Laura his arm. He was far better suited to escorting women than hunting fugitives; Laura read as much on his men's wooden faces. They started off together and the last ten minutes began to feel very much a dream.

The whole main square was alive with men and lorries and lights and cafés with doors hospitably open to the softening spring air. Laura expected Young would be meeting Pim in a café. But he led her to Fifth Army headquarters instead.

It had been built into Poperinghe's town hall: a sensible building repurposed for war. Telephone wires looped the outside in swags, and endless messengers, on motorcycles and bicycles and horseback, hurried to and fro.

"My uncle insisted on hosting dinner," explained Young. "He was so impressed, you know, by Mrs. Shaw, her courage, you know." Was he babbling? He must be properly in love, to sound so nervous. Then she thought, *Is that love?* He sounded so— apprehensive.

She said carefully, "Any success in your search for the German? He is in Pop, you believe?"

"I—" Young seemed distracted. "No, we haven't caught him yet, no. But we heard—there was a report—we suspected he was here— it's only a matter of time." He sounded as if his mind was elsewhere. "I am so glad you are here, truly, Miss Iven, I think you will be a great comfort to your friend."

Laura was puzzled. She knew of Pim's distress, but wasn't it strange that Pim would have confided in the hapless Young?

They went into HQ and up a flight of stairs and it turned out that dinner was not an intimate affair, at all; there were other officers present and a few volunteer nurses of better birth than Laura. Three of the nurses knew her; there were exclamations, a flurry of reminiscences. Laura tried not to look distracted. Pim was already seated, talking to Gage. Young's eye went straight to her as they walked in; he looked at Pim as though she were a mermaid fished up from the deep.

Pim glanced at Laura. For a second she wondered whether Pim was displeased to see her. Her expression went strange. But then she smiled, got up, and hurried over, a hand outstretched. "Laura! I thought you went back to Couthove hours ago, my dear; I am so glad to see you."

Gage was looking at Pim with an intent expression. Was he in love with her too? But she thought she detected some disquiet there as well. Laura didn't understand. Young said, "Here's a surprise for you, Mrs. Shaw. I found your friend coming up the street—such a coincidence—I knew you'd be glad to see her."

"Indeed I am," said Pim, smiling.

A glass of wine appeared and Laura sipped gratefully. It was a solid step above the one-franc variety sold in the estaminets.

"I had such a lovely day," Pim was saying. "We went riding, and then the lieutenant showed me how to use a pistol— Oh, I was so frightened, but it was quite easy, really. And there's other news— General Gage is going to pay Mary a high compliment."

Laura wasn't particularly interested in Gage's compliment. *Did you go try to find Faland's hotel?* Laura could not ask in company. *Are you going to?*

She couldn't ask right then, so between sips Laura gathered that the compliment *was* a high one: Elizabeth, none other than the queen of Belgium, was hoping to visit a hospital, wearing a nurse's uniform, accompanied by photographers. Pim had suggested Couthove. Probably, Laura thought cynically, because the fine atmospherics of a ward in a ruined ballroom made an appealing backdrop for photographs. Certainly there was nothing picturesque about the sheds and tents of nearby Mendinghem.

Gage was smiling. He was going to accompany the queen, if he could get away. He would be delighted. Enchanted. He proceeded to pay Pim, and Laura and Couthove, a dazzling run of well-phrased compliments. Why did he look so ill at ease?

Laura did not think the queen's visit a fine idea. A royal visit would mean the routine of the hospital thrown into disarray. It meant scrubbing and laundry, and tucking men into sheets without a wrinkle and ordering them not to move, not to groan, and if possible, not to bleed or look ghastly or smell. "I am sure Mary will be delighted," Laura said. She got her glass refilled. Mary *would* be delighted. She'd invite a pet newspaperman and use the whole event to winkle more donations out of people.

Pim touched Laura's arm comfortingly, as though she understood.

Dinner was served. It wasn't luxurious, but there was chicken, there was butter, there were eggs. Laura's wine quivered with the impact of some distant explosion. She tried not to imagine what was happening further up, while they ate and drank and talked. Tension in Pim's spine, in her face, in her hand on the glass. But still she charmed both Gage and Young, smiling, listening. The evening was warm; the long front window was open. There was a lull in the conversation. In the brief silence, Laura heard the sounds of men and raucous laughter on the street below.

The melody of a single violin filtered, lonely and insistent, through the night.

Laura almost spilled her wine; without hesitation, Pim pushed back her chair, right in the middle of one of Gage's well-turned anecdotes. She hurried to the window, leaving him sputtering. Laura collected herself with vague excuses and hastened to follow.

There was no violinist out in the street, but there was a great number of men. More than usual? The music wound between them, a shining thread of sound.

Pim stood perfectly still.

The music shifted. A high terrible sound shot from the strings, and somewhere beyond the reach of the lights, Laura heard glass breaking. Beside her, Pim stood rigid.

A man sprinted across the square as a voice shouted "Halt!" There was another crash of glass. A crowd, shoving, had formed in the square. Laughing, breaking things. Laura thought she saw the shine of tears on one man's face. Whistles, bellowing, came from those trying to reestablish order, but to no avail. The whole scene had dissolved into chaos. Laura couldn't hear the violin anymore, but it didn't matter, somehow the melody echoed still in the sounds of riot. As though the violin had breathed madness into their minds or perhaps simply reminded them that some men ate roast chicken while others died, that the burdens of the war were unequal, and always had been. Someone was trying to lead Laura and Pim away from the window.

And then Laura saw—or thought she saw—a head of ash-colored hair, thin shoulders in a civilian suit, caught in a gleam, then gone in the gloom.

Suddenly Pim was gone from her side, breaking free of the solicitous officers, running down the stairs. Laura was turning to follow, when she faltered. Outside, on the square, stood her eyeless ghost, face turned up, the scarlet pits fastened on Laura.

Laura swore. At herself, or her ghost, or at Pim, she didn't know. Then she ran. Someone below was calling her name.

It was Young. Laura joined him at the bottom of the stairs. He said, "Miss Iven, you must stay here, I'll go get her—you must calm yourself."

Pim had gone outside, then. Laura turned toward the door. Young, behind her, protested, but Madame's warning was clear in Laura's mind. She pushed her way out into the chaos. Did Young follow? She didn't see. Three steps and she knew she'd made a mistake, underestimated the crowd, overestimated her own strength. The mob was like a riptide now, its noise like water on rock. Somewhere in its clamor, still, she seemed to hear the echo of Faland's music. Laura's eyes struggled to adjust. Pools of light, violently bright, gave way to thick shadows. A man knocked her sideways, but she hardly felt the jar, her mind alight with adrenaline.

And then her mother's bleeding ghost was right in front of her. She bit off a scream, afraid for her sanity. Or was she hoping for absolution? There was nothing, again, but that pointing finger. Following the line of it, Laura saw neither Pim nor Faland nor Freddie but a man, a stranger, crouching in a doorway, watching the madness with startlingly blue eyes.

Then her leg betrayed her. It folded, cramping, and Laura fell, and for a second she was pummeled under a hundred heedless boots, rolled in oily dust.

And then a shoulder was there, a body, creating space. An unfamiliar hand reached and seized her, yanked her, gasping, to her feet, hauled her back into the shallow shelter of a doorway. A voice said, "Are you all right?"

Her lip was split and bleeding. Her body was bruised everywhere. The light was behind her savior. "Thank you," she said, panting, and then stilled. He had a big-boned face, stubbled with beard like sand, hair a shade darker, as though the sand had got wet. He was a big-framed man, wasted thin. His face was stoic, his expression watchful.

The sleeve of his coat was empty.

Kate's words and Young's jostled for room in her mind: *A German spy, escaped. He brought news of your brother. He didn't think that Freddie was dead. I believed him. I believed him.*

He couldn't possibly be here, brazenly walking the streets of Poperinghe, with half the British Army running mad through the street. And yet . . . Laura had not time to think of what that pointing finger had meant. He was saying "Better stay here, miss," and turning to go. She caught his empty sleeve.

"Are you called Winter?"

Alarm filled the blue eyes. He wrenched free. She spoke hastily, "My name is Laura Iven. I am a nurse at Château Couthove."

He stilled. His eyes fastened on hers.

She said, "I am looking for my brother."

A stout detachment of military police was coming across the square, swinging clubs, shouting. Had they seen him? They might have. He'd gone out into their line of sight, into the crush, to save her life. Did she dare ask? Could she stop herself from asking? "Winter," she said. "Did you know my brother?" And then, the dangerous question: "Is my brother alive?"

The military police were coming closer. He opened his mouth as though to speak, cut his eyes right, pulled himself free, and disappeared into the crowd.

33

DREAM NOT OF OTHER WORLDS

.....

THE RIOT WAS BROKEN UP. WHISTLES AND LOUD VOICES FILLED the square; military discipline slowly reasserted itself. Laura stayed in the safety of the doorway until it was done, scanning for Pim, for Faland, and, although she told herself she wasn't, for a glimpse of Freddie's russet hair. But she saw no one she knew. Not until she stumbled back to HQ and saw Pim, as composed as ever, talking again to Gage with Young hovering earnestly. When Laura, bedraggled, finally pulled herself through the door, Pim turned to her at once, with an expression of concern. "Oh, Laura, I'm so sorry. Did you go out looking for me? I didn't—well, I didn't get anywhere at all before I realized what a ninny I'd been—thought I saw someone I knew, as I told the general. Then I turned right around like a sensible woman." Pim peered worriedly into Laura's face. "Your poor lip."

They were offered a lift back to Couthove in the general's car, and they accepted. A pensive line, fine as floss, ran between Pim's brows, and she was terribly solicitous of Laura. The car was ordered, and a man was tasked to follow on Mary's motorcycle. There were ten thousand things Laura wanted to say, but none she could say in the presence of their driver. So silence reigned between them, all along the road to Couthove.

. . .

Jones met them at the door, took one look at Laura's face, and his expression turned dark. "Can take care of herself, she said."

The drive back to Couthove had acquainted Laura with a large number of previously unnoticed bruises, and she was in no sweet temper. "Nothing a wash and a rest won't mend." Pim had already murmured "Good evening" and was disappearing upstairs. Laura made to follow.

"Iven," said Jones.

"Doctor," she said, shoulders stiff. "I don't want—"

He made an impatient sound. "I will not say a single censorious word, if you will let me look you over. You look as though you've been in a four-day bombardment. What happened to your lip?"

"A mishap over dinner."

"Some mishap." He turned to the sterilization room, then just as quickly turned back. "There are three orderlies playing cards in there—will you come upstairs? I can call Shaw back if you want a female with you." He looked uncomfortable as he said it, then impatient with his own discomfort.

Perhaps that was what made her say, dryly, "I suppose I'll brave the lion's den. But I can't take a scolding tonight."

He looked relieved. "I won't, however much I'd like to. Now come up, before you drop."

. . .

Jones had a better room than Laura and Pim; it had been one of the château's proper bedrooms before the war, although it contained nothing more than Jones's spartan cot and his trunk, with an old-fashioned writing case and a book lying by. The window was open to the warm spring night.

His back was to Laura as he turned on the light and Laura said, "Do you think I'm mad?"

He turned around. His expression was cautious. "No, Iven."

She was at the window, looking out at the lights of war on the horizon. "Is that your medical opinion?"

She heard his step cross the room, felt him at her shoulder. "You are very trying, to a man who promised not to pry, Iven. But yes, it is. Your mind's all right, although your dress has seen better days. Come into the light."

She looked down at herself. Saw rips, stains, dust. Jones took her elbow. Said, in a carefully neutral voice, "Someone kicked you. There's a boot print there."

"It was an accident," said Laura.

"Was it?" His face was hard, but he didn't ask. He pressed his palm to the print, and she flinched despite herself. "No pain round the ribs?"

"Only bruises," said Laura. Why had she come? She could check herself over very well. Why had she agreed to this, to come to his room, to stand by his bed? She felt her own vulnerability. Very carefully, Jones took her jaw in his hand, turned it in the light. Touched the bruise on her jaw, another round her eye. Palpitated it delicately. "Any loose teeth?"

She shook her head. Men had clutched at Laura in pain, in fear, in loneliness ever since she joined the army. She had an arsenal of professional defenses against that. But had no armor at all, she realized suddenly, against his precise, undemanding fingers, and the concern in his eyes. She drew away, afraid of her own fragility.

"Iven?" said Jones, as she backed away.

"I—I'm sorry, Doctor," she said. "I'm all right."

"I can get you a salve for the—"

She fled.

. . .

Laura went straight upstairs, and thankfully, Jones did not follow. She prayed that Pim was asleep already, so that Laura could submit her emotions to her pillow in silence and get up calmer tomorrow.

But Pim was not in bed. She was at their little table, a lantern burning before her, paging through her notebook. She didn't turn around when Laura came in.

Laura sat down on her cot to take off her boots. Pim closed her notebook and turned. "I hardly dared ask before—did you get news of Freddie?"

"Yes," said Laura.

Pim's silence was expectant.

What could she tell Pim? Not that she'd spoken to a fugitive whom Kate White believed, against all logic, had escaped to go look for Laura's missing brother. She hardly knew what to think herself. "His CO said he died on the Ridge."

Pim's eyes filled with sympathy.

Laura fumbled her damp stocking as she unrolled it. "Pim, how are you?"

"Me? Oh, but Laura . . ." She caught Laura's eye and said reluctantly, "I'm all right. Quite well. Wasn't dinner nice?"

"Did you go out looking for Faland?"

Pim gave a shamefaced nod. "It was silly of me. I couldn't find him."

"Did you and Young go looking for his hotel today?"

"Oh—no. I—I listened to you and saw sense. No point in hurtling all over looking for it. And of course Faland doesn't seem to want to be found. I'm done looking."

Laura stood up to take off her dress, relieved. "That's probably for the best. You're very thin. Mary's working you too hard."

"Not harder than you." Pim's mouth was set in that concealing smile that nice girls were taught in childhood. "I'm glad I've been writing so many letters. I hope it comforts people. I'd have liked a letter myself. In Halifax. From someone who was with Jimmy. And a sketch. What do you think of this one? I did it this morning. For Mila." She reached again for her notebook, turned a few pages, pulled out a loose drawing of a grave, backed by a sunset. The headstone Pim had drawn in looked much nicer than the white wooden cross that Mila had actually got, and the imaginative tumble of flowers looked lovely. It would certainly comfort his mother, if they ever discovered who she was.

"This is beautiful," said Laura. "But you ought to rest."

Pim said, "I'm all right, honestly." She hesitated. "Laura, I know you're tired. But will you do something for me?"

"If I can."

Pim didn't reply in words, but reached up and began unpinning her hair. It was still plaited from dinner. Section by section, she took it down. It looked especially lovely, poignant somehow, falling loose in the wood-floored attic. Pim ran her fingers through it, scalp to hips. "I washed it yesterday. It was cold, so it took ages to dry. And I keep imagining I feel the feet—little louse feet—" Pim's hand trembled as she dug into her bag and pulled out her shears. It was quiet enough in the room to hear the endless nighttime rustling of the wards below.

"Pim," Laura said. "Why now? It's not just about lice, is it?"

Pim looked away and said, "The general—he was so charming at dinner. So *civilized*. But I—I didn't want to be beautiful for him. Or for anyone. Do you know, I felt more sympathy for the men in the street, running and shouting and breaking things? Sometimes, I should like to scream myself."

Laura took the scissors.

Clean gold fell like light over her dress and Pim's. Laura almost asked her for a lock of it, like a foolish knight, or a fond Victorian aunt plaiting hair into mourning bands. But she bit her tongue and finished the job in silence. Then she did the only thing she could think of. She set the shears aside and wound her arms round Pim's shoulders. Pim didn't cry, but she buried her face awkwardly in the crook of Laura's elbow. They sat there together, weary, the warmth of their skin bleeding together, an instinct older than Armageddon, until Laura turned off the lamp.

34

TO LOSE THEE WERE
TO LOSE MYSELF

.....

FALAND'S HOTEL, PARTS UNKNOWN,
FLANDERS, BELGIUM
WINTER–SPRING OF 1917–1918

FREDDIE STILL DIDN'T TELL FALAND ABOUT THE PILLBOX. Sometimes he thought it was mere pointless defiance, not giving Faland what he wanted. Sometimes he thought he couldn't bear to forget Winter's eyes.

He didn't know. But he wouldn't talk about the pillbox.

Faland didn't give him another candle to leaven the darkness, and he didn't come now when Freddie woke up screaming. Freddie started to wander the empty hotel by day, shuddering at every whisper. Sometimes he glimpsed the dead man waiting around corners.

The wine turned sour on his tongue, like it was corked, and even the mirror, though he stared at it with a madman's desperation, began to seem insipid. He'd look at Laura's face and think, *She'd never smile at me like that, she'd ask me what the hell I'm doing.*

Winter wouldn't smile either. He'd tell me I have a duty. Real people were difficult and hurt you, and left you, and no mirror could ever . . .

And still he told Faland stories. Other stories. But they'd all grown so vague. He'd grope for words sometimes, grope for the sequence of events, and shake as he spoke, as though his very soul were a wall beginning to crumble. He almost begged Faland to play the violin, to remind him of his forgotten self. But he was afraid of the person whom Faland might conjure, afraid he wouldn't recognize him—or perhaps that he would, only too well. So he bit the words back.

Sometimes, as he walked the hotel corridors, Freddie told himself he was trying to find the door that led out, but he wasn't. He didn't have enough hope left to really try. All his doors were locked, and the hotel was his entire world.

Finally, every time he slept, he woke screaming.

But he still would not let go.

"Tell me," Faland said, avarice still lurking in his eyes, his voice gentle enough to make Freddie want to cry. "And be at peace. I'll make such music of you, Iven."

He was going to yield eventually. His mind was failing. He knew it, and Faland knew it. *Tell him now,* he thought. *Don't wait until you're an empty wreck.*

Faland seemed to sense the change in him. His lighter eye glittered.

But then between one terrible hour and the next, some utterly unmarked space of time later, three women walked into the hotel, and one of them was his sister.

She was pallid, filthy, and soaked. She looked the way he imagined she might have, dying wounded in the mud at Brandhoek, her hair plastered to her neck, the scars prominent on her hands. Perhaps she was a ghost, like the drowned man.

And then he thought, with a strange quiver of his heart, would a ghost look so *very* much as she'd looked in life? Irritable at being wet, her expression skeptical, watching Faland finish playing his violin and ply them all with wine? Would she be so painfully real, so as to reduce the image in the mirror to a vague sketch, sfumato, without life or self?

Would a ghost make all his absent memories hurt so much?

And then Freddie glimpsed Faland's face, and stood very still. For he could have sworn Faland was angry, even perplexed, even though he'd crossed the room smiling, and then the thought broke through the haze in his mind like a ninth wave: *That's my sister and she's in the hotel and she's alive.*

He lurched forward. But Faland flickered a glance at him and the thought shattered into shards of *Is that really her? It can't be her. And even if it is her, why would she want me? I'm not Freddie anymore. I've forgotten too much, changed too much. I'm no one.*

With clenching hands, he saw Faland bring them wine. Saw one of the other women, the beautiful one, go to the mirror. Heard her scream. The mirror made men cry, but scream? Freddie glimpsed a flurry of motion in the woman's reflection, a red like blood.

His sister was on her feet, her face full of concern. She limped when she crossed the room. Why was she limping? He wasn't even aware of moving toward her. Blind instinct was deeper even than the apathy Faland had nurtured in him. That was Laura, and she needed him.

Then he saw Laura see him. To his shock and fear, and something too painful to be delight, he realized she was staring into the mirror, staring back at him. She could see him in the glass. He couldn't look away. Their gazes locked, and he half-saw her turn round, heard her cry, her living voice calling *"Freddie!"*

I must be the same, because she knows me. Faland doesn't. He just knows the pieces. He shoved toward her. Then the crowd got between them. He had time to hesitate, to think, *Does she? Who are you now, Wilfred Iven?* The memory of who he'd been wavered in the half-fallen edifice of his mind. He didn't even know all that had been lost between them. His limbs were weak; had he drunk so much? He thought he saw Faland standing by his sister, hands clamped on her shoulders. When he tried to cry a warning, no sound came. The crowd was so thick. Where was she? Now he glimpsed Faland standing face-to-face with the beautiful woman. Her golden hair was a few shades darker than his. She was shaking her head.

Faland's lips moved. He was smiling. "No?" he said.

He couldn't tell if it was rage or terror on the woman's face. Unholy delight on Faland's. Where was Laura? He was trying to call her name.

Then the world dissolved, and he jerked awake, again in his own bed, with a sick headache. He lay there gasping, eyes shut tight, trying frantically, as he had so many times before, to figure out what was real, and what he'd already lost in the wasteland of his mind.

WHAT HATH NIGHT
TO DO WITH SLEEP?

·····

CHÂTEAU COUTHOVE, FLANDERS, BELGIUM
APRIL 1918

LAURA'S SLEEPING MIND REGISTERED THAT THE TEMPO OF DIS-
tant firing had increased just as a bell began ringing below, and
she was out of bed before she came properly awake. "Up, Pim,"
she said, already dressing. "They'll want every pair of hands."

There were violet smudges under Pim's eyes, and her newly
shorn hair stuck up round her head like dandelion fluff. She rolled to
her feet. Laura watched her sidelong, worried. Pim had never seen
a hospital ward during a push. She was unprepared for what was
going to happen.

When they hurried downstairs, they found the hospital in a ferment: Jones in the operating theater, arranging his scalpels; Mary
intent and bustling. Hurtling past, she called, "Triage, Iven, for
now, and keep Shaw with you."

Ambulances were already sweeping up the drive. A glance outside showed the orderlies pulling out men wrapped in dirty blankets. Laura and Pim went out to the carriage house. The orderlies
carried them in and laid them down, and suddenly Laura was too
busy to think at all.

Time was reduced to a series of images, each etched sharply in her mind: A man grinning despite a thigh laid open; he knew he'd live and get a ticket home out of it. A man gray-white, his head lop-sided. Patient after patient. Mary directed the orderlies with their stretchers, so that the men in each row touched without a break.

"—Put him here."

"No, we can't save the foot—"

"Water, for God's sake, Sister," said a man on the floor.

Slit boots piled up in heaps beside the stretchers. Orderlies went by with buckets of soapy water to wash the yellow-nailed feet. Laura went from man to man, examining, comforting, deciding who needed emergency surgery and who could wait. "Here!" she called. "A lung, here, hemorrhaging." The man was swept up and taken away.

A voice, urgent: "Sister, Sister, what do I do? This one's brain came off with the bandage. I put it in a bucket."

She gave the man morphine. "But Laura, isn't that too much?" whispered Pim. Laura didn't answer and Pim fell silent. The patient's breath shuddered out of him.

At some point, she grew aware of hands on hers, an acerbic voice speaking. "Doctor," she said.

Jones said, "Iven, if you looked in a mirror and saw your own face . . ."

She said, "I know my limit."

"Has it occurred to you," said Jones, "that your limit has perhaps diminished after a hearty round of pneumo—" He didn't finish. Three voices were calling for him, and others for Laura. "Iven, if you collapse, you'll have me crowing I told you so."

He strode away.

It was near dawn. The influx had slowed a little. How many hours since the rush began? Laura paused to ease the growing ache in her back, and that was when she heard Pim scream from somewhere outside. Back forgotten, she ran toward the sound. She'd seen patients turn murderous before, the war more real in their minds than anything else. The scream had come from somewhere between the carriage house and the château. Laura stopped in the grass-grown drive, seeking.

A glimpse of stained uniform, and there was Pim, staggering, holding up a man deep in the shadow of the building. Laura ran, managed to get an arm under him before he fell.

As Laura and Pim eased him down between them, she saw his set face.

His blue eyes.

He was wounded. He was staring fixedly at her.

"Laura, I thought it was Jimmy," Pim was gasping. "I mean, I saw—his hair—he—"

Laura had no time to answer. Her hands were flying over Winter's body, looking for the source of the blood on his clothes. He was clammy. She found the bullet hole in his left side, small caliber. Perhaps it hadn't perforated the intestine. Nicked his liver, though, and he'd been bleeding for a while. His pulse was a thread; she didn't think he'd been strong to begin with. His open eyes were still fixed on her face.

She had a split second to decide what to do.

"Pim, get Jones. Get him *now*. Only Jones; no one else. All right?"

Pim took one look at Laura's face and ran off, her feet quick on the grass-grown gravel.

"Laura Iven," said the man on the ground. His eyes searched her face. "Laura."

"I'm Laura," she whispered. "Laura Iven, and Wilfred is my brother."

Winter looked fleetingly perplexed. "How am I here?" His eyes were half-closed.

"I don't know. You're wounded," said Laura.

The German whispered, "I saw him yesterday. Wilfred."

Her heart gave a single great thump. "Where?"

Winter didn't answer. He looked like he was struggling to stay conscious, like a man in a shipwreck, braced for the next wave. Laura bent nearer. "Do you know where he is now?"

Before Winter could speak, Laura heard Pim's voice behind her: "Just here, Doctor, oh, I think he's very poorly."

And Jones's voice answering, sharper than usual with tiredness, "What's he doing collapsing in the hedges, though, could he not come inside like a sensible man?" And then he was dropping to his knees beside Laura, handing Pim a pocket torch to hold. "Tell me, Iven," he said.

"A bullet. Liver, I think," said Laura, trying to marshal her thoughts. "And he's—" But Jones had stilled, wary surprise in his tired face, taking in the hazy blue eyes, the stubbly sandy hair. Possibly the irregularity in uniform, and certainly the healed stump. Jones was no fool. He'd heard the story of the elusive German.

Winter seemed to shrink from Jones's suspicious eye, as if he might be able to stand, slip away, hide himself again in the chaos. But he was at the end of his strength. "It's all right," said Laura, although she wasn't sure it was.

"He won't get away without help," Winter said to her suddenly, as though he'd made up his mind to speak while he could and damn all hearers. He caught her wrist in a bony hand. "You have to help him."

Laura crouched close, heedless of Jones and Pim. "*Where is he?*"

"He's with—" Winter tried. "He's lost—" Perhaps English was failing him in his exhaustion, for he said a single word, the blue eyes burning. "Faland," he said. Then he fainted.

Laura heard Pim's small gasp. The light in her hands wavered.

"Christ," said Jones, harsh. "Young's German. One arm, rags, accent. What's he doing here?"

Laura, eyes on Winter's slack face, whispered, "He came here to tell me that Freddie is alive." *With Faland, with Faland. So when I saw him—I must have seen . . .*

But, Freddie, what happened to you? Why didn't you come to me?

And then—*He knew, didn't he? That bastard with his violin. He knew. He lied.*

Her thoughts stuttered to a halt. Jones had rounded on her. "He said—and you *believe* him? Iven, he was just saying the first thing to come into his head. Playing on your sympathies."

"He knew my brother's name," said Laura. She was staring at Winter. So was Pim, her face quite blank.

Jones said, "He could have learned it. If I save him, then they'll come for him. They'll interrogate him, and hang him."

Laura shook her head, not disagreeing. But she said, "I need to know what he knows."

"Your brother's dead," said Jones.

She just looked at him.

Almost pleading, Jones said, "Tell me why you believe him. One real damn reason. Iven—give me something."

Laura said, "A friend told me—someone I trust. That this man came off the battlefield with Freddie's things. What he knows—I need to know too, Jones, I *have* to."

Jones ran a hand over his stubbled face. He didn't ask why she'd not said anything about this before. "Iven, this can't end well."

Laura knew it. It was one thing to be careless with herself, but this was a risk to people who had not asked to be endangered, people who trusted her, and to whom she had a responsibility. She still didn't hesitate. "Please."

Jones nodded slowly, eyes fastened on her face. "All right, then, Iven. All right. We'll get him into surgery. Shaw, could you—?"

But Pim was already running across the grass, and a moment later two orderlies came with a stretcher. Pim was still with them. Her eyes met Laura's, a long look. But Pim, voluble Pim, did not say a word.

· · ·

The orderlies took Winter, still unconscious, into the X-ray room and then into surgery, where Jones and Laura faced each other, alone over his unconscious body. Jones's hands were steady as he laid out his instruments, but his voice was harsh. "Iven, you say he brought in your brother's things—but you know he could easily have got them off a corpse. He could be a madman. The area is absolutely teeming with mad—" He broke off. "He said 'Faland,' didn't he? This man you think is the fiddler. The legend, the charlatan?"

She was arranging the mask, the cotton for the ether, counting Winter's pulse. "I saw Freddie," she said.

"What?" said Jones.

"That night I spent with Pim and Mary. In Faland's hotel. That I told you of. I thought I saw Freddie that night. In the crowd. I thought—I thought he was a fever-dream. Perhaps he wasn't."

"Or perhaps he was, and you are grasping at straws. Iven, I don't want to see any patient of mine dragged away to be hanged."

She was silent.

Jones added, "And if it's discovered we aided him, well, they might hang us too. Or close down Mary's operation and send her back to England. They'd like to, you know. Replace her with a man."

"We'll plead ignorance," said Laura. "If it comes to that. In the chaos—the fighting. Say we were moving through patients, we were tired, he didn't speak, we didn't realize." She was preparing Winter for surgery as she spoke, cutting away his clothes, swabbing the surgical site.

"You're taking a risk with all of us," said Jones.

She was. He didn't look accusing, but she could see the question in his face: *Why, Iven? Tell me why?*

The only answer she could think of was one that made her throat close, her hands cramp. One she didn't want to give. But she owed it to him. She was asking him to go against his own judgment, his own ethics. Asking him to trust her. So she said, in a voice she hardly recognized, counting Winter's breaths as she spoke: "When the ship exploded in Halifax, I wasn't at home. I wasn't in Veith Street, by the docks. I was working. I'd just got a job. Looking after a trio of old ladies. I should still have been at home in bed. My leg hurt, I was limping. I saw the explosion, out of their front window—a flash of light, and a noise, loud enough to crack the glass. It sent me straight to Flanders. I threw myself flat, quivering like jelly, and for—I don't know—a quarter hour—I couldn't *think*. I was back in Brandhoek, with shells incoming. Just *useless*, paralyzed. The old ladies helped me. Smelling salts, and a warm blanket." Her mouth twisted in self-derision. "It was only after that—when I was coming round—that I realized what must have happened at home. We lived by the docks, you see. Me and my parents. I looked out the window. I could see the fires already starting to spread. I got up. And went. I couldn't run, my leg wasn't so steady. I walked. All the way there. It was—God, sometimes I go to sleep and find myself still walking. Houses flung to matchsticks, sparks falling, fires everywhere. And the screaming. It was just the time when kids walked to school, you know? Mothers were screaming for them. Sometimes they were buried themselves but still screaming." She swallowed. "I got home and I saw—well, my mother had been at the window. Watching, you see, the ship on fire in the bay. It was quite a spectacle, and of course my father was out there. Trying to put it out. The explosion—it blew in the window glass." She paused. "Perhaps there was no way I could have saved her. There was so much glass in her eyes. In her face. She hardly had a face anymore. But I keep thinking I might have. If I'd been quicker. Cleverer. If I hadn't spent a half hour flopping like a fish. So if there's a chance to save Freddie, I have to take it. I've—Jones, I've nothing else."

She fell silent. Felt the world come back slowly. For a moment she'd gone very far away. It was as though that day in Halifax had carved its own place in her mind, and even a careless word was enough to take her back and hold her there, lost. Winter was ready for surgery on the table, if only Jones would . . . She met his eyes and held her breath.

"All right," Jones said. "All right." He started rolling up his sleeve.

"What are you doing?"

He gave her a testy look. "I'm type O, myself. A lot of the units on our shelves were mine. How do you think I found that some blood always worked and other blood didn't? Mine always did. Now go and get me some tubing, Iven. He needs blood, and we've no more jars left."

Speechless, Laura went. Within minutes, blood was running into Winter, and a little color was coming back into his face. Laura, watching the patient, whispered, "Thank you. I'm not sure why you are doing this. But thank you."

Jones's eyes traced the lines of tubing, considered the color of Winter's face. Finally he said, "Because you asked me to, Iven."

She didn't look at him. *No,* she wanted to say. *No, it's not real, whatever this is. Good things don't grow in this rotten earth.*

Jones huffed. "I can almost hear you being dramatic and you haven't said a word."

. . .

They got Winter through surgery, and he woke from the ether still alive but only half-conscious. Of course, now there was the question of where to put him. It wasn't as if the château was empty. It teemed with nurses, orderlies, doctors, patients, the Belgians who came in every day to cook and do laundry.

They considered hiding him. But finally, Laura said, "What guilty fools we should look if he's found bleeding in the pantry. The main ward in fresh pajamas will do for now. I don't think anyone's up for noticing the Archangel Gabriel with his trumpet after all this, let alone yet another wounded man."

Jones was still unhappy. "Look," he said to the dazed Winter, "whoever you are, you are not to speak. Be like those men who come through a bad bombardment; don't say a damned word, just look vacant, all right?"

The blue eyes flickered; impossible to tell whether he'd understood. "I'll keep an eye on him, Iven," said Jones.

"I can—"

Jones said drily, "I am well aware you can. I am not sure you ought."

She was silent, suddenly aware of stabbing pain in her feet and ankles, her calf cramping, the residual ache in her chest.

Jones said, "Go and sleep for an hour. I'll tell you if he says anything. You won't do him or your brother or anyone else any good if you relapse."

She hesitated. Trust—gratitude—what strange things to feel. "All right," she said.

Their eyes met. "Get along, Iven," said Jones, and she went.

Pim was in the foyer.

Her skin was damp with sweat, her uniform stained and sticky, curls of her chopped golden hair escaping her veil. Her eyes were glassy as water. She looked as wrecked as Laura felt. "Come with me," said Laura, taking her arm. "You are having some rum and a chocolate bar and a few hours' sleep."

Pim shook her head. "I— No. No, indeed, Laura. I'm all right. They need me."

"Now, Mrs. Shaw," said Laura.

She chivvied Pim up the stairs. At the door of their room, Pim broke free and burst out, "Who are you to give me orders? I know you lied, Laura, didn't you, when you told me what happened, while you were out searching? You said that you knew for sure Freddie was dead. But you—you didn't look surprised at all to see that man tonight. You didn't even look surprised when he said 'Faland,' did you? You've been telling—telling me to stop looking, and all the time you were—"

"I heard—rumors," said Laura. "In Poperinghe. But they were so strange, I discounted them. Go inside, for God's sake." She closed the door behind them.

"What rumors, Laura?" said Pim.

"Pim, you're exhausted, you're—"

"You're worse off than I am," retorted Pim, with a ferocity that Laura had never heard from her. "You've got cramps again, don't you? In your leg. And you're bossing me anyway. *And you lied to me.*"

Laura, not replying, stripped off her dress, sat down on her bed, undid her garter. The muscle in her right calf was like wood, and her ruined, exhausted fingers were spasming too hard to apply pressure.

"Let me," said Pim abruptly, kneeling at her feet.

"Pim, I can—"

"Let me help you." Bitterness in her voice. "Or don't you trust me, Laura?"

Laura let go and leaned back. Pim had taken off her scarf; her hair stood out in spikes as she began to massage. "And then?" said Pim, not looking up. "Laura, is your brother dead?"

"I don't know."

Pim nodded, working away the cramps. "And the patient, the blond man—he's the one Young told us about. The German."

Laura felt a flicker of fear. "Pim, please—"

"I won't tell Young," said Pim. "I won't tell anyone. I wouldn't, Laura."

Voice thready with weariness, Laura said, "My friend told me about Winter. Told me that Young's spy was the man who brought my brother's things down off the Ridge." Laura faltered then, gritting her teeth through another cramp.

Pim pressed harder. The only thing Laura could see of her was her hands and the top of her golden head. Tears pricked her eyes from the pressure, but the worst of the tension eased. Laura said, "And during the riot, Winter saved me; he pulled me out from under it. Not—he didn't know who I was. He did it for kindness." She didn't mention coincidence, if that's what it was: the bloody, pointing finger that led her straight to Winter. "I recognized him from my friend's description—blue eyes, one arm. I asked him if he knew my brother. He didn't answer. I didn't know what to think. But then he appeared, wounded, in the hospital, and said Freddie's name, and that he is alive, and said *Faland's* name and *Christ*, Pim." Laura heard her own voice go harsh. "Do you think I know anything at all? Any more than you? Winter could be mad, he could be a liar. And if he's not—then I *still* don't understand."

Pim's hands faltered, fell away. Then she looked up. "But it will be all right now, Laura, I'm sure of it. You'll find him."

"How?" said Laura.

"You will," said Pim, and somehow her voice made Laura shiver.

"Did you find Faland, Pim?" said Laura. "In Poperinghe? I *know* you went looking."

Pim hesitated fractionally. Frowning, she shook her head. "No," she said. "But I will. You'll see. It will be all right now. I know you're tired, but you must not give up."

"I'm not giving up, Pim."

Pim turned away and got undressed, and they each sponged off the worst of the muck and crawled under their blankets, lay in silence. Laura was mortally tired, but wound up like a clock-spring. Apparently Pim was too. "Why are we here?" Pim asked abruptly. Her voice was small.

Laura forced her eyes open. "At Couthove?"

"No," said Pim. "It's not— Oh . . . How did we get *here*? How did it all come to this?"

Laura didn't really have an answer, but she found herself saying, haltingly, "I was at a party once, with a great military scholar. He got very drunk. One of the things I remember he said was that the reason the Germans couldn't call it off, invading Belgium, back in '14, was that they'd already got their train tables down precisely, and any deviation from the schedule would ruin it."

"So you think train tables got us into the war?" said Pim, skeptical.

"No," said Laura. "Or maybe a little. But it's not just train tables. The whole world's made up of systems now. Systems that are too big for any one person to understand or control, or stop. Like the timetables. Alliances. Philosophies. And so now we're here, even though no one wanted to be."

"Why did God let it happen?" whispered Pim. "I tried to understand—all those days in Halifax, after Nate passed, and I heard Jimmy was missing. I'd go to church and tell myself that God has a plan for each of us. But how can we know?"

"I don't know," said Laura. She wouldn't blurt out the heretical thing she was actually thinking: *What is God if not another system?*

"I want to hate someone," said Pim. "But I can't hate the Germans. Isn't that strange?"

"No," said Laura. "Not the men out there. They're caught in it just as we are. Go to sleep now. I'll wake you when the shift changes."

But Laura still couldn't sleep. And judging by the rustling, Pim couldn't either. "Come into my bed," said Laura finally. "I'm cold. There's enough room."

It was a measure of both their weariness that Pim—chatterbox Pim—didn't say a thing, but got up wordlessly and slid under the blankets in her chemise. They curled up together, and Laura put an arm over her, and blew out the lamp. They were asleep in an instant. Laura could not remember the last time she'd been so warm.

PANDEMONIUM

·····

FOR THE FIRST TIME, FREDDIE WOKE IN THE HOTEL NOT WITH an absence, but with a new memory. Faint as cobweb, blurred, but there. He'd seen Laura. Alive. Limping. In the hotel. Reason told him he hadn't seen her. It could have been some new trick of Faland's, a mirror-image that his mind tried to insist had been real.

But the memory persisted. The things in Faland's mirror faded the second you looked away. But this woman looked back at him from his own mind's eye, as unforgettable as a wound: wet, scarred, furious, vital, threads of white in her tawny hair. He could not have imagined her. It was Laura.

He'd forgotten so much, changed so much. But he hadn't forgotten her. Nearly every memory of his childhood contained his sister. Seeing her, he remembered that he was a person too, however shattered. He wasn't a single agonizing note in Faland's patient hands.

He didn't know how much time had passed since he'd seen her. He'd long since stopped caring about day or night. But now he thought, *How long has it been? Where is she now?* With a ferocity that surprised even him, Freddie got up and went downstairs.

He was a few feet down the corridor when the first bars of music hit him. He cringed back at the sound. Faland was playing a piece he hadn't heard before, and the sound of it was shocking. Jagged, glorious, insane.

Then the music stopped and began again, more tentatively, as though Faland, for the first time since Freddie had met him, was feeling his way through something unfamiliar.

Freddie followed the sound down the corridor, down the stairs, to the archway to the foyer.

Stopped.

The foyer was empty. The foyer was a ruin. It smelled of mold and mice, the furniture overturned, broken glass on the floor. And the worst part was, Freddie wonder for a moment what had happened. Because it was just like waking up, when your vague dreams dissolve in the cold light of morning. Of course the foyer was like this.

A scrape at the fiddle seized his attention, and he realized that Faland was sitting on the edge of an overturned ammunition crate, oblivious to the wreckage. He tried again to play the new music; briefly it soared, glorious and mad, and then fell apart. Faland was frowning.

He glanced up at Freddie, the same as he'd ever been, a little shabby in his checked suit, sardonic, the ghost of a terrible beauty still lurking somewhere in his face, beneath the cynicism and dissolution. He seemed almost more at home in the wreckage than he had in the intact hotel.

They eyed each other.

Faland seemed to study him and then he said, "Look at you, the toy soldier remembering he is a real boy."

Freddie said the only thing that mattered. "I saw my sister."

Faland began to play his violin again. An ordinary run of notes now, flavored mockingly with longing. "Did you?"

He had. He knew he had. The rush of emotion was too violent, too shimmering and fragile even to name. *She's alive.* "Where is she now?"

A little curling smile. "Gone off into the bright world, mon brave. Do you think that shining girl wants to lurk in the shadows with you?"

It shouldn't have hurt. Freddie told himself that it didn't. "She was limping."

Faland said nothing.

"She looked ill."

Faland's answer was in music, a melody like a caterwauling of childish plaints. Freddie gritted his teeth and said, "I'm going to go find her."

"Indeed?" The music took on an exaggerated nobility. As though Faland was laying out all the leaves of Freddie's soul, and finding them shallow and obvious. "Allow her to lament the remains of the man you were? Make her aid a deserter? Will you let her watch when they shoot you, or let them shoot her along with you, when she tries to help you?"

Freddie floundered. How could he risk— Fumblingly he said, "No—I can't— She's alive. I have to go to her. She—she won't care what I did. I'll go in secret, I won't stay, I . . ."

The violin music shifted to a major key, bright with ferocious courage, and Faland said over the sound, "Do you think she'll accept it? That amber-eyed girl? No, she'll turn traitor for you, harbor you, a deserter, without a qualm, she'll try everything she can to save you and when they arrest her for it, she won't flinch for a moment. She'll go to her death alongside you. Or am I mistaken?"

Freddie hated himself for shivering and falling silent.

Faland added, "If *she* won't hesitate to risk her life, are you going to *let* her?"

Imagination failed him. He was so much less than he'd been.

"I didn't think so," said Faland.

Freddie bit his lip. "I have to know she's all right at least."

A faint gleam in Faland's lighter eye and the tumble of half-mocking music went silent. "Well," he said. "I could help you in that, perhaps."

"Can you?"

"Yes." He was looking straight at Freddie now, and the dusty silence in all the ruin was far worse than the background of violin music.

"What do you want?" Freddie whispered. He thought he knew the answer.

But Faland surprised him. He did not ask about the pillbox. "Tell me a story that frightens you."

"Why?"

"You are full of questions for a man solely concerned with the fate of his beloved sister."

Freddie still hesitated. "And if I tell you . . ."

"Then you will see her, and not endanger her life. I swear it."

Freddie said, "But you know what frightens me. I've told you—" He didn't remember what he'd told Faland.

Faland began tuning his fiddle, as though in anticipation. "Not that. Tell me why you scream at night."

"No," Freddie whispered. The memories that woke him screaming all involved Winter. He wasn't ready to—

Faland said, "Leave her to her fate, then, what do I care?" He drew his bow lightly across the strings, made a moue of dissatisfaction at the sound, tuned the violin again.

He couldn't go to Laura. That much was clear. The brother she'd loved had died in the pillbox. But if he could do even this small thing, from afar, to ensure her welfare, then it was cheap at the price of any memory. And again, he felt himself yield. "Your word?"

"Yes."

Freddie was silent, then. What frightened him? Memories were growing harder for him to dredge up, and when they came they were fainter, like ink too much handled. And Faland wanted to hear about one of the days that had no words, that should stay in his mind, always unvoiced. He thought of the night he believed Laura had died, opened his mouth with the road to Brandhoek already glittering foully behind his eyes. But he was suddenly afraid that the memory of grief was part of the edifice that fixed his love for her in his mind. Could he not rid himself of sorrow without losing the rest?

Faland waited.

What, then? Was he afraid of the hotel? No. He was afraid of how much he never wanted to leave the hotel.

Without consciously deciding, he found himself speaking of the walk from the shell hole to Ypres. It all came back to him: the noise, the smell, Winter's hands holding him back from the water, holding his soul together. His courage, leavening the horror, the only reason Freddie had come out alive, and sane. He retched on the words, and didn't know whether it was from the memory or his sorrow at losing it. Already the color of Winter's eyes seemed less immutable in his mind. But he told it.

This time Faland listened with his lips a little parted. As though he could drink up Freddie's whole life, swallow it for nourishment.

At the end, Freddie was weeping, and Faland let out a long, delighted sigh.

Freddie said nothing. He looked up and the hotel was beautiful, warm and gilded, although shabbier than ever and the broken glass was still on the floor. Reality was a crumbling thing, a rotten tree.

"Is this place a ruin?" he whispered.

Faland reached out and tucked a strand of Freddie's hair behind his ear. Freddie hadn't noticed how long it had grown. Caressingly, he said, "Not to you, little soldier. Not as long as you're with me."

The fire was so warm. Faland's fingers were tangled in his hair. "I saw a ruin," he insisted.

Faland said, "Don't look at it. Look at me instead."

And wasn't that the damnable part? Freddie couldn't look away.

. . .

He didn't know how much time passed after that. The world moved more and more to dream logic. He didn't know if hours had gone by, or days. Freddie said, "You promised. I don't have much time," and knew it to be true. He didn't know if it was his mind failing or his body, but after he told Faland his first memory of Winter, he lived in a wrung-out daze. He was fairly certain he'd be mad or dead now, if he'd not seen Laura. He told the memory over and over in his mind: how she'd looked, the tone of her voice. And he hung on. "I have to see her," he said. "You promised I'd see her."

Then, between one hour and the next, Faland came to him where he lay asleep, and shook him awake.

Freddie looked up, and briefly thought he saw the roof fallen in over his head, a single star shining, and with the dim light behind him, Faland a specter of avarice and despair. Freddie would have called him inhuman once, except now he knew better. Whatever Faland was, it wasn't inhuman. Inhuman was out there on the Ridge.

"Come with me," said Faland, and put out a hand.

Freddie took it just as Faland glanced up at the star himself. Shook his head a little, and when he turned away, carrying his violin, Freddie followed. It was night, and the air smelled of spring. Freddie felt the weakness of his limbs, the dimming of his eyes. Wept a little, as he walked.

They halted in a cemetery outside a crumbling old château. "Where are we?" Freddie whispered. He was so tired.

"Watch," said Faland, and he turned his head, so that Freddie was fixed with the darkness of his left eye. "And do not say a word." The moonlight eased some of the lines in Faland's face; the grandeur of him was ascendant, his face alive with what might have been curiosity. And there Faland set bow to string.

For the first time, Freddie realized that Faland in his hotel had been merely amusing himself, trying this melody and that, a musician at play. On Christmas, true, he'd filled the air with anger, perhaps disturbed the nights of his hearers. But he'd been humoring Freddie, giving him a taste, nothing more. He hadn't meant it.

Perhaps he rarely meant it. But he did now, for Faland stood there and played pure terror into the night.

Freddie listened with a fist over his mouth. It wasn't music. It was the fear of a man in a frontline trench, jumping at every noise, it was the fear of a man in a hospital when supple-winged Death visits the bed beside him. It was terrible and primal and it was *his*, the road to Ypres, with the falling shells and the bodies and the ghost, and Freddie wanted to scream for Faland to stop. Too much of it and horror was all Freddie would remember; he'd be nothing more than a memory of crawling dread. *Laura,* he thought. *Laura.*

Soldiers stripped the war of emotions as best they could. They'd go mad if they did not. But Faland was relentless; he poured long-denied fear into the night until men shouted in terror from behind the château's dark windows.

In the midst of the clamor, Faland stood still as the eye of a hurricane, sketching Freddie in sound, until Freddie had utterly forgotten anything besides being afraid. Until he was on his knees but didn't know it, his arms wrapped round his head.

Finally the violin dropped to Faland's side, but the music didn't die away. It seemed to Freddie that the essence of it had been taken up by the sounds in the château: screams, orders, moving lights. He raised his head; he was covered in cold sweat, snatching desperately at memory-fragments, anything to anchor him through the fear. There was nothing. He felt like he was drowning in mud. Somewhere behind his eyes, the dead man smiled at him. Faland just stood poised, waiting. His eyes were on the window.

A light hurried in, and in it, Freddie saw Laura. She was herself, straight-shouldered, neat in her uniform, authority in the lines of her body. She was all right. *Laura,* he thought. *Laura, I'm frightened.* She turned toward the window; he saw her face clear in the lights within. His breathing started to settle. A patient was standing in his pajamas, facing the window. More lights had come into the ward. His sister spoke to the standing patient, then caught him when he fell. A doctor came, helped her ease the patient back into bed.

Again Laura glanced toward the window.

Instinctively Freddie shrank into the shadows but he was so caught up in the sight of her—now she was bending over a patient, a tall dark-haired doctor beside her—that he failed to notice the woman who slipped out the château's front door until she was half-way across the drive, her steps tentative in the dewy grass. Faland stirred, and Freddie turned and recognized the woman. From the hotel. With the golden hair.

Her face changed when she saw Faland. She crossed the space

between them, slowly, and stood still, facing him, colorless in the moonlight. The music still seemed to echo, in the dying clamor of the château.

The woman said, "I've been talking to the men. They say such things about you. Are they true?"

"What do they say?"

The woman was silent.

Faland smiled. "Perhaps they are true, then."

"I won't do it," the woman whispered. "You know I won't. It doesn't matter what I saw." She was so beautiful. Freddie wanted to say something, but his throat was locked tight. She had not once looked away from Faland.

Faland's voice was softer than Freddie had ever heard it. "And yet you came outside."

She said nothing, but in her face was a strange and terrible desire that made Freddie's flesh creep. Faland was watching her as though in fascination. Then she shook her head, whispered, "No—no—I don't even know how I would do it."

Faland said, "Oh, I think you know exactly how."

The woman stood still, her lips parted. Then she wrenched herself round and ran back the way she'd come.

Faland turned away, whistling. "Well, that's done."

"Leave her alone," said Freddie. "That's my sister's friend. Leave her alone."

"Did I ask her to go out wandering at night, arguing with bad men? Leave me to my pleasures, Iven, the world's so dour now."

"What does she want?"

Faland said, "What does anyone want? Her heart's desire. Enough. I'm going. Come back with me or go to blazes, boy, which is it?"

"Damn you," said Freddie. "What about my sister?"

"You saw her, she's perfectly well," said Faland.

He didn't move. "You lied. You came for that woman. You didn't come to show me Laura at all."

"*Laura* was ill," said Faland, with precision. "Influenza, and

pneumonia. She survived, evidently. She is now working in that—"
He pointed at the château. "A private field hospital. Happy as a rabbit in clover. Anything else you want to know?"

"How did you know all that?"

"I am an inveterate gossip," said Faland.

"Leave my sister alone."

Faland snorted. "If she leaves me alone; she's the righteous, meddling kind, you know."

Freddie strained his dimming faculties. "And that woman? What do you want with her?"

With exaggerated patience, Faland said, "I think your question should be what do I want with you?"

"I know what you want with me," said Freddie.

They shared a long look. *It is not far from love,* Freddie thought somewhere in the embers of a mind that had been a poet's. *The tie of hunter and prey.* "I want to see Laura again."

"I said you'd see her, and you did. You could have gone in."

He couldn't have. Faland, that bastard, knew it.

Faland said, "Stay or go, Iven?"

He was already walking away, over the dewy spring grass, whistling a little to himself, as though trying out a melody. Without a word, head bent, Freddie followed.

· · ·

More time passed. No one came to the hotel anymore, as though Faland had suddenly got tired of playing at hospitality. Freddie drifted through corridors that he did not always recognize; lived in a world that was nine parts dream. He couldn't remember when he'd last eaten. But still he clung to the scraps of himself. Laura was out there. She'd survived, she'd come back. He didn't have the strength to go to her. But he couldn't bear to leave her either. Not when she hadn't left him. Perhaps he'd see her again, he thought vaguely. Even from afar. So he wavered, a stranger to himself. Hour after hour.

Faland spent every moment on a piece he could not seem to master, love and madness twined in a nauseating swirl. Freddie kept telling over memories that felt like they'd happened to someone else, trying to reweave the fabric of his soul as quick as Faland tore it apart. And at the end of each day's story, when Freddie was slumped, crying, feeling like he'd clawed pieces off himself with his fingernails, he'd ask, "How is she?"

"The same," Faland would say.

And finally Faland answered instead, "She's left the hospital. Your sister."

"Why?" said Freddie. But he knew why. Deep in the remains of his soul, he knew, whatever his mind tried to tell him. His heart beat faster—was it in fear or delight? *She's looking for me.*

Don't find me, Laura. I don't want you to find me. He hated himself for being glad that she was looking.

"Do you wish to see her?" said Faland.

He tried to fight his way through lethargy, like clawing away cobweb. Why would Faland ask? "Yes."

Faland touched Freddie's face with a wounding gentleness. "All right," he said. "I shall take you to her. But first I want you to tell me what you see, all those times you've fled from nothing, when you look behind you in my hotel."

He saw the shell hole, the soldier's face as he drowned. Winter. The shell hole was one of his hoarded memories of Winter. Of course Faland wanted that.

"I—" He couldn't say no anymore. He wanted to see Laura. Perhaps the sight of her would tell him what to do, how to live, or when he could die. Perhaps he'd grown too tired at last to carry the weight of himself. "Listen, then," he said.

Faland smiled at him, with heartbreaking gentleness.

Freddie told him about taking refuge in the shell hole, the night they escaped the pillbox. About the drowned man, and how Winter had looked Freddie in the face, after he killed him. What color were Winter's eyes? They'd been dark, hadn't they? No.

"Come with me," said Faland afterward. He was glowing, as though Freddie's love and terror were things he could hold, wear, possess. "I know where she is."

"Where?" said Freddie. He was slow as a tired child.

"Poperinghe," said Faland.

They walked, and sometime later—he'd no idea how long—Freddie saw the lights of Pop all around him, wavering as though underwater. Perhaps, months ago, when he'd first come to the hotel, he'd have been afraid. Afraid that the sheer, pulsing life of Poperinghe, its edge-of-death giddiness, would draw him back into the world's bloody maw. But now he wasn't. He was too far gone to be afraid. His tie to the world was thin as a silk thread.

Poperinghe was full of men, loud as a holiday, and Freddie watched them with distant eyes. "Where's Laura?"

In answer Faland bowed his head and set his bow to his strings, and loosed music like a flight of arrows into the night.

This time it wasn't fear that Faland conjured. It was rage, close kin to madness, unleavened by understanding, or sorrow. The hot rage of a soldier on a trench raid, the poisonous anger of men in the back area told they must polish their buttons between spells in the line. The rage that had drowned a man in a shell hole in No Man's Land, under Freddie's unflinching hand.

It was the worst thing he'd ever heard. It conjured it all, true as life: The sounds the soldier had made as he died, the color of his face, the smell of the rain, and Freddie's entire existence shrank to that one moment, to that one wretched self—murderer. That was all he was. All he would be, forever and ever, amen. There was nothing else. He was screaming. But no one heard. The entire town was screaming.

Because they'd heard his anger—and answered it. The same violence lay at the heart of every man there, and Faland drew it forth like a conjuror. Between one note and the next, music morphed into the sound of riot: screams and running feet, shouts, and wild laughter. Glass broke, wood smashed, and the streets were *packed*, everyone mourning, rowdy, drunk. Freddie was screaming with the rest. They might walk and laugh and fight like men, but they were all screaming underneath. Faland knew. Of course Faland knew. Faland might be oblivion with hands and a face and a quicksilver tongue, but he knew them all. He'd been a soldier too.

The crowd swung dizzyingly past. He thought he saw Faland standing face-to-face with the golden-haired woman. Her eyes were as wild as his. His lips moved. "Shall I show you?" he said. They disappeared in the turmoil.

He didn't follow. The tumult was all around him, the tumult *was* him. He was going to drown in it. Laura wasn't here. *Please let her not be here. Let it all be over.*

But before he could move, he froze. He'd seen a ghost in the crowd.

A ghost he knew.

Not Laura this time, but Hans Winter, a point of stillness in all the wild movement. Their eyes locked. The left sleeve of Winter's jacket was empty. Freddie realized Winter was fighting to get to him. Realized that he was doing the same, shoving forward. Winter hadn't gone. He hadn't forgotten. His eyes weren't dark. They were a shattering blue.

They would despise you, Faland had said. Laura and Winter. But there was no scorn on Winter's face. They pushed toward each other, and Freddie felt his mind slowly clear, felt reason briefly return. For a second, he was himself, and he thought, *I am needed. Why should I give my soul to that dilettante musician?*

Now Freddie heard running footsteps. A voice shouted, "Halt!"

There was fear in Winter's eyes. Of course Winter would be a fugitive. How else could he be here? Their hands were almost touching when a pistol cracked from an unknown source, the crowd heaved, and Winter jerked back, his hand coming to press against his side.

Freddie saw the stain blooming.

Blue, desperate eyes stared into his.

"Hold on, Iven." And then Winter ran again, stumbling, and vanished in the crowd.

. . .

Freddie went straight to Faland, although it took far too long to find him, darting in a panic from lights to darkness, his head swimming with the sound of the gunshot, the look on Winter's face. Freddie found Faland sitting in a café, of all places. He had a glass of something and an expression of heavy-lidded contentment. To Freddie he said, "You seem to have had a pleasant evening." A gleam of knowing malice there. "See anyone you know?"

"Winter's alive," said Freddie, panting.

Faland lifted both brows, sipped his drink, made a face. It occurred to Freddie to wonder how much Faland knew, how much he'd planned, but he shook the thought away. It didn't matter.

"He's wounded—shot—they're looking for him. I have to help him."

"Do you?"

Bitter admission. "I can't, alone." He couldn't do anything alone. He could hardly exist.

Faland rolled his glass between his fingers. "And what will you give me, if I help you?"

All the air seemed to leave his body. "You know," said Freddie. "There is only one thing you want from me. And—and you planned this. To get it from me."

"Well? Did I get it?"

"Yes. Damn you, yes. Anything."

Faland got to his feet. His eye sparked. "Very well. We'll take a leaf out of your book, Iven, and take your poor hunted friend to your sister. A fair price, would you say?"

Freddie was silent.

Faland fixed him with a faintly smiling gaze. "And afterward, Wilfred, you will tell me at last about the darkness, and how you came to love that man."

AND I SAW A NEW HEAVEN,
AND A NEW EARTH

.....

I T WAS STILL DARK OUTSIDE, THE COLD, STICKY HOUR BEFORE
sunrise. Laura woke, with sleep still heavy in her eyes, and saw
her mother in the shadows.

She rolled to her feet without thinking. The darkness was empty.
But Laura reached out anyway. For the first time, her first thought
was not a wordless scream of horror and guilt. Her first thought was
Are you there?

Her second thought was *Why are you here? Did you lead me to
Winter?* It was, although she had told no one, the other reason she'd
been ready to trust him.

Are you helping me?

No answer came from the darkness, but Laura stared into the
empty corner, and neither experience nor reason could suppress her
hope: *I'm not alone.*

Then Laura realized that Pim was gone.

She didn't know why her stomach knotted. Pim could have
slipped out for any number of reasons. But even as she reassured

herself, Laura was reaching for her dress, thrusting her feet into damp boots, and pinning her veil as she turned to the door.

. . .

Pim wasn't in the main ward. A glance told her that, but Laura went in anyway, her electric lantern a blue-white pool in the darkness. She stopped here and there, offering one man a bedpan, another a drink of water. Asked the ones who were awake if they'd seen Mrs. Shaw. Sighing, they admitted that they had not.

Where, then?

She came to the silent Winter. She'd bandaged the healed stump of his shoulder to conceal the fact of the old injury; she made a show of checking it, then turned to the bullet hole in his side. He hadn't bled through the bandage, although his skin was hot and dry. She thought he'd do. Her sense of the stages of dying was unerring. Jones's blood had helped, and the ether had worn off.

All the men nearby were asleep, although a few tossed in a pain-filled doze. A boy was whimpering. Laura turned away to give him morphine, feeling Winter's gaze, then she returned to him, and gave him some water, and under the cover of her helping him sit up, holding the cup to his lips, he said, "Your brother's with a person called Faland."

They had only moments: *How, when, why* were questions she could not ask. So she whispered, simply, "I have met Faland. Tell me."

Winter said, "We were in Ypres together, wounded, when Faland found us. I was close to dying; perhaps that was why I feared him so. He looked like the war to me. Devouring. I tried to tell your brother, but he didn't understand. He saved my life, but went away with Faland. That's where he is. That's where I have to find him."

She didn't ask why he'd do so much for her brother. She knew enough of soldiers to understand the ties that sprang up between men out there: thicker than blood and selfless. "Did you find him?"

Winter said, "I saw him. During the riot." The blue eyes stared at the ceiling past Laura's shoulder, and she thought how it must have been for him as a fugitive, searching, stealing. Almost to himself, Winter said, "The ghost pointed and I saw you. And the same night—I saw him too. It felt like a miracle."

"Ghost?" said Laura, despite herself.

"Front's full of ghosts," Winter whispered. His gaze wandered a little now. She laid the back of her hand against his forehead, felt his temperature rising. "How many dead men? A million? More? Tombs are open. Wasn't it written? They said that would happen, at the end of the world. *And I saw the dead, great and small.* They can help you. They helped me. People thought I was one of the wild men. That's why I wasn't captured. The dead—they told me— Haven't you seen? New heaven. That was written too. New earth. New hell too. That's not in the verse. But it's true. You've seen, haven't you—how the new world and the old world share space . . ." He shook his head.

"How do I find Faland?"

"The ghosts," he said. "You have to ask the ghosts."

She was afraid her hope would pull her into madness with him. Afraid she was already there. Afraid they both were sane and the world was infinitely stranger than she'd thought. She was a creature of her senses: diagrams, bodies. She wasn't equipped for this; *she* wasn't a poet. "Winter, who is Faland? What would he want with my brother?"

The lucidity was fading from Winter's face. "To eat. Just like the war does. Only he savors. Does that make him better? The ghosts said his world ended too."

"I'll find him," said Laura. It was a vow. She got to her feet and said as an afterthought, "Have you seen my friend? She has yellow hair."

A small perturbed frown, but he shook his head. Laura turned and left the ward.

. . .

Pim could not be found in the château at all. In the sterilization room, Laura found only two orderlies playing cards, and Jones, stirring cocoa powder into steaming tinned milk, his eyes red-rimmed. He looked pleased to see her. "Iven, you must come with me and see Trovato's leg. I thought we might have to have it off after all, with the artery severed. But the small vessels are doing the work, no necrosis of the foot—"

Then he noticed the worry on her face. "What is it?"

"I can't find Pim."

"She's a grown—" He seemed to realize that Laura was really worried. "Well, she's not here."

"She's not in the château. I have to find her." She left the sterilization room, words trailing away in Jones's startled silence, pulled open the front door, breaking the hospital fug with the smell of early spring. She peered out into the predawn gray.

Jones followed her into the foyer. "Iven?"

Laura was scanning the grounds, the drive. Dead ahead, the rusted iron gate of the château, and beyond the road, marked with the lights of lorries, running east. To the left was the ruined orchard, and beyond lay the hospital cemetery, enlarged every week of the war. Was that a light, there, among the crosses?

Jones had seen it too. He was staring narrow-eyed into the night. "I thought Shaw looked peculiar, yesterday evening, when you came back from that dinner. I suppose it was too much to bear, dining in luxury after weeks of tending to men in pieces? And Mrs. Shaw *would* crack picturesquely, and go out wandering the moors in a nightdress or something."

It cut too near the bone to be amusing, but Laura was glad of Jones's presence as they went out together, through the slick grass at the edge of the drive. Laura could almost talk herself into an innocent explanation, convince herself that Pim was upstairs. The cemetery was on the far side of the overgrown apple orchard. They cut between the trees, whose shadows were just visible under a faintly graying sky.

The light reappeared in the cemetery. Laura thought she heard a voice. "Did he say I had him?" It wasn't Jones's voice.

Laura could not hear the answer, but the speaker laughed. "Oh, he told you, did he? Will I come if you do it? Yes, of course I shall. But don't think that—"

The voices faded. The gleam of light had gone again. But Laura's eyes found movement in the graveyard. Too tall to be Pim. Thinner than Jones. The light was so uncertain. Was it Faland? Was there really, in their wonder-stripped world, a monster she could placate, to get her brother back? Pim's voice, shaking, said, *"Please."*

Laura's brain started working again. Why would Faland be here? How would Pim have known? What was she doing?

Then Jones's light caught Pim running. There was no one else there.

"Mrs. Shaw," Jones called peremptorily.

But Pim wasn't looking at him. "No!" she called, running still. "Wait, I said I would, I—"

No one was there. Pim slowed to a walk, then stopped, panting. She stared blindly at the graves. Laura saw her shoulders shake. Then she turned toward them, collecting herself with the startling speed of a gently reared woman. Laura had seen her in profile, lips parted, a face full of some tormented emotion too complex to name, but Pim was smiling by the time she turned. "Laura, is that you?" she called. "And Dr. Jones, good heavens. Were you looking for me? Oh, lord, have I made a ninny of myself? Forgive me, please, both of you." She brushed grass from her skirt. Jones hadn't said anything; he looked suspicious. Laura wondered what he'd heard, what he'd thought, of that broken exchange in the shadows. Pim kept right on talking: "Was I sleepwalking? I suppose I must have been. You know, I had a maiden aunt prone to sleepwalking. Terrible thing. I think it's the overstrain. Do you think it's too early for a cup of tea?"

Oh, Pim, Laura thought. There were a dozen questions on the tip of her tongue, but a glance showed her Pim's eyes wary behind that beautiful smile, and Laura didn't think she'd get an answer. Not with Jones standing right there.

In the château, then. The instant she and Pim were alone.

But solitude wasn't so easy to come by. Day was breaking and a dozen voices greeted both Laura and Jones the instant they passed the front door: a clamor of emergencies. One man had bled through his dressing, a nurse had seen signs of gangrene in a man's leg, they were getting more Frenchmen that day, anything to relieve the strain on the overstretched regular hospitals. The rhythm of it all swept Laura up, and Pim didn't let herself be corralled; she was on her feet without a break, fetching, carrying, sketching, while men dictated letters.

Young came at noon, the gravitas of his bearing only a little marred by his ears. He was closeted first with Mary, then with Pim, leaving the staff all eager to know what was going on.

"He's still looking for their escaped German prisoner," said one of the nurses, the one shameless about eavesdropping. "The fellow was actually *seen* in Poperinghe, it seems. They are searching abandoned buildings nearby. And the queen of Belgium is coming to us! At least that rumor's true. This very evening, on her way to supper, and General Gage is coming with her. And a newspaperman. Oh, Mary's going to have us all in a fury of scrubbing."

THE FRUIT OF THAT
FORBIDDEN TREE

·····

WINTER HAD BECOME FEVERISH, SINCE THE DAWN. LAURA stopped at his bed when she could, to check his wound and sponge cold water on his face. Once she came into the ward and saw Pim and Winter with their heads together, whispering. Winter was shaking his head.

Laura came nearer, heard Pim say *What other way*, but before she could hear more, the patient beside her tugged her sleeve. When she looked up, Pim had vanished and Winter looked troubled. Laura went across. "What did she say?"

Winter said, "She is determined, your friend."

"To do what?"

"Help you."

"How?"

Winter hesitated, and then Laura, damnably, was already being called away. The whole hospital must scrub itself spotless, overseen by a martial-eyed Mary. "Royal patronage is a splendid thing to gain at the cost of a little scrubbing," Mary told them. Laura bit back on her flaring temper. At least Winter was safe. She had already boiled his thermometer, surreptitiously turned him sticky and pallid with petroleum jelly. Most experienced nurses had a flair for malingering;

there were always patients—the odd fifteen-year-old soldier mostly—that they tried to keep in hospital as long as possible. When Laura was through with him, Winter looked ready to die on the spot, and it was child's play to have him huddled away at the far end of the ward, where his imminent demise could not disturb Her Majesty.

Pim was wound tight as a clock-spring and trying to hide it. Laura wasn't fooled, and Jones saw it too. Laura caught him giving Pim an unflattering once-over from the far side of the ward. "I don't care how much she brightens the men," he said to Laura, after. "She looks positively fey. Riding for a fall. And what was that outside, this morning? Looking for her fiddler again?"

Jones was too perceptive by half. "I'll talk to her," said Laura. "I would have before, if it weren't for Mary's strictures. Down with all monarchies, I say. I think I'll move to Russia and join the Revolution."

"Throw your lot in with those murdering Bolsheviks? You may as well come to America, where we have no tsar and no kaiser either."

Jones did not look away when Laura stared at him. "And what," she said, "would I do in America?" His eyes were so very dark. They studied each other.

But if Jones meant to answer, other voices intervened. "She's here!" cried one of the nurses keeping watch at the front window, and a wave of chatter went through the staff.

"Right," muttered Jones. "Now I'm with you. Vive la révolution."

Laura snorted. He grinned back, looking suddenly younger.

Scrubbed and starched, the whole staff assembled to greet the queen. The sun was slanting west. Laura wished Her Majesty had come earlier; most men were in pain by evening. She saw strain on faces all over the ward. And not only patients. Pim's whole body was radiating tension as a beautiful white car swept up the drive. Perhaps the visit would be brief, Laura thought. It was dinnertime.

The woman who got out was dazzling too, as she walked into the château on General Gage's arm. She was wearing a sort of Red Cross uniform, but an experienced tailor had got hold of it, and darted it to flatter. The whiteness was blinding. No one, Laura thought, had been sick on it. Bled on it.

"Welcome, Your Majesty," said Mary.

The queen smiled, remote as a white peacock. She didn't seem real. *Strange world,* Laura thought. It had changed so fast, so suddenly, that you wondered, over and over, what was real anymore.

Maybe more things than she'd thought.

And again her mind circled back to Faland. *Freddie.*

A decent stretch of tedium followed. Laura could feel a restless Jones shifting from foot to foot beside her. Gage made himself charming, full of swift Irish repartee, and Young, who had come with him, said inane things and looked longingly at Pim. Were they still talking? Didn't they have a war to run? The queen wished to meet the men. A newspaperman had indeed appeared—Laura didn't know if he was Mary's or the queen's—and he set about industriously snapping pictures.

In the main ward, Laura positioned herself where she could best distract the curious from Winter. He'd buried himself in the covers, looked like nothing more than a heap of blankets. No one glanced his way. There were too many other green-tinged faces vying for the queen's attention, and to her credit, she didn't flinch at any of them. She went from man to man with kind words and bits of chocolate. Laura could almost have been in charity with her, were it not for the camera snapping and flashing, setting the men on the jump, and herself too. At least, she consoled herself, the queen was efficient, and her newspaperman too. With any luck, she'd be gone before dark.

Laura was wondering how to get to Faland, what to say to Pim, when the report of a gunshot echoed through the ward.

Half the men shouted, and most hurled themselves off their cots in instinctive search for cover, then howled again as they jarred their wounds. Laura threw herself flat too, on the same pure instinct, then looked up, uncomprehending. Pim was staggering backward, down the middle of the room, grappling with—grappling with *Winter* for a pistol. What in God's name? How had he even managed to get up? He was feverish, bloodlessly pale, but on his feet. How had he got hold of a gun? How had he got past her? Had he tried to shoot—whom? The queen? Christ, why?

The gun went off again, and as the bullet whined past his ear, Gage jerked, lost his footing, and fell heavily. The ward erupted with more shouts. A patient was lunging for the struggling pair, as the general stumbled to his feet, shouting. But before anyone could reach them, Winter clipped Pim on the jaw, sending her crumpling to the ground.

Then Winter stood panting, almost doubled over, the gun in his hand. He stared wildly around the room; his eye fastened on Laura. He glanced at Pim, then back to Laura. Raised his eyes briefly to the window. There was a furious message in his gaze, but one she could not read. "I'd do it again," he said. His accent was damnably German. He'd dropped the pistol. Then his knees buckled.

Gage was sweating with shock and fury; the queen was white and shaken. It had been a close call. Laura scrambled for Pim, just as Jones went for the fallen Winter. He seized the pistol, knocked the rest of the bullets out of the chamber, and passed it swiftly to Young, who was trying clumsily to get past Laura to Pim. Then he turned Winter over to check his dressings, cursed at the scarlet stain; Winter had burst every one of his stitches.

"How did he get a pistol? How did he get in?" Gage roared, bending over Jones, who said nothing. He didn't look at Laura. Young had paused, frozen in abstraction, the gun in his hand.

Laura had her arms around Pim. Her friend was sitting up now, looking from Gage to Winter with a look of abject horror. Her face was already swelling.

What the hell had happened?

Winter was bleeding fast from his reopened wound. Jones was fussing over it in a competent manner, but not, Laura noticed, working enormously hard to stanch the blood. He looked grim.

"Save that man's life!" Gage was thundering. "Save him, damn it! He must be questioned! It's him—it's the spy—trying to assassinate—"

An assassin? Had she been so deceived? Pim was looking out the window. So was Winter, and there was a likeness to their gazes, dazed and desperate.

Laura looked too.

For just a moment, his face vague in the just-gathering dusk, she saw Faland, watching them all with mismatched, glittering eyes.

. . .

Pim was trembling violently, trying to speak. Mary said, "Hush, dear, not now," face drawn with bewildered anger.

"Save that bastard's life, damn you!" bellowed Gage again.

Jones's eyes were coldly black, his face set, expressionless. "Get everyone out, if you want me to save him. Give me some room," he said. "Damn you," he added, low, to the German. He still didn't look at Laura.

Winter reached up and caught Laura's wrist. "Don't you see? He came for this."

Despite herself, Laura glanced again at the window. Faland was gone. He might never have been there.

Mary was pulling a trembling Pim out of the room; Young made to follow, his expression troubled. Winter's eyes stayed fixed on Laura even as they rolled him onto a stretcher. There was a frantic message in them.

Laura turned away, and ran out of the ward, out of the château.

INTO THIS WILD ABYSS

·····

CHÂTEAU COUTHOVE AND PARTS UNKNOWN,

FLANDERS, BELGIUM

APRIL 1918

THE DRIVE WAS EMPTY, EXCEPT FOR THE QUEEN'S CAR AND THE shadows of the orchard, cast long over the gravel. The crosses in the cemetery cut lines in the fading sky. The spring air felt cold on her face, and Laura was somehow not surprised to see a bloody figure among the shadows of the trees. It pointed, and Laura looked and saw movement; a brief anonymous flicker near the gate. She didn't question anymore, or doubt or fear. She just ran toward it.

Faland was by the gate, and turning into the dusk, his hair the same color as cloudy sky. She was nearly upon him before she saw him, and then she seized him by his sleeve and spun him round.

To her surprise, he didn't resist, but stood watching her with narrow interest. "I know perfectly what they were hoping for," he said. "But I wasn't sure you'd believe them." He looked dissatisfied.

She set her jaw. "Where is my brother?"

"'Great is the battle-god,'" quoted Faland. "'Great, and his kingdom.' Gone, of course."

"You are a liar." Laura kept expecting that Mary's voice—

someone's voice—would call after her, inquiring, demanding. But the front door of Couthove didn't open. The driver of the shining car didn't turn his head.

"Perhaps I am," said Faland. "But he is gone. All of him is mine now. Everything that matters. He gave it to me." Faland spoke as though it was nothing to walk through the wreckage of the world, amused and curious and avid for the human soul.

She didn't care. He was no more terrifying than Brandhoek, the bad nights and worse days. Her rational mind still protested, but she told it to be quiet. Her beloved was out there somewhere, in the abyss. And she was going after him.

"You're wrong," she whispered.

"Am I? Will you bet your life?" He fixed her with a narrow gaze.

"Yes."

"He won't go," said Faland. "And you won't be able to get back. Not where I'm taking you. Not this time."

"Lead the way," said Laura.

. . .

Laura would have said she knew the forbidden zone of the Ypres Salient. She knew its rest areas, its aerodromes, its crumbling towns, the lie of its roads, the color of its sky. Knew how men lived there, what they ate, how they joked. Knew how they died, and where they were buried.

But she never remembered that walk, could never recall the path they'd taken, although later she dreamed of seeing things that weren't there: a river, a great, crumbling wall. She remembered that the hotel took her by surprise, that at first glimpse she thought it was a palace, standing ruined against a fiery evening sky. But it was just Faland's hotel. He opened the door onto an empty foyer, silent and dark and smelling of dust. It made her think of Faland himself, the glitter of him, the air of years and slow decay. The room was as she'd last seen it: a ruin, dead and cold.

But Freddie was there.

He knelt, staring at nothing. A broken mirror hung over his head.

"Freddie!" The cry scraped Laura's throat. She lurched across the room, sank down beside him.

Her brother didn't look up.

"Freddie, it's Laura."

He looked like a ghost himself. He didn't even acknowledge her. "Freddie, what's happened to you?"

She tried to take his hand. He removed it gently from her grasp.

"Freddie, for God's sake—"

His brows drew together. He didn't look at her. "Are you dead?"

"No, I'm not. I'm *not*, Freddie, I'm here. I came back to find you. Freddie, *please*."

There was so little of her brother left in this hunched, gray man. She turned on Faland.

"What have you done to him?" At Brandhoek, and after, during all those long days on the hospital train, on the hospital ship, despite the pain, she had not cried. But she was crying now.

Faland's voice was almost gentle. "At least I know his name. I'm sure you've seen men worse, and at the hands of their fellow man."

Laura was silent.

"Stay," said Faland. "As my guests. You'll be together. What's the world got for you anyway?"

"Is that what you told him?"

Faland didn't answer. He'd taken out his violin, his fingers rest-less on the neck of it as though he could pull music from her love and sorrow. Maybe there was no way to reach her brother. *We have to get out,* she thought. Out under the sky, into a world that some-times made sense. "Freddie, we have to go."

He was like a puppet when she pulled him to his feet.

Which door had they come through? There were too many. All alike. She dragged him to the nearest. Turned the handle.

It was unlocked. The door opened. She recoiled. Freddie cried out.

It wasn't the way out. It wasn't anything Laura understood at all.

· · ·

The door opened, with a gust of frigid air, onto an iron-hard daylight, with bitter rain falling. Laura wavered; the ground had fallen away. She had to grip the doorframe to steady herself.

They were standing at the edge of a trench.

Laura stood still, disbelieving. Beside her, Freddie made a small sound, of fear or sudden comprehension. It was cold, and the rain was falling just behind that ordinary wooden door. There was the sound of guns, the smell of wet wool, and excrement, and corpses. Men waded along the trench, not glancing up, mud to their waists, holding rifles over their heads. One leaned in to the other and said, grinning, "They'll have to bring in the navy soon, to bring us up. Too wet for the infantry . . ." just as a section of a trench gave way, and a body, half-rotted, slumped out of the revetments . . .

Freddie made a low, agonized sound.

Laura slammed the door. Freddie backed up. Horror was trying to break through the blankness in his eyes. "No," he said. "No, I'd forgotten."

Faland was watching them.

She pulled herself together, caught Freddie's unresisting hand, tugged. "We just have to get out. We'll try another door. Just one more, Freddie."

But the next opened into a hospital, and now it was Laura's turn to freeze rigid in the doorway. For they'd bundled a dead man up into a sheet, with orderlies preparing to lift him, and a sister lurched forward, calling, "No, wait, be careful—"

But they'd lifted him too quick, and his broken body simply— slid apart . . .

"Laura," Freddie said then. "I can't." It wasn't dramatic. It was just a statement of fact. The door was still open. The memory-hospital was sharply real, down to the smell. She slammed the door shut. Freddie was shivering as if he was sick.

"Do you want to come with me?"

"No," said Freddie.

Her heart crumbled. They'd have to try the doors to get out. Door after door. What more lay behind them? Could she ask him to face it? Did she have a right to decide for him at all? "Then—do you want to stay here?"

"I don't want anything," he whispered. "I'm not—I'm not anything. You don't want me."

She caught his face between her hands. "Never say that. Never. You're everything I have."

For long moments, he was silent. She thought he wouldn't answer. Then his ragged-nailed fingertip came up and blotted her wet face. "Laura?"

"I'm here," she whispered.

"I'm—I'm not the same. You don't love me. The Freddie you loved—he died."

"I don't care."

"I'm a traitor," he whispered. "I remember that. I—I did a terrible thing. I killed—" His voice stuttered. "I ran. I'm not brave."

"You don't have to be. Not for me."

The blankness was trying to slide across his features again. But then he clenched his jaw. He said, "I don't want—" He stopped. "I don't know if we can leave."

"We can. I know we can."

He looked so frail. "I'll try."

He was shaking so hard it vibrated up her arm when she took his hand. They tried another door. And another.

None of them led out. They led back through his mind. Through fear, boredom, envy, anger. Waste, disillusionment, cold nights and dark days. Laura didn't know she was crying until she tasted the salt. A man's head blown from his shoulders, but his body still running. A shell that had fallen on an observation post, and Freddie given a sandbag and a shovel, to retrieve the bodies.

She began to hesitate before the hammer-blows of each door, but her brother's blank face had slowly taken on an insane determination. Now he pushed ahead of her, opening door after door, as though looking for something. As though there were some truth about himself, something he needed, contained in one of those monstrous minutes.

A single glance back showed Faland on his feet, watching.

Then Freddie opened another door, and didn't go on to the next. He stood there rigid. Laura, at his shoulder, saw Freddie, in memory, tumble into a shell hole, followed by a big man whose sandy hair was plastered flat with rain. Then another man, in a soaked Canadian uniform, fell into them, screaming. She saw the screaming man strike at the man with sandy hair—*Winter*, Laura thought. Freddie and Winter. Saw the Canadian stretch to his full height, bayonet raised. But Freddie was there, dropping his shoulder, tackling the man, sending them both flying into foul water. They writhed a moment, one uppermost, then the other, until Freddie got his feet under him.

Held the other man down until he stopped moving.

In the hotel, in the doorway, Freddie stood still. "I killed him." His voice was perfectly flat. "I wanted you to see it. He was one of ours and I killed him."

She didn't touch him. She thought he'd flinch away. "You didn't mean to."

"Oh, I did," said Freddie. They were still looking through the doorway, where, in memory, Freddie was crawling up the ice-slick slope of the shell hole. Winter caught him around the shoulders before he could fall, and put a canteen to his lips. They were staring at each other. As though each contained the other's entire world.

Laura bit blood from her lip. Thought—and for the first time, really regretted—*Winter's going to die.* He'd had a bout of madness—or patriotism—and tried to kill a general. He was going to be interrogated and executed.

She stayed silent. Freddie was staring into the dark. But he wasn't looking at Winter. His eyes were on the body, floating facedown in the shell hole. "I'm sorry," he whispered to it. "It should have been me, not you. I'm sorry." Freddie reached out and slowly closed the door. He looked old. But the blankness did not come back into his face. "I needed to remember that." His voice was a croak. "And there's something else I have to remember."

"What?"

"I'll know when I see it."

. . .

Laura did not know how many doors later, but finally one of them opened onto nothing. Onto darkness like the beginning of the world. And in the darkness, she heard snatches of voices. "—Sunlight in the pines. Blackberries—"

"—the sea. I love the sea."

A verse of a poem. Voices that mingled in the emptiness. She realized that she was crying again.

Freddie whispered, "I remember now. It was so dark."

"And Winter was there," said Laura.

"Yes," said Freddie. "He was there." He turned. And it was her brother's hazel eyes looking into hers. Exhausted, sad, with horror lurking in the back of them. But he was there. "I'll go where you want, Laura," he said. "As long as you can. But I'm still a traitor. I'm still a coward and a murderer."

Laura held his hand and said nothing.

Faland was watching them. Had been that whole time. "Really?" he said. "I open the secrets of my hotel to you and this is how you answer? Go back out there and live with it?" He was stalking across the room. Freddie and Laura both stood very still. "But didn't you scream for your mother to run, that night in my hotel, Laura? I heard you. You want to remember *this* for the rest of your life?" His hand was on the knob of another door. He flung it open.

. . .

It was their parents' bedroom, in Halifax, full of broken glass. Their mother in the middle of it, lying in her own blood. The room was filling with smoke, sparks falling outside. Their mother was trying to cry, but her tear ducts were gone.

Freddie went perfectly still.

And Laura darted forward, into the memory, and knelt beside her. All she could think was that she finally had a second chance. Back in the heart of her own nightmares, she could do it over again.

And again. And again, until she got it right. Until she saved her mother.

But someone was pulling her away. She didn't want to go. But the arms held her, and she found herself sobbing against her brother's chest. His arms were tight around her. They were together in the memory, in the burnt living room in Veith Street.

"When?" he whispered, into her hair.

Her voice was almost unrecognizable. "In December. Mother and Father are dead. The house is gone. Everything's gone."

Freddie was silent. They held each other, shivering. How do you go on from the end of everything? She didn't have an answer, and neither did he. They were frozen by it, at a standstill. In the doubt-filled darkness, Faland's voice came and wrapped around them again. "You don't have to go on. You don't have to remember."

He was right, Laura thought. He'd pour them wine, if they asked. He'd play his fiddle. They wouldn't need anything else. She could see the truth of that in her brother's haunted eyes. They could both just stop. A look of triumph came into Faland's face.

But then Freddie said, "I couldn't leave, for myself," his voice thin as a thread. "But Laura can't stay here. Laura—she has to help people. Do you hear me, Laura? I won't let you stay here."

Freddie's words made Laura think of Jones. Jones who did still believe in the future. Perhaps there was something beyond all this, something she couldn't see.

"I won't leave without you," she said.

"I don't know how to get out," Freddie whispered. "I don't even know how to try."

Stop trying doors, Laura thought. The doors weren't the way out. *Faland* was. She felt in her pocket. She had matches, from lighting the Bunsen burner in the sterilization room. She glanced up. Crossed the room. Faland was leaning on a table, watching her carefully. She struck a match and held it poised. "Let us out," said Laura, "or I'll set the place on fire."

He looked unimpressed.

The match was pitiful; it was burning her fingers. Laura stepped closer to him. Closer still. He looked impatient. Then she threw the match. It arced, and his eyes followed it.

As they did, she lunged forward and snatched his violin, raised it, poised to smash. "Now," she said.

He went very still.

"You can't escape," he said. "Even if I let you out. There is nowhere for you to escape to. Don't you understand? What future can you expect, out there? In the wreck of the world? Haven't you even seen all the ways you are ruined?"

She didn't answer. She was afraid to; she might find herself agreeing. Instead she clutched the violin by the neck and started to whip it down.

"Stop!" he snapped.

She waited.

"You think this is a victory? It will only end in ashes."

Laura said nothing. Finally, unwillingly, his head turned. She followed his gaze, and where there had been only wall, she saw another door.

"With my malediction," said Faland. It was almost gentle.

"I am not afraid of you," said Laura. She took her brother's hand and walked outside.

HOW CAN I LIVE
WITHOUT THEE?

·····

CHÂTEAU COUTHOVE, FLANDERS, BELGIUM
APRIL 1918

FREDDIE'S PULSE WAS RAPID; HE WAS EMACIATED, HIS LIPS cracked. She could feel him trying not to lean on her, but he wasn't very strong. Laura took his weight as best she could. They were outside the hotel, in the courtyard, with ruined buildings on all sides. It was night. Pure moonless night, without a star visible. She looked for the road, for a landmark.

Nothing.

Nothing but buildings, and paths, and darkness. She was lost. Did the abyss have borders? Could the monsters be placated, at all? *Maybe not. It's a new world after all.*

Faland's slick, persuasive whisper sounded in her ear. *Come back inside. It's better inside. At least I will remember your names, Laura.*

Freddie was trying to stand upright. "Laura, I'm frightened. I can't see the way."

You ask the ghosts, Winter had said.

You trail your ghosts like penitent beads, the Parkeys had said.

I don't believe in ghosts, Laura had said, over and over. But had it mattered? The ghost had followed her anyway. Laura had thought her a conjuring of her own guilt and grief. But perhaps she was a little more.

Laura whispered, like the child she'd not been in ever so long, "Maman, I'm lost. Can you hear me? We're lost, Freddie and I."

Silence.

A hand brushed hers. Warm fingers, a little rough with glass. *Ghosts have warm hands.* She didn't open her eyes. She didn't dare. Looking would burst her fragile soap-bubble of belief. She didn't look even when that familiar hand wound its fingers with hers, and pulled her forward. Holding on to Freddie, she walked. And then, some unnumbered steps later, the hand let go. Laura opened her eyes and saw that she and Freddie were behind the château of Couthove, seen only hazily through the mist of her tears.

. . .

Faland was gone. He hadn't followed them. But Freddie was drooping against her, and Laura could feel the other monsters circling now, in their way far more implacable. Law, regulation, custom. Waiting to claim a deserter. To claim them both.

A light drifted from one of the bedrooms above, and Laura counted the windows. Realized whose room it was. Without stopping to think, she swiped a handful of pebbles from the drive, and threw. They rattled on glass.

Jones's window flew open. He thrust his head into the gap. Saw them both, standing in a bit of light. Just as quickly, he vanished.

Her heart sank. She could feel Freddie's strength ebbing. "Where?" Freddie mumbled. His head hung low. "Laura, where are we?"

Laura did not have time to answer before Jones came round the house and crossed to her in quick strides. He said, "What the hell, Iven?" And then he got a closer look at Freddie. They weren't terribly alike, but shocked comprehension broke over Jones's face anyway, as he reached to take Freddie's weight. "How?"

"I found him," said Laura. "He was trapped—he was— It wasn't his fault."

"Come inside; you're shivering," said Jones, after a pause.

"We have to get away from here." *It should be all right,* she thought tiredly. They were together, they spoke French, they . . .

But then Freddie stirred and said, "Winter."

Jones's jaw tightened.

"Winter," Freddie said again. "He was here. I remember. The château. We brought him here. Where's Winter?"

"You *brought*—" began Laura, but Jones had seen straight to the point and he had a surgeon's instincts: Cut in order to heal.

"No saving him," said Jones. "He tried to murder a general, in the teeth of a massive German offensive. They took him right off, never mind his wound, and they'll be interrogating him now. And then they're going to hang him." To Laura he added, "We need to get your brother inside."

"No," Freddie whispered, and Laura felt a sinking fear. Perhaps Freddie's body would survive, if by some miracle she got him home. But the rest of him was so ragged. Would his mind survive, if he got out, but Winter was left behind, executed? She remembered how the two had looked, in memory, in that shell hole. Why had Winter fired the damned gun?

"I won't let them arrest my brother," said Laura to Jones, her voice jagged.

"I know," Jones said. "But you both look like you're about to collapse. Let's get him inside. Then we'll think, without drama, what to do."

The last time she'd asked for his trust, it ended with a gunshot. He ought to be disgusted with her. He shouldn't be risking his neck. Again. But here he was. "All right, Doctor."

"Call me Stephen," he said. He sounded irritable. But his fingers were gentle when he took Freddie's weight from her. "We've a ways to go yet. I'll look after you both."

. . .

Laura's hope—and she imagined Jones's as well—was to slip Freddie into the château unseen. Get him settled, get some food into him, some tea. Let him sleep, for God's sake. And then—well, he was officially dead, so perhaps with some bureaucratic chicanery they could slip him out. She didn't have the money for passage back to Canada, but first things first. She could take a job, she spoke French . . .

So ran her thoughts, as Jones, with Freddie leaning on his shoulder, slipped in through the servants' entrance and made for the back stairs, with Laura behind.

They met Pim coming down.

She was fully dressed and neat, despite the hour, and she didn't see them at first. She was calling behind her as she walked. "No, I telephoned already, you can't stop me, Mary. I'm going."

Mary was in the stairwell a few steps behind her. "Have you even considered, for a moment, that it's better not to draw attention—" She caught sight of the trio at the foot of the stairs.

Everyone stopped.

Mary recovered first. "Where have you been, Iven? We were—" She'd seen Freddie. "Who's that? Get him in the ward, for pity's sake, is he—?" She stopped again, seeing the looks on all their faces. "What?"

Pim had understood. With a swift step, she got to the bottom of the stairs and flung her arms around Laura. "You found him," she said. Her eyes were starry with tears. "You found him."

"What in God's name?" said Mary.

Laura, suddenly full of a sinking fear, tried to marshal her thoughts. She hadn't actually planned for an *after,* when the miracle had happened. She shouldn't have come here at all. Mary was not sentimental. She wouldn't risk her hospital to help one tattered deserter.

"It's Freddie, of course, Mary," Pim threw over her shoulder. "It's Laura's brother."

At Pim's voice, Freddie lifted his head. A strange look came into his bewildered eyes. "I remember you," he said. "Whatever he told you, he lied."

"I beg your pardon?" said Pim.

"I saw you." Freddie struggled for words. "I saw him—" His eyes swept the room. "Where is Winter?"

"Where did you find him?" demanded Mary.

"Trapped," said Laura.

Mary looked scornful. "Deserted, you mean. And you brought him here, Iven, Christ. You know I'm going to have to—"

No, she wasn't. Laura opened her mouth, furious, but Pim spoke first. "Mary Borden, how *dare* you?" Not for the first time it occurred to Laura that Pim's slightly foolish manner was a construct, a shield maintained so perfectly for so long that she herself forgot sometimes what lay beneath.

"You are going to help them," said Pim. "Because if you don't, I'm not going to smooth over the—incident with Gage today. I'll tell Young when he comes that *you* knew who Winter was when you took him in, that you pitied him. I'll tell Young all kinds of things."

No one said anything. It was as though a mouse had roared.

Mary set her jaw. "Shaw—"

"I mean it," said Pim. "I'll do it. They'll be so angry. Make you close up your hospital. Or you could do the kind thing for once in your life, Mary."

"Very well," said Mary, bitterly. "All right, Pim, you wretch. You'll go to Poperinghe, you'll smooth things over with the general. And take Iven with you. I don't trust you not to do something rash."

Laura had missed something. "Tonight?"

Pim said, "I telephoned Young. I want to see the general. There were a few things I remembered, that—that Winter told me. I thought they would interest him." She glanced at Mary. "And I thought—I can make sure that they're not angry at us over it. Young's coming to fetch me. Soon, actually. But lord, Mary, there's no call for Laura to—"

Laura wasn't listening. It didn't make any sense. If Pim could telephone Young to tell him that she had information, why not just pass it along, then and there? A glance at Mary's face showed Mary didn't entirely buy it either. What, then?

"Winter?" whispered Freddie.

"It can wait," said Jones, in a tone that allowed for no arguments. "You can barely keep your feet."

Laura said slowly, "You're going to Fifth Army HQ tonight, Pim?"

"Yes," said Pim. "But of course I don't need Laura to come with me, Mary, that's quite all right. She ought to be here, of course, with her brother—"

"No," said Mary. "You've backed me into a corner, Penelope Shaw, and I'll let you go on that one condition, that Iven goes with you. I don't know what you're playing at, but Iven will keep you out of trouble, if only for her brother's sake. *You* will make sure that no one at HQ blames the hospital for this wretched contretemps. In exchange, we shall put Laura's brother in a bed quietly, and I shall arrange for them to leave the country. All right?"

Pim was shaking her head. "No—Mary, I'd rather not—"

"I mean it," said Mary. "That, or I send Iven's brother straight back to the Canadian Army and they deal with him. I have no more patience for any of this."

Pim looked suddenly tired. "All right."

Jones said reassuringly, "The quicker you go, the quicker you can come back. I'll find a bed for your brother."

Freddie was shaking his head. "No," he said. "Can't you see?" It was as though he fought to make sense, but could not.

"Stephen," Laura said, low. "Take care of him."

THE UNCONQUERABLE WILL
AND STUDY OF REVENGE

.....

YOUNG APPEARED IN THE DRIVE RIGHT AFTER LAURA HAD had the quickest wash of her life, and flung on a clean uniform. In the meantime, Jones had hustled Freddie up to his own room. When Laura paused to look in on them, her brother was sitting on Jones's bed with his boots off, his shoulders tense. "Malnourished," said Jones, eyeing him. "In fact I don't know what the hell he's been living on. Look at his teeth."

Laura didn't answer. She didn't think Freddie even knew where he was. He sat very still. She crossed the room, knelt. He raised his eyes to her face. A hint of trust there, a question under the confusion. How, after all this, could she possibly leave him?

Jones seemed to follow her thought. "If Borden says she'll do a thing, she'll do it," he said, from behind her. "She meant this. Do it and she'll get you both out."

She thought he was right. But she was still afraid to go. As though, if she let her brother out of her sight for one more instant, it would snap the last thread that bound them to their past, and to each other.

She felt Jones's hand on her elbow. He drew her to her feet. Looked her in the face. "I'll take care of him, Laura," he said.

He was impatient, unsentimental. He gave her brother his bed. He'd taken a terrible risk, gone against his own judgment, used his own blood to save Winter's life. And then, when Winter threw their trust back in their faces, he hadn't said a word. She said, "Why, Stephen?"

He shrugged a little.

She waited.

"I would like you to go home," he said at last. "And I want to hear you laugh one day. Go on, Iven."

Laura put a hand on Freddie's stiff shoulder. He glanced up, but he didn't speak. Then she went.

. . .

Young waited outside the car, looking boyish in the soft spring night, his ears absurd, the adolescent slope of his shoulders concealed by his uniform. To his credit, only a little disappointment crossed his face when he saw Laura loping along at Pim's heels.

They got in the car and sped off. "Are you all right, Mrs. Shaw?" Young asked. "Such a dreadful ordeal. Your heroism, stopping the spy—"

Pim didn't answer, but when she smiled and touched his hand, he fell stammeringly silent. Then Pim said, "I just wish I'd recalled sooner what that man said."

What did he say, Pim? The question penetrated the fog of Laura's tired mind. Something didn't add up.

"Something that rascal said to you?" said Young, echoing Laura's thought. "Oh, lord, when I think of him—so sly—there beside you and you unsuspecting, and the gun might easily have—"

He swallowed and fell silent. Pim had put her hand over his again. There was again that strange distress, not quite love, in Young's face. "It's all right," she said. "I'm all right. I must only see the general. So kind of him, to take a moment."

"Well," said Young with disarming frankness, "it's got everyone on the jump—spy on our doorstep, very nearly assassinated a general. And the Germans attacking—it's really dreadful up there now, Ypres all to pieces with the shelling. And they had to pull back from the Ridge. It was indefensible, you know."

Pim had known that, as had Laura, but the color briefly left her face anyway. Her son had died taking the Ridge. Her eyes and Laura's met, just briefly, in the darkness.

• • •

Poperinghe was in a ferment greater than Laura had ever seen. Cars, lorries, horses. Bicycles and motorcycles and people on foot. Telephones, messengers, men calling news. Troops going up, the wounded coming back. The noise of shelling, drumroll-fast, the whole sky stabbed through with wild light.

The car drew up in front of HQ. Young spoke to some men, turned back to them. "My uncle's with the prisoner now," he said. "You can wait to speak to him. Or . . . there is some hope that, in your presence, perhaps, when he learns what you shall reveal, he might be induced to say . . ."

Pim had gone just briefly still. "All right," she said.

His voice a little hoarse. "If—you are sure, Mrs. Shaw?"

Pim said, "I'm sure." She took his arm to escort her into the building. "I'm quite brave, you know."

"Oh," said Young fervently, "I know."

They would see Winter. Laura didn't know how to feel. He may have owed a debt to her brother, but he'd been a loyal German in the end. Seen a chance to kill a general, and taken it. It was only luck, and Pim, that had thwarted him. Perhaps it was right that she'd be there. If she could tell him somehow that Freddie was all right. For her brother's sake.

Reason pricked her, told her that didn't explain Faland's presence outside the château or Winter's gaze locked on hers.

Perhaps she'd never know.

• • •

Young took them to a cellar room with a strong door, a room that might have contained liquor, or town money, once upon a time. Now Winter was there, in a chair, with bruises on his face. Laura supposed they'd no time for gentle interrogations, not with an attack literally in progress. Rationally she knew that. But her every instinct rebelled at beating a wounded man. She crossed the room in three strides, her fingers finding the pulse beneath the cold sweat on Winter's neck, turning so she could see the blood on his side where Jones's painstaking work on his burst stitches had torn again. His eyes fixed instantly on her face.

She gave him the barest nod. *I found him. He's alive.*

He closed his eyes.

"Miss Iven," said a voice. Laura turned. The room was not empty. There were Young and Pim, of course, behind her. And Gage himself, standing, with an aide seated, and another man wearing the uniform of Military Intelligence. "So glad to see you again, my dear. Your charitable impulses do you credit." A faint irritation in his well-bred voice; of course he didn't want the prisoner comfortable. But he didn't remonstrate with her. He'd turned to Pim, luminous even in the harsh light, and said, "Tell me now, Mrs. Shaw. What did this man admit to you? Hurry, hurry, I must go back up in a moment."

Winter had raised his chin, and Gage obviously saw it; he turned his head, watching Winter's reaction. But Winter surprised them all. His eyes were locked on Pim, but he spoke to Laura. His split lip cracked and began to bleed when he said, "Iven, take her out."

Even as he said it, Laura heard a disturbance in the corridor. A crash, shouting. Then, strangely, someone laughing. Everyone in the room tensed. *Sabotage?* Laura wondered first, and Gage obviously had the same thought. "Edwards, Boyne, go see," said the general, and the intelligence officer and the aide hurried to the doorway, peered down the corridor.

Then she happened to catch Pim's eye, which was wild and cold and entirely unsurprised. *"No,"* said Winter, trying to rise.

But Pim had turned toward the door behind the two officers. She slammed it, and shot the bolt. Laura, startled, was slow to react when Pim pulled a pistol from her pocket, got behind the indignant general, and pressed the gun just behind his ear.

Everyone froze.

Gage, holding himself rigid, whispered, "Have you gone mad?"

"Pim?" whispered Laura.

Young stood frozen, his mouth a little open. "Penelope?"

"I warn you, young woman," said Gage. "Stop this nonsense at once, or—"

"Or?" said Pim, in a low, terrible voice. "You'll kill me, just like Jimmy?"

The air seemed to leave the room. Pim's back was straight, and her eyes were cold, cold, cold. Was that madness, there in the glitter?

"Penelope?" said Young again. His voice was small and strained. "I told my uncle he shouldn't have told you. He's sorry now. He's sorry. Put the gun down."

Winter was rigid under Laura's hands, his face salt-white. "Talk to her," he whispered. "Don't let her do this."

"Pim," said Laura again. But she didn't have words, didn't understand in the slightest the expression on Pim's face.

Strangely, Young seemed to know better than Laura did. "I am sorry. It's a—well, a hell of a thing to hear. I know that. You—maybe I'd have been unhappy too. Truly. But this isn't right. Put the gun down. Please."

"It's not worth it," said Winter to Pim.

"He's not worth it," echoed Laura, finding her tongue. "Pim—whatever the reason—it's not . . ." She trailed off. The despair in Pim's face was absolute, and it frightened her. Fearful sweat poured down Gage's face.

"Maybe not," said Pim, and pulled the trigger.

. . .

It was loud and it was messy. The general lurched and sank down. Laura crossed the room and kept him from crashing to the floor. His gaze was already fixed, his body twitching.

Pim dropped the gun. There was noise in the corridor outside, shouting, banging. Young, standing rigid, had not reached for the bolt, had not opened the door. Christ only knew what they thought was going on inside.

Gage's blood pooled on Laura's skirt.

Pim's breathing was hard and noisy in the confined space.

"You—" Young started, then stopped. He licked his lips. "Is this why—from the beginning?—to get to *him*?"

Pim nodded. "You can arrest me. It's all right."

Laura said, "Pim, *you* tried to shoot the general in the hospital, didn't you?" Then she understood. "Winter stopped you."

Passionately, Pim said, "I never meant for him to die for me. I'd have told everyone. But first I had to do this."

"But why?" whispered Laura. "For God's sake, Pim, why?"

OUR TORMENTS MAY
BECOME OUR ELEMENTS

.....

FREDDIE CAME BACK TO HIMSELF BY PAINFUL DEGREES. He
was in a dark place that smelled like old fabric. It wasn't the
hotel. It was colder, harsher somehow, the insulation of wine
and music and lost memory gone. He was back. In that moment, he
didn't want to be. He yearned after vanished oblivion. Where was
Laura? He'd come back for Laura. And for—

Winter.

He's going to die, someone had said.

The thought roused him. *Coward,* Faland had called him. Maybe
Freddie was. But he was a coward with a purpose, and he'd been
long enough a soldier to see how purpose strengthened even the
weakest men. He forced himself to open his eyes and sit up and exist,
for the first time in months, in a place that was neither shielded nor
confined by Faland's overwhelming presence.

The room was dim, bare, and prosaic, but there was no smell of
dust or decay. Just something mildly astringent. He was lying on a
bed, with a trunk at its foot, a folding table beside him. A man was
sitting next to him, a man with big, bony wrists. Brilliant dark eyes

softened a hard jaw, a hawklike nose. Freddie remembered him, vaguely. He'd called his sister Laura. Freddie raised himself on one elbow. "Who are you?"

"I'm a surgeon. Name of Jones," came the measured reply.

"Can you tell me what is happening?"

The dark eyes regarded him levelly. "If you'll do the same. Damned if I know, really."

Freddie tried to organize his mind. He remembered the hotel. A beautiful woman with golden hair. He'd seen her head bent near Faland's—where? In the hotel? Somewhere else? A dark place. Both of them wrapped in music. No—in noise. The wide blue eyes. What had she seen in the mirror? What had Faland told her? Then? And later? Where was Winter? Where was Laura? Freddie said, sharply, "Tell me first; where's my sister?"

Jones's dark eyes measured him. "In Poperinghe. With her friend Mrs. Shaw. Who was behaving very peculiarly."

Freddie caught Jones's wrist, his mind ticking over faster, like a watch newly wound. "She's the woman with the yellow hair, isn't she? We need to go to them. Something's wrong. He's not done with us. We need to go."

Jones shook him off. "You're ill, you've had an ordeal, and you're still in considerable danger. Which, frankly, I'm not sure I would care about, except that I care very much for your sister. So for her sake, I am going to keep you—"

This time Freddie's fingers closed with desperation on Jones's forearm. "Let me explain. And you decide. But I don't think there's much time. You see, I've seen that woman, Mrs. Shaw, before."

The black eyes grew sharper still. "Talk then, Iven."

. . .

There was no regret in Pim's face. Only endless unassuaged anger. "I'm sorry, Laura," she said. "I'm sorry you had to see. But I thought you wouldn't mind. You hate him too. For Brandhoek, for what happened on the Ridge . . ."

"*Wouldn't mind?*" she whispered. "Pim, he wasn't—they're going to arrest *all* of us. What in God's name possessed you—" She looked from Pim's still face to Young's. "Tell me what happened, Pim."

"Jimmy ran away," said Pim. Her eyes pleaded for understanding, for benediction. "After Passchendaele. After the horrible battle on the Ridge. Jimmy survived, but then he ran. They caught him. At Le Havre. He was trying to get on a ship. Trying to get back to m— Anyway, they caught him. Took him back for his court-martial. He was convicted. Sent to—the firing squad. At dawn. In Poperinghe, behind the mairie. Faland—Faland showed me where. The courtyard, the post. The cell they kept him in. The night of the riot, he showed me. He told me. He knows so many things, Faland."

"I'm so sorry, Pim," Laura said. Icy sweat poured down her ribs. She groped for the right words. "But what did Gage have to do with it?"

"Gage—he was out walking—that morning, when they were leading Jimmy to . . ." Pim spoke as though she could not get enough air. "Gage saw him. Pure chance. He stopped him. Asked—what he'd done. They said what he had done. And Gage told Jimmy—" Pim's voice wavered. "That Jimmy had erred and he was dying for it. So that other men wouldn't. So in dying—the way he was, he was serving the cause of the war after all. He couldn't even get free by dying." Her voice broke at last. "And Gage was the last person on earth that Jimmy ever spoke to, at all. The last voice."

"And he told you all this?" said Laura, realizing. "Gage told you in London, didn't he? When he called you into the library?"

"Yes," said Pim. "I think he thought I'd somehow be relieved that Jimmy hadn't died in vain." Her voice dripped with bitterness. "I think he meant well."

"Why didn't you tell us?" asked Laura.

"I didn't have words. It was such poison. I hated him. Oh, Laura, I've never hated anyone before. Not like that. I've hated him ever since. The hating was eating me up. He could have saved him, I'm sure of it. Sent him back to me. That night in Faland's hotel, when I looked in his mirror, I thought I'd see Jimmy. Of course that's what I wanted most. My boy. But it wasn't that. Instead, I saw myself killing Gage, and stamping on his bones." Pim's thin shoulders heaved. *"How dare he take my son."*

Laura shuddered. Laura had fought her monster, and Pim had found herself one. It was so much easier to hate a man than a system: vast, inhuman, bloodstained.

Pim continued, "And so—well, there was Young, and I knew he liked me. That gave me the idea. He offered to teach me to ride, and I asked him to teach me to shoot as well, like it was a great joke." She wrapped her arms around herself. "But it wasn't."

When Young spoke, it was the last thing either of them expected. His eyes were wet. "I'll say the German shot my uncle," he said. He looked at Winter. "If you'll say the same."

"I will," said Winter, without hesitation.

Young took a step nearer Pim. His eyes were blind with devotion, while Pim's had been empty with rage. Christ, was anyone sane? "He was—I mean—I'm sorry. I don't think that killing"—his voice cracked—"killing him gave you anything back. But I can get you away from here."

"No!" cried Pim. "No—*no!*" She drew herself up stiff. "I'll tell the truth. Do you think I want anyone to die for me? I knew what I was doing. I wanted to do it." She turned with determination to the door.

"No, wait, Pim—" Laura began, but Pim had already slid open the bolt and flung the door wide. Laura expected a mass of angry aides, and military police, to be standing there. But there was only Faland, leaning against the opposite wall.

"Took you long enough," he said. He looked at the general, lying in a heap on the floor. And he laughed.

"Penelope?" Young echoed, staring with astonishment at the fair-haired stranger, the empty corridor. "Who is this?"

Pim lifted her chin, faced Faland squarely. "You didn't think I would."

"On the contrary, I knew you would," he said. "I don't underestimate people, as a rule. With occasional exceptions." He shot Laura a glance. "And now? Going to own up to it? Confess, and die along with the spy here?"

"Do I have a choice?" said Pim.

"Oh, yes," said Faland. "That boy there wants to rescue you."

Their eyes locked. "And you?" whispered Pim.

"I want to ruin you," said Faland. "Which shall it be?" Noise echoed in the corridor, shouting, footsteps coming closer.

Laura said, "Pim, for God's sake, he had Freddie. Freddie was a—a husk when I saw him. Don't—whatever you're thinking. Don't."

Pim was still looking at Faland. "If I go with you," she said, "will you get them away?"

Faland said equably, "I suppose I could. I'll even take a leaf out of Iven's book."

Laura didn't know what he meant, but it soon became clear. Faland knelt beside the dead man, rifled his pockets. Pulled out a book of matches. With deft fingers, he got some priming out of the gun. Struck a match. It caught with surprising speed. Smoke billowed through the room. Laura's eyes stung.

There was no time to find a handcuff key. Laura had to set her jaw and dislocate Winter's thumb so he could pull his hand free. He submitted to this without a sound. Then they went up an empty staircase, coughing. The silence in the building was eerie. She didn't see Faland anymore. She didn't see Pim. She felt hollow with shocked betrayal as they emerged into a spring night that roared with moving cars and moving men, shook her head as though she'd crawled out of a dream.

Where was Pim? Young was turning in a wild circle as though he too searched. There. She was standing facing Faland. Neither moved. Young would come to his senses and give the alarm in a minute. Laura, still supporting Winter, crossed the space between them, her feet awkward in the dust. "Pim, come on, come away. We'll go back to Halifax. We'll—"

Pim turned her head a little. But Laura's voice died in her throat. Winter's hand tightened on her arm. She'd had years of schooling in the hardest, coldest reality—and she recognized the look on Pim's face. It was the look a wounded man got sometimes, a man who was not mortally wounded, perhaps, but who had simply had enough. Who meant to leave the world behind.

"Pim, he's not—" But she met Pim's eyes. Stopped again. Felt Winter quiver, as he fought to stay upright.

Pim said to Faland, "You'll help them get out. All the way out. To safety. To the ordinary world."

Faland's gaze was fixed as though in fascination on Pim's face, as though he could read the unsteady play of emotion there like sheet-music. He said, "And you will tell me everything. Every night. What you love. What you hate. And why you're afraid. Until you remember nothing at all."

"Yes."

"Pim, don't," whispered Laura.

Faland smiled a little. "Enjoy the pieces of your brother, Iven. Or rather, enjoy watching him enjoy them. Do you think any part of dear Freddie is yours anymore? It isn't. It's his. And a little bit mine."

Laura swallowed around a great, furious knot in her throat, but Pim merely turned and kissed her lightly on the cheek, and said, "It's for the best, Laura."

Laura was silent. Because she'd seen Pim at last, through the gauze of her bright, sweet nature. And what moved under the skin was wounded, and ruthless, and certainly a little mad. She realized that she was crying, and saw that Pim was too.

Faland had his violin. His eyes were still on Pim. "How's this, then, sweet?" he said. "I finished it." He put bow to string.

It wasn't so much music as a mad scream, of rage and grief and insane determination, jagged and wretchedly beautiful. Laura heard Pim's voice in the howl of it. The roar of the crowd echoed the sound of the music, the churning rhythm of war all around them. Laura stood there for a moment caught between Faland's poisonous refuge and the world's dangers. She could have turned to him then. Faland probably knew it. Winter was silent, but she could feel him shake beside her. Any moment, the alarm would come and then—

And then Jones was there. "What in hell, Iven?" he said.

THROUGH EDEN TOOK
THEIR SOLITARY WAY

POPERINGHE, FLANDERS, BELGIUM
APRIL 1918

WITH NO OTHER MEANS TO HAND, FREDDIE AND JONES walked to Poperinghe, stealing through shadows, hurrying through the two miles or so that separated Pop from Couthove, almost impossibly taxing on Freddie's drained limbs. The city was in warlike chaos, and the noise shredded his nerves.

With Faland, it felt like nothing else in the world could touch him. But now the world was all around him, raw and bright and painful, its dangers immediate, its ugliness obvious. They kept their heads down as they passed the outskirts of town, dodging frantic traffic in bad light until they got to the town square, which was packed and heaving with men. He wasn't sure how, in the bewildering midst of the crowd, his eye found Laura. But he found her. She was standing beside Winter, supporting him, his arm over her shoulders.

Winter's eyes were narrow with pain, his face set. There was blood on Laura's skirt, and the remains of tear-tracks on her face. How were they—

Then Freddie's senses cleared a little, and he heard the music beneath the crowd's noise, realized that it moved not to the demands of modern war, but to another power entirely. Faland was there. He was playing his violin.

Jones broke away, went to Laura and said, "What in hell, Iven? Are you all right? Where is Shaw? What the hell are you doing with . . ." He gave the half-conscious Winter a very unfriendly look.

Freddie had followed Jones, trying to ignore the music lurking in the crowd's rising noise. Winter raised his head a little. Their eyes met. Winter said, "Iven—why did you—?" A billow of flame, pouring like wings from the town hall, cut him off, and there was the music again, insistent, underlying the noise of the crowd.

There were shouts of fear, of anger, the sound of car horns, as though Faland were dragging sheer madness up from where it lurked beneath the surface of their minds. Or perhaps they were just reacting to the fire. Freddie couldn't tell what was real anymore. He felt quite insane.

What now?

He raised his eyes and caught Faland's gaze. As though he'd always been there, eyes heavy-lidded while he waited for Freddie to notice. He wasn't playing his violin anymore, but that didn't matter. The essence of it had been taken up by the crowd.

Faland wasn't alone. The beautiful woman was with him, and Freddie understood the expression on her face, the terrible decision. Magic and oblivion on one side, and a whole broken future in their new world on the other.

Jones said, "Mrs. Shaw—what are you doing?"

Freddie knew what she was doing. He felt a surge of jealousy. He'd chosen the new world, chosen Winter, chosen Laura, chosen the wasteland of his life, with whatever green shoots he could coax out of the parched terrain of his soul. He saw that the woman had made the other choice, to go into the dark with the stranger, and allow herself oblivion.

For a second, *he* regretted. For a second, he almost called to Faland, his whole heart twisting suddenly with longing. Faland watched him, waiting. But Winter's arm was tight around him, and Laura was leaning on him from the other side, and they were all anchoring each other in the madness, and he couldn't have broken that connection, not for anything.

Mrs. Shaw's delicate face was twisted up with longing, and her eyes were on Laura. She hesitated.

"Pim," whispered Laura, barely audible over the madness. "I need you too." Their eyes, amber and blue, were locked together.

She just shook her head a little. Freddie saw that she had bloody hands. She looked up at Faland and said, "Well?" He could see the shine of her tears in the billowing light. Freddie wanted to cry too, but his mind and his memory were in too much chaos.

"We have to get out of here," said Jones.

"That way," said Winter.

Laura said nothing, and neither did Freddie. But they both turned when the other two prompted them, and the echoes of Faland's music chased them out of Poperinghe. The crowd heaved with the emotion of it, and at the very edge of hearing, Freddie thought he heard Faland's voice.

"Farewell, Iven," said Faland, and laughed. "Try not to think of me too much."

. . .

They walked. Winter, leaning on Freddie's shoulder, alone of them all seemed to have some idea where they were going, which lanes and roads would conceal them. Perhaps that was how he'd survived, all those months. When he stayed. Looking for Freddie.

Freddie didn't know how to feel.

They walked until it felt that they'd always been walking.

Jones spent the whole time insulting them, chivvying them, ordering them to keep going. And Winter set his jaw and kept going, as he had on the battlefield, his courage as bright as it had been there.

So they went.

Finally—and Freddie could not have said exactly when it happened, except that day was breaking and he was utterly spent—they stopped walking and found themselves on the outskirts of an ordinary town, with the mutter of war quieter than the send and suck of the sea. Freddie didn't know how far they'd gone. He could not muster enough of himself to care. He felt like he'd wakened from a dream, and half-wished he hadn't.

Laura's face was still streaked with tears; she was gray in the morning light and her skirt was bloody. Winter's face was expressionless, but he and Freddie had held each other up, that last distance, each instinctively seeking the other's strength. "We must find a rooming—house—run by Belgians," Laura said. "A modest rooming house. And pay them well. So they won't ask questions. Or talk."

"I'll go," said Jones. He looked as though he'd no idea what had happened. But he was the only one of the four neither bloodied nor wraithlike. His glance lingered briefly on Laura. Then he went.

It hardly took half an hour, which was good because they were all, to varying degrees, on their last legs. It wasn't even that difficult. No one, in those bad days, would turn down hard currency, no matter how strange the appearance of a doctor and a nurse, and two hollow-eyed men that kept to the shadows. They took two rooms, and locked the doors, and then it was quiet, and Freddie didn't know what to do. He and Laura took one of the rooms, Jones and Winter the other. Freddie didn't say anything. The darkness was prosaic now, the world's horrors gray, unleavened with Faland's malice, his painful empathy. Freddie stood there, feeling hollow.

. . .

The mattress was suspect and the plumbing shrieked. Freddie hadn't said a word. But Laura was too tired and too grieved to worry about that; he was *there*, alive, dragged back to her against the odds. She'd saved him, she reminded herself. She'd come there to save him, and she'd saved him. Even if she could not save Pim.

It hurt to think of Pim.

She took off her stained dress and put it to soak. Stood there in her combination and stockings, wrapped a blanket around her shoulders. Freddie was still standing there, looking around at the homely room as though he could not quite believe it was real. When she went to him, he was passive; let her help him peel off his clothes, washed his face when she put the cloth in his hands. "Is this real?" he asked her once, low.

"Just rest," she told him.

And finally, he went to bed, and fell into a restless sleep. His white-threaded hair stuck to his cheeks. Laura sat awake, watching, as though she could make it all right for him if she just never looked away.

She could not, of course. Freddie woke screaming, at some point, in the darkness. No effort on her part, no pleading, no comfort, no touch, no words, would quiet him.

Preoccupied, she didn't see Winter come into the room, didn't hear his halting footsteps until he was standing beside the bed. He'd been with Jones next door; Jones had cleaned and dressed his wound. She would have thought he'd be dead to the world now. But he was there, standing by Freddie's bed, his expression guarded.

Freddie raised his head, looked at Winter as he had not looked at Laura. He said, "It's dark."

Winter said to Laura, although his eyes never left Freddie, "Sometimes, waking, I'm back in the pillbox with no way out. There's no light. There's no air. I would have died, if I'd been alone. I'd have gone mad, if I'd been alone." Pause. "I think for him it's the same."

Like sharing the same death, the same birth. Laura understood. She also felt an unholy jet of rage. How dare he? This German, this enemy. He'd have killed Freddie out in No Man's Land but for a strange quirk of fate. How dare he stand there, looking at her with steady eyes, as though he knew her brother, the last family she had, better than she ever could?

Her brother who'd all but forgotten her. Her brother whom she loved. Who was all she had left in the world. Whose eyes were open wide, stark and afraid. He'd given up oblivion to try to come back to her. She'd saved him from that.

But she could not save him from this.

Perhaps they'd never find their way back to each other. But they had a chance to try. Because he was alive.

She owed Winter that.

She stepped away silently, until her back was to the connecting door. She paused in the doorway. "He is all I have," she said to Winter. It was half apology and half warning.

"I know," said Winter. And, strangely, she thought he did. It was that understanding, and that alone, that gave her the strength to turn her back on her brother, to go through the door and leave them alone.

· · ·

Jones was on his feet, by a refreshed fire. Well, of course he was awake, he'd heard Freddie screaming. And did Jones ever sleep, anyway? Even at Couthove, he'd always been doing something. He was in his shirt and trousers now, his sleeves rolled halfway up. He looked from her to the doorway, and said, "Come and sit by the fire."

She had forgotten that she had a blanket wrapped over her stockings and combination and little else, until she felt the fire's heat on her bare shoulders, and realized how cold she was.

She sat on the shabby armchair, and Jones leaned on the mantel. Finally, he said, "I'd dose your brother, if I'd anything to give. I gave what I had to Winter."

Laura shook her head. "It's not that. There are demons that we can't fight. Not even you." She tried to smile. "A dose won't help him, I think. If anyone can help him, it's Winter."

Jones said, "She's gone then, is she? Shaw?"

Laura flinched. Jones waited. "She wanted to go with Faland," said Laura. "She didn't want her life anymore—she'd lost her husband, her boy. I couldn't—I couldn't hold her. I could hold Freddie. But not her."

Jones's pragmatic voice was tonic. "You can't save everyone, Iven."

Laura bowed her head. He stood there looking down at her, and she wished he'd go away, wished he'd say something, wished he . . . "Laura," he said, and at the new note in his voice, she looked up. "May I hold your hands?"

His eyes were black in the firelight. He waited. Without a word, she put out one hand to him.

He knelt, in silence, on the rug beside her, and took her right hand in both of his. His fingers were as clean as ever, cool and dry and precise, as he tested the scar tissue, the range of motion in the joints, massaging where they were swollen. He took up her other hand, tracing the deadened lines of scar tissue, pressing so she could feel the sensation, diffuse, beneath. She could not have stood sweetness, or sentiment. But he had a surgeon's touch, gentle and a little ruthless, and trust eased some of the knots in her soul. There was utter silence from the room next door.

Laura said, "They need each other." *More than he needs me,* she was too proud to say. *I got him back and I lost him . . .*

"That's how they survived, I think," Jones said. He was still looking down at her hands. "Needing each other. You can't change it, and you shouldn't try. But you got him back."

She was silent, but after a long pause, she let her head fall onto his shoulder. His hand came around her head to hold her there, tangling his fingers in the short, tawny curls. It all felt too big, too strange for emotion. Pim and Freddie, Winter and Jones. She didn't know how to feel.

"I don't know what to do now," she said, against his shoulder, feeling his fingers in her hair. "I didn't—I didn't expect—"

"Understandable," said Jones. His voice had roughened a little, but his hands were precise as ever, in her hair, between her scapulae. "You will go home, of course. Take them both home, and sort it out there, out of earshot of the damned Front. You have time now. A whole future in front of you. No more war for you, Laura."

Laura didn't lift her head. Very softly, she admitted, "I don't know how to get them home."

Jones said, "Winter will need identification. So will Wilfred. And three berths on a ship. I'll help you get it." His hands fell away as she lurched back from his shoulder.

"Stephen—" she began, his name still strange in her mouth, and saw color rise in his face. But he interrupted, pragmatic as ever, before she could say anything else. "Don't be proud about this. How else are you going to get home? Are you going to stay here until someone wonders what on earth the three of you are doing?"

She said, struggling for sense, "And you? Are you going back to Couthove?"

He might have hesitated. "Yes. I have patients. Obligations."

She said, "I don't want to be an obligation."

"You're not."

"I don't—I don't want it between us. I already owe—"

"Christ, Laura," he said. "You don't owe me anything because I won't let you. I want—" He didn't finish that thought. Laura didn't know if she was glad or sorry. "Well, there's time enough for that later."

Somehow the harshness of him touched her own rough edges and smoothed them. Low, she said, "Then come and find me. After it's all over. And tell me what I owe you."

"Nothing," he said, and he was close enough for her to feel the brush of his hair, against her ear and throat. The vibration of his voice. "I already told you."

"Come and find me anyway," said Laura.

. . .

Out of the depths of his nightmare, Freddie heard a voice, and it was saying *"Wilfred,"* oddly careful. His head cleared a little. The door had closed behind Laura and there was only Winter. Freddie didn't know what to say, didn't know how to say it.

Winter looked strangely foreign, with his stiff fairness, his single arm, standing by the bed; utterly out of place. Winter said, "I—fall asleep and I dream it's the pillbox, and there's no way out." There was half a question in his voice.

"So do I," said Freddie.

Winter said, "But we got out."

Freddie wasn't sure he had. The hotel had held it all in abeyance, but it had mended nothing. And he'd opened every single door in the place to get out, and now all his worst memories swam round and round his mind.

Winter sat down, very gingerly, on the bed beside him, not touching. Freddie felt the heat of his feverish body. There was no music here, no oblivion. There was the familiar sound of Winter breathing.

"Winter, I—"

Winter said, "It's all right, Iven."

"I was a coward."

"You were a man. I'd have gone with him, if our positions were reversed."

"I'm a ruin," Freddie said. "I let him have—my mind, myself. And I got back—only the worst things, I can hardly remember anything else." *Except for you,* he didn't say. *I remember you.*

"You came back, though," said Winter. His spine was more rigid than ever.

"You stayed," said Freddie.

"I swore," said Winter, "that you weren't going to die. I knew it was the last thing I was ever going to do. I don't break my promises."

"I promised the same thing," said Freddie.

"And we are alive," said Winter.

"Are we?" said Freddie, with bitterness. "I might as well be dead."

Winter said with sudden ferocity, "Do you dare say that, Iven? Do you think I stayed because I believed that? Do you think your sister came back searching for you because she believed that?"

Freddie was silent, but his silence was resentful. He wasn't looking at Winter anymore, and so he started in surprise, when Winter caught his chin in his hand. His eyes flew up and found Winter's. "He filled your ear with poison, didn't he?" said Winter. "Faland."

"He said the world had ended and that I am a coward," said Freddie. "And he wasn't wrong."

He could see the muscles tense along Winter's jaw, but Winter said nothing, for a moment. "No, perhaps he was not wrong," said Winter at last. "But that doesn't mean he told you everything."

"What else is there?" said Freddie.

Winter had let go of Freddie's face, and Freddie found himself wishing that he hadn't. Winter was real in a way Faland had never been.

Slowly, as though thinking it out for himself, Winter said, "That there's no such thing as a coward, or a brave man—not out there. There's no man's will stronger than the war. He might as well have called you an angel as call you a coward, the—distinction—is just as valuable. That is to say, not at all. And of course the world ended. But it went on too."

Winter had turned a little as he spoke, drawing one knee up so they were facing each other. Each watching the other, a little wary, measuring. He *did* still have a soul, Freddie thought, in some wonder. For what else could it be, the thing inside him, linked to Winter, like interlaced hands? It was not a kindly bond. They'd lied and suffered—even killed—for each other. With Faland, whatever you did, there were no consequences, not really, except for the single, great consequence: the utter loss of self. But that hadn't seemed to matter. The war already made him forget he was a person.

But he was a person and there were consequences now. Reach a hand to Winter, and Winter might draw away.

Reach a hand to Winter, and he might be angry.

Reach a hand to Winter, and he might reach back, in equal, drowning desperation, and Freddie didn't know which frightened him most.

"Winter, what happened? After—at Brandhoek. After I left. What happened?"

"I was ill," said Winter. "Very ill; I ought to have died. It was your idea that saved me, to give your sister's friend a reason to value my life. I didn't die." He didn't look at the place where his arm had been.

"But—you could have—you could have *gone*. Once you were

well. Gone to be a prisoner, safe. You nearly died because you didn't go."

Winter said, "I knew you'd gone with Faland, Iven. Do you think I didn't understand? I saw him, when they were taking me away. I tried to warn you. I wouldn't let him have you. So I searched. I hid. I stole. I felt like a madman for trying, or a ghost myself. Or one of the wild men that poor boy thought we were. I was on the edge of despair that night in Poperinghe."

Freddie reached out then—his fingers brushed down Winter's face, jaw to throat, and he felt Winter go still, the blue eyes finding his.

But Freddie had yanked back; the touch sparked a sense-memory, remorselessly strong. He was suddenly *there,* back in that shell hole, his hands on a different throat, also warm, thrashing against his, tension running through the cords of the neck, wet. There was rain and there was water and there was drowning, his own desperation, and he didn't want to be alive, he didn't want to remember.

"I can't," he said. His voice cracked, right at the end. "Winter, I *can't.*" He couldn't articulate what he couldn't do—not love, so much as live. He'd said he would try but it was no good, he *couldn't.*

"Iven—"

"I can't," said Freddie.

"You don't have to do anything," said Winter. "Just be here. Stay, Iven."

But Winter was a man, and he did not lie, like Faland, beyond the bounds of the world, beyond what the world called right and wrong. There would be a morning. And perhaps another morning, and another.

But the world ended, Freddie thought, in strange wonder. *Mother always said the world would end, and it did.* As a child, he had imagined that it would be glorious. As a soldier, he'd thought it meant something gray and hopeless.

But now, with the first feeling of hope he'd felt since—since he couldn't even remember—he thought, *Everything's different now. What does it matter if I reach for him, here in the dark and . . .* He didn't let the thought finish forming; he reached for Winter's arm, and said, hearing his voice rough and abrupt, "Are you cold?"

He felt Winter go perfectly still. The arm under Freddie's hand went steely and rigid. He saw the blue eyes black in the dark, the blunt-featured face, the sandy hair.

Time stopped. The question hung there, and the room was utterly silent.

Carefully, so carefully, Winter's own hand came up, and closed on Freddie's, where it curled round his arm. "Yes," he said.

Slowly, awkward with his wound, he slid under the wool blankets, lying on his good side. Freddie could hardly see him, but it was better that way. He'd always—perhaps always would—know Winter better in the dark. Winter didn't move, when Freddie touched him, but his heart beat hard under Freddie's hand.

"Why did you stay?" said Freddie. His voice was just a stirring—even less—in the dark.

"I promised," said Winter.

"Is that the only reason?"

Winter made a harsh sound. "Can you ask? Iven, we were dead together, we were born together. I cannot live without you." He didn't sound happy about it. In fact, he sounded much the way Freddie felt, as though he'd been changed against his will, and was marking out the new boundaries of himself.

Freddie's hand trembled now, where it lay marking the swift tread of Winter's heart. "I remembered you," said Freddie. "I was losing everything else—but I remembered you. I'd wake up listening for you—"

Winter moved forward, sharply, and kissed him, his body warm, his grip almost bruising. It was shocking. It was inevitable. It was home. It was the first time Freddie had felt alive in his own skin since the night he went up Passchendaele Ridge.

He kissed Winter back, his own hands rough on Winter's face, gentle on his wounded side. Winter drew away, but only to a finger's breadth, close enough for Freddie to see his pupils blown wide, his face afraid. Neither of them, Freddie thought, was who he'd been. But if they'd never changed, they wouldn't be here, together, in the dark.

"Stay," said Freddie, and twined his fingers with Winter's, bit his lower lip. Felt him breathe.

"Yes," said Winter.

BUT THE REST OF
THE DEAD LIVED NOT AGAIN

·····

THE *ARCADIA*, OUT OF CALAIS, AND
HALIFAX, NOVA SCOTIA, CANADIAN MARITIMES
SPRING 1918–SPRING 1919

JONES REFUSED TO TELL HER, HOWEVER MUCH SHE ASKED, what he'd paid, whom he'd bribed, to get documents for them all, and clothes, and berths—all plausible enough to get them home instead of arrested.

"No, Iven," he said irritably, when she asked for the fourth time. "I won't tell you. It's done, anyway. You're going back to Canada where you belong, and Godspeed." The spring air was warm around them. They were standing on the deck of the ship. Freddie and Winter had already gone below. Winter was still feverish. He was a wealthy young American, according to his papers, maimed in combat. Laura was his nurse, and Freddie his servant. To the east, the war convulsed the very air; they could faintly hear the guns, even there in the port at Le Havre.

Laura said, "I am in your debt, then."

Jones was smoking restlessly, not quite looking at her. "Winter's wound—the stitches will—"

Laura took a step nearer him, and his voice died away. She said, "I am capable of managing Winter's stitches."

"I know," he said. He tossed his cigarette overboard, watching her.

Very carefully, she touched his face, palm to cheekbone. She was angry at him for being high-handed, but perhaps it was merely her reflexive distrust of someone trying to help her. It was a novel experience, after all. He didn't move. *Come with us,* she hadn't said. Jones was like her. He knew his duty, and while he still had strength, he would not turn aside. Laura's duty lay below, with the last of her family, resurrected.

"Write me," he said. "Let me know how you get on."

"If you do the same," said Laura.

They paused again. Finally Laura huffed, and pulled his head down and kissed him. Four years ago, her behavior would have shocked the deck; now no one even looked their way. When Jones drew away, his eyes were brilliant. The whistle blew for departure.

"Hell," said Jones, and kissed her once more. Then he turned, and walked down the gangplank and away.

. . .

The voyage was slow, and quiet, and private. They kept to their staterooms. Laura would wake up, weeping, remembering the voyage out, and Pim. But Freddie comforted her, and Winter too. Winter was observant, in his quiet way, and they'd come and sit together in the library when no one else was there. Winter proved to have a bone-dry sense of humor that carried them all through the harder moments. Such as when Freddie, gravely, asked Laura, the first night, if she'd tell him about himself. Told her why.

So, evening after evening, she told over their childhood for Freddie and Winter too. Inconsequential memories. Funny memories. She told him about the boy he'd been, and had the painful pleasure of seeing her brother—if not become the person he'd been—at least begin to resemble him.

She saw how it was between Freddie and Winter. She didn't begrudge it, not really. But it made her lonely.

. . .

They arrived in Halifax in late spring.

Laura, lacking anywhere better to go, took them all straight to Blackthorn House, hoping to throw herself on the sisters' mercy, at least until she could plan their next step. It still stood square and stern on its plot, rambling and old, in sight of the sea. Laura and Winter and Freddie were all wearing the civilian clothes that they'd got in Belgium, although now they were sweating in the clear sun.

All through the taxi ride, Laura was thinking, *I'll have to get work. Lord knows what I'll do about Freddie and Winter . . . Freddie's officially dead, and Winter. . . .* Her thoughts had run along much the same lines all through their trip across the ocean, without a solution. Worry nagged her still, so much so that she hardly saw the house even as the taxi dropped them off. Or at least she didn't see it until Winter frowned and said, with the censorious tone of a punctilious German farmer, "Look at the garden."

Laura looked, really looked, at the garden that had been the Parkeys' pride and joy. At this time of year, the irises ought to have just been coming in, and the poor climbing roses, with the peonies nearly done, but still rippling in colorful profusion, in the wind off the water. But the garden was overgrown, unweeded. The red beetles had got at the planting of lilies that stood by the door, and their stems stood sadly naked. And the house—there was something strange in the house's stillness.

The door was locked. Had the door ever been locked?

No one came to Laura's knocking.

Finally Laura groped, not really expecting to find it, for the hidden latchkey, behind a loose piece of siding. To her surprise, it was still there. Hesitating, she put it into the lock. The door swung open.

The house was empty, and still. Dust, and dust sheets, covered the furniture. "Miss Parkey?" called Laura. "Miss Lucretia? Miss Clotilde?"

Silence. The deep hush of a house that contained only its ghosts. Had they died?

"What's this?" said Freddie from the front hall, a few steps behind her. "It has your name on it."

Laura turned. Saw a letter on the hall table, addressed, in an elegant, slightly shaky hand, to Miss Laura Iven. A much thicker envelope lay beneath the first. Laura snatched the letter up and slit it with her pocket lancet.

She saw the same handwriting on the letter, which read:

My Dear Laura,

So you've got back, have you? Well done. We've gone, you know. But we've left you a few things. You've earned them. Take your rest, my dear.

Yours sincerely,
Agatha Parkey

Laura stared at the odd missive. Stared and stared, and finally handed it to Freddie while she opened the second envelope, only to stare in astonishment at a will leaving the house, effects, and funds of Agatha, Clotilde, and Lucretia Parkey to one Laura Elizabeth Iven.

· · ·

So they had a place to live, after all. When Laura went to the Parkeys' lawyer, she learned, to her shock, that they had money to live on as well. Enough for respectable clothes, and for proper food, to bring all three of them back to some semblance of health.

It was even enough money for Laura, walking dazedly through the vast, dusty old pile, to think, *Could I do it? Could I open a sanatorium here? Could I help the people the war broke?*

But not yet. There were a thousand details of life to work out first. Winter, on the second day, went outside to the toolshed, found the heaps of rusty gardening implements, and set about cleaning and sharpening them. Overnight, it seemed, the garden was trim and weeded and fertilized with fish meal. They had not time to sow a spring crop, Winter explained to her, but they could have lettuces. Parsley. Cabbage. Even potatoes.

He brought flowers into the house every day.

Freddie helped Winter in the garden. But Laura had bought him a sketchbook and an easel, pencils and chalk, and later oils, and soon he was busy with his paintings. The images were jagged, done in violent colors, and made Laura's skin crawl. But Freddie was always a little happier, a little livelier, after finishing one.

And so they mended, bit by bit, in their little rambling haven of a creaky old house. Across the ocean, the war went on, through that summer and into the autumn. *The Allies are advancing now,* Jones wrote Laura. *They've had a victory near the Marne. I resectioned a bowel today, poor man, we shall see . . .*

It feels like the end, Kate wrote. *But people are still dying.*

They were. People died and died and died that summer. From influenza, and hunger, and war. The horsemen galloped, disembodied, and the old world writhed in torment, giving birth to the new.

They never spoke of Faland. Freddie would not speak of his time in the hotel, except once he painted a jagged room of peeling gilt, and colors soaring like sound over the abstract canvas. Laura saw him looking at it, with a strange sickened longing on his face. Then he thrust his palette knife into the painting and ripped it end to end.

"It's over," said Laura. "It's all right."

"But I'll never hear music like that again," said Freddie, and he looked ashamed of himself for saying it.

Laura crossed the room and took his hand.

It was September when Laura and Freddie finally went together, alone, at dusk to see where the house in Veith Street had been. It was suppertime, and everyone was indoors. Freddie was muffled up so the neighbors wouldn't recognize that dead soldier, Wilfred Iven.

Laura had bought herself a motorcycle and a motorcar, and practiced in determined laps, until she could drive both rather well. So she and Freddie motored down to Veith Street and got out of the car, and stood together, in silence, where the house had been. There was nothing left, really. The timber had been cleared away by their enterprising neighbors; anything beneath had long since been taken up by others or hauled away for scrap. There was only a cellar-hole, and memories.

Laura said, "We should sell it. The land will be worth a bit. Or perhaps I shall build a new house—not like ours, different from ours—and rent it to boarders. Young women, maybe." *Build something new,* she thought. *Something else to remember.* For all her memories of this house from before had folded into the one—blood and glass and smoke.

Freddie nodded, not looking at her. "I remember how it was— what I saw. In the hotel. When the ship exploded. Was it really like that?"

"It was," said Laura.

Her mother had not come to her, dreaming or waking, since she'd led them away from Faland's hotel. A miracle for her beloved children, who never imagined that the world contained either the mysteries or the doom that she had believed in so fervently.

For the first time, Laura asked, "Was the pillbox like—like what I saw, in the hotel?"

"It was."

"I'm sorry."

"Mother was right, you know," Freddie said. "About the world. Requiescat in pace."

And he bowed his head into his palm, and for a moment neither spoke. Laura put an arm round him and he put an arm round her, and for a moment, they were as united as they'd ever been in childhood, as though Armageddon had never come between them. Then Laura said, "Come on. Winter's waiting for us."

And she saw, with pleasure and a little pang, the light come into Freddie's face.

They turned and left Veith Street together, for the last time.

· · ·

Laura had thought that they would get better there. The house had a silence that was conducive to healing. They would build new lives there together, and new selves. Gardener, painter, nurse. They'd be all right.

But September became October, and Laura began to wonder whether Freddie was indeed healing. Day by day, his art grew stranger, and he grew thinner, and paler, and he was often silent, holding a book in his lap without reading it. Sometimes she'd hear him moving restlessly about the house after she'd gone to bed, and hear Winter's measured step, going to find him, hear their voices together in the darkness.

October became November.

It was the eleventh of November, an early morning, when they were all awake, and gathered at the breakfast table, when the bells began. Every bell in the city, church to church, rising and rising, a wild clamor. Laura heard feet running, people shouting.

She'd been dishing out eggs when the noise began, her head full of schemes for solariums and treatment rooms. She dropped her serving spoon at the noise and put her back instinctively to the wall. Winter and Freddie both leapt for the cover of the table. They were all three of them frozen for a moment, staring at each other.

Laura realized first. "It's over," she said. "The war's over." The joy was palpable in the noise in the streets. But she didn't feel it. For a moment she could almost smell the bog-reek of the hospital, feel blood under her fingernails. See Pim's blue eyes, blank with mad rage.

Winter had bowed his head. Freddie reached out and covered his hand with his. *We won,* screamed the people outside. *Don't they know,* Laura thought, *we all lost?*

But it was over. The fighting would stop. The killing would stop. And perhaps the world had learned. Perhaps this was the war that would end war. Perhaps.

For long minutes, no one spoke.

Then Freddie burst out, passionately, as with something long thought but never given voice, "We can't stay here."

Laura was still bemused by the noise. For a moment, she didn't understand. Then she did, and the realization struck her like a blow. Winter sat slowly back in his chair, his eyes concerned. Freddie went on talking, the bells outside a strange backdrop to his voice. His words tripped over each other; he spoke as though his courage would fail if he stopped talking.

"Laura—we can't stay here. In Halifax. I can't stay in Halifax. It's too—too loud here. Too many noises. Too many walls. I can't— Wilfred Iven's dead, remember? How can I make a new life, hiding?"

Laura whispered, "I don't know." People were still whooping outside. "Where would you go?" she asked, with an effort.

"Cape Breton," said Winter, in a tone that meant they'd talked about this, planned it. All those nights, when Laura had heard their voices. *Don't be angry.* She had no right to be angry. Winter went on, carefully, "It is wild. Isolated. No one will care who we are. There will be sheep. And cattle, perhaps. And snow. And silence. Peace, there, for us. Wilfred can paint."

Laura nodded slowly. She said, her voice harsh, "You know I can't go with you."

"I know," said her brother. She could see the love in his face, and regret. But mixed with that was eagerness to be gone. For a moment, there was that petty anger again, that she'd saved him for someone else.

She let that feeling go. "Just promise me—" Her voice cracked, and she tried again. "Promise me that you will live. And try to be happy."

Freddie glanced at Winter, and the light that came into his face was brief and blinding.

They left the next spring, with the melting snow, bearing the deed to land near the wild, rocky coast of Cape Breton Island.

. . .

And then Laura was alone, where she'd begun.

Until, one day, when the peonies were blooming, there came a knock on her door.

Laura went to answer it. Standing there, she saw a man with close-cropped hair and eyes infinitely dark. Something in his face lightened, when he saw her. "I have come to call in a debt," he said, stiffly. "From a woman who insists she owes me."

Laura stood staring at him. A smile kept trying to climb onto her lips.

"Come in," she said. "And tell me."

THE GREAT WAR IS NOT AN AMERICAN PREOCCUPATION. OUR country entered the war late and helped finish it quickly; it wasn't until 2014, the centennial of the war's beginning, that construction of a memorial in Washington began. As of this writing, that monument is not finished. For many, the overriding impression of the war is of a quaint, gray-tinted conflict: muddy men in funny hats hiding in holes. One remembers, vaguely, a reluctant skimming of *All Quiet on the Western Front* in high school and perhaps a documentary in class, full of grainy footage and British-accented narration. In the American imagination, World War I is wholly eclipsed by its bloody, momentous successor.

However, it is worth mentioning that the largest American military cemetery abroad does not overlook the landing beaches at Normandy. Rather, that dubious distinction goes to the Aisne-Marne American Cemetery in Belleau, France. This vast stretch of graves contains American dead from the First World War.

World War I deserves our attention. The hectic, violent years from 1914 to 1918 set the stage for the rest of the tumultuous twentieth century and laid the groundwork for the modern world.

I spent years working on *The Warm Hands of Ghosts*. Over those years, many people asked me to describe the time and place that was taking up so much of my imagination, and the descriptor I found myself using over and over, sometimes humorously, sometimes seriously, was *steampunk*. The years of World War I were as close to a

moment of historical science fiction as we will ever get: an indescribable mash-up of changing mores and technologies. And its par-
ticipants, like time travelers, were people of one era flung without
warning into another.

It was a time of shocking juxtapositions. Artillery could kill from
seventy-five miles away, yet armies still communicated via messen-
ger pigeon. Suits of armor went up against machine guns. Cavalry
charged at tanks. Combat nurses wore corsets and carried gas masks.
Primitive hand-to-hand combat with bayonets and trench knives
alternated with precisely calibrated artillery barrages, and, famously, generals ran the war from luxurious French châteaux while
their men, a scant few miles away, slept in wet, corpse-ridden
trenches.

These contrasts are what initially drew me in. They give the war
a hint of the fantastic, or at least of the darkly surreal. Some of the
most indelible literary images to come out of the war did not find
expression in historical tomes or works of realistic fiction but rather
crept their way into fantasy and horror: The 1938 French war film
J'accuse! has the mutilated bodies of the dead rise and come sham-
bling out of No Man's Land, a clear precursor to the modern zombie
film. More famously, in *The Lord of the Rings*, J.R.R. Tolkien based
his descriptions of Mordor and its neighboring lands on his wartime
experiences. The unforgettable descriptions of Frodo and Sam
crossing an alien landscape of slag heaps and smoking pits, with any
water they can find burning their mouths—Tolkien didn't imagine
that. He lived it.

It is perhaps not surprising that a substantial part of the Great
War's cultural influence was filtered through fantasy. It was a time
so rawly traumatic that its survivors barely had language to describe
it. Millions disappeared. Millions died. Millions more went home
maimed. Huge swaths of France and Belgium were annihilated
under tens of millions of shells. And in 1918 a flu pandemic swept
the globe, killing more millions, often quickly and gruesomely.

Europeans in 1914, rich with plundered colonial wealth, believing
wholly in their cultural supremacy, discovered that they were capa-

ble of sending their children off to live in holes and murder each other. That knowledge stayed with the survivors all their lives.

The break with the past was so sudden and so traumatic that many writers have framed the war in apocalyptic terms. A 2014 French documentary about the war is called, simply, *Apocalypse*. Dan Carlin called his WWI podcast series *Blueprint for Armageddon*. A 1916 Spanish novel about the war is titled *The Four Horsemen of the Apocalypse*. This is not surprising. The Western concept of the end of days is shaped by the biblical Book of Revelation, and it is not difficult to map imagery from those pages—plague, war, famine, death, the sun turned black, a rain of fire, the martyrs crying out—onto the war years.

I, too, considered the war through an apocalyptic lens, and in doing so I kept returning to this biblical quote: "And I saw a new heaven and a new earth, for the first heaven and the first earth had passed away."

The question I would have asked this long-ago prophet is: "Did you see a new hell too?"

Because humanity did.

Hellscapes are a feature of the Western literary tradition, from Odysseus's trip to the underworld to Dante's nine circles to the golden city of Pandemonium in *Paradise Lost*. But the twentieth century provided us with earthly hellscapes: Hiroshima, for example, and Dresden, and Auschwitz, and, before any of those, in 1917, the Battle of Passchendaele.

Of course, the West's fantastical hellscapes also have indelible masters; think of Hades or Dante's three-headed Satan or Milton's charismatic Prince of Darkness. But what kind of master, I asked myself, do these twentieth-century hellscapes have? Do they have one at all? What would a devil of the old world do if he found himself in the hell of the new one?

Because in any of his mythic or literary guises, Satan, the silver-tongued antagonist, the musician, Milton's antihero—the West's original compelling monster—would surely find himself at a loss in the face of such impersonal, inhuman devastation. What use would the lover and exploiter of mortal flaws have for a place that torments without accounting for vice or virtue, a place that renders the infinitely interesting human soul a number in a ledger, a body in drab?

What would he do, what do humans do—what do any of us do—when thrown, unprepared, into a strange new world?

These are the questions I asked myself at the outset of *The Warm Hands of Ghosts,* and for years I chased the answers. I am still looking.

But thank you for making the journey with me.

Katherine Arden
April 2023

ACKNOWLEDGMENTS

THERE WAS A TIME WHEN I THOUGHT THIS BOOK WOULD NEVER be written, and I am still a little surprised that it was. It isn't the longest book, but for draft after draft after draft, it simply refused me. Refused to work, refused to exist. Every chapter, every sentence—sometimes it felt like every word—was hard-fought. I couldn't have done it alone. So many people stood by me at every stage, listened to me cry, listened to me complain, held me when I couldn't hold myself.

So many thanks to my editor Jennifer Hershey who read every single one of those drafts, with unvarying patience and incredible wisdom. To the many amazing folks at Del Rey Books who worked on this endless project: Wendy Wong, Erin Kane, Scott Shannon, Tricia Narwani, Keith Clayton, Alex Larned, Loren Noveck, Pam Alders, Jane Sankner, Simon Sullivan, Paul Gilbert, Regina Flath, Scott Biel, and Rachel Kuech. To my publicity, marketing, and social media team: Ashleigh Heaton, Tori Henson, Sabrina Shen, David Moench, Melissa Folds, and Maya Fenter. To my copy editor, Emily DeHuff, and to Debbie Kaiser, who saved me from grave errors in German. Thank you to David Lindroth for the amazing map.

Thanks also to my international publishers, in particular Mitopeja's Vladimir Sever, whose kindness and keen eye were invaluable. To the publishing team at Century in the UK: Selina Walker, Rachel Kennedy, Sam Rees-Williams, Barbora Sabolova, Kristen Greenwood, and Ben Brusey, thank you for championing this story.

To my agent, Paul Lucas, who endured actual years of listening to my frustrations and fears and never stopped believing in this novel. To my team at Janklow and Nesbit: Eloy Bleifuss, Stefanie Lieberman, Molly Steinblatt, Adam Hobbins, Michael Steger, Lianna Blakeman, and Emma Winter. And, of course, the folks in the UK office: Nathaniel Alcaraz-Stapleton, Ellis Hazelgrove, and Hellie Ogden.

To the many, many booksellers who have championed my work, especially Katya D'Angelo at Bridgeside Books and the entire team at Phoenix Books, including Tod, Robin, Christy, Sean, Phil, Ruth, Ali, Jenna, Eliza, Sofie, Riley, Miriasha, Coco, and Drew.

To Naomi Novik and Peter Brett, who read all the drafts, encouraged me, listened to me, and went on writing retreats with me, over and over, until I got there. Thanks, guys. I love you.

To my friends outside the book industry, invaluable for keeping any author sane: RJ Adler, Pollaidh Major, Tanya and Chad Miller, Garrett Welson, Meghan Condon and Sam Reed, Tisa Watson. I spent a year telling everyone it was almost done, and no one called me out on my blind optimism. Thanks so much.

To everyone in my family, who have always stood behind me, even when I am tackling overambitious, melodramatic projects like this one. I love you all.

To Evan and Moose: I don't have words for everything you are to me, but you were both with me through all the ups and downs of drafting this book, and I could absolutely not have finished without you.

And, finally, to the dead, who felt so alive to me as I was working: the men and women who fought in the Great War and whose voices came to me in memoirs, reminiscences, and letters. To Will Bird, whose unforgettable account, *Ghosts Have Warm Hands,* gave my book its title. To Edward Thomas, whose beautiful poem "Rain" I excerpted as the work of the fictional Wilfred Iven. To Edwin Campion Vaughan, Robert Graves, Wilfred Owen, J.R.R. Tolkien, Kate Luard, Vera Brittain, Mary Borden, Ernst Junger, J. F. Lucy, Louis Barthas, Philip Gibbs, and all the others whose names I have lost. You put the color and texture of your lives into words at a moment when it seemed as though the whole world was on fire, and I hope your acts of witness are never forgotten.

ABOUT THE AUTHOR

KATHERINE ARDEN is the *New York Times* bestselling author of the Winternight trilogy and the Small Spaces Quartet. In addition to writing, she enjoys aimless travel, growing vegetables, and running wild through the woods with her dog. She lives in Vermont.

katherinearden.com
Facebook.com/katherineardenauthor
Twitter: @arden_katherine
Instagram: @arden_katherine